Mythanimus

Mythanimus

A Collection of Stories

Storm Constantine

IMMANION
PRESS
Stafford England

Mythanimus
By Storm Constantine
© 2011

http://www.stormconstantine.com

Cover by Danielle Lainton
Interior Design by Storm Constantine
Illustrations on pages 107 and 146 by Storm Constantine

Set in Souvenir

IP0025

An Immanion Press Edition
8 Rowley Grove
Stafford ST17 9BJ

http://www.immanion-press.com
info@immanion-press.com

ISBN 978-1-904853-60-2

Books by Storm Constantine

The Wraeththu Chronicles
*The Enchantments of Flesh and Spirit
*The Bewitchments of Love and Hate
*The Fulfilments of Fate and Desire

*The Wraeththu Chronicles (omnibus of trilogy)

The Artemis Cycle
The Monstrous Regiment
Aleph

*Hermetech
Burying the Shadow
Sign for the Sacred
Calenture
*Thin Air

The Grigori Books
*Stalking Tender Prey
*Scenting Hallowed Blood
*Stealing Sacred Fire

Silverheart (with Michael Moorcock)

The Magravandias Chronicles:
Sea Dragon Heir
Crown of Silence
The Way of Light

The Wraeththu Histories:
*The Wraiths of Will and Pleasure
*The Shades of Time and Memory
*The Ghosts of Blood and Innocence

Wraeththu Mythos
*The Hienama
*Student of Kyme

Short Story Collections:
*The Thorn Boy and Other Dreams of Dark Desire
*Mythangelus
*Mythophidia
*Mytholumina
*available as Immanion Press editions

Contents

Introduction

Mythanimus is the fourth of several anthologies, in which are collected all of my published and unpublished short stories and a few surprises – in the form of half finished stories I was able to complete and include. There is only one exception, *Lacrymata,* which was written for a game system that is still thriving, so therefore I am not permitted to reprint the story myself. *Lacrymata* is still in print, in the Games Workshop anthology *Deathwing*, should anyone wish to read it.

The first short story collection I published through Immanion Press was *Mythanima*, which appeared in 2009. I intended to collect *all* of my uncollected stories in one volume, but with hindsight and now more knowledge of book design, I can see what a bad idea that was. I was never happy with the small size of the font, which was unavoidable; otherwise the book would have been prohibitively huge and expensive. But since that time, I've regained the rights back to all my stories, so decided to publish them all, in four volumes, with type that is easier to read. The other collections, published through Immanion Press, are *Mythophidia*, *Mythangelus* and *Mytholumina*.

What follows are my thoughts on the inspirations and ideas behind the stories, as well as information on where they were first published, if applicable. Some of the pieces here were first written way back when I was a teenager – since rewritten, naturally – and all of them to me speak of the 'myth inside'. We create our own mythologies constantly; we are drawn to archetypes and live out archetypal dramas. In the depths of our dreams and our most soaring imaginations, we are creatures of myth, capable of anything.

Owlspeak

This story concerns how we each live in our 'reality tunnel', and sometimes even the language we speak is alien to people occupying other 'reality tunnels'. In our interactions with others, we can take for granted they understand where we're coming from, what our beliefs are and so on. But sometimes there is no common language, only bewilderment.

This story first appeared in a collection published through Newcon Press in2008, called *Myth-Understandings*, edited by Ian Whates.

An Elemental Tale

This story first appeared as a chapbook published by my information service, *Inception*, way back in the 80s. For a long time, I never considered selling it anywhere else, because money from this publication helped keep Inception functioning. But since that incarnation of the info service is no more, and all remaining copies of the chapbook passed to me, I wanted to make this story more widely available.

In some ways, this is a very personal story too, since I wrote it for a friend who was undergoing some miserable circumstances in her life. In story form, I sought to work magic for her, to make things better. Whether this strange little spell was responsible or not, things did change in her life. The tone I wanted for it was that of an old fairy tale.

I wrote the piece during the time I was working on *Burying the Shadow*, which is why the soulscape makes an appearance.

Dancer for the World's Death

The original version of this story was created for one of Games Workshop's Warhammer 40K collections, but never made it into the final selection. As I liked the story, I 'filed off the serial numbers' that connected it with that universe and rewrote it. Again, it was published as a limited edition chapbook by my information service *Inception*, and it only ever appeared in my original story collection *Mythanima*.

Panquilia in the Ruins

This story is based on a very old idea of mine, which I actually wrote when I was about fifteen, in the hall at school where I was sitting my 'O' level English examination. I'd finished the exam and was waiting until everyone could leave the hall. To make the time pass more quickly, I decided to write a story. I still have the original of this piece, written in turquoise ink on official Cambridge Examining Board note paper. It was only two sides, and concerned a warrior wandering off after a battle into a strange, ruined city, where phantoms drove him mad. I rewrote the story in the mid-80s, giving it more of a plot and a more satisfying denouement, but never sent it off anywhere. I called it *Gampander in the Ruins*.

In 1990, the Midnight Rose project (helmed by authors Neil Gaiman, Mary Gentle, Roz Kaveney and Alex Stewart) was putting together a number of shared world anthologies, and approached me to ask if I'd like to submit some stories. I did, to all of them. One of the collections concerned a character called Redfox, who was the brainchild of an English comic artist, called Fox. Redfox was a feisty female adventurer, and I decided to write a story about her, based on my old Ruins piece, which I called *The Wasteland Haunt*. Unfortunately, Fox's collection never made it to print, and my story didn't get used. I intended at some stage to rewrite the piece and remove all the obvious trappings of Fox's created world. When Stark House was working withme to compile *The Oracle Lips* collection, I was inspired to dig out and polish up a number of old stories, which were either half finished or needed serious rewriting. *The Wasteland Haunt* was one of these, and I renamed it, as the original title no longer seems appropriate.

The Preservation

The story appeared in the short-lived SF magazine REM that

was around in the early 90s. Its inspirations are early South American culture. It explores another recurring motif in my work, that of repressive religion and what its fanatic adherents can do in the name of their beliefs. I also attempted to show that what people regard as sacred is wholly a part of the reality tunnel they inhabit, and sometimes those tunnels are too far apart for people to reach a common understanding. In that case, the stronger will prevail, but what constitutes strength?

I created two white chalk illustrations on black parchment for the magazine edition, and after some digging around managed to find the originals and scan them into the computer so that they can accompany the piece here too.

Priest of Hands
This story eventually became the novel *Calenture*. I had to change the gender of one of the protagonists in order to sell it, but not for the usual reason of any homo-erotic content. The story had first been sent to a female editor who reacted strongly to it. Originally Ays had been a priestess of hands, rather than a priest, and the terranaut had been male, but the editor implied it was 'anti feminist' and said something along the lines of: 'no woman would give away her power in that way'. Needless to say, it was rejected. So, wearily, as I'd had to do before with other stories, I changed the genders around, with the understanding that it would be ok for a male to give his power away to a female. Rather than send it back to the same editor, I sent it to Interzone, and the editor there accepted it without argument. When I started to expand the story into a novel, Ays was female again, but somehow it just didn't work. I wrote about forty pages and got totally stuck with it. So I changed Ays to a male once more, and the story began to work. Very odd that!

Joy in Desire
I wrote this piece not long after the extreme flooding that

submerged a large part of England in 2001. It appeared in *The Seven Deadly Sins* anthology, edited by David Howe. My 'sin' was Lust, and for inspiration, I chose the similarly named Tarot card from the Crowley Thoth deck that in most other decks is usually called 'Strength'. I really enjoyed writing this piece; it just had a tone and a feel to it that made it come easily.

The Fool's Path

This story was written for a collection based on the Qabala, edited by Ed Kramer. I don't think the book ever made it into print, as I never got a copy and when I checked on the Internet found no sign of it! The story is based very loosely on a supposedly true tale that was told to me by a friend, but the characters themselves are very different to the ones in real life.

Quite often, people who are 'unbelievers' in the occult or the paranormal want to challenge it or demand proof to their physical senses that unseen realities might exist beyond them. This story involves a young woman who recklessly challenged The Cosmic Joker, the archetypal fool, who is a lord of chaos and chance. As I've said, I was told that this story really happened once, but I never met any of the people involved or even learned their names. This is my version of events, what *might* have happened. Naturally, I embellished the original tale that was told to me!

The Time She Became

I wrote this story for David Garnett's *Zenith II* anthology in 1990. To me it has a particularly strong mood and atmosphere, and is one of my favourite stories.

Some stories are quite difficult to write and I'll create them over weeks, months or in some cases even years, but others just pour out in little more than a single session. *The Time She Became* was one of these. I loved the idea of cities that continually moved and recreated themselves, and explored it in more depth in my novel, *Calenture*. This story contained the seeds for that longer work.

Where the Vampires Live

Ian Whates of Newcon Press asked me for a story for his *The Bitten Word* collection (2010), and this was the piece that came to me for it. The vampires, if such they are, do not resemble the creature typically found in fantasy. They might not even be vampires at all.

I feel there is a novel lurking here, and have ideas for it, and have even tried to write more. But the voice that came to me for the original piece, the feeling and ambience, I found hard to replicate once the last lines were written. Perhaps it is meant to remain as it is – a snapshot.

The Deliveress

This is a light, humorous piece, which I enjoyed writing immensely. It first appeared in the *Villains* collection, which was part of the Midnight Rose project. For *Villains* I played with several fantasy tropes. There are many novels, in which the protagonist is an average individual from our ordinary world who undergoes some kind of magical journey and is whisked into an alternate reality. Invariably, these people simply get up, brush themselves down and set about saving that world from some calamity or another. They generally accept their predicament without too much trouble, which to me seemed extremely unlikely to say the least. In *The Deliveress*, I wanted my heroine, Jenni, to react and behave in a realistic manner. She is an ordinary girl, with an ordinary job and an ordinary lover. Suddenly, she is catapulted into a fantasy world, where special-effects magic is a daily hazard and muscle-bound barbarians roam the land looking for quests. Rather than mounting her horse, reaching for her magical sword and galloping off to do heroic deeds, Jenni worries about the slow decay of her disposable contact lenses, the lack of feminine hygiene products and the general unsavoury nature of the primitive culture in which she finds herself. What Jenni has to realise is that in a fantasy world, anything is possible. Magic solves everything, and there's bound to be short-sighted wizards around.

Candle Magic

This story appeared in Pete Crowther's *Blue Motel* anthology. I initially wrote it way back in 1985, before my first Wraeththu novel became published, but in its original form it wasn't really good enough to sell. However, some years later, I dug it out of my files and reworked it. It's a prequel to the story *Such a Nice Girl*, which appeared in the collection *Mythophidia,* also published by Immanion Press.

Candle Magic is about the power of obsessive desire, that all-consuming passion, which can lead to mental illness. The object of the protagonist's desire might or might not be real, but what *is* real is the girl's inferno of longing, which leads her down a dark path indeed.

Of a Cat, But Her Skin...

Near my home town, there's a stately home called Shugborough, which is the seat of the Earl of Lichfield. Shugborough has a long history of being connected with the occult. Outside, in the grounds, there are many fascinating follies. One of the monuments, known as the Arcardian monument, has carvings that are reputed to conceal esoteric knowledge. There is also a Grecian temple, the Temple of the Winds, and once hidden away down a neglected woodland track, (but now easily accessible since renovations to the gardens), the cat monument. This was the setting for *Of a Cat, But Her Skin*. I'm intrigued by Victorian occultism, and many local mansions and stately homes have legends associated with magic. The Victorian gentry, it seems, had a penchant for all things esoteric.

The title for the story comes from the saying 'what can you own of a cat but her skin?' which to me says in a nutshell that whatever physical restraints we are under, our souls are always our own, untouchable. Cats are the living embodiment of this. They might find it convenient to live with us, they might even quite like us most of the time, but no cat owner is really under any doubt that a cat, if it could speak, would certainly never say it belonged to anyone. Owning them is a comforting little illusion we humans have.

This story is also about relationships. Most people will have had experience of a jealous and possessive partner at some time in their life. These tendencies are extremely destructive, not just to love itself, but to both partners' self-esteem. All too often, a partner's obsessive jealousy becomes too hard to cope with, and the sufferer will do anything just to keep the peace, to avoid yet another argument. Nina, the protagonist in the story, believes she finds self-empowerment through the magic of the cat stone, but in reality she merely discovers a part of herself that has been lying dormant. This discovery is salvation, not just for her, but for her lover, who lives in a self-created hell of fear and insecurity.

The Silver Paladin
The final two stories in this collection are utter rareties. This one, co-written with Sian Kingstone, was created for a game world. The story was never used by the game developers, and never really completed, so I filed off any remaining serial numbers connecting it to the game world, and polished it up. I quite like this little piece and thought it was too good to languish for ever in the back waters of my hard drive

The Farmer's Bride
There is a poem of this name by Charlotte Mew (1869-1928), which when I read it absolutely stunned me with its imagery and language. For many years I wanted to write a story based upon it, and even began one, but never got round to finishing it. Then, once again, a game company asked me to produce a piece as an intro story for one of their books

and I finished off *The Farmer's Bride*, giving it a new name and adding details pertinent to the world of the game. The game did not last and is long out of print, so I did my usual job of filing off the serial numbers and reinserting bits of text that appeared in the original version.

Because the poem is so wonderful, I've included it here in the book before the story. As the poet has been dead for nearly a hundred years, I'll assume I'm not breaking any rule of copyright here. The woman herself was fascinating, and sadly forgotten. I've copied below a short biography I found on the internet by someone (un-named) who attempted to rekindle interest in this extraordinary poet. Unfortunately, the site is anonymous and there is no way to contact the author.

"Charlotte Mary Mew, esteemed by Siegfried Sassoon, and Ezra Pound was born in London on November 15, 1869. She took her own life on March 24, 1928. Haunted by unrequited passion and tormented by fears of madness she, nevertheless, produced poems of unique beauty and passion. Although her life was lived for the most part in poverty and despair she was still recognized by Vita Sackville West as a poetess of distinction. Virginia Woolf called her the greatest living poetess, and Marianne Moore, a quarter of a century after her death, considered her work 'above praise'. Thomas Hardy accorded her extraordinary praise and others believed she approached poetic genius."

I hope including the poem in this book, and the story it inspired, will do something to expose the haunting, beautiful work of Charlotte Mew to others.

Storm Constantine
September 2011

Owlspeak

In the 26th year of the Burnt Star, King Leonald defied Fate. Cenaggara, Lord of Destiny, became enraged and sent out his seventeen Slaughterers. Ten of the Slaughterers pursued the monarch through many levels of reality for several lifetimes; the rest imposed curses upon the Royal Family from which, to this day, it still reels and suffers. It is not prudent to displease Cenaggara. When he calls you, you bow and then dance to whatever tune he deigns to play. If you defy him, he will not forget you. It is in everyone's interest to be ignored or forgotten by Fate.

Shay was born into a family that followed the laws of Strixion. He did not go to the squat grey church with his mother every night, and said he did not follow her beliefs, but still he lived at home with her, and the family she controlled. Once he told me that when he was younger, he slept in a bed with six brothers, and on two occasions, in the midst of the winter, he had woken up to find one dead beside him. The first time, it had been from the Blacklung; the second , his eldest brother, who was fat, had slept on a young one and smothered him. Now Shay slept alone, because he was older, in his twenties, and it was therefore inappropriate to sleep with others.

The laws of Strixion are very particular. A human life, it is said, must not stray from the narrow path that winds between the cliffs of experience. The goal of our brief existence is to reach death, having reproduced as much as nature allows. We should not aspire to greater things, and to follow the instincts of the heart is not just folly but sinful. A devout Strix follows the footsteps of his or her parents, and their parents before them, way back through the generations, so that the footprints are kept perfect. Footprints in the mind.

Shay was trampled from the day I met him.

Under normal circumstances, Shay and I would not have become friends; we were so different. I had no family of blood, but lived with others of my kind. We were followers of Lady Onyxx, which our detractors might say means we didn't follow very much at all, since Onyxx enjoys hedonism in her followers and despises anyone who bows a knee to her, never mind a head. But we did believe in destiny and magic, and that we could make a difference in the world. We believed that each person has a responsibility to evolve themselves as much as they are able, and that to retreat from life's challenges is weakness.

I had been taken in by my mentor, Dwine Estos, in my fifteenth year. Ten years had passed since. Dwine was in his forties even then, but a perennial dreamer who appeared far younger than his years. Dwine knew the state of the world, yet still he believed in its potential and had hope. From him, I had learned nearly everything I knew – how to shape reality, how to make dreams come alive. Ten of us lived in the house of Dwine, who had grown rich on the purses of gullible city folk needing guidance and magic. We, his younger followers, stayed up all night and slept all day. We did not want to grow old and scorned doing what we thought of as ordinary things. We scorned ordinary people too, and sniggered covertly at those who came to Dwine in despair, although he would have been disappointed in us if he'd known that, because we were supposed to be tolerant of others. But we were young then, somewhat arrogant I suppose, and determined to be extraordinary. When we were awake, we talked endlessly or created things together; works of art, stories, ideas, new systems of belief. Or else we worked our magic - shivery rituals beneath the midnight stars to make the world a better place. Sometimes we would have fires in the garden at the back of our house. We would get drunk on plum brandy and toast the most capricious of the spirits. My mentor later said to me that on one of these nights I had accidentally asked the universe for Shay to come into my life. Unwittingly, perhaps secretly desiring it, I had committed some magical act – perhaps a wish thrown with drunken joy into the night sky - that had made him happen to me. I had tempted Destiny. I can't remember doing so, but Dwine is no doubt right. He says we can trace everything back to an initial idea, when it was born.

As to how Shay and I met: well... It was during the Plague of Owls a couple of years ago. Conditions had been deteriorating in the city for several years. Our queen had gone senile and the ministers who now ruled in her name appeared to be mad. They instituted pettifogging laws constantly, some of which contradicted one another, while overlooking the greater ills that sorely needed a firm hand. While no one was now allowed to walk in the middle of a road because it was dangerous, the pavements were littered with rubbish, where vermin bred. Exotic new diseases were uncurling everywhere. People were becoming selfish and suspicious, and it was as if a plague of stupidity was taking over every mind, one by one. No one cared about anything any more, not the things that really mattered. Steadily, our once affluent society was falling into decay and no one truly knew why. Mismanagement, yes. Complacency, yes. But it was more than that. My friends and I talked about this a lot, how we had a duty to try and stem the inexorable tide, this nausea, this sickness. We called it the Yellow Wave, and it seemed unstoppable. Then the birds came.

No one knew where they came from nor why: a shadowy, whirring host of doom owls that brought twilight to the noon day. They came to roost upon the highest points of the city and turned the white towers to a midden. They were round-eyed in the daylight, perhaps wondering how they had got there and what to do next. The owl is a symbol of wisdom and of teaching. Why had these wise birds gathered in our stumbling city only to act like imbeciles, peering and blinking and uttering ugly cries?

People came in their hundreds to view the extraordinary sight. I went to look because it was phenomenal and beautiful and strange. I also went alone because my best friend, Theo, was called away by a boy she was in love with, seconds after we had put on our shoes to leave the house. I didn't mind. The experience was wonderful, whether shared or not. Poor owls. Had they come to teach, only to be horrified by what they'd found at journey's end? People pointing and making a noise, picking up the feathers that dropped, but no one really asking: why?

Shay was there with his family; they had brought the younger children to see. There were so many people. Easy to get lost in a crowd. A small boy ran into my legs, almost knocked me over. I was looking upwards, thinking how the wings that sometimes expanded from the towers above me looked as if they were trying to lift the city into the heavens.

'I'm sorry,' a voice said.

And I looked into eyes that were like the sky. I didn't have to lower my gaze from the city summit that much; he towered over me. 'For what?' I asked. It was then I realised I had a child attached to my legs.

'My kid brother,' he said. 'He ran off, nearly floored you.'

Why had the child chosen me to cling to? I don't know. Cenaggara was in him. 'There's no need to be afraid,' I said to the child. He looked up at me with those wonderful eyes that belonged to his family. Strange how so repressed a breed could gaze upon the world through starlight. It was clear they were Strixes: the austere clothes, the cropped hair, the somewhat rigid body posture, even in the child, the skin that looked too scrubbed, almost raw. I noticed that their ears looked strangely vulnerable and naked. What they thought of me in my multi-layered clothing of many colours, the tassels, and bright rings and necklaces, I can only conjecture, but I doubt it was favourable.

'The birds are dark,' said the child.

I smiled at him, touched his face. 'That's just their colour. They're lost, that's all. They were going somewhere and forgot what they were doing. They are more afraid than you are.'

The child's brother laughed then, in a not altogether pleasant way. My hackles went up. 'Perhaps if he hadn't been scared, he wouldn't have run off,' I said accusingly. 'Do you teach your children to fear the natural world?' I disengaged the child and pushed him back towards his brother. 'Yours, I believe.'

It was the sort of moment when you should walk away, having ended the encounter, but unfortunately I was exactly where I wanted to be and had no desire to move.

We stood next to one another in uncomfortable silence, a pocket of stillness in a tempest of noise and activity. He did not move away and rather than wondering why, I simply found this annoying. But as the moments progressed, I realised I could feel a strong pulsating energy emanating from his body. That did not speak of Strixion; it tasted familiar to me, which was odd. As I was thinking about this, and what it might mean, he said, 'Aren't you bored with this now? Shall we walk?'

I examined him for some moments. As I said, it had been clear to me from the start he was not of my kind, but there was something about him that was compelling. 'Why do you want to?' I had to ask. It wasn't a coquettish question, just that usually his type avoids mine and vice versa.

He shrugged. 'I just do.'

If only I had said no. Why didn't I? He was a contradiction and that should have warned me rather than intrigued me, but then this must have been Cenaggara's influence again, sniggering away in his Halls of Torment. 'Where shall we go?'

'Let me lose the kid first,' he said.

'Again?'

He laughed, this time in a different way. It was altogether

agreeable.

We went to the Swan's Neck Bridge, so named because, long ago, a princess had looked over the wall and had seen the Swan's Neck constellation reflected in the river water. She had seen ghostly birds fly out from it and they had spoken to her. She never revealed what they had said, but the bridge had been renamed. It is enormous, a suspended highway lined by stands selling food and trinkets. In summer time and the midst of winter there are fairs over the water, and a thousand fey lights mimic the heavens above us.

Shay told me his name and bought for me a cheap necklace made of metal swans. It would make my skin itch and presently be discarded, I thought. The sun was beginning to sink and the river turned to blood beneath its dying light. We leaned against the rosy stone, in a niche where benches had been placed, and gazed in the direction of the distant ocean that we could not see. The tide was coming in; the water seemed alive.

'Look,' Shay said, and pointed up at the sky. The clouds there were multi-hued, as if fashioned by a painter of landscapes. 'There are the tides and their king, riding into the light.'

A shiver went through me at those words. They seemed to me wonderful. I looked at him askance. 'I would not expect you to say such a thing.'

He shrugged. 'Why not?'

'Just that... well, you're a Strix, aren't you? Isn't such fancy against your laws or something?'

'I don't believe in anything,' he said. 'I can't help who raised me.'

We stared at one another, and I thought that I would never again be able to break away from his gaze. 'I think we were meant to meet,' I said.

'I don't believe in fate,' Shay said.

'I do. I believe in magic too.'

'Of course,' he said, 'you're a Nixie. So there we have it. Meeting on a bridge.' He laughed. 'Ironic really.'

'I'm hungry now. Let's eat.'

He nodded. 'Where do you suggest?'

Naturally, I took him to one of my haunts, which I hoped would impress him. It was a Nixie inn, decorated in vibrant colours, and filled with customers who had earnest things to say while getting very drunk. Even from that moment, I had a desire to reach Shay. I wanted to turn his head in my hands, so that he faced a different road in life. Perhaps if he heard the way my people talked, he would start to think. When he laughed, when his eyes lit up, I could see within him a shining light. It was like looking through the bars of a cage at something wonderful and winged that could not stretch or even breathe properly. But there was very definitely a cage and it was his sanctuary as much as his prison. For every step towards me, he retreated half a step. The creature in that cage was wild; suspicious of a coaxing hand.

After a few glasses of plum brandy I was ready to believe I could save this trapped soul. And so I wove with words my own philosophies on life. I spoke about that which we cannot see, that we are meant to see, even though the laws of his religion would forbid such things.

'Anyone can see there must be change,' I said, 'and it is our responsibility. We are ruled by fools.'

'The ministers are doing the best they can,' Shay said, somewhat too primly for my taste. 'It is the people who are falling into decadence, not them.'

Did he really believe that? 'But can't you see the way people are manipulated? Yes, most of them are sheep who can't raise a bleat in protest, but in many ways they are innocent.'

Shay snorted. 'Some people spend too much time thinking and listening to their own voices, when they could be doing something useful. We are animals; we should live as animals do, and not in the way you're thinking right now. We should live our lives according to what is natural.'

I wasn't completely sure what he meant by those words and in all honesty shrank from asking. I was sure the answer wouldn't please me. Instead, I put my head to one side and said: 'Aren't you just the tiniest bit curious about what I do?'

He had taken drink too. 'Actually, yes,' he said. 'I'm not sure I believe you can change the world, in any way, however big or small, but I'm curious about how you try.'

'We could work magic,' I said. 'Are you brave enough?'

His responding laughter was nearly a coughing fit. 'Brave enough? Is that a challenge?'

'It was you who said you didn't believe anything. What if I could prove to you that you *can* change reality through the power of your own will, and that it is the most natural thing in the world?'

He shrugged, grinned. 'I'm open to having my mind changed.'

I believed him.

And that was how our friendship began. At first, it was heady. When in his presence, I felt that together we would create miracles. There was power and huge potential inside him, plain to see. This appeared like flashes of starlight off moving water, almost too fleeting to glimpse, but when it did so, the light was amazing. It silenced me. Sometimes, when we were together, I would bring my work – poems or pictures – and when I was clawing my face in despair because I couldn't, just couldn't, get a detail right, and it threw off the whole work, Shay would just take a look at the piece. 'Here,' he would say, taking the charcoal from my hand. A few deft strokes later and there it was: the spirit of the picture brought to life. The same happened with words too, not just licks of pigment on a page. But when I suggested to him he should write or draw himself, he'd only laugh. 'I can't,' he'd say. 'I'm not creative. I can simply offer ideas and solutions, that's all.' He hadn't even tried. And why? I had no doubt this was because his mother would have considered such a thing fanciful and meaningless. He would be ashamed to be caught by her creating something beautiful with his own hands.

For Shay to lose himself in a life of Strixion - simply breeding, doing menial work, eating, sleeping and then dying, having achieved nothing - was obscene to me. It was up to me to fan the embers of his being into life. Surely, this was a vital task that had been put in my path. I took it very seriously.

My friends were not so enthusiastic. I let a few of them meet Shay a couple of times, but realised very quickly it was better to keep him apart from them until... until later. Theo, who never contains a thought if one pushes into her mouth, was most emphatic. 'You're mad,' she announced. 'You really are. Why are you wasting time on that Strix? He's curious, yes, but there will come a point when he'll run from you. There is a line he will not cross. Don't get attached to him.'

Dwine was not so caustic. I went to him for guidance and he listened to my impassioned description of Shay's potential without interrupting. Eventually I ran out of words and Dwine regarded me silently for some moments. Then he said, 'If you feel you must pursue this path, then continue. There is always a lesson in everything we do.'

As for what I showed Shay of magic, I opted for slow and gentle progress. We meditated together in places of beauty – the white stone fountain in the deserted Aurish quarter; the aspen copse on Sentinel's Tor outside the city; the Swan Pool in a corner of the City Park where no one ever goes. I tried to encourage visions within him, taking him upon guided journeys into fabulous landscapes. This was intended to open his mind to glorious possibilities. I think he enjoyed the experience but that was not really magic. After we meditated, we would drink watercress wine that we bought from a girl who made it herself, and who always sat at the gate to the park. Shay would come alive then. Even though we were so different, we discovered we were uncannily alike in many ways, saw humour in the same things.

We could only meet a couple of times a week, because Shay spent most of his time with his family, which was huge. He had duties and responsibilities at home, and his mother ruled him severely. I never met her, and never wanted to, but sometimes she was a third person at our meetings. There was a father, but he seemed to be like a ghost, a shadow, with hardly any presence at all. Shay rarely spoke of him. For all that Shay professed to be something of a rebel, it quickly became clear that in most ways he wasn't. Even if he claimed not to believe in the religion, he did believe in the narrow, restricted life he had been raised in and appeared to revere it. If the mother called, he ran, even if he had other arrangements planned. Once I listened, sickened, as he told me about the girl he would marry in several years' time and how he was looking forward to 'settling down', as he put it. There would be no outside social meetings then, and he just accepted this as what should be. The girl was a clone of his mother, approved by her. He would run from one breast to another, without ever learning to feed himself. But still, he could not keep away from me and, I thought, was clearly fascinated by what I knew. I realised I had limited time in which to make him think for himself. I tried to make him aware of his own potential. He did not have to become a fully-fledged Nixie, but he could stand up for himself, do something different, have a rich life, both inwardly and outwardly. I did reach him to a certain degree. For a while, I think he too believed that together we could work to create positive change, even if this was only in our small corner of the world. Over the weeks I began to feel a certain impatience building within him and concluded the time was ripe to show him something more concrete. I told him this. 'But first, we must establish a psychic link to enable us to work together properly.'

He nodded, barely frowning. 'Very well.'

We were by the Swan Pool, because it had become our

favourite place. The sounds of the city were muted there, as if we'd stepped out of time. The air smelled fresh, always with a hint of springtime, when all hope is renewed. 'We must create a symbol,' I said, 'something that captures our very essences. This will bind us. We must sleep with it close by.'

He agreed to this ritual act. Three nights later, we took parchment and the blackest of inks out to the Swan Pool, and beneath the light of a quarter moon and what seemed to be millions of stars, we created our symbol. Lines upon a page, some curling, some straight, delineating the essence of our friendship, the dreams we shared and those we might share in days to come. 'Tonight, we will visit each others' dreams,' I said. 'Look out for symbols there. First we must call upon the Needles of Onyxx to empower our work. You know what they are?'

He shook his head. 'No.'

'They are servants of the Lady,' I said. 'But ruthless. They will serve us too, but it's important that they recognise you, so they do no harm.' Something occurred to me then. 'Shay...'

'What?' He was staring at our parchment, turning it in his hands to look at it in different ways.

'You must realise that through this act you will step upon the Path of Wyrd. You do understand that, don't you? If your eyes open to reality, if you ask for the Needles to work for you, that will be it. You won't be able to sleep again. By that, I mean you won't be a sleepwalker in life, not really *seeing* anything... the way... the way your church teaches you to be.'

'I never was asleep,' he said abruptly. 'I've told you. It's not my church.'

I sighed. 'I don't think you get what I mean, but please just be aware this is a responsibility. There's no going back.'

'Yes, I understand,' he said, still looking at the parchment.

I dreamed we met in a garden. There were fruit trees on lawns, and snaking pathways of smooth slabs between them.

It was winter time, very cold, everything rimed with frost. We sat on a bench together and I had a pile of papers on my knees, covered in scrawled writing, as if they were hastily scribbled notes. Despite the cold, my hands were fever-hot. I was trying to make Shay understand something; I can't remember what now.

He was speaking over me, not listening. 'We can't do normal things,' he was saying. 'I can't take you to my home. You can't meet my relatives. That is what should happen.'

'It doesn't matter,' I said.

He looked at me sadly, said nothing.

'We haven't had this conversation yet, but we will,' I assured him. 'I can't be in your world, and perhaps you can't be fully in mine, but remember we can meet on a bridge.'

'There's no bridge here,' he said, but I could see that he was looking for one.

We met up the next day. For two people to have the same dream is no ordinary thing. I'm used to such occurrences, of course, but as I described what I had dreamed, I saw the colour drain from Shay's face before me. His dream, he told me, was not identical, but too similar for comfort. There had been a garden and a conversation, but he couldn't remember what about, only that it had made him feel strange. When I heard this, I was excited and pleased. It meant our experiment was working. He had stepped upon the Path and it had welcomed him. This should be the beginning of wonders.

I was too enthusiastic. 'This is it!' I cried. 'Shay, it's wonderful. There is so much we can do, so much we can try.'

'It's difficult for me,' he said, troubled, but at the time I was too elated to take any notice of that doubt.

I took his hands in mine, shook them. 'Can't you see?' I pleaded. 'Please see, Shay. Think about how you can be great. You can make your mark upon history. You don't just have to live a cipher of a life. I can really feel it. Stand up! Own your power. Together, we can achieve anything. Don't you realise what we have achieved? But it's only the first step.'

He pulled his hands from my grasp roughly. 'My life means so little to you, doesn't it?' he raged. 'You despise it. You think you're better than I am. But I want my life. I don't want to change it.'

I was confused. 'But Shay,' I said gently, 'you said you wanted to see what I did, and I showed you. You did it willingly. Everyone wants to better themselves, don't they? I have great faith in you. You're not supposed to have a little life doing exactly what your parents did. There is more to life, much more.'

But for Shay this was not the same as it was for me. He hadn't expected our dream experiment to work. I couldn't see this at first. I thought I had allayed his doubts, assured him I only had his greater good in mind. Yes, I did despise his life and was convinced that he could achieve so much more than what his mother had planned for him. What I didn't account for was the strength of blood.

He didn't say anything further on the subject to me but, from that moment on, things changed. A few days later he informed me that he was very busy with family commitments and our meetings would have to be less frequent from now on. I took this badly, even though he assured me it wasn't personal. We still met, but whenever I suggested carefully that we do some more work, he would change the subject, deftly start talking about something else I was passionate about – a new picture, a destitute girl I'd seen dying on the street, the colour of the sky. I sensed a distance in him, sensed he was slipping away from me, even though at the same time we were drawing closer. We hardly ever touched, but when we were together an energy fizzed between us that could have illuminated the grandest summer fair. It was like the building of a sea storm, rolling inexorably to land. I could feel his moods even when we were apart, and thought that perhaps he experienced the same. If only we could direct this power towards a particular goal, I was sure we would achieve amazing results. But I suppose I was a relentless cudgel, crashing into the walls of his sanctuary, smashing and destroying, when I should have been a slow moving river, slowly eroding the bricks away. If only I could have communicated my feelings, mind to mind. But we were not that much in tune and words were not enough. To follow my way of life, to whatever small degree, would mean he'd have to disobey his mother, change his future. Cenaggara had challenged him, perhaps. There was a fork in the road. One way was certain; the other, while more exciting, was fraught with danger.

One day, the owls lifted from the towers of the city where they had roosted for so long and, to the astonishment of onlookers in the area, threw themselves as one into the river. They made no sound and did not struggle with the water. They merely floated as a sad sodden mass towards the sea.

Shay did not come to our meeting that night. I waited alone at a toddy booth on the Swan's Neck Bridge, watching a scum of feathers bobbing about the bridge supports where they met the water. I knew he would not come. I felt it in my heart. I was surprised by the pain and realised, too late, that I loved him. I took from my throat the cheap necklace he had bought me. The metal had dyed my skin black and now the swans themselves were blackened and tarnished. Without thinking, I threw the necklace into the river, far out.

Shay sent me a note some days later. 'I'm sorry,' it read. 'I'm not the person you thought I was. Don't try to contact me. It's best this way. Goodbye.'

I held the note in my hands, absorbing the essence of Shay that lingered in it. I felt his confusion, his desire to take up the challenge, and also his fear and conditioning, which were iron bars that broke his limbs so he could not run. I realised that all this time, as we had drawn closer, bound by what I had thought was magic, he had felt uncomfortable but had not said so. It had not been the magic that had kept him coming, but me, our friendship. And now all that I was had come between us. There was no bridge.

Our parting tortured me. I felt as if some vital organ had been wrenched from my body. I hope never to feel that agony again. It's been over a year now, yet still the wounds will prick me sometimes; scars from a battle I did not win. I wondered how he felt, convinced the wrenching must be similar for him, but he had clung to what was safe. This had made him strong enough not to give in, to contact me. I waited for so long, stood on that bridge so many times at sunset. But he did not come.

Dwine, as ever my comforter, told me, 'Yes, you and Shay were a destiny. That's why you feel you are being pulled apart. But Shay wasn't ready for it. There is plenty of time, many lifetimes.' He paused, touched my face. 'Just not this one. I'm sorry.'

Someone called me in my sleep last night. It was a call over space and time, a scream into darkness. This was his voice: I was certain. It woke me up and I sat panting in the bed. There were no echoes in the room around me, but an echo in my head rebounded through eternal abysses. When you step upon the path there is no going back, and to walk that path alone with no guidance or experience is a terrible thing. Cenaggara had given Shay a destiny; we were meant to meet. I think now it was only that, and the magic had been secondary. He and I ourselves were magical. But he'd been afraid. What he'd felt and experienced had compromised his heartfelt beliefs, his whole being. Where did I fit into the world of what his mother desired for him, and the faceless girl who already had her mark upon him? I wish he'd spoken of this. Instead, he had remained silent and thought he could retreat back into his narrow life to lick the wounds an inconvenient love had inflicted upon him, but now he was discovering that he couldn't. He would never speak of it, but there would be Needles upon his path, for ever. As his life closed over him, that tiny box, he would lock a madness in there with him. Owls into the river. Drowned wings.

I still have a copy of the symbol we created, in a drawer of the small cupboard next to my bed. Now, with cold fingers, I take it out and look upon it. Did we weave pain into that design? I don't know. I light a candle with a dull ember from the grate. 'Cenaggara, be merciful.' My words are a steam upon the air.

I hold the scrap of paper as it burns in the candle flame, hold it until my fingers hurt, as I would the hands of someone dying, someone holding me too fast, but inexorably fading away.

An Elemental Tale

There are many tales to tell of the soulscape, my children, too many for a single eve. Draw close to the fire, pretties, for if I cannot tell you all I know, I can spin a yarn or two against the night. See here, see my hand. There are the lines you see, the lines that make a man or woman, lines we are born with and which shape our destinies. Think we can change those lines, my children? Think again.

In the soulscape exists all the lands that ever were or ever could be. Because there are so many lands – even for an infinity which, of course, the soulscape is – the horizon is three times as far away as that beyond your window. When you wake up, you can look out into a morning of a hundred miles away, and that is far, believe me. Now, this is a tale belonging to a single land, and to a single woman, too. Imagine this.

There are black and grey mountains going down into a still, dark sea. Along the shore are places where boats can be hired for a schekel or two. The sand is white and colourless, but sparkles beautifully under the light of a round moon. If you have a fearless heart and the moon-madness is upon you, you may take a boat, one with a silver sail and a bold eye on the prow, and sail west into the mists of twilight. Sometimes the long, smooth backs of fishtailed serpents will cut through the water, parting the curly mist. Oh yes, there is mist; banks of it, shrouds of it, dense and white as wool, with a perfume of ice-flowers, those fey blooms found where the glacier weeps into the rock. You are going into the realm of the soul's cup, you see, and its path is veiled. Pay no heed to the calling voices, even though they sound so mournfully like your mother calling you back from peril. Pay no heed to whatever rises up and peers over the side of your boat. Eventually, if you are true to your course and not distracted by the way-taunts, the mist will draw apart like a gossamer curtain and you will beach upon the pale, blue shores of the Sorrowing Isles, where all the colours are those of the soul, deep and watery.

You are back in time, of course, for this is a tale of the past. Travel on, my children.

At one time, the Sorrowing Isles were known by a different name and were a place of radiance. The colours of night, of witchery, were edged with the silvery light of the lady moon, or else a sheen of the sun god's ray came down through the mist like a kiss. Always a land of mystery, of course, for that is the way of the soulscape realms, but to walk its fields was to walk in peace, in serenity, with the heart filled with gladness. But now, the golden days are past; the mist lies everywhere, as lint over a wound, and all the beasts are silent, sleeping beneath a heavy coverlet of cloud. Still, if you keep to the path and do not waver, ignoring, as on your sea journey, any calls or movements intent on tempting you aside, your feet will lead you to the palace of the Queen and you may mount its frozen marble steps. Your skin will be trembling, my dears, dripping with icy cold droplets of despair and you will find your innermost heat, the spark of your soul, getting smaller and smaller until, if you have no knowledge of protection, it will freeze quite away. Only the very brave or the very wretched make this journey.

The Queen of the Sorrowing Isles has only a small kingdom, but it is hers, and hers alone. She has watered it with her tears. Her name is the Lady Rio.

Once, in that land (when it was known by the name that was not Sorrow), the Lady Rio went down from her whispering halls to the silvery shores of her private lake, where she bred dreams and desires. Mostly, its surface was still, so it lay like a vast mirror beneath the clouds. Time is a strange thing in the soulscape. Sometimes, it does not move at all, but in those moments as she paced the lake shore, Rio had made a morning feeling all around her, for her own pleasure. The hem of her gown sucked up the dew and left a dark trail in the azure grass. The lawns carried on growing right under the lake without any difficulty and small creatures scurried between the two realms of air and water without noticing the difference. Lady Rio walked up and down beside the lake with a sweet and secret smile on her lips. Soul-birds wheeled about her head and she was attended, at a respectful distance, by a pair of grey lynxes. 'Today,' Rio said to the birds, 'I shall have a lover.'

'A lover?' said one of the birds. 'Is that not the way of humankind, to have such things?'

'Today, I am a woman and it is my way,' replied the Queen. She had a mind to impress her friends with her daring, they who loved only angels who strayed too close to the soulscape clouds and whose wings became waterlogged, making them rather easy to catch. With a laugh, she extended her hand out towards the still waters and, after a few minutes heartfelt concentration, conjured forth an elemental being, bidding it shape itself into the semblance of a man. Now, the Queen was of a watery nature, for that was her element, but she understood the principle of man to be that of fire. Therefore, if she was to hex herself a creature to love, and if it was to be male, it must necessarily be of a fiery disposition. This was a mistake, but an easy one to make when the heart is intent on its purpose.

The surface of the lake began to bubble and steam. What came forth from it was not a watery entity at all (as perhaps it should have been), but something that set the leaves on the trees beside the lake quaking in alarm. Rio was quite taken aback by what she saw. The man she had fashioned stood, ankle deep in boiling steam, stern as a newly-forged blade, intensely radiant as a star. She had not anticipated her conjurations would be so potent. However, she knew this was not a time for infantile bewilderment, so straightened her back into a rod of ice and raised her chin importantly.

'Follow me!' she ordered, and the man of fire did so.

She took him up the marble steps into her palace, and where he walked, he left scorch-marks in his wake. Soon, the island would bear his mark in many places, and they would be burnt extremely deep, believe me. You might say that a man of fire, even created by the Queen, had no business in that territory, and many would agree with you, but the truth was that Rio needed the comfort that only the arms of another elemental being could bring. Because of her watery nature, emotional bliss was an intrinsic need (at least from time to time), and in creating her man of fire she had sought to fulfil a longing that had nagged too long unheeded within her. Even as she stalked, in her regal way, ahead of the man into echoing halls of her home, she began to question the wisdom of attempting to curb such a wayward element. But a need was a need; if there were risks to his inhabiting her landscape, she thought they would be worth taking.

At first, things went very nicely, thank you, in the ways that things do between a man and a woman discovering certain delights at the same time. They made a beautiful steam together, and Rio grew to like the way her halls came to be perpetually misty, advertising the trail of the man of fire. However, she knew in her heart that, where inside she had a cup overflowing with the waters of love, the man of fire had only a hard coal. He kept this well away from the spilling cup because he was aware that, if these inner parts of their beings ever touched, the water of the Queen would quench his fire forever and, being what he was, such a drastic transmutation made him feel rather afraid.

For a long time, Rio tried to ignore this essential difference, or dilemma, between them. Steam was intoxicating, steam was exciting. She purposely did not think at all about the consensual flowing of two rivers, waterfalls cascading into limpid pools or waves crashing in harmony together upon the shore. In her heart, the cup ceased to overflow. It gradually became stagnant and when the heat of the man of fire came near, it dried a little, a few drops at a time.

Now, it happened that the Lady Rio had a coven of friends, other Queens like herself, but of different countries. Their borders touched in the evanescent way that territories nudge each other in the soulscape, and it was no difficulty for an adept traveller, such as Rio, to hop over from her watery realm into a place quite different to the reality she knew. Although their forms and their handling of incarnation varied considerably, the Queens' essential femininity resonated in harmony. Rio had spent many a happy time in one kingdom or another, netting angels with her friends. They had a secret habit of confining these etheric princes in cages of silk so that they became confused and could be stroked to gather sparkling aether dust from their skin. Other, more audacious pursuits concerning these magnificent hostages were conducted in darkness and were discussed openly among the Queens only on occasions of bacchic abandonment. Impulsively, Rio had freed all her captives since the man of fire had come to stay. Now, impelled by an increasing unease, she knew she needed guidance and that visits afield were called for.

One day, resolute in her purpose, although far from happy about it because she feared what might be said to her (especially about freeing the angels in her charge which were usually circulated out of courtesy), she crossed the waters and flipped into existence in the kingdom ruled by the Queen of the Healing Light. This Queen was named Mavren and her lands were very green. Mavren had a brick tower on top of a forested hill as her home; its battlements were littered with netting equipment. Rio hurried there directly, hardly bothering to pause and sniff the foliage – so different to that of her own land – as she normally did.

Mavren greeted her as usual, noting only, 'Rio, you seem a little dry.'

'Mmm, I do feel that way,' Rio admitted, reluctant to say more now that she had arrived.

Mavren took her to a high balcony where a seraph was chained by crystal links to the stone wall of the tower, shading his face from the sun with two of his wings. Rio glanced wistfully at him, unable to resist wiping a finger along his arm and then sucking the rich dust from it.

'So, you are desiccate; tell me,' Mavren said, and Rio, aware it would be folly to attempt a lie with this shrewd being, told her the problem.

'Ah, that is easy solved,' said the Queen of the Healing Light. 'I can't imagine why you haven't realised; it is so simple. You and the man of fire were never meant to be together. Send him back into the lake so he may return to his natural realm. Then you will both be happy. Spend some time with me here; I will restore your flow with delights.' And she eyed her captive seraph meaningfully.

'Perhaps you are right,' replied Rio, but in her heart, she did not think so. Her promises to heed Mavren's advice were made vaguely.

Rio vowed to discount what the Queen of the Healing Light had said to her. She could not imagine what it would be like having no man of fire around her. However, it was very hard to dismiss the problem. Often she awoke from sleep choking, unable to breathe, her throat as dry as sand. The man of fire slept quietly beside her, giving off a powerful heat. In moments of darkness, honesty came out from the deepest places, and she knew the man of fire was killing her.

At length, unable to force herself to send the man away, she crossed the waters and tumbled into being in the land of the Queen of Cats. This Queen was named Pasht and was the governing principle of all things feline. She lived in a stone warren made of warm, yellow stone, with plenty of nooks and crannies where cats can curl up contentedly. Pasht, for her part in the sport of Queens, had confined a vigorous archangel who flapped sparks in her face and promised unimaginable torture for her effrontery. It must be noted, however, that she confined her angel without chains and that he wandered about her labyrinth without restriction, all the while bemoaning his captivity, and making a great deal of wind and noise with his huge wings. He was a prisoner in her realm because of constraints more subtle and enduring than chains.

'Rio, my pearl-string of shimmers!' Pasht exclaimed delightedly as Rio squeezed past the etheric prince of immense magnitude into the solar den where Pasht and the archangel spent most of their time. 'How wonderful to see you. Here, damp your skin at my well. My precious has quite dried you with his gustings!'

'I am not dry because of your prince,' sighed Rio and threw herself into a pile of cushions wriggling with cats. 'Oh, I am unhappy!'

'Then tell me,' said the Queen of Cats.

Rio did so. 'I could not bear to lose him and yet together our love withers daily. What can I do?'

The Queen of Cats considered for a while before she answered, throwing down a handful of divining cards to help her along. 'In all truth, if you need a man, it should be a man of water,' she said, showing Rio one of the cards to prove it. 'If you are wise, you will endure the pain and send the man of fire back to his elemental realm. Stay here a while with me when the deed is done. I will have a choir of sarim fan mist onto your skin for a brief eternity. You will enjoy it. Then we can see about finding a man of water, if you like.'

'Perhaps you are right,' said Rio, but in her heart, she did not think so.

For a while, Rio tried to continue as normal. She took deep baths regularly and walked in her gardens seeking the moist, breathing dark of the most hidden corners. On occasion, she also strolled beside the lake, but she had noticed, with sadness, that the lake had shrunk considerably and was looking undeniably rank about the edges. Therefore, she did not walk in that place very often, because the sight of what had happened to it hurt her. Everywhere were the marks of the man of fire; burned footprints in the azure grass, withered trees, pools of boiling mud that had burst like abscesses beside the stagnant water. Rio sighed and closed her eyes tightly as she walked. There was someone else she could talk to, one last friend she trusted enough to confide in.

The Lady of the Scrolls lived in a gigantic castle that covered all of her land. She was named Petra and was very wise indeed. Rio knew that her friend was not without problems of her own for she had once captured a particularly fractious angel with whom she had created a child. This meant she was loath to free him, even though areas of the castle had been rendered quite uninhabitable by his fits of temper. She listened patiently to Rio's impassioned outpourings and thought in silence for quite a long time before answering. 'It is clear to me that you must talk plainly to your man of fire,' she said at last. 'Tell him the effect he is having upon you, and suggest a co-mingling of essences, thus producing two entities of compatible elemental constitution. I think you will find this should solve your problem.'

The Lady of the Scrolls believed deeply in the magick of communication, and with regard to her own problem, experimented with it endlessly. So far, her endeavours had met with little success owing to the fact she and the angel she lived with spoke different languages, but she was very persistent.

'Yes, I'll do that,' Rio replied brightly. She liked this advice the best of all because it did not suggest an ending.

'Ah, the folly, the folly of our love that we immolate ourselves in its name!' cried the Lady of the Scrolls with feeling.

Rio was quite sure they were utterly in accord in this matter.

For an eternity of eternities, the Lady Rio attempted to initiate a searching conversation with the man of fire. She wanted him to surrender his hard little coal of a heart, because she could make it full and lush with her healing waters. In return, he would make her elemental flow warm as human blood. 'Be more like me!' she urged.

The man looked at her askance. 'I would like to eat a punnet of plums,' he replied, as ever avoiding the point.

Eventually, the Lady Rio looked inwards painfully, and faced the miserable little pool that was all that was left of her flowing soul-cup. Within it, she confronted the bitter knowledge that she would have to send the man of fire away, if only to save her life, for his dry, searing heat was killing her slowly. Was fire so much stronger than water that she had no defence against his heat?

Gathering the shreds of her strength about her like a veil of raindrops, she sought out her lover as he smoked his way along the pathways of her garden. 'Leave me,' she said, with sorrow. 'I give you your freedom and the gateway to the realm of fire. Leave me.' Her tears flowed like a mountain stream and where they hit the ground, they hissed.

The man of fire went willingly enough at first, streaking like a comet to the place above the clouds where the sky is hot and scorching. Then he fizzed as a searing bolt of flame into the heart of the realm of fire, and the welcome of his salamandrine siblings in that place consoled him instantly. But, as time went on, in the wayward manner it does in the soulscape, he found himself thinking about the time he had spent in the realm of water, and that the Lady Rio might soon create for herself another lover, this a man of her own element, who would be all that she desired and would keep her soul-cup forever full. This thought filled the man of fire with rage. He did not want to live in the realm of water, yet he could not bear to think of Rio with another, especially someone who would be as she was. With a hot scream, he plummeted up from the fire pit, along the starstreams, casting bemused angels from his path, and down, down through the clouds, towards the Isles where Rio ruled. Angrily, he knocked her mist-tailed peacocks from his path, leaving a sizzling trail behind him where everything died, and presented himself beneath the Lady's window.

Rio had just begun to adjust to this change in her life, and the pathway was stony for her. Daily, she was coaxing her watery strength to return, but it was not an easy process. She was alerted by the commotion in her garden and went out to the balcony. Her heart hissed in anguish at what she saw; the man of fire as a crescendo of furious flame, burning away the grass beneath her window. 'Go away,' she said, feeling her fragile strength begin to bubble with steam. 'You will only hurt me.'

'I cannot bear to live without you,' he replied. 'And I will not go away. I will haunt you forever. Let me back into the palace.'

'No! Never!'

'You need me! You made me come to you! If you deny me, you mock yourself and the feeling you have for me! Don't be foolish, Lady Rio. Let me inside!'

'Will it be different?' Rio asked in a whisper. He may have heard, he may not have, but it took only a short time for him to wear down her arguments and make her change her mind.

Ah well, thought the Lady Rio later on, as she lay beside the man of fire on her bed of vapours. *I must make the best of things. It seems we are destined to be together, whatever happens, so I shall work to keep us both content.*

It took a long while, and many a time Rio wished she had not let the man of fire back into her heart. He still did all the things that burned her soul. He still would not surrender his fiery heart to the cool mystery of her waters. Yet, despite this, she told herself and told herself that she loved him, and in the end, she convinced herself utterly. At that moment of surrender, the seed of the Sorrowing Isles was sown in the soulscape and took root.

One day, she thought to herself, *Now, I am like he was. I cannot live without him.* Then she flinched away because he had spat fire at her again. *I love him,* she said to herself. *I really do.*

The man of fire realised he had totally ensnared the heart of the Queen. Always, though, she would insist on making allusions to their bonding, which made him very uncomfortable. If he was to stay with her, she said, they should become one in harmony. It was only sensible. The man of fire, however, liked his element. He liked it rather more, it must be supposed, than he liked the Lady Rio. Their lives, such as they were, were a pleasure to neither of them. And yet both lacked the power to give the other freedom.

It happened that the Lady Rio had to go away for a while. Occasionally, she had to convene with others of her kind – water women, and all of them witches of one colour or another – in order to manipulate the essence of their element in the substance of the soulscape. She knew this would be a healing time for her when she could gather strength and moisture from her people. In a spirit of resolution, she said this to the man of fire before she left. 'I shall set a timeseed in the fabric of this Isle and, by its reckoning, will be away for seven days. When I return, we will become one, melding our souls into a true union of elements. Are you agreeable to this? You must know that it is beyond time, and I need your commitment.'

The man of fire replied quickly. 'Of course. It is time. On your return, we shall do as you say. Now, be safe on your journey, my beloved. I shall wait for you.' He blew her a kiss which parched her skin and burned the tip of her nose.

Left alone in Rio's palace, the man of fire stalked from room to room, driven by a frantic anguish. Why had he returned here? It was a prison, and she, his beloved, the keeper of the keys. He thought her insistence on their melding a cruel and selfish thing. Why could she not appreciate him for what he was? Didn't he care for her? Wasn't that enough? The man of fire was blind to the depredations his harsh element made upon her soul. While she was away from the Isles, he paid visits to his old home in the fire pit, weighing up the differences, measuring preferences. When Rio returned to the palace, he had come to a decision (in his favour, not easily made, though helped along by certain persuasive factors), and told her he was leaving the realm of water. Leaving forever.

At first, Rio was stunned. 'But why?' she asked. Several times. Having rehearsed his scene, he spoke smoothly of how he did not want to dry her up to nothing. He said that he cared for her and wanted what was best for her. Rio listened in silence. In truth, the man of fire had found himself a slippery little tongue of flame to tickle his spirit while she was away, but he did not speak of this.

This time, when he left, the Queen felt as if all heat had left the Isles. The mist came down all at once and the beasts of the fields and the air fell into an impenetrable sleep. Every sweet voice was silenced. Even the silver fish of the lakes and the shores sank motionless to the bottom of their respective homes and did not stir. Only a drab peacock paced the faded azure lawns of the palace, his feathers all plucked from his tail, calling out in a terrible voice of betrayal and loss. Rio cocooned herself in a veil of despair. It was cold and damp with her tears. The cup within her spilled over now, as of old, but the waters were grey and murky. All around her palace and its gardens were the black footprints of the man of fire. She felt they were all around her heart as well. She became the Queen of the Sorrowing Isles and all who trod its fields trod them in peril of their souls.

One by one, her closest friends came to the palace, to see what ailed the Queen. They enfolded her in their arms, but it was only a temporary comfort. After they had gone, Rio was once more alone in her silent halls, silent but for the echo of laughter, dead and dry. Occasionally, the man of fire came to torment her. He was a ghost of course, but very solid, hanging in the air beyond her window, asking as to her welfare. It was a dismal mockery. Eventually, Rio had to draw all the curtains, but still she could hear his voice.

'I hate you!' she said aloud, wishing it were true.

One day, the Queen of Cats came to the Sorrowing Isles. She brought with her a little pot of radiance she had milked from the skin of her magnificent archangel, and she and Rio sat around it to warm themselves. 'This won't do, Rio,' said the Queen of Cats.

'I am full of hurt, my heart-waters are soured,' Rio replied. 'What can I do? He has burned me from the inside out.'

The Queen of Cats shook her head. 'Stuff and nonsense, Rio dear! Hold out your hands.'

Now Pasht did not have fingers like we do, but a sort of paw. Rio carefully laid her hands down, palm up, between the outstretched claws. You can be sure she was afraid of a scratch. The Queen of Cats shook her head. 'Tch, Tch!' she said and then made a sound like a little hiss.

'What is it?' Rio asked, her despair quite forgotten in the face of the alarm she felt at her friend's tone.

'Well, this'll have to go for a start!' declared the Queen of Cats and deftly, swiftly, drew one curved claw across the palm of the Queen of the Sorrowing Isles.

'Ouch!' Rio cried, quite justifiably. When she tried to

draw her hands away, Pasht held onto them firmly.

'Now, don't take on that way,' she said. 'It was only a little scratch. No pain at all, my silly. Here's what I'll do. Cut you a new life.'

Rio was staring in disbelief at the red beads swelling from her scratched palm. 'Cut me a new life?' she whispered hoarsely.

'Be sure. Here!' Snick! The Queen of Cats cut another line.

'Oh!' cried Rio.

'And here! And here!' Snick! Snick!

Rio almost screamed. Her hands were running with blood. 'There! That wasn't too bad, was it?' asked the Queen of Cats. Without waiting for a reply, she licked all the blood away from Rio's hands, and when she put them down again, there was no sign of any scratches at all.

Rio was astounded. She peered closely at her palms. Only smooth gentle lines ran across it, though quite different to how they were before.

'What have you done?' she asked.

Pasht shrugged. 'Well, someone had to,' she said.

'It is so strange,' Rio said wonderingly. 'I feel so...'

'Damp?' enquired the Queen of Cats.

In amazement, Rio ran to her window. She threw wide the drapes and if the ghost of the man of fire was hanging around outside he was dismissed summarily by the force of her actions.

'Pasht!' Rio cried. 'Come here! Come look!'

The Queen of Cats yawned and stretched and wandered over slowly. 'So?' she said. 'A realm of water. So what?'

Outside, a rainbow luminosity embraced the sky. Fountains of diamond droplets cascaded upwards from a dozen dry pools. The azure lawns glowed with the most dazzling brilliance. Birds thronged the air, their wings entangled, their voices combining to a sweet, poignant euphony. The willow trees put out fresh buds (as a whim,

Pasht had directed them in Rio's palm to have kitten's tails as
blossoms) and all the beasts woke, blinking into the intense
silver-blue light. 'My lands, my isles,' breathed the Lady Rio.
'They are restored.'

'And you are now Queen of the Moonsilver Isles,' said
Pasht, 'as you were before.'

'No, it is better,' declared Rio.

Pasht shrugged. 'Maybe. You are a bigger person now.
Some might say tainted by the element of fire, others might
say enlarged by it. Me, I go for the latter. Oh, look Rio!'

'What?'

'Over there, by the path to the lake. What do you
suppose that is?'

He was slim as a willow with eyes the colour of the sea;
ever-changing. He was naked as a babe, dripping with shining
droplets, his skin white as polished moonstone beneath. His
hair was a riot of waving waterweed. He was quite, quite
beautiful and very obviously male.

'Well!' said Rio, half in wonderment, half in delight, with
just a frisson of wary awe.

'Well what?' Pasht replied. 'Where are your manners, my
dear globule of iridescence? Go down and invite him in right
away.' She shook her head.

'You are a minx,' said Rio, planting a kiss on the head of
the Queen of Cats.

'I hope so,' Pasht replied.

Rio hurried away, her footsteps splashing loudly on the
wide marble stairs.

Pasht waited by the window and caught sight of the man
of fire hovering, wraith-like by the casement. She sniffed
discontentedly.

'Tell her I've changed my mind,' he said plaintively. 'Tell
her I'll make the bonding. Tell her...'

'Not likely!' said the Queen of Cats and blew strongly
over her claws in his direction. The realm of water had
regained its strength entirely and it was easy for her to blow

him right out of existence in this elemental kingdom where he did not belong. He vanished with a feeble puff of acrid smoke.

Rio was coming back up the great stairway, leading her beautiful man of water by the hand. 'What was that, Pasht?' she called. 'Did you speak with someone?'

'No,' Pasht replied. She did not, under the circumstances, consider it a lie.

Dancer for the World's Death

Lariel Farbuinnen, student and protégé of the terpsichore, Firfirieth, had kept the vigil, as instructed.

He had lit a taper of pure heartwood and its incense filled his head with quiet. He had danced to the ancestors upon a prayer mat of three colours beneath the five eternal lights of spirit and body. He had prostrated himself in the gesture of submission and performed a Limb-Twining of Measured Respect. His body glistened with paint and sweat, yet despite the disciplines, Lariel could not summon any confidence about the journey to come. Executing a final saltation of entreaty to Gespath, the Smiling God, lord of all terpsichores, he ended with a flourish and sat panting upon the mat.

At that moment, as if he'd been waiting outside, Firfirieth swept into the chamber. He parted the curtains of silvery smoke with the blade of his body, energy and excitement pouring off him like heavy perfume. 'So, Lariel, I trust you have seen to all the spiritual preparations for our little excursion?'

As usual, Firfirieth's voice was full of laughter; Lariel still couldn't decide whether it was genuine amusement with life or cynical condescension. The terpsichore's voice implied: 'See me. I am of the ancient line of sacred dancers: I leap, I fly, I bewitch the eyes of all who behold my art.' And his speech was the dance, the light in his eyes, ever-changing, and his movements; always the dance.

Lariel assumed a posture of respect and answered, 'I have performed as you suggested.' Which was the expected answer.

Firfirieth smiled – another part of the dance. 'Come then,

faythling. We'll see to more mundane matters.'

Part dancing priests, part mercenary seers, the terpsichores travelled the world, taking their sacred art to the courts and houses of the rich and powerful. By nature, they were adventurers, and many of them lived perilous lives, devoted to penetrating the secrets of history, in their fight against the powers of the abyss, a realm forever hungry for the souls of men and women. Firfirieth was a creature full of curiosity. There was no doubt that he was wise, but he could be reckless and he craved excitement.

To Lariel, it now seemed very long ago that he had prepared to leave home, packing a few belongings in the company of his precious sister, Sareth'in. She had confided to her brother that she believed the terpsichore Firfirieth to be utterly mad. 'It is hardly surprising, of course,' she said, 'for it is said all terpsichores are touched by the Smiling God, but I do not envy you this education, Lariel, and I question our father's wisdom in accruing it.'

Sareth'in's words had been justified, Lariel felt. Firfirieth was a dangerous companion because, to him, all of life was a dance; a feat of balance and rhythm, and the dance was essentially exciting. Difficult manoeuvres must be performed regularly to keep the spirit of the dance bright and strong within the flesh. Lariel, since being in Firfirieth's charge, had learned to run very fast indeed, but wasn't yet sure whether his ability to dance had improved significantly.

Firfirieth and Lariel had been guests of the Lord Summoner in the ancient city of Thoughts of Far Deeds for several days now; Lariel engrossed in the spiritual preparations for what lay ahead; Firfirieth paying his respects to all the dignitaries who would have been most affronted had he snubbed them. Perhaps an anomaly amongst peripatetic terpsichores, who were renowned for being solitary creatures, Firfirieth maintained a high profile within society, flitting from city to city, courting attention and income through his dance and psychic counsel. Lariel had been taken to a reception during their first day in Thoughts of Far Deeds. He had padded self-consciously behind the charismatic figure of his mentor, only to be introduced as 'This is my apprentice, Lariel Farbuinnen. A pretty jewel for my cape, eh?'

Lariel had endured this treatment stoically, tolerantly believing Firfirieth was unaware how humiliating his introductions could be at times. It was no easy life being indentured to the man; communication was often a problem and translation of the terpsichore's quicksilver thoughts and suggestions was often impossible. Their interaction was best described as accidental, understanding attained on those rare occasions when their thought processes happened to coincide.

Thousands of years ago, the Muinish, Lariel's people, had held dominion over a score of worlds, and had enjoyed millennia of plenty. Then, centuries of horrific war with the denizens of the abyss, the Kleepoq, had stripped them of their kingdoms. The Muinish had retreated to a single world, Mahkouf, and all the gateways to the other worlds had been locked with a thousand seals and disguised with illusions. Mahkouf was an ancient world, its sun weak and faltering. The Muinish needed to regain their lost domains, but all those who had held the secret knowledge of the gateways were long dead, and their secrets had died with them. Only certain terpsichores still attempted to find the gateways, certain that with their higher knowledge they would one day lead their people back to what was rightfully theirs.

The reason Firfirieth and his protégé were dallying in Thoughts of Far Deeds was because of a key that had fallen into Firfirieth's clutches during some arcane transaction with a huddle of disreputable bone merchants in an isolated hostelry, scoured by the Great White Desert. Naturally, the key was special. Firfirieth claimed, upon insistent enquiry from Lariel, that it could open one of the forgotten gateways that would lead to a lost and devastated world. The gateway, so the terpsichore's source had told him, lay within an abandoned section of this city.

Lariel had greeted this information without enthusiasm, but Firfirieth had only sneered at his concerns. 'Really, Lariel, there is little to fear. The devastations happened thousands of years ago. It's likely the world is empty, or else some remnant of the Muinish has blossomed there again. Aren't you eager to lay eyes on the ancient lands, to witness the reality of our past and perhaps lead our people off this mouldering cinder to a bright, new future?'

Lariel said nothing, but looked sceptical.

Firfirieth glanced away. 'Anyway, I am looking for something, something precious there. It is precious for you, too.'

Lariel was more concerned about falling prey to whatever now might still linger in the lost territories. He could only hope that this gateway, like others Firfirieth had discovered, would lead to nowhere.

'Have you checked the weaponry, Lariel?' Firfirieth asked, pacing lightly around the luxurious apartment the state dignitaries had bestowed upon them.

'Twice, my light. All are in order.'

'Good.' The terpsichore perched briefly, like a bright, restless bird, upon the edge of a table. 'Light of foot we are, but if fleetness fails, a fine dart should suffice.' He frowned. 'Ammunition?'

'Three times checked, my light!'

The terpsichore nodded distractedly. Lariel knew he alone was responsible for physical safety, bringing up the rear with a ready weapon while Firfirieth fairly flew into danger like a fizzing flame. Such had been the way of things so far into their alliance and Lariel could not foresee any change in this arrangement. He had been the comet's tail in many excursions into unknown territory chasing some rumour or another. True, Firfirieth had a knack for wriggling out of danger at the last moment, Lariel behind him, wondering if he was still alive or victim to some ghastly death-throe hallucination of freedom, but such luck could not last forever, surely?

'Well then, we are ready to leave, it seems!' Firfirieth decided, jumping up. 'Where is my mask?'

'Behind you, on the floor.' It was the custom for all master terpsichores to mask their faces in public. Firfirieth had dozens of masks, but the one he had chosen for their quest was that of the Angel Warrior, a fierce, leering visage.

'Ah yes!' Firfirieth slipped the mask over his fine, grinning features. The artificial grin was just as cynical, just as crazed. 'There! A last pageant for the fair citizens of this worthy Perusal of Old Myths!'

'Thoughts of Far Deeds, my light.'

'Quite! Shoulder the baggage, Lariel. It is time to march!'

Thoughts of Far Deeds was not a large city, consisting merely of two ramshackle, dome-sheltered sister boroughs that seemed to cling to one another as if some far-gone collision had brought them together in a partnership, from which both were too idle to extract themselves. The population too was modest, a mere four and half thousand or thereabouts.

'A failing organism; hear her sigh and die!' Firfirieth declared as he led the way through gently curving passageways beyond their apartment.

Lariel had to admit he'd experienced a nagging discomfort throughout their visit. Thoughts of Far Deeds really did seem to be just fading away, all life melting softly into the twilight of the dim sky.

Here, in the populated areas, the covered streets were clean and quiet. Lariel and his master walked through a vast solarium that, at night, channelled the brilliant star rays down onto a plaza where the shops were closed and dark. A single bird pirouetted near the crystal panes far above, its feathers rattling as it hit the barrier. Firfirieth sighed and reached above his head with curling fingers. He turned, ran backwards a few steps, before leaping nimbly up, buoyed by the sighing power of his aerial belt. He spiralled upwards, spinning with the bird that cawed and scratched against the crystal, shedding two black feathers in alarm. Lariel watched the feathers spindle down. He picked one up and tucked it into his tunic. The terpsichore tumbled and soared high above, his mask a frozen smile that flashed in and out of sight. Lariel watched, and shook his head with a reluctant smile as he walked across the empty plaza.

'Do you know where we are going?' Lariel asked, for perhaps the fifth time since they had left the apartment. Firfirieth had explored several corridors in the last few minutes, all of which had led to locked areas, where the lighting was dim and tired.

The terpsichore waved a careless hand behind him. 'I consulted a dozen scryers down Mazepit Alley, then a dozen mathematicians in the city hall. From their utterances, I intuited explicit instructions how to reach our destination.'

'Then why aren't we getting anywhere?'

'The fault is mine. My attention wandered. Ah, this looks promising...'

'My light, we can't go down there. There is dampness and stray wiring. We could be burned to nothing.'

'Nonsense, Lariel! It is too dark for you to perceive any such hazard. Come along!'

'What is this place?'

'An old recycling terrace, I believe.' Firfirieth had already disappeared into the gloom.

Lariel shrugged his baggage into a more comfortable position and followed, sourly. The grillway beneath his feet felt positively unsafe and he was sure he could hear the walls creaking. Caustic rot had set in. It was likely this abandoned section of the city would soon crumble away from the main structure and the wound would be covered with a skin of metallic plastic.

Bulky, ancient machinery brooded silently, stained with

tears of rust and corrosion. Sagging ropes of conduit cable hung like desiccated vines, dusty with the spores of a sharp-smelling fungus that filled the air with acrid powder when Lariel brushed against them. Firfirieth wove his way between these obstacles without collision. He was humming a tuneless melody. Lariel wondered how he'd managed to divine the location of so secret a place. Surely no scryer or mathematician would have assisted Firfirieth if they'd known his intentions. The gateways were hidden and sealed for good reasons. Lariel had been brought up to fear of the past. He wondered what was persuading him to keep his feet on the path and not run away, deserting the mad terpsichore for good. After all, there were a multitude of places to hide in the world of long shadows and half-abandoned cities. This awareness was an escape clause in their contract, Lariel felt, and perhaps the only thing that kept him faithful.

Up ahead, Firfirieth laughed, causing a ripple of discomfort to work down Lariel's spine.

'Some of us possess the art of persuasion!' came the mocking voice, which seemed uncannily like a response to Lariel's musing.

Art? Lariel thought. *Sorcery, more like!*

'Here, I think. Round here somewhere.' Firfirieth had abandoned any psychic prying and was now sifting through a jumble of rubbish on the floor.

'Is that the disguise for the gateway?'

'Stupid boy, no! It's a pile of rubbish!'

Lariel sighed and eased the bags off his shoulders. 'Would you like a drink, my light?'

Firfirieth's half-hearted assent was enough to give Lariel an excuse to sit down and burrow in the luggage for their beverage flask. He hunched against a wall, trying to ignore the popping, groaning vastness around him, the tall shadows that seemed to move just on the edge of his vision. He sighed miserably.

Firfirieth squatted down beside him and hitched up his

mask. Beneath it, his handsome face was smeared with dust. He ignored the cup being offered and helped himself to Lariel's own. 'Sometimes, faythling, I feel you have an unhealthy lack of adventurous spirit!'

'There are good reasons not to pry into what is hidden, my light, that's all I know. And my guts agree with me on this!'

For a moment, Firfirieth looked almost serious. 'That's not guts, faythling, that's learned fear, sucked from your mother's teat. I don't believe we should forget what happened in the past, but face it with teeth bared. How else may we remember what we should avoid? Hmm? Come now, your mouth is sagging. Bad for the muscles, bad for the spirit. How will you ever come to dance the Joyous Madness with your face set like that?'

'How did you find out about this hidden place?' Lariel asked cautiously, trying to smile. 'What do you want from it?'

Firfirieth sighed. 'Was it me who taught you to question? I suspect it was, damn my teeth and breath! How I came to know of this forgotten place does not concern you. What I will look for there is precious beyond belief. Now, no more questions. Part of your indenture concerns trust, I believe...'

'You are sure we will be safe?'

'What a ridiculous statement! Have you learned nothing from me?'

'You mean no one can ever be sure of anything,' Lariel recited miserably. 'I remember, my light. I fear for our souls!'

Firfirieth shook his head and grinned. 'All that fear! And yet you still cling to my heels, even when the sanctuary of flight and desertion hungers for your presence!'

Lariel gathered up the cups, averting his face. 'My family have bought your time for me,' he said, embarrassed.

'Your family have bought me – for you! Aren't you lucky? Come along now, on your feet. I need a moment's silence to sniff the way.'

It looked like any other section of wall; ochre-streaked

and frail with corroding age. Firfirieth laid the palm of his hand against it, made a few glottal noises of deep thought and then produced a thin, enamelled wafer from within his jacket. The key. 'Turn away, faythling,' he said. 'There may be acid light.'

Lariel obeyed, and when he turned again, the wall had melted into a dim opalescence. Firfirieth kept the secret of it to himself. Lariel had followed Firfirieth into many gateways, none of which had ever led to a lost world. This was different. Where some gateways had unfolded space-ways before the mind's eye like glowing ribbons stitched with colours, inviting travellers to tread the rainbow path, and others had appeared as steel throats, lustrous as an eye, this was lightless and virtually invisible. It could be perceived only as a kind of greyness, but without perspective of any sort. Lariel was wary of venturing inside it, but Firfirieth, apparently unaffected by any misgivings, tipped his mask into place and stepped forward. 'Come faythling!' he said. 'Let us not keep our appointed destinies waiting!'

'But what if... what if we should both die?' Lariel squeaked, hanging back.

Firfirieth laughed. 'Such little faith!' he declared, and the greyness covered him.

It was a place that should be sealed forever; this was clear. What had happened at the nether end of this tunnel was bleached into the very fabric of it, coterminous with the material, and it was no longer a highway through space. It was without true form and whatever it led to must be worse. There were strange echoes, as if they walked through a passageway of stone, their feet invisible within a dust of swirling grey. Firfirieth loped along in his habitual swinging style, as if travelling towards some longed-for liaison. Lariel could only be conscious of the vast nothingness beyond the un-walls of the tunnel and the inevitability that must yawn at its end. He had lived this fear before; in nightmares. He could not speak in that place, sure the sound of his voice would attract unimaginable horrors. A sudden feeling of pure hatred towards Firfirieth rose within him, with such strength Lariel was afraid it might be a miasma of the abyss wrapping a tendril round his heart. He attempted to banish it. Firfirieth was strange and whimsical, but also wise and cunning. He wouldn't be making this journey if he really believed his life might be threatened. So Lariel attempted to comfort himself, and Firfirieth, whether he was aware of his student's inner conflict or not, did not look back even once.

How long they walked, Lariel could not tell; time as well as space became a grey murk in that forgotten, damned place. He thought about how once someone had stood in the recycling plant of Thoughts of Far Deeds and sealed this tunnel shut. What dreadful things had they sought to contain? That was the worst of it, of course. The tunnels were sealed to keep things in, as much as keep people out. But it had all happened so long ago. Nothing lived here now, no one had trodden this path for millennia.

They'd taken no chances, however; the gate was also sealed at the other end.

Firfirieth, complaining about inconvenience whilst grudgingly admiring their ancestors' thoroughness, produced the enamelled wafer once more and began to make the passes of restruction. His body swayed, a half dance quivering in his attenuated limbs.

This is it, Lariel thought. *No dead end. We've arrived somewhere!* Terror filled his mind, dizzied him. Impulsively, he threw down his baggage and hurled himself at the terpsichore. 'No!'

Wire-strong hands gripped Lariel's wrists. He found himself lifted right off his feet, his face drawn close to the grinning mask. He could smell the spice scent of the terpsichore's breath, his legs kicking uselessly in air as he hung suspended. 'Don't,' Firfirieth said gently.

'You can't!' Lariel sputtered, wriggling. 'You can't! They sealed the place! If you open it... if you do... Gespath, my light, *what will you let out?*'

'Discipline has become a problem with you, hasn't it?' Firfirieth said, dropping Lariel into the grey dust around the gate. 'You set yourself above me, faythling, to criticise my decisions. I admit to pride. I don't like criticism.'

Lariel felt tears of humiliation and anger gather in his eyes; also tears of other things too convoluted to label. 'What is it you're looking for in there? What?' he asked miserably.

Firfirieth folded his arms, the mask impassive, staring down. He tapped a single finger on his sleeve. 'Get up, Lariel,' he said. 'Find your spirit. You might need it later.'

It was a night world they came upon; cloudless sky netted with bright stars and a pair of moons, irregular and tumbling. A gentle hill sloped down from where they stood, the desiccated soil fretted by a low wind that sounded like a tormented soul wriggling on its belly across the land. Lariel's heart had frozen within him. He followed his master out onto the dry, powdery clay of the land, looking back once at the eroded gates behind them. They stood like enormous pylons of rust-streaked stone, a lightless black sealing the way between them. They were surrounded by fallen buildings, tumbled bricks that had once enshrined the passage to other worlds. There were neither demons nor spirits apparent in the landscape.

'This land turns her face from the sun,' Firfirieth said, striding down the hill. 'See, faythling, the lack of light has killed it. Some great tumult ceased the world to spin. On the other side, I expect it is burned to ashes, and burns still in fierce sunlight.'

Lariel did not ask how Firfirieth could know this. He was alert for movement and peered nervously into the black and white of their surroundings.

At the bottom of the hill, they climbed onto a high, cracked road. It was bare and dust-scoured, bordered by avenues of flayed trees; some still garlanded by stubborn rosettes of petrified leaves that fluttered on the questing wind. Beyond the road, the land was flat, the only features being humps of dark that may have been old buildings, or else just rocks.

After some minutes, shapes appeared out of the shadows up ahead: the eroded towers of a dead city.

'If you look closely, you might see bones,' Firfirieth said, indicating the oscillating dark beneath the trees. He spoke as if he was pointing out some delightful feature of interest.

Lariel did not answer. The wind used the outflung branches of the dead trees as a voice box and he was worried that other beings might use this din as a shield for their own corrupting songs. He found it hard to imagine this had once been a thriving land, for there was no sense of history about the place, even though it was clearly ancient. This world seemed scoured utterly of memory; it was the province of hallucination, or the deepest, most excoriating of meditations when a person traverses his own soul's blackness, just to be aware of its existence.

Lariel hoped that Firfirieth would find what he wanted quickly, so they could leave. There were no lessons to be learned here that he could not experience in his own heart on a dark, lonely night, far from home.

As they approached the city, which became more and more ruinous in Lariel's eyes as details of its destruction were revealed. Spots of sullen red light sullied the surface of the land. At first, Lariel's heart leapt with terror. He thought they were fires, and though he had more or less decided not to speak to Firfirieth until they had returned to Mahkouf, could not refrain from blurting out some anguished enquiry.

Firfirieth laughed politely. 'No, faythling, no hand or claw built those. They are merely cracks in the soil revealing blood-tears still wept by the core of this world where life lingers.'

'Could this place ever revive?' Lariel asked. 'If it began to spin once more, would it remember how to live?'

Firfirieth shrugged. 'Perhaps, but then, whatever taints still linger would also be revived. We must hope the world does not remember her dance before we leave!'

Lariel frowned. 'I thought you wanted to revive this world. You said you wanted to bring our people here.'

'Did I?' Firfirieth affected distraction.

Lariel shuddered. No doubt the terpsichore would eventually reveal the purpose of their journey. 'I feel no taints,' Lariel said. 'I feel nothing here. Do you?'

'More can be learned from what is not than what is,' Firfirieth replied.

There were no walls to the city, not even any crumbled remains. This seemed to signify it had been built in secure and prosperous times. Now, it was a nothing place, without ambience or proper form. Picking his way neatly over rock-falls and crevasses, Firfirieth led the way inside, where the brooding, broken towers cast dark blue shadows right over them.

If Lariel narrowed his eyes, he could believe they walked through a natural labyrinth of weathered rocks. 'Is it here, what you're looking for?'

Firfirieth paused and looked about himself. 'We will find a temple,' he said, 'and there you will dance for me.'

Lariel uttered a shocked exclamation. 'Dance! I have no inspiration to dance! I just want you to find whatever you've dragged me here to find, so we can get out of here quickly!'

'Want, want, want,' Firfirieth said, sighing. 'I've dragged you here to dance, faythling, so you had better find the inspiration somewhere!'

Lariel's first impulse was to exclaim angrily at this, make plain his discontent and march swiftly back to the gateway. Unfortunately, Firfirieth had led him so deeply into the maze of tumbled spires, he was unsure he could find his way out. *But,* he assured himself, *when we are away from here, it is the end, I swear it. I will not follow his capricious madness any longer.*

They fought their way up what had once been a wide boulevard. Spikes of pocked stone mantled its verges; perhaps the remains of columns, the roofs they supported long gone. For much ofr the way, they were forced to scramble over rubble, which shifted alarmingly beneath their feet.

Cresting the apex of a particularly high scree, Lariel twisted his ankle and fell forward, his hands grasping stone, baggage flying, flesh scoring from his fingers.

Firfirieth stood, hands on hip at the bottom, watching him fall. 'I hope this won't mar your performance,' he said. 'Because we have reached your venue.'

Shakily, Lariel picked himself up and tested his limbs, which appeared sound. His clothes, however, had been ripped by the cruel stones and his hands and knees were painfully skinned. It was beyond him to speak, not just because of his feelings towards the terpsichore, but because of what lay before them.

Beyond the rocks lay a wide, debris-free street, flanked by buildings that were mainly still intact. Not far from where they stood, a long flight of shallow stone steps led up to the portico of a graceful fane. Tiers of columns filed backwards into darkness, their abraded surfaces catching the raw starlight; they glittered as if studded with gems. Lariel was astounded. Everything had become too insane. He knew he must dance, simply to escape. One did not argue with lunatics.

There was warmth in the temple and the voluptuous smell of burning resin. 'There is someone here,' Lariel said, dully. Somewhere on the street outside, his autonomy lay bleeding.

'That would seem to be a possibility,' Firfirieth agreed, apparently oblivious to his protégé's state of mind. 'A short investigation should reveal the truth of the matter.'

He strode into the dimness. Lariel followed, limping.

They ventured into a dream. This was the only way Lariel could describe it to himself. The warmth, as they investigated the high-roofed passages of the temple, bloomed into light, ruddy and kind to the ancient stone. They entered a chamber, where an altar of fire presided over a shining, empty floor. Carved representations of divine inner aspects of the ancient Muinish stood to attention round the edges, supporting the roof upon their heads. It was, without doubt, a sacrosanct place. *I have been deceived,* Lariel thought. *This cannot be a blighted world. It is all an illusion he has spun. He has brought me to an inner sanctum of his kind. It is another trick; all of it.*

When pale, robed figures began to glide from between the columns, Lariel was not surprised. Nothing would have surprised him. The figures, definitely female, advanced with stately grace. They wore the full-head tragic masks of priestesses, the faces of which represented the Fallen Bright Ones, creatures of myth.

Firfirieth seemed to know these women. He bowed extravagantly at their approach. 'Greetings, sisters! It is I, the terpsichore Firfirieth an Guirienn ur Sorreth.' He straightened up. 'If I may intrude upon your privacy once again, I request that you grant us permission to use the fane.'

One of the women advanced cautiously towards him. 'Face!' she snapped. It was a dry voice, but not old.

Firfirieth, without a pause, lifted his mask from his head. Lariel was astounded his master obeyed such a demand. The sight of the terpsichore's face was a privilege he granted as sparingly as his affections. However, Lariel was sure the strange females would now acquiesce to the terpsichore's request, simply because he was standing there in the altar-light, lithe and quivering with energy, his face beneath the mask another mask of beauty. Firfirieth ran his fingers through his hair, seemingly to push it from his face, but Lariel knew this was simply a seductive gesture.

The woman nodded. Lariel thought she seemed pleased, although her mask could show nothing but hideous grief.

'Greetings to you too, terpsichore. Too long since we last met. Too long. I will ask my sisters if they accept your petition.' She turned to the others, who were arranged in an ordered row behind her. They all inclined their heads. 'You see, you have bewitched them,' said the priestess. 'And I, Arnainn, as High Priestess of this fane, speak for us all and grant you the license you require.'

Firfirieth turned a radiant smile upon his apprentice. 'The dance, faythling,' he said.

'Which one, my light?' Lariel asked, perplexed. He was unsure he could muster the right ambience to dance in such an eldritch place.

'An Invocation of Progression, up to the third interval.'

'Firfirieth!' Lariel felt as if he'd woken up abruptly. The terpsichore was tormenting him again; must be. Both of them knew the dance he'd suggested was an intensely private performance, an assimilation of spiritual flowering, and always performed naked. That Lariel should be asked to do this before an audience of strange women was unbearable. He was young and his body still mainly an alien territory to him.

'These are exceptional circumstances, Lariel,' Firfirieth said, and his voice was the coldest Lariel had ever heard it.

You are trying to break me, Lariel thought. *I won't let you!* 'I have no percussion,' he said. 'It will be difficult to muster the rhythm.'

'You have your heart,' Firfirieth said, 'and, if that is not enough, I will clap for you.'

'I cannot bathe. My skin is unoiled.'

'You do not need such fripperies to execute the dance,' Firfirieth said. 'It is internal and the shapes should manifest through your bones whether the flesh is oiled or not. Come now, hurry up. Undress yourself.'

'Why?' Lariel demanded. 'What are you trying to do to me? Why bring me here for this? What is the purpose?' His angry voice hung on the still, warm air, echoing round the columns, twisting between the disapproving features of the sentinel statues.

'Just do as I ask you,' the terpsichore said. 'Remember; trust me.'

'Trust you?' Lariel cried. 'I cannot trust a madman!' He could not bear to look at Firfirieth's face. He had gone too far. It was finished; all of it.

Then, there was a rustle of cloth and the High Priestess Arnainn glided over to Lariel. She laid her hand upon his arm. He saw that her flesh was white, smooth, the fingernails perfectly formed. 'Shame on you, terpsichore. You bully the boy!' She squeezed Lariel's arm gently. 'It is not often people seek this temple. A dance of any kind would bring us reassurance, but the Invocation would be a blessing, of which there are too few in this place. Dance it for us, terpsichore's shadow. If you consent, I and my sisters will bathe and anoint your body in preparation.' Her voice was beautiful, the former dryness moistened with soothing concern.

Lariel sensed an ally and addressed his next words to her alone. 'I thank you sister. Because you asked, I will perform the dance.'

Firfirieth tittered. 'Go with them, Lariel. Let them touch you. Just make sure the dance is all they need!'

Lariel felt his face flame. He let the women lead him away.

They took him to another chamber, this carpeted with fur, the walls hung with draperies of indigo silk. Bowls of light were scattered around the floor. The women turned their sad masks towards him and came forward to remove his tattered clothing. It was as if they grieved for his youth. Their ministrations were reverent and without familiarity. It did not cause him shame.

'Who are you and why are you here?' Lariel asked. 'What is this place? Where am I?'

The women did not berate his questions as Firfirieth did. 'We are slaves of the Smiling God,' said Arnainn.

Lariel was confused. 'He does not have slaves, does not want them.'

The woman shrugged. 'It is as we choose, nothing more. This place is a dimple of life in a dead world. Not many come here, but those who do come to dance. It is a function of the temple.'

'Other students, other terpsichores, come here?'

'They do.' The priestess applied anointing oil to his knees and palms, which numbed the sting of his abrasions.

'Was this place a great city before the devastations?' Lariel asked.

'It is a lost place, bereft of dreams.' The woman rose, putting a stopper in her vial of oil. 'You are ready, terpsichore's shadow.' She bowed her head. 'We salute you.'

They cast a cloak of midnight velvet round his shoulders and one of them brought forth a covered item on a tray. Arnainn bowed reverently and removed the cloth. Beneath it lay a mask, and it was as if the sleeping face of a lovely boy reposed there; decapitated, flayed, a sacrifice. Lariel was intrigued. 'Such artistry,' he said.

'For you,' the priestess replied. 'Put it on, terpsichore's shadow.'

Lariel lifted the mask from its tray. It was light as skin, smooth, and warm to the touch. Silken hair fell from its brow; sad, heavy hair. Until the time Firfirieth decided that Lariel should undergo the rite of passage into becoming a fully-fledged terpsichore, he should not mask himself to dance. But the women had offered this holy thing to him. He should not refuse it. Lariel slipped the mask over his head.

He was blind! There were no eye slits! Stifled! Panic!

Uttering a cry of disgust, he lifted his hands to remove the mask, but a cool fan of fingers stayed his arm.

'No, you must wear it.'

Lariel's voice was shrill. 'But I can't see! How may I dance if I'm blind?'

'If you have the art, truly have it, eyes mean nothing,'

Arnainn said firmly. 'This is the way it must be.'

The priestesses took hold of his arms, to keep them away from his face, and guided him from the chamber.

Imprisoned within the mask, Lariel could only experience sound, of which there was little save their swishing feet, and smell and taste, which were all of the mask; musky and faintly sweet.

The temperature grew warmer; the floor beneath his bare feet felt smooth as glass. Somewhere, unseen, the terpsichore Firfirieth was watching. Of this, Lariel was acutely aware. In his mind he resolved that, as well as being representative of his own progression and experience, the dance to come would also suggest resentment and repulsion. *For you, my lord terpsichore,* Lariel thought. *This is the last dance of mine you'll ever behold.*

The hands left his flesh and, save for his head, which felt confined within the smallest portion of the multiverse, Lariel experienced the stretching vastness beyond his skin's surface. It was an entirely malleable material, into which he could insinuate his limbs and draw forth significant shapes. To the dancer, air is as clay to the sculptor.

As promised, the sharp sound of clapping hands conjured up a rhythm. Lariel tested the mechanisms of his muscles with a few introductory stretchings. The machinery felt good; oiled and ready to race. He executed a few running steps, and found, as if the oil had made his skin more sensitive than usual, he could sense the boundaries of the temple by a faint cold, and the altar of fire by its warmth. If he paid attention to these things, there was no risk of him colliding with some obstacle. The priestesses had been right; eyes were not necessary for what he had to do. In time to Firfirieth's slow percussion, Lariel began to extrapolate his soul's innocence.

Where am I? his body queried. *What is my place in the multiverse? What is my true name?*

His limbs wove and swayed, illustrating the heart-rending passion of the uninitiated seeker, the loneliness and poignant need for knowledge, the surety in the heart of hearts that is essential to walk the fire, be burned and cindered, to understand the question of existence. *There are no answers*, said Lariel's body, *but to know the questions is enough.*

Such was the intensity of the dance, he felt tears spring from his eyes. His heart ached with terrible sadness, and beyond the mask came the muffled sound of women weeping. Women alone, mummified in an ancient, forgotten fane; she-wolves, mateless on the blasted plains, howling for love.

Also, though it may only have been the beating of blood in his ears, it seemed to Lariel as if a thrill of drums had started up, speaking the rhythms of the dance. He could no longer hear Firfirieth's hands.

Wildly, he flew into the heady exultation of the second interval; the quest. Leaping, flying; it felt as if his head brushed the roof of the temple, and he with no aerial belt to aid it.

The women's keening had become part of the music. Lariel was a blade cutting dross, cleaving its way to the heart of all knowledge. And then, at the climax, at the brink of the third interval, when the eye of Gespath opened in the dancer's face to reveal terrible questions, the closed lids of the mask opened.

Lariel was so intoxicated by the dance, for a moment he did not question this odd development. Then, he accepted the oddness as being inevitable and proper. The fane was full of smoke, bitter incenses that brought a taste of burning meat to the throat. Lariel balanced on tiptoe, arms flung high, a reed of taut fibre, a sword of flesh.

He was a dancer at the world's death.

Looking through the lids of the mask, Lariel saw he was no longer in the fane, but somehow outside of it, standing on the marble steps; not swept now, or scoured by flaying wind, but marked with soot and dark, wet patches. A hurricane shrieked in his ears as he stood there, poised in the position of the sword. The mask's heavy hair was blown into his own, streaming out like a ripped flag. The wind was hot and full of smoke and screams. Figures ran through a flame-dashed murk. Everywhere was noise and tumult. The sky above boiled like an angry cauldron in which souls bubbled and merged. Wicked lightning, like swift, spirit hands, grasped the ground in serpent-strikes, throwing up soil and brick and bodies.

Two figures threw themselves at Lariel's feet. They held out clawing hands, mouthing nonsense that he knew was a plea for help. 'Dance!' they seemed to cry. 'Dance for us, pale shadow. Dispel the abominations!'

Lariel could not move. His body was frozen to white stone. He was, in fact, a statue, benign and beautiful, prayed to, adored, but inevitably, utterly without power of any kind.

He wanted to turn his face away from the carnage, seek the darkness of the temple, and yet the dance still had him, a rhythm pounding through his veins that held him motionless, because stasis was simply part of the performance.

And then a huge shape began to fill the sky, shadowing the burning, collapsing city like a god. At first, not being part of anything his mind could catalogue, Lariel could not see it as a thing of substance, but merely an idea of vastness and power. His fingers curled, a movement shuddering down his arms, forcing them into a new configuration of the dance. His thighs quivered.

The shape coalesced before him, shining and coiling, rearing a torso of exquisite milk and pearl. Eyes that were green stars opened and sought his own. A mouth, a gash of blood yearning kisses, smiled beneath them.

'Here I come,' said the god-shape. 'I am the harvester and the artisan. From this corn of souls I shape the sustenance of stars and brooding powers. Come to me, shadow-dancer, for the best sit on my shoulder. The best ride the storm of my passing, clinging to my neck, and it is a ride like no other...'

Lariel's body turned slowly, describing a tremulous query.

The god-shape laughed; a sound of seasons turning, a sound of reaping scythes. 'Come now, beloved, no gawky remonstrances, please! Climb my hands. Put your warm, naked limbs on my flesh and climb.'

The Shape extended it hands, each the size of a plaza. The fingers opened and closed. Lariel felt the heat of unbearable beauty scorch his skin. Around him, the ground shook and gulped stone. Bodies trembled and fell. It was no longer a cataclysm but a battle. Nimble darknesses flitted through the smoke, leaping onto fleeing forms, drinking screams and blood.

Lariel's body arched forward; his spine creaked and flexed. The toes of his left foot hovered above the vast plate of the flexing hand. He could feel the inner fire of it, terrible and seductive. One step, one tiny step...

'Take off the mask, Lariel.' The voice came from nowhere; everywhere. He hesitated and drew back his foot.

'No!' said the god-shape. 'The mask is beautiful, Muinish sweetmeat. Keep it on and come to me.'

'Take off the mask, Lariel!'

'Who calls?' Lariel cried. 'Who calls me?' His body spun and the world became a sickening blur, the god-face flashing in and out of sight.

'Your ancient lover calls you!' screamed the Shape. 'Lord of this domain!'

'And I, Lariel! Firfirieth, your master, also calls you!'

Lariel spun helplessly, a white incandescence. His head ached and seemed to swell, pressing painfully against the confines of the mask. The god-shape crooned promises across his flesh, searing promises of unbearable delight, while the mad terpsichore urged him to remove and mask and finish the dance.

'Obey me!' Firfirieth ordered harshly. 'Trust me, Lariel. The dance must end as it is ordained. Finish the movements! Remove the mask and end it!'

'Do not listen to his mewing,' said the God-shape confidentially. 'Trust me, beautiful, for I offer you eternities of everything.'

'Eternities of corruption!' Firfirieth cried.

'Corruption is pleasure and sweetness.'

'Corruption is decay! Lariel, do not listen. Come back! It is Lithuin calling you; the Lord of the Kleepoq. He is the Power that destroyed this world; turn away!'

Lariel felt tears on his face again; he was unsure what emotion moved them. 'Why should I come back?' he asked. 'Tell me!'

'Because I ask it,' Firfirieth said. 'That's all. I can offer nothing more. The rest is up to you. Now please: take off the mask.'

There was no reason why Lariel should obey. Firfirieth had become a bane to him; a dangerous bane. And yet, his sluggish limbs moved achingly from their poise to grasp the edges of the mask. Above him, huge as eternity, Lithuin roared and snarled, hurling white-hot threats that burned like ice, that pierced Lariel's flesh like spears of ice. 'Go to him and you are lost, Muinish brat! He has betrayed you! Made you suffer! Go to him and I curse you to oblivion!'

'He is my master; my family bought his time for me,' Lariel said, dazed, and lifted the mask from his head.

He stared through his own eyes at the world around him. Kleepoq spawn flowed over the city, hacking and devouring, raping and mutilating. The awful Power presided, a composite being of crawling souls that flowed into rivers of flesh resembling a face, eyes, a torso, arms. Lariel turned his head away. Behind him stood Firfirieth, close and yet so far away.

'Dance to me, Lariel,' he said and held out his hand. 'Believe me, when you reach my side, I can teach you little more. You will stand beside me, Lariel. In every way.'

Feverishly, Lariel tried to move his limbs. They screamed in agony as if every muscle was ripping. A field of blades had blossomed between him and his master; to reach Firfirieth, he must dance across them.

'I cannot... reach... you,' Lariel said, gulping the foul air.

'Do it!' said the terpsichore. 'Do it and you will be as I; you will have danced the dance of Inner Power. It is the last lesson and the first of what is to come.'

'I... cannot!'

'I believe you can, Lariel. Dance! Dance!'

Blood greased the blades, blood was the music of the dance. Lariel felt the sweat of pain course down his flesh and knew, as he danced, that his feet were ruined, cut to pieces. He would never dance again, never walk even. By the time he reached his master, he would be cut, boneless, to the knees. And still he danced, an everness of movement and despair. Behind him, Lithuin laughed, tasting his agony like a fine wine.

'I am dying!' Lariel cried, his body faltering.

'No, you are with me. You are here,' Firfirieth said, and Lariel collapsed against him.

He awoke and found himself lying on the floor of the fane, his head in Firfirieth's lap. Grasping at consciousness greedily, he tried to rise. The priestesses stood some distance away in the shadows of the columns, wreathed in incense smoke. Now, the temple smelled of ancient tombs and grave-dust; no sweetness here, no gods. The women seemed fearful.

'Get up,' Firfirieth said, and dragged Lariel to his feet.

Lariel cried out, afraid, but when he looked down, his skin was unmarked by blood or blade. He was whole. Some feet away, lay the discarded mask. It was easy to see now what it truly was. A scalp, a skin, perfectly preserved, but still the face of a corpse.

'Yes, look long and remember,' Firfirieth said, supporting Lariel against his shoulder. 'That is the face of the last who came here.'

'The last who... danced...?' Lariel swallowed; his mouth felt cracked and dry.

'Yes. You can hate me still, faythling, if you wish, but the task I set has been fulfilled. You are a terpsichore; a young one, maybe, and with much to learn, but you have taken the test of ultimate pain and passed. The rest is easy in comparison.'

'And this is what you sought? The precious thing?'

'Your strength,' Firfirieth said, and kissed Lariel's brow. 'We are guardians you and I, sentinels of our race, warriors of the aether, enemies of the Kleepoq; forever. You have much to learn of your calling yet, Lariel, but..' Firfirieth tapped Lariel's brow with his fingers, 'it is all mind training and learning the secret arcana from now on.'

Ahead of them, the line of priestesses hissed through their grieving masks, backing away.

Firfirieth burrowed in his coat and threw them a handful of coins. 'Take that and be off, vermin!' he said. 'You gambled and lost, thank Gespath!'

The High Priestess uttered a mocking laugh. She stepped forward, and bent to retrieve the flung coins with a wizened, mummified hand. Her mask flashed upwards. 'Don't be so cocky, terpsichore,' she said, straightening up. 'You'll be back, and next time perhaps, not so lucky.'

'Yes, I'll be back,' Firfirieth said softly. 'I'll be back with new souls to test.'

'You are a fool!' spat the woman. 'You sacrifice your children to Lithuin in the name of pride.'

'No hag, you are wrong. With each who fails, more of my soul bleeds into the abyss; each surrender is a death for me. Do not think I do this lightly. It is you who are the fools, you who are proud. You think to best us, we the sharpest of terpsichores. You think it is easy measy when we test our students in this fane. But you are wrong. We forge the strongest alloys in this accursed place, which we turn against you. Take the coin and use it if you can!'

The priestess spat thickly at the terpsichore's feet. 'Yah, take your stripling, clown! Make him a posturing dandy like you! The day will come when you are all crushed, for all your vanities and tricks!'

Firfirieth bowed smartly. 'Good day to you, madam. I thank you for your hospitality and grieve I must leave you empty-handed.'

The priestess cackled and retreated to her sisters. 'Next time, terpsichore, next time! You, or one of your fellows, will submit a soul to Lithuin, young and fresh as a sweet fruit for our lord to suck!'

'If a soul submits to your master, then it is hardly sweet, but rancid,' Firfirieth remarked dryly, and dismissed the women from his attention. He wrapped Lariel in the cloak of midnight, which somehow had become old, ragged cloth. 'It is time to leave,' he said.

The priestesses set up a cacophony of profanities to sing them from the fane.

Outside, the wind hit Lariel like a curse. Yet even though his eyes clouded with blackness, he climbed without faltering over the fallen stones, following Firfirieth back to the gateway and sanctuary. He sensed that things had changed between them.

When they emerged into the rusting corridors of Thoughts of Far Deeds, Lariel sank to the floor, hardly able to move. For a few moments, Firfirieth stood over him, silently, then squatted down beside him. He raised his mask and put a hand on Lariel's shoulder.

Lariel raised his head. 'That world can never be reclaimed,' he said. 'You have known of it for a long time, haven't you? You've been there many times before.'

Firfirieth dropped his eyes for a moment, then sighed and fixed Lariel with his gaze. He nodded. 'Yes. All terpsichores know of that place. It is the dark side of Mahkouf, a distorted reflection, and was never a world of ours.'

'What is our function, my light?'

Firfirieth squeezed his shoulder. 'Later, my light, later.

You are tired.'

'No. Tell me. Do the lost worlds still exist?'

Firfirieth smiled tightly. 'Yes. But we are not yet ready to begin the fight to reclaim them. Our order, the terpsichores, will one day be an army to fight the abyss, but not yet. For now, we protect this small cinder of a world from invasion with the strength of our spirits, which we manifest through the dance. That forlorn place we visited is the testing ground of our warriors. This is our secret, Lariel, of which you have become privy.'

Lariel shook his head. 'This is incredible. My father just wanted me to be a sacred dancer. If he knew of this...!'

Firfireth laughed. 'My dear Lariel, it was we who chose you. It was nothing to do with any choice your father made. You believe he paid for your apprenticeship, but he did not. He was required to surrender you to me, at the will of our Emperor and his hierophants. We are adept at spotting... talent. You will learn this skill too.' He leaned forward and kissed Lariel briefly on the mouth. 'Come, you are exhausted. There will be plenty of time for questions.'

Together they retraced their steps to the waiting apartment, and in the silence they left behind, the old passageways closed in a veil of rubble and decay to hide the secret of the ancient gateway until the next student came to be tested in the cursed fane.

Panquilia in the Ruins

She was woken by a bale of hay falling across her face - for an instant bringing dreams of suffocation - and the rough voice of the carter saying, 'Well, your ride ends here, my lass. Liven up!'

'My ride ends where?' Panquilia, demon hunter and traveller, sat up, pulling straws from her hair. She had fallen asleep wrapped up in her cloak, but could tell the air was much colder now. Dusk was creeping on, too.

'Hussard's Inn.' The driver was laconic, although he had been amenable enough to let her beg a ride. Panquilia burrowed in her pouch and then offered the customary chip of currency, which the carter accepted with a stiff nod.

'Hussard's Inn,' Panquilia said, eyeing the dark building. 'Not many lamps lit, are there.'

'You'll find the door open,' the carter said. He clucked at his mules and they began to move again. Panquilia was obliged to leap awkwardly over the wheels.

For a moment she stood on the furrowed track, observing the Inn. This land was unknown to her. Until recently, she had been travelling with two colleagues: Thomathy Versaille and Ilander Groomblack. They had been commissioned to contain a rogue angel, who had been pleasuring itself with sleeping boys in a boarding academy. Once they'd completed the job successfully, the three companions had gone on a spree, wandering from town to town, drinking and playing jacks for currency. Ilander had taken up with a one-eyed woman she'd found, and had been left behind. Thomathy had become bored and went back to his home in Aphlex. Panquilia, fascinated by the land, had declined the invitation to accompany him, although she had arranged to visit him soon. In the event, she wished she'd gone with him when he'd asked, for her interest in the quaint customs of the land quickly diminished once she travelled alone. She realised it had been Thomathy and Ilander who had made the journey interesting. Also, there had been no sniff of work, and her funds had dried up.

Now, she wondered whether it had been a mistake to sell her horse back in Holy Hand. The idea of comparative wealth had seemed attractive at the time, but the reality of having to find alternative transport east proved troublesome. Not many people travelled across the eastern plains it seemed. At first, Panquilia had been amused by the reaction her request had conjured from the townsfolk; hurried signs of protection against evil, whispered charms, effusive spitting into the dust. Later, this behaviour had lost all quaintness in her eyes, and became merely annoying. The penultimate pathfinder she had approached had offered her his throat. 'Cut this now,' he had said. 'It will save time.' The gesture, she supposed, had been dramatic, but the memory it conjured within her filled her vision with boiling motes of light.

Panquilia replied, 'Look, I need to get across. You are a guide. I have money.' Her smile was faint by this time.

'Go south,' he'd advised. 'The journey, though longer, is easier.'

Eventually, she'd been directed to the carter - a dull stone of a man - who had been about to set out on a journey to deliver a wagon of hay further north. It was said he could at least take her to the lip of the plains.

Hussard's Inn looked no different from the countless other travellers' retreats Panquilia had patronised over the years. It was set in a bleak land - no wonder fodder had to be brought up from the south. Behind the inn, a low sprawl of stables could be seen, and the brick wall of a kitchen garden. Beyond this, the dim humps of the northern mountains nested in a pillow of foothills; the sky above them devoid of cloud, although uniformly grey. Panquilia sniffed, rubbed her nose vigorously, and marched into the inn.

She had not expected there to be many patrons, and was quite surprised to see about half a dozen men sitting at a long table at the back of the room, the remains of a meal pushed out along the wood. The room was quite plain; a flagged floor rugged by goatskins, crude wattled walls, low beams. Her entrance, predictably, conjured a silence.

'Is the landlord about?' Panquilia asked, moving to where a lively fire filled up an immense grate, perhaps the only decorative feature of the room. Behind her, the clientele sat up to attention as she threw back her cloak. Such reactions always pleased her. She considered the gratification of vanity a small sin, in the face of all the other gratifications she denied herself. She turned around expectantly, making sure the men caught a glimpse of the long, slim blades hanging from her belt in expensive leather sheaths. She did not want to have to deal with any untoward advances.

One of the men stood up and moved towards her. 'I am Hussard,' he said. He was dressed in shirt and breeches, without the customary apron to signify his position.

'I'm breaking a journey here,' she said. 'You have a room I can make use of?'

He nodded.

'Splendid. I also need transport further east...'

'Are you travelling alone?'

Panquilia thought she detected disapproval in his voice, and smiled in her most feral manner. 'Yes, I generally travel alone.'

One or two of the men around the table laughed. They doubtlessly considered her a mercenary or a whore. Deploring, yet again, the narrowness of men's minds, Panquilia marched over to the table and dropped herself heavily into a chair. Nonchalantly, she laced her fingers together, extended her arms to display tight, wiry muscles and one or two scars, and cracked the knuckles. She did this to illustrate that the blades hanging from her hip were more than decoration. 'I could use a meal,' she said.

The men sobered and watched her warily, one or two burying their noses in tankards.

She had sat next to a young man, whose eager smile signified that he was either an innocent or a moron. 'This is a not a good point to travel east from, lady,' he said. His companions nodded.

'Oh?' Panquilia sensed the imminence of unwanted advice.

He shook his head. 'No. You'll have to go south a long way first. The Duke has forbidden anyone to travel into the deserted lands from here.'

'How inclement of him.'

Another man shook his head. 'It's a protective measure.'

'Don't tell me - you have monsters hereabouts. No? Demons, ghosts?' She grinned at the unsmiling faces. 'Perhaps you Duke has vast treasure out there he has a mind to keep.'

'We have a ruin out there,' the second man answered. 'Big ruin.'

'I see. Danger of falling masonry then.'

'Danger of losing your life - or your mind.'

'I was right about the demons, it seems.' She could have told them she dealt with such things on a daily basis, but the company did not interest her enough to begin a tale.

Hussard returned with a bowl of dark, aromatic pot-stew. Panquilia's stomach churned with yearning at the sweet perfume of it.

'You'd be wise not to scoff,' Hussard remarked. 'Like Avro said, you'll have to go south before entering the plains. The ruins have claimed too many people, including one close to the Duke himself. He is a just man and does not pass laws unfairly.' He thrust a shallow, wooden spoon into Panquilia's hands. 'You want bread with that?'

She nodded. 'Bread, ale, everything. I've not eaten since morning.'

Panquilia had consulted a map in Holy Hand and there

had been no indication of dangerous ruins on it at all. Perhaps she would have to buy some kind of animal transport again if she wanted to cross from here. A nuisance. It would debilitate her purse. She'd anticipated the funds from her horse sale would keep her amply until she reached Aphlex.

'This is really very good,' she said to the landlord. His smile was still guarded. 'So, tell me why I can't go east from here. I don't want legends - facts. Is it just physically dangerous?'

'That depends on what you mean by physical,' Hussard said, sitting down again. He replenished the tankards of his companions with thick, dark ale from a huge jug on the table. 'People got lost in there regularly. Place is a labyrinth. But it wasn't until Gampander went missing that any positive indictment was made against going in there.'

'Gampander?' Panquilia said. 'Can I have some of that ale?'

The landlord pushed a tankard across the table towards her, filled it carefully. 'The Duke's son. There's a tale to it.'

'There always is.' She leaned back in her chair, her stomach comfortably filled. Having spent most of the day asleep in the back of the cart, she did not feel particularly tired. And, she was in the mood for a good story. 'Tell it to me, then.'

Hussard settled himself comfortably. 'Well, it all began as a bit of a lark. Young men will be that way, won't they? Seven sons of seven noble houses, they were, bored and looking for diversions.

'The Duke of Sar Pendrous has green lawns before his palace; watered and preened. The royal boys rarely leave this environment; they canter their ponies up and down beside the lakes, sometimes hunting vermin in the long grass.' Hussard frowned. 'I suppose Gampander was never popular among his peers.' Clearly, such implied affront to the local nobility did not rest easy with him.

'So, why was that?' Panquilia asked.

Hussard shrugged. 'Jealousy, perhaps. The Duke denied him nothing. Sons of lesser families would be considered spoiled allowed his privileges. Anyway, one day, mischief was afoot. Gampander's companions led him to the brink of the wilderness, into the rattling grasses, where you can see the grey-water, and the first slabs of the ruin, through the canes. At best, it is an arcane place. Then, Gampander's friends galloped their ponies off in all directions, thinking to leave the boy alone with the unhappy ghosts of the place; only their laughter remained. Gampander was unused to being out alone. He must've tried to find his way back, but somehow lost his way.

'By sundown, the Duke was beginning to worry. He questioned his son's companions who, at first, were reluctant to admit their culpability. None of them had imagined Gampander would have been stupid enough to wander off in the opposite direction to home. The Duke sent people out to search. They followed the prints in the grass cut by the pony's hooves, which led out of the safe grounds, along the withy way, to the shores of the lake and the road to the ruins.

'The trackers returned with their news, and the Duke, who by this time had lost all pretence of patience and tolerance, had the six youths taken into custody. This was despite the protest of their parents, who also happened to be very good friends of his. You can imagine the bad feeling it all caused. After but an hour in confinement, savouring the company of rats and the stink of slime, all six youths were eager to admit their folly. The Duke, who, in spite of his grief, was a fair man, exacted no punishment other than a brief flogging for each of them.

'The Duke himself led a search party into the wilderness. They found Gampander's pony standing upon the cracked road - ruins to either side - as if it was waiting for its master to return. It took them a further few hours to find Gampander himself. He was lying beneath a crumbled arch, his head upon stone. He was naked, his clothes strewn around him, as if they'd been torn from his body by frenzied hands. His father thought he was dead, of course - and it would have been a blessing if he had been. The boy's eyes stared unblinkingly upwards, the pupils wide and black. Upon his face, there was a smile. His body was warm.' Hussard's eyes had assumed a faraway look.

Avro finished the story. 'They say Gampander will never speak again, never wake up properly. It's said he's been shocked into silence by ghouls that haunt the ruins, frightened to silence. He will never be whole again - his mind is ruined. I have heard that, on moonlit nights, he goes to the window doors of his bedroom and goes out onto the terrace. He looks up at the sky, staring at the stars.' He made a wide gesture with his arms. 'The servants can't coax him back inside, even if it is a cold night. Maybe, at those times, he listens to the voice of the part of himself that stayed in the ruins. It's possible. Maybe he hears wondrous things that he can never share with anyone else. Perhaps,' and here Avro made a dramatic pause and lowered his voice, 'perhaps that is the price!'

The landlord snorted and waved a derisory hand at the boy. 'Fool!' he said. 'You look for romance, but there's little in that bestial place. Whatever took him hasn't left him with the ability to feel pleasure, that's for sure.'

'You've seen this Gampander yourself then, have you?' Panquilia asked.

Hussard bristled. 'No, but sometimes the Duke's staff come drinking here if they've been afield. They talk.'

'Don't they!' Panquilia agreed. 'Personally, I don't see any proof of ghouls being involved. Wouldn't you say the most obvious explanation was that Gampander was assaulted - by creatures most definitely human. There must be vagabonds in the ruins - such places are natural territory to that type.' Her hand strayed to the faience collar she wore around her neck, mostly hidden by her clothes. She wondered at her own motives for refuting the story. Didn't she know herself just how possible such hideous events were?

'Believe me, we know what happened,' Hussard said. '*We* live around here. You're a stranger. Gampander wasn't the only one to lose his mind in that place.'

'Perhaps you're right.' Panquilia told herself she had lost interest in the conversation, ignoring any other inner remarks that prompted otherwise. 'Would you show me my room now?'

It was not a large room; the bed filled most of it. From superstitious habit - a result of past events - Panquilia turned the misted mirror to the wall. For some reason, she hardly undressed to sleep, and lay awake for a long time, thinking about what she should do the next day. As her mind churned, her fingers crept beneath the collar around her neck, and traced the lightning branches of the scar that lay beneath. It was perhaps no coincidence she hadn't found any work since her companions had left her. Consciously, she might not admit this, for she strove to conceal her inner fears from both herself and her friends and colleagues. But the talk of haunted wastes had brought the past back to her in frightening clarity. She saw herself, young and inexperienced, cowering in the shadows of the collossal pylons of a shattered temple. She heard the screaming breath of the demon as he burst like fire from the darkness: Zebellion. He lived in ruins, and once in youthful bravado she had dared to try and match him. She knew better now, and to recall the episode made her feel ashamed and uncertain. She had spoken of it only to the healer who had found her, nearly dead, after Zebellion had streaked away like a comet from her blasted body. Not even her mentors knew of what had happened then. Later, adepts of her Order had entrapped the demon and sent him screaming into the hinterland; the realm between life and death. But sometimes, Panquilia still felt his presence. Her fear conjured him. She felt they had unfinished business.

Now, she had second thoughts about crossing the ruins beyond the inn. That alone annoyed her. Was she still driven this way and that by the whip of fear? Would she let that whip drive her south, away from Aphlex? No. She had a compass and a destination. She could find her way across the ruins; ghoul-infested or not. It would only add days to her journey, if not weeks, if she took the longer route south. There could be nothing in those ruins she could not deal with.

By day, the saurian outline of the ruined city could be seen hazily towards the east. Hussard pointed out the great flagged highway, some of which was still used by locals, as it led out of the wasteland towards market towns in the south. Panquilia fought the urge to heap reassurances upon the landlord's head concerning her safety. There was no point. He meant nothing to her, and his opinions were undoubtedly riddled with ignorant superstition.

With regret, she surrendered some of her funds and purchased a mount from the inn-keeper. The beast was a narrow, young pony - not long broken, by the skittishness of it. Panquilia was filled with apprehension, realising, as soon as she climbed on its back, that the journey was going to be far from comfortable. The pony shimmied and skipped about as she tried to adjust her position, and it was through sheer good fortune she managed to salute the landlord, in a kind of extravagant, swashbuckling way, as the animal began trotting mercilessly away from the inn.

She had tied her compass firmly round her neck and did not intend to waver one inch from her direction. The pony made quick progress and soon came to be jogging along a stretch of the road where headless columns formed an avenue to either side. The road was made of immense slabs that, through the years (perhaps centuries), had come to list drunkenly in their foundations. Sometimes the pony, which had not changed gait since they'd left the inn, missed its footing and lurched alarmingly. Panquilia cursed aloud on these occasions. Her thighs were already protesting painfully; a torment she had to ignore. Only a death-like grip on the animal's flanks kept her on top of it.

Ancient statues were interspersed between the columns on either side of the road: orators and kings, all gesturing meaningfully with broken arms; their faces, though disfigured with age, humourless and filled with self-importance.

Presently, Panquilia came to a place where remnants of a city wall protruded through the surrounding debris. Little remained of the ceremonial arch into the town, and the road was so littered with rubble, the pony was forced to decrease its pace. Panquilia, though grateful for the physical relief, was uncomfortable with the slow progress. On either side of the road, eerie, shadowed mounds of tumbled masonry stretched as far as she could see. Occasionally, lone, broken columns punctuated the rubble. She saw a flight of marble stairs that ascended only into air, the house once surrounding it having long since crumbled to dust. Panquilia wondered what kind of civilisation had once thrived here - and what had happened to it? From the size of the ruin, the city must have once been an affluent place, and densely populated. All around her were relics of a past opulence: a massive villa, broken and roofless, marked only by rows of columns; a single terrace of splintered tiles; a forlorn alcove that sheltered a weathered, faceless statue. There was no sign of anything corruptible among the stones; no rags, no bones, not even a single plant. The air was utterly without odour. She extended her senses to see whether she could detect any spiritual presences around her, but there seemed to be none.

Examining her compass, Panquilia realised she'd have to leave the comparative safety of this major highway and find a path for herself through the ruins themselves; not a prospect she viewed with pleasure. Much of the place would undoubtedly be impassable. There were signs of subsidence here and there, so her path might often be blocked by rubble. Still, no time would be saved worrying about it. She must trust her compass and her sense of direction.

Giving the pony a few desultory kicks in its skinny ribs, she hauled its head to the left, and followed the first road available to them.

The silence itself was a sound that whistled in the ears, barely audible. Panquilia hummed a tune beneath her breath. The melody comforted her and she began to beat a percussion on the front of the saddle. Behind these sounds, she fancied she could hear music accompanying her; the bray of some wind instrument, the chink of small bells shaken in the air. After a few moments, Panquilia considered this was not just her imagination. Perhaps there were other people in the ruins, hiding among the stones; nomads and vagabonds following in her wake, playing her a tune before they jumped her. She fell quiet and swung round in the saddle, but there was no sign of movement behind her, and whatever sounds she had imagined had stopped. She drew in a deep breath in preparation to resume her song, and her nose filled with perfume; an overwhelmingly sickly sweet odour of flowers. This could not just be in her mind. She sniffed repeatedly, and the smell was still there; a heavy aroma, as if to mask the less flavoursome odours of sickness. For as far as she could see, however, the ruins were only bleached stones, with no indication that anything lived amongst them, no splash of colour to betray the presence of flowers. Perhaps grave-blooms cowered in the shadows. Now, her singing was confined to a vague hum. She felt uneasy, as if she was no longer alone.

The ruins gradually became less fragmented. The buildings on either side of the road here were intact. Over the noise of the pony's hooves, she thoughts she could hear the buzz of city noise; human voices, the creak of carts, heavy objects being moved, music, animal cries. Was it possible a part of the city was occupied? After all, the buildings, as far as she could see, appeared habitable.

Turning a corner, she came upon a crossroads. It was here she found the first sign of life. In the middle of the pale, dusty road sat a child; a little girl, wearing a red dress, her hair tied up with ribbons. In her small hands she held a wickedly curved, long silver knife, and was so absorbed in the task of scratching patterns in the dust with it, she did not even look up as Panquilia approached her.

Panquilia reined her pony in and, for a few seconds, watched the child warily. She did not appear to be more than four or five years old, and Panquilia wondered why she was out alone, allowed to play with such a potentially dangerous toy.

'Hello!' Panquilia called.

At that, the child looked up. For a moment, there was an expression of bizarrely adult cunning on her small face, which was swiftly replaced by a sweet, gap-toothed smile.

Panquilia urged her pony forward at a walk. 'I didn't expect to find anyone here,' she said to the child. 'You live here?'

The girl nodded slowly. Her pudgy hands twisted the knife in a disarmingly proficient manner.

'Are there any shops near here?' Panquilia asked. 'Somewhere I can get something to eat and drink?'

The girl nodded again. She pointed up one of the streets.

'Thanks.' The child was clearly a little crazed. Her smiling silence was unnerving.

Don't give in to these feelings, Panquilia told herself. She was just a child.

Walking her pony in the direction the child had indicated, Panquilia was again conscious of noise, but there was still no sign of any people, as if all activity was taking place one street away. She heard laughter, and now the air smelled of fruit - fresh and rotting - and the fatty aroma of frying food. Buildings to either side of the road were shuttered, but appeared to be freshly painted. Perhaps nomads had adopted this derelict place; there had been something suggestive of gypsy blood about the child.

Suddenly, from a doorway ahead, a young woman, dressed in white, ran out into the street. The pony shied in alarm, and Panquilia's hand instantly sprang to her sword-belt.

The woman pawed air blindly for a moment, and then turned towards them. Panquilia couldn't help uttering a cry of surprise; the woman's white bodice was liberally splashed with shining red - the unmistakable bloom of life blood.

The woman lurched towards Panquilia, holding out her hands in front of her to display a gruesome coating of thick gore. Her voice was a low, continuous moan of despair. Panquilia had seen plenty of blood before, but something about this tableau deeply repelled her. She felt nausea rise in her belly as she saw the spatter of scarlet droplets on the woman's white neck and pale cheeks. Panquilia drew her sword, and brandished it in a way to suggest she did not want to be approached too closely. The woman edged, arms still outstretched, around the perimeter of Panquilia's reach. Her pitiful keening did not change in tone, as if she did not have to draw breath at all. 'Are you hurt?' Panquilia asked. It was impossible to tell whether the blood was the woman's own or someone else's.

The woman shook her head, hiccuped a few squeaks as if she was about to speak, before hurrying off down the street, crying, 'It's all like this, and this, and this!' Her voice was so ragged, it sounded as if her throat was raw from screaming.

Panquilia was quite shaken by the confrontation, and did not feel inclined to put away her weapon. She was beginning to wonder exactly what kind of people inhabited this isolated place.

After venturing down a few side-streets, she eventually emerged into a large square. Here, it seemed, the local inhabitants were all gathered together. It was a comfortingly familiar scene; market stalls laden with goods, people moving among the stalls, haggling. Children played noisily, running in and out of the market stalls. There was no sign of an inn.

Panquilia dismounted from the pony and began to lead it up one of the alleys that radiated away from the square. Here, the ancient buildings leaned toward each other, their balconies festooned with flowering vines. Clean washing hung drying in tiers from wall to wall, high above, flapping gently in a faint breeze. Panquilia gazed up at the wafting sheets as she walked along, her eyes filled with white. Perhaps she could sell the pony here and acquire transport east on someone's cart. Surely, the people here must travel that way. How else would they get the merchandise that filled the stalls of the market?

A movement in the corner of her eye prompted her to look round and, for a moment, she thought one of the sheets was drifting past her up the street. Then, she realised it was a huge white horse. At first, she thought the animal was untended, but saw it was followed by a teenaged boy, who was holding onto its tail. From his milky, upturned eyes, she deduced the boy was blind. Still, he might know where she could sell the pony.

'Excuse me,' she said, 'but can you tell me if there's a livery stable anywhere near?'

The horse stopped and looked at her through a dark eye.

'You can find anything if you look hard enough,' said the boy.

'Perhaps I need a guide like yours,' she replied, rather sharply. 'I'm a stranger.'

'Who isn't.'

The horse snorted, stamped a front hoof and then began to walk on.

Are all the people here deranged or have I just picked the wrong ones to ask for directions? Panquilia wondered. The street had become dark, and damp underfoot. Around her, the buildings sagged in disrepair. Perhaps she was venturing beyond the inhabited areas again.

Just as she was about to turn round and retrace her path, she saw a man leaning against a wall up ahead. Because he was in shadow, she hadn't noticed him immediately. He was dressed in garments of dull yellow and green, a grin upon his face. He was juggling what appeared, to Panquilia, to be either small animals or brown furry balls.

She walked up to him. 'Hello,' she began. 'I'm not from around here. Could you help me out with a little information? I want to know where I can find a livery stable. Or perhaps you could recommend a decent inn?'

The man didn't stop juggling. He rolled his eyes.

'Are those rats you're throwing around there?' she asked.

'Catch!' he replied and threw all three of them at her. She yelped and ducked, embarrassed to see three wooden balls clunking down around her. 'You have to be quick,' said the man.

Panquilia brushed her hair from her eyes and fondled the hilt of her sword in what she hoped was a meaningful gesture. 'Well, will you answer my question or not?'

'Did you ask a question?'

'I asked about a livery stable, transport, an inn.'

'Livery, livery, liver. Is that a stable made of liver, or one whose stalls are peopled by wobbling organs freed from the flesh?'

'It's a place where horses are kept.'

'Livery. Live. A building full of the living, no doubt. Do we have such a thing. If so, why?'

I'm wasting my time, she thought. 'Well, thank you anyway. I suppose I'll just keep looking.' She turned around and headed back the way she had come. As she walked, she noticed things had quietened down considerably. There was no longer any sound of activity coming from the square and, overhead, all the housekeepers had taken in their laundry. 'Town shuts early,' she told the pony. The sun was still high overhead; perhaps everyone took a siesta at noon. This assumption appeared to be correct for, when she stepped out into the square, it was completely empty of people. Sighing, Panquilia hauled herself back into the saddle and set off at a brisk trot in an easterly direction. She wouldn't both to try and find an inn. She had water and dried supplies in her saddle-bags. That would have to suffice.

Nothing blocked her way. No bloodied women burst from

the silent doorways, no jugglers leapt into her path, no blind boys led by horses. The ruins were occupied only by the sunlight that bleached everything to the colour of bone. Panquilia tried to think comforting thoughts of her friend Thomathy, waiting in Aphlex for her arrival. In her mind, she wove her recent experiences into an amusing anecdote, which could be delivered over a meal later. Panquilia's spirits began to lift. She even made herself smile as she thought up descriptions in her head.

Then the boy appeared in front of her and she was not so sure the events she'd witnessed were at all amusing.

He was slight of build with long, black hair, dressed in finery that had seen better days. He was young and, despite an air of confusion as he felt his way forward with groping hands, was quite handsome. His eyes were very dark, although Panquilia suspected he might be as blind as the boy who'd followed the white horse. She also felt - and there was no real reason for doing so - that this boy was as much a stranger to these parts as she was. She felt she was being given a vision of how she might appear, should she be unable to find her way out of the ruins. A superstitious desire to allay Fate, rather than altruism, prompted her to rein the pony in once more, and ask, 'Are you alright?'

The young man turned his head towards her, his fingers twitching. He seemed surprised she had spoken.

She dismounted and approached him. He drew back a few steps, perhaps frightened. 'It's alright,' she soothed. 'Don't be afraid. What's wrong?'

The boy's face creased into an expression of grief. He blinked at her; she could see he was not blind.

'Can I help at all?'

'They...' he said. 'They...'

'Who? They what?'

The boy shook his head miserably. 'No, no time. My flesh! My flesh!' With a cry, he stumbled off down a side alley, careering off the walls as he went. Panquilia watched in astonishment for a few moments. Then, irresistibly drawn, she followed in the direction the young man had taken.

After some minutes, she entered a realm of shadows. The stones of the ruins were dark blue around her. She could just make out the staggering form of the boy ahead, and kicked her pony into a trot in order to catch up. 'Wait!' she called, certain he wouldn't. He didn't.

They came to the foot of a vast flight of steps, once polished marble, but now rough and weathered and, in some places, splintered away entirely. Panquilia could see the boy leaping up the steps two or three at a time, and urged the pony to follow.

The steps led to the gloomy facade of an ancient temple - in parts roofless - whose high corners where thronged with diurnal bats, squeaking and rustling about their business; the walls were stained with their droppings. Panquilia had lost sight of her quarry, but thought she heard the echo of a cry, from up ahead in the dimness. Keeping in the saddle, in case she had to make a quick get-away, she forced the pony - which, by this time, was exhibiting signs of disquiet - to enter between the columns. Many lightless passages lined the main aisle and, although she knew the boy might have disappeared down one of them, she had a strong reluctance to investigate. On a purely practical level, there might be danger of falling masonry, ruptured floors or, less likely but still a possibility, predators.

The aisle led to a large chamber, perhaps once used for worship, which still bore the signs of an ancient religion. The walls were decorated with detailed murals, which Panquilia thought might depict religious myth, and there were several altar shrines, where the statues of old gods squatted in the shadows. Yet this was also a place of desecration. As if by an agency of insane fury, the wall pictures were gouged and dislodged, the statues disfigured, as if they had undergone inhuman torture. Eyes were hacked away, noses broken off, hands severed, breasts chopped from torsos. Looking at the devastation, Panquilia was conscious of a rising unease within her. Had the young man done all these things?

Keeping her pony in the light, she advanced up the chamber. At the end was a magnificent altar - untouched by dissolution - behind which stood an equally magnificent statue. Panquilia's heart nearly stopped. If this was a god, it was a mockery. There was something hideously familiar about the flamboyant garb, the haughty, sneering smile, the outstretched curved claws, the spreading, ripped leathery wings, with their hooked joints. Was it her imagination, or was the idol before her truly a representation of the Lord of Screams, Zebellion? Terror welled up within her. She should not have come here. Her worst fears swooped up from the blackest corners of her mind to haunt her. She must not believe an image of the arch-demon Zebellion reared above her. It would be too much of a coincidence if it was he. It could be any hideous deity. She wasn't commissioned to investigate this place. It was none of her business. She must leave here now. Shuddering, she turned the pony around. She would spur it into the fastest pace it had ever taken. She would teach it to surpass itself - through severe pain, if necessary.

When she turned, her path was blocked.

A priestess stood there, garbed in a pale blue habit that revealed as much as it concealed of the slender body beneath, due to its extreme transparency. She looked very young; dark red ringlets of hair fell from beneath her veil and curled seductively over each small breast. Her lips were parted in a smile, which was rather too red.

Panquilia was only aware she'd drawn one of her blades when she actually saw it held out in front of her.

The priestess raised her hands. 'Please, I pray you, do not raise weapons in the house of our Lord.'

'I see no lords here, only demons,' Panquilia answered. 'I suggest you move.'

The priestess ducked her head and stepped lightly aside,

revealing that the boy Panquilia had followed to this place was crouching behind her. Hardening her heart, Panquilia urged to pony to walk past him but, at that moment, the boy raised his head and stared at her with such a poignant expression of wordless entreaty, she pulled the animal to a halt again.

'You can come with me,' she said. The priestess had no weapon; there was no apparent danger.

'Alas, I must inform you that is impossible,' said the priestess. 'You are a stranger here. That is rare, and worth examining for its own sake, but there are limits to how much I can tolerate in this fane - especially of a heretical nature.'

'It seems to me you have tolerated much in the way of heresy already,' Panquilia remarked, indicating the walls and the broken statues. 'Or are you and your demon merely encamped in someone else's temple and responsible for the damage yourselves?'

The priestess narrowed her eyes, but offered no immediate response.

Panquilia spoke gently to the boy. 'You have nothing to be frightened of. Walk out of here with me.' She directed a swift glare at the priestess to show she was not above a fight, if necessary.

The priestess laughed. 'He can't leave. He is not whole.'

'What does she mean?' Panquilia asked the boy.

'I am not whole,' he replied, head hanging. 'My father took some of me away, and now I am not whole.'

'Who are you?'

'Son of a great house. Taken by the weir, delivered to the waste. Taken. Taken.'

Panquilia examined him with more attention; he had a well-bred face. 'Would that great house be Sar Pendrous?'

The young man scrambled to his feet, a ghost of pride coming into his voice. 'There is only one great house in this land, and you have named it,' he said.

'Then I must have the honour of addressing the soul of Gampander, Son of the Duke of Sar Pendrous.'

'His soul?' spat the priestess. 'No. His father took the soul. *This is his body.*'

Panquilia frowned. 'That cannot be. Gampander lives, apparently mindlessly, in his father's house. How can a soul take on flesh?'

'You know nothing,' replied the priestess. 'This is no ordinary place. The energy of Gampander's flesh here anchors his soul to this plane. If this body should die, the soul would dissipate and be unable to incarnate in any plane, sphere or realm. It would have no point of reference.'

'So why not let his body go free, so that he can reunite with his spirit?' Panquilia traced a faintly threatening finger along the edge of her blade. Thoughts of paternal gratitude and subsequent reward were not far from her mind.

'You have no intelligence!' the priestess cried and, with a smothered curse, stamped her foot and performed a vibration that made Panquilia's head ache. In seconds, the priestess had transformed herself into a predatory beast of startling appearance; still female, but hideously fanged and clawed. 'He is mine,' the beast woman roared, 'as are all the memories of the temple. As are all the phantoms of the day and night. As you will be, very soon.'

'I would not, in your position, address such remarks to a woman carrying a sword,' Panquilia said. She flexed her sword arm and decapitated the apparition in one stroke. The body continued to stand there, extending its talons and spraying the surrounding area with an unsavoury ichor, while the head shrieked obscenities from the floor.

Gampander shook his head. 'She will take on another form soon enough and, because of the way you just insulted her, will make the tearing of the soul from your flesh doubly horrible.'

'I don't intend to linger here,' Panquilia said. 'Follow me. Quickly!'

'I can't.'

'You must. You must call your soul back.'

'Impossible - here. She wouldn't allow it. It would give me back my freedom - at least in a physical way.'

'Gampander, if I may address you so informally, you must fight your fear and flee. Now, you have a chance. What is that creature anyway? Are all the other people in the city of her kind? Come on, tell me as we go.'

They began to hurry back down the temple, the boy sprinting alongside the pony, who was so desperate to escape the place, it had broken into a canter of its own accord. 'There are no people,' Gampander replied, gasping, as he ran. 'Those you have encountered are merely memories of the past, memories of the time when the Lord of Screams and his followers amused themselves at the expense of the population of this place. All that you have seen here are just reflections of an ancient madness. As for the priestess, she is An'd'yanae, a handmaiden of the demon, Zebellion. She was human once, or so she boasts, but now...'

Panquilia was cold with dread. 'But Zebellion is trapped in the hinterland; he has no power on earth.'

'An'd'yanae is collecting it for him,' Gampander replied. 'She is his last follower. She collects the souls of the unwary - be they beast or human.'

They had come out into the shadowed sunlight. Panquilia felt light-headed with relief. All they had to do now was run.

Then the air shimmered around her. It happened so quickly. She had one last glimpse of Gampander's horrified face before reality began to fade away and a dry freezing wind chilled the blood in her veins. She could no longer feel the pony beneath her. An insatiable darkness, where there was no life at all, pressed down upon her. She knew this place; it haunted her nightmares and lurked like a ghoul at the edge of her mind at all times. The wind shrieked more keenly around her, becoming, at length, a hideous and inhuman laughter.

Panquilia was on her knees in the blackness. A dreadful pain stabbed through her body and there was an appalling warm gush at her throat. The wound had opened. Her lifeblood was pouring out once more. The Lord of Screams had taken her once again. She would be lost to the never-ending death, never-ending torment, and the extinction that is conscious.

Cruel laughter swelled and ebbed around her, fading at last into the sussurus of wind through leaves. The blackness faded. Panquilia looked around herself and recognised with relief the mighty hascody trees of the ancient forest of Durawn, a spiritual realm of dreams and tranquillity. She would find peace now. No demons could follow her there. This was sanctuary. She was surrounded by a whispering verdure, and walked through the trees towards a place she knew well: the Pool of Spirits. It was time for her to look into it once more. The pool was a mirror of black water. Sighing, Panquilia leaned forward and saw her reflection looking back at her from the water. A mirror of truth. Then, her hair began to lift from her shoulders of its own accord, hissing like serpents. Her face contorted into a wicked sneer, her eyes burning with a sullen fire of destructive lust and vengeful power. She had lived this moment before. She cried out and tried to turn away, but could not move. As she gazed at her reflection, she saw a red mark steal across her throat. It opened like a second mouth that drooled red ichor. It became the smile of Zebellion. The face no longer looked like her own at all. Hideous beauty. The demon had come for her again, to take her body, drink her soul.

Everything rushed into darkness once more, and Panquilia knew she was in the hinterland, the exile-haunt of Zebellion. She perceived a faint wavering light approaching her; hardly more than a slim reed of luminous energy. But it was approaching fast, growing, expanding in her awareness. Panquilia's spiritual form could not blink against this radiance. Her whole being was concentrated on its advance. Gradually, the light became a creature of flesh before her, a familiar face and body. Its scent surrounded her, the scent of Durawn, and this scent had a name. 'Kavael...'

Could it be true? Had he come to assist her? He was an angel warrior, conjured often by members of her Order in their work. His face hung before her, its expression that of kind concern. In gratitude, held out her arms to him. 'Take me away from here... Help me...'

Then, she heard manic laughter, and felt steel claws close around her body. It was not Kavael before her, but Zebellion himself. She was looking upon his insane face; she could not turn away, or break free of his overwhelming strength. He would possess her now, completely.

In the city of ruins, the sun sank gradually in the sky and the tumbled stone became lit by mysterious lights. Sad reflections of the past issued forth like smoke from the gutters to ape the ways they'd once lived: a juggler juggling, a blind boy led home for eternity, a child in the dirt with a knife. A darker shadow slipped between these aimless lights, ragged as an ancient bat. It melded briefly, intimately, with the clustered shades about a tomb mouth beneath the temple. It flashed a white, startled face back the way it came, before slipping into the black mouth of rock.

There was nothing but pain in Panquilia's world. A crack stole through her soul, through the tender place where mind and spirit join. Soon, that join would be sundered. She could see nothing in that dark place. Neither time nor space existed there. But there was knowledge.

She was a weak creature. She had let the demon claim her once. She'd told the healer he'd ripped her throat, but the old woman had known otherwise. She'd known the truth, even though she hadn't spoken of it. Her eyes said it all.

Zebellion had possessed Panquilia's body, and part of her had welcomed it. She had sensed the immense power of the demon, and how as his acolyte, it could become hers. She could not resist him. She could not expel him from her flesh. Not with the force of her will alone. She'd taken desperate measures. Before the desire to become one with him had overtaken her completely, she'd found the strength to slit her own throat and force the monster out. He hadn't attacked her. If anything, he had attempted a seduction, because he had recognised the frailty in her.

The healer had known this, but Panquilia had never spoken of it to anyone. It was a hideous threat that hung over her continually. She was an insult to her order, tainted. Zebellion could sniff her out wherever she ran in the world. He knew she'd find him again, help free him from the hinterland. She had only one destiny. She had no strength left to fight it.

Then, a flash of light splashed across her mind. She could open her eyes. She found herself lying upon a catafalque in what appeared to be an ancient tomb. Gampander was crouched on the ground nearby. At the foot of the slab stood a man in ragged clothes, his face lined with filth. Behind him was only darkness and the damp reek of old stone. The man reached out to touch Panquilia's ankle, and her flesh contracted as a single organ. She allowed no-one to touch her, but she could not pull away.

'Look,' said the man.

Look where? Again, the flash, a harsh brilliance. Panquilia saw that the man held in his hands an instrument of truth, a thing she feared because of what she might find within it: a mirror.

No! Panquilia whimpered and tried to turn her head away. No mirrors, no!'You must look,' the man said. He walked to the head of the catafalque and dug his fingers into her hair, dragging her face towards the glass. 'Look long and deep.'

She had no choice. Wide, panicked eyes stared back at her from the polished surface. Her mouth hung open in horror. She waited for a hideous image to impose itself over her reflection, but it did not happen. There were no demons in the glass. She blinked and the image blinked too. She smiled a little and the image smiled back. That is me,

Panquilia thought. I am in there.

Then, the ragged man said, 'Now, look deeper.'

She tried to move her head, but again, the man pulled her hair and said, 'find yourself!'

Myself? She blinked at her image. All she could see was the collar around her neck that concealed the old scar. She never looked at it; she avoided mirrors, or any reflective surface. But now, she wondered what the scar looked like. It had been some time since the injury. Her hands seemed to lift of their own accord. She unclasped the collar, unpeeled it from her flesh. In the mirror, she could see that the scar was no longer livid, and she did not feel ashamed to look at it. It had taken spirit to do that to herself. Ultimately she had vanquished the demon. This scar, this reminder, was just as much a part of her as any other. She struggled into a sitting position on the stone catafalque, and the man adjusted the mirror so she could still see into it clearly.

'Now you see,' he said, nodding his head. 'You see *all* of yourself, and that is the true power.'

Panquilia sat up on the stone, staring at the bearded vagabond, who still brandished the mirror in front of her. 'Who are you?' she asked.

The man balanced the mirror on the edge of the tomb and rested his forearms on it. He smiled. 'At one time, very like you,' he said. 'I look upon myself as a sentinel for these parts. The demon's bitch tried to claim me once, but couldn't manage it. For some reason, I am exempt from her dominion, but...' he shrugged mournfully, 'I can no longer live in the world I loved. My only satisfaction in life is to deny An'd'yanae her own desires. In a way, you have helped me fulfil my own destiny, because it was through chasing the boy here that I lost myself to the ruins. I have been searching for him for a long time, but she kept him hidden. Only when she smelled your life did she release him onto the streets to lure you to her.' He straightened up and handed the mirror to Panquilia. 'Here, you take this. You may find a use for it.

Now, hurry and get out of here. Take the boy home. When he confronts his soul he will be able to resolve the separation. But make haste, An'd'yanae will soon be back. She believes your soul is in the process of separating from your body. She will return to gather this sustenance for her master. Go quickly!'

Panquilia did not even pause to thank him, but leapt from the catafalque and grabbed hold of Gampander, who appeared nearly witless, huddled against the cold stone. She dragged him back out into the street, intent only on escape. Gampander uttered strange little cries, which seemed to comprise both fear and relief. Panquilia still felt shaky, and did not want to risk another confrontation with the priestess. She was relieved to find her pony loitering about outside. Muttering a hurried prayer to all the angels of protection, Panquilia helped Gampander mount the pony. She would run beside it.

Then, a dismayed screech splintered the evening air. Panquilia looked up and saw An'd'yanae come hurtling out of the temple behind them. She was evidently resentful of Panquilia's unexpected escape and intended to remedy the situation immediately.

Gampander expelled a squawk of terror, while Panquilia shrank against the pony's flank, expecting another psychic assault on her tender mind.

'Ride, Gampander...' she began, but another voice cut into her instruction.

'It is really quite clear.'

Panquilia look round. The ragged man was standing in the doorway to the tomb, smiling, his hands hidden in his sleeves.

'It is?'

He nodded. 'Reflect upon the problem.'

Panquilia narrowed her eyes at him, and it seemed that time froze over for several seconds. The priestess was arrested in her flight, obscenities held in her gaping, black mouth.

'Oh yes,' Panquilia said. 'I see.'

Even as An'd'yanae came yelling towards her, Panquilia raised the mirror she still gripped beneath one arm. She held it up to the priestess' face. 'What do you see?' Panquilia said.

Something less than beautiful, it seemed. The priestess uttered a further squawk, cut short, as her image gathered in the glass. Then, she emitted a stream of black smoke from her mouth and, quite gracefully, separated into a million firefly particles.

Panquilia turned to thank the ragged man, but he had disappeared.

'I knew him,' Gampander said. 'He once worked for my father.'

Panquilia remembered the stories she'd heard in Hussard's Inn, especially that of the man who'd emerged from the waste with a broken mind. Perhaps not that broken.

The Duke of Sar Pendrous was unstinting in demonstrating his gratitude to the woman who delivered the body of his son back to the noble house of his birth. Panquilia had succeeded where all his men had failed and, for that, must be rewarded. She could name her own payment. Transport and an escort to Aphlex were among Panquilia's modest demands.

The Duke ordered that a banquet should be laid in her honour, and Panquilia found herself seated next to a newly reconstituted Gampander. He paid her amorous attention, from time to time his glances stealing furtively to the collar around her throat. She'd covered the scar again, but she knew the next man who took her fancy would get to nibble her neck before she let him nibble anything else. She felt in receipt of a delicious freedom, and it had been hard won. She deserved the laurels.

'So,' Gampander said, with a flirtatious gleam in his eye. 'Are you still going to cross the ruins to reach Aphlex?'

Panquilia fixed him with an equally coquettish grin. 'Dear boy, I have decided, in order to make the most of your father's generosity, I will take the longer route.'

Gampander aped a moue of disappointment. 'I thought you were an adventurer.'

She picked up her wine goblet and smiled into its depths.

In the morning mist of the following day, several servants saw a white horse leading a blind boy across the lawns of Sar Pendrous. Panquilia left the court a couple of days later, departing so early in the day that no-one saw which road she took to Aphlex. When her escort returned to the Duke, they might tell, of course, but then again, they might not. Panquilia knew now she had powers that demons had no name for and it was quite possible she might use them, on the road.

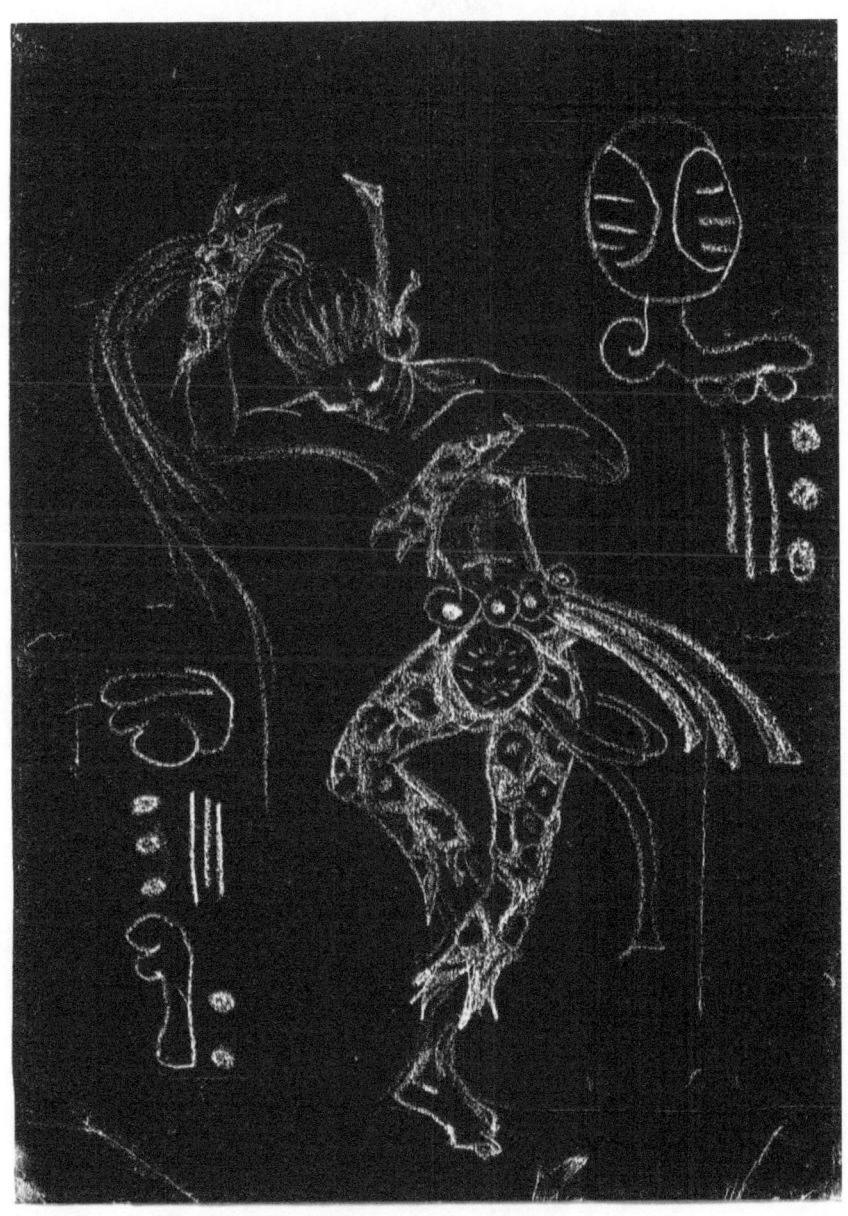

The Preservation

My mother was the only one who wept when Tila went to the flame. I can still remember standing there beside the smoking hole, looking down at the gilt-wire embroidery on my new slippers, thinking how fine they were, how lucky I was to have them, with the sound of my mother's muffled whimpering somewhere behind me. I did not look at my sister when she walked by, her head a mass of nodding feathers, a stupor-smile where her mouth should have been. The crowd was all around me, our neighbours in their ritual best. They commented on Tila's beauty, casting disapproving glances at their own daughters who, with downcast eyes, hid their shame at being inferior morsels. I did not look when Tila, Child of the Temple, danced a few last faltering steps on the lip of stone.

'Aaah!' sighed the neighbours, hands locked on their breasts.

I was hot with envy, thinking, *Well, at least I have my slippers!*

Tila made no sound when she jumped, but the priests shook their rattles, stamped and cried. All that was left of Tila was a plume of vapour. I looked up, you see, when I was sure she'd gone over the edge.

We marched back to the village after that, everybody singing, even the inferior daughters. Spinning spirits buzzed overhead, high up, and blazing with day-time stars. Although I felt happy, I wanted to walk alone. Now, I was eldest daughter of our household. One woman came to take my hand, perhaps thinking I mourned Tila's absence, (a common thing among the relatives of the blessed), or maybe she thought I looked unwell. I remember it clearly. Her skin was very dry and she had a cracked finger nail that pinched when she squeezed me.

'You are a lucky girl!' she said.

I couldn't think why.

My mother was quite overcome with emotion by this point and was being helped along by two of our neighbours ahead of me. Dust was flying everywhere, obscuring the rank, withered corn beside the trail. Now the fire was sated, rain would soon come. We all knew that, and no one was sad or worried any more. Tila, bright image, was gone. I wondered what she was thinking as she turned into a goddess.

Because it was a special day, the priests stripped and danced for us in the sacred square, the heart of our village. Women brought out the honey wine and hard, sweet cakes. Men clucked and yodelled, clapping their hands; music of the flesh. Mother was being feted, staggering from group to group, throwing up her arms, proclaiming, her face blood-hard and very shiny. One of the young priests, Xiln, took her shawl and wound it into a dance. It seemed to me as if he thought he was the only creature alive that day. When he danced close to me, I could smell the tincture seeping from his skin. Tila's clothes were brought out from our house, folded upon a mat of woven reeds. She had been wearing most of the jewellery she'd owned, of course, but I saw her lesser beads glint in the sun, cushioned by a tumble of silky, green cloth. All of this was burned. Later, children would poke the cinders with sticks and carry off her forlorn, tarnished beads to hide as talismans.

Next morning, we found fish lying in the fields, but there was no rain.

I assumed the position of eldest daughter with nonchalant ease. My mother had no husband. She'd been a beauty in her time, and both men she'd chosen - Tila's father and, later, mine - had been her physical echo. Pregnancy had prevented my mother from making her own offering, but she'd presented her men to the gods in her place. Now, but for

Tila's baby, we were alone. My mother was no longer beautiful, being too full of hip and cheek, and I, with my short limbs and lacklustre hair, was no fit avatar for our people. I would live until the foulness of age amplified the shame of my longevity. Yet this disappointment was tempered by my being allowed to speak in the temple. I was a good speaker, even as a girl. Once I heard someone say to my mother, 'The gods have their ways of compensating.' I took heart from this and spoke with passion.

'She will be a priestess one day,' my mother said. Often, the ugliest girls were made priestesses as a privilege, because they'd never enter the flame, never bring life to the people. Only the beautiful gave themselves. It had always been this way. A flawed body would not only insult the flame, but perhaps damage it in some way. Pure fire, after all, is pure beauty, which can be dangerous, and it is best not to provoke it.

On the first worship day after Tila had given herself, I was permitted not only to lead the chanting, but speak the story as well. It came straight from my spirit; I did not even think about what I would say on the way to the temple as I often did. Midway through my speech, a crack of thunder drowned me out, and everyone ran outside. I felt cheated and ashamed of myself because I thought more of my story-telling than I did of the rain beginning to fall. Luckily, my displeasure was not noted. People swore my strong narrative had been the final incentive that persuaded the cloud goddess to loose her flow. I was pleased about that. Later, one of the priestesses offered to instruct me in the mystery of medicine and I knew my path had been smoothed with flat stones forever.

Judd didn't like fanatics. They made him twitch; the only evidence of controlled fear. Filtered sunlight, smouldering in through the rotor's visor, fell across his hands and still managed to interfere with his notefile's display panel, despite pilot Morton's adjustment of the polarisation. Judd blindly key-stroked his way through his orientation notes, reading nothing. He skipped the animation; it was bad quality anyway. *Why me?* he wondered. Was it deliberate? He kept his paranoid thoughts to himself.

Nothing intentional about this allocation. Just do the job and file the report. Just do it. He swallowed, and tasted something bad. Central Arbitration for this zone, Judd's employers, had been approached by a group of people reporting an infringement of the Amity Convention in their community; arb-speak for murder. The group were unconformists - a religious organisation aping obsolete cultural mores. That spoke trouble to Judd; hysteria, faulty neuro-sets, obsessions. He questioned Central Arb's judgement in intervening. The organisation had opted out of society; as far as he was concerned, they should be left to get on with their crazy manias, contraventions and all. It seemed the perpetrator of the transgression had already left the community anyway.

'Morton, I can taste the days ahead,' Judd said. 'I hate this kind of spooky shit.'

'Nah,' his pilot replied. 'All you can taste is the recycling plant. It's east; near to here.'

'That's not what I meant.' Judd glanced out of Lady Coyote's transparent flank. Companion bird, Cheyenna Wing, was close behind; the two craft were predatory shadows on the yellow ground below.

'So you mean we're heading towards crazyland, yeah?' Morton laughed. 'What's new? I thought this outfit we're eyeballing was licensed, though. How come Central Arb've got involved?' As usual, he had neglected to examine the preliminary information.

'We were asked to intervene,' Judd replied patiently. 'License or no license, there was a contravention. That's what I don't like. These characters usually think they're above consensual agreement.'

'Then why bother to call us in?'

'Panic,' Judd replied. 'And my mouth is full of its sour flavour.'

The rotors carved north in the cloudless sky, passing over the Altamina Reclamation Zone. Their destination wasn't far off now. Judd attempted to concentrate on his note-scryer's directives: *Light's Fair Children - religious group, license number, 01566-T16, license granted 10:12:46. No settled location: temporary lease of obsolete research facility. Belief system: nomadic lifestyle, monotheism, pacifism.*

It sounded harmless. There were no known anti-social tendencies connected with the group.

'There's the old Research Complex up ahead,' Morton said. 'Looks quiet.'

'The fire was days ago,' Judd said and pressed the communicator pad. 'We're here, Cheyenna. Tammy, shoulder the med supplies. In case...'

'The fire was days ago,' Morton repeated, grinning below his insect shades.

'I hate this spooky shit,' Judd said. 'Why can't people be civilised?'

I carved Tila's icon myself, from a piece of bleached, silky wood. That was another of my fortunes; I was good with my hands. I took her to the god-chamber annexed to the temple, and walked up and down beside the shelves of icons, to find her an appropriate place. Some of the carvings were crude and I was surprised the gods ever inhabited them. Tila, as she had been in life, was beautiful. I spoke to her, hoping she would give some sign concerning where she wanted to be placed, but it appeared very little of her substance had yet entered the wood. I had coloured her lips and breasts with a mixture of red clay, spit and a tiny amount of the menstrual blood-powder she'd left me for this purpose; I expected this pigment to become wet when she had chosen her place. It did not happen, however. Some perversity or whim made me put her back beneath my shawl, even though she no longer belonged among the living. I decided I'd come back again when Tila had put a bit of herself into the wood. It was a blessing I did that, for the next day strangers came from the world outside and took all our gods as prisoners.

My people had become used to invaders over the centuries. It was an inconvenience as cyclic as the seasons, or so the wisest said. Lessons were to be learned from the fact that our people existed still among the ruins of a thousand other cultures, evident beyond the forest and further south along the flat river-bank, but no one Outside was ever clever enough to heed them. We, like the corn, bend and sway in the winds of history. The winds just blow themselves out eventually, or else wail on somewhere else. There are other tribes living some days' walk from us, but we have little to do with them, other than the occasional visit for bartering. If a person was to walk south for many days in a row, they would come to the end of our world, and the place where Outside begins. It is considered bad magick even to see that place, and the vine people living closest to it have constructed a barrier of woven trees so the skeleton towers of Outside can never be seen. Sometimes, however, people from beyond the barrier come into our territory - Outsiders, flatpaws and softskins - who covet the treasures of the mountains that rise to the clouds and beyond, behind our village. Gods live in the mountains, silent and terrible and jealous of their kingdom, but this is a tribal mystery, not to be spoken of to anyone from Outside. Let the stranger take his life in his hands, if he wishes. We will not warn him.

So, Tila's icon was wrapped in my pillow shawl when the strangers came. At first, as many of them do, they pretended to be our friends. They came up out of a morning haze, leaning on staffs and singing together; maybe eight of them. Everyone came out of their houses, attracted by the noise of strange voices. We saw people wearing earth-coloured clothes in the Outsider style, who hid from us the fact that many more of their fellows were concealed in the long forest beyond the river. But we knew anyway.

'People! We never expected people!' they said, lying.

We laid out food for them. They ate. We offered them honey wine. They drank. All the while, their eyes were never still, travelling from throats hung with talismans to rich silk shawls to the creamy temple walls. I felt that they, as did all conquerors, could smell the metal and the finery so strongly, it eclipsed the smell of the food, the wine, the damp ground, the quick, fleshy flowers growing on the walls of our buildings. I felt I knew then what kind of people we were dealing with; those whose perception of treasure was warped.

Even so, the day was one of celebration. We knew what we knew; the strangers wore their hearts in their eyes. Fires were lit as the afternoon sought rest in the fields, and the slippery twilight came to bed it down thoroughly in a curtain of mist, borrowed from the river water. When they thought they could hide their desires in the darkness, our visitors dragged leather sacks towards the fire. 'Look, we have gifts,' they said. We nodded. Membranes marked with sigils; we had seen these things before. It was known that Outsiders believed all their wisdom existed in such marks, and that some of them were even worshipped as having god-life of their own. Our priests told us never to scoff at other people's beliefs but, privately, I thought their religious motifs lacked mystery. There was no challenge in staring at the black marks, none like staring the Fire God in the eye, because he is made of stone.

Our most beautiful priest, Xiln, picked up one of the gifts and stood in the firelight, tawny as polished wood. One of the strangers said, 'That is a holy book,' arranging his hands in a special way. Some kind of blessing, I supposed. Already, Xiln's mentors, older men, were eyeing him messages. They were counselling him to silence. He could not have mistaken what they signalled, but still threw down the gift so that it sent up a spray of sparks at the edge of the fire. I saw the stranger stiffen, the muscles flex beneath the skin of his face, but he kept a steady smile there. 'Would you like me to read for you?' he said.

Strangers had said that to my people before. I'd heard the legends. It did not mean, as was usual, looking up at the sky and understanding the language of the clouds, nor did it mean pool-gazing for god-speak. It meant staring at the black marks and speaking aloud whatever came into your head. Perhaps Xiln was curious. Perhaps his anger at this intrusion was presented as yielding. He said, 'If you want to speak, do so. You are our guests.'

The stranger picked up the gift Xiln had cast at the embers, and brushed it down carefully with his sleeve. His companions all shifted into new positions, their faces assuming serious expressions. It struck me just how much they must believe in their strange rituals. Always, it is said, they ask to read to us.

The stranger opened his book and studied it for a moment, frowning. Then he said, 'Ah!' and cleared his throat. He told us a story about a potter, a man of great skill. His gifts, apparently, had come from the Sky Master himself. This potter had lain in bed at night thinking his skill might even rival that of the Sky Master. One day, he'd discovered a wonderful new clay and had thought to himself that it almost resembled flesh without life, and perhaps might be the raw material of a man. Confident of his ability as an artist, he decided to try and make a man out of the clay. He kept his door barred to all of his neighbours and, after six days, had finished his creation. All that remained was to bake the clay. However, later, when the potter took the clay man out of the oven, the surface of its clay skin had been as dry as a desert road, and there seemed to be no life within. The potter pondered for a moment and then went to his well to draw up a pitcher of water. This he poured over the body of the clay man. The dark red skin hissed and sizzled, sucking up the water greedily. The room was filled with steam. The potter's neighbours, hearing the hissing noise and observing what they took to be smoke pouring from the workshop, hurried to see what was happening. They blinked into the steam and saw the potter extend his arm to a young man lying on the work table. They saw this person sit up, take the potter's hand, and pull himself from the table. He stood in a wrapping of curling steam and the neighbours could see that this person was perfection. The potter told his neighbours, proudly, that he had made the man with his own hands.

At this, the neighbours had gasped, the women burying their faces in their aprons. The stranger had screwed up his face at this point in the story and clenched his fist in front of him. He said that just to hear such blasphemy as the potter had spoken could have damned the whole community. One of the neighbours, braver than the rest, had told the potter to take back his words, because no one but the Sky Master could create life. The clay man should be destroyed before the Sky Master could punish everyone. The potter had been annoyed by this and had refused to destroy his creation. At this, the neighbours had shaken their heads and moved away, because they did not want to look upon the foolish and evil man who challenged the Sky Master, or his abominable creation. As good people, faithful to their Lord, they locked the potter inside his house, though he called to them from inside. Then, they took kindling and stacked it up around the walls. The potter, by this time, was banging on the shuttered windows, begging for release, calling out that he was sorry for what he had done and would destroy the clay man. He would take whatever penance they suggested, only, please, let him live. The people, whom the stranger called 'good' and 'pure', knew they must not listen to his pleas. The potter had sinned against all that was right in the world, and nothing he could say would erase that fact. So, they set fire to the potter's house and watched it burn, closing their ears to the cries of the potter that could be heard above the flames. Then, the stranger told us, these people all went to the nearest shrine and offered thanks to the Sky Master for the important lesson he had given them. Because of their humility, He gifted them with plenty for the rest of their lives.

The stranger snapped his book shut. 'Now, what does that tell you?' he asked.

Most of us were silent; the message was obvious.

Xiln, however, could not keep silent. 'It shows,' he said, 'that the Sky Master of these people was a small and powerless god.'

The strangers all made noises of indignation, but the speaker raised his hand for quiet. 'How does the story suggest that to you?' he asked patiently.

Xiln shrugged. In the flame light, he looked very much as I imagined the clay man of the story to have been. 'That is simple. First, the Sky Master is a fool if he thinks the creation of life is his province. Men and woman create life continually. Any of them who do not realise that are as foolish as their so-called god. Secondly, once the potter proved he could create life from clay, it negated the point of having a creator god at all. At that moment, the Sky Master was indeed redundant, and should have been forgotten by the people of the city. They should have fashioned new, more suitable gods for themselves.'

The stranger smiled and shook his head. 'You do not understand,' he said. 'The Sky Master *is* life itself. We are all His children. To try to imitate His actions is an evil, suggested by demonic forces. Also, you cannot make a god. He made us. We are His children, just children, but we must be alert for obscenities against His name.'

Xiln laughed. 'You are one of the neighbours,' he said. 'Aren't you.'

There was a silence, and the crackling flames of our fire brought back the horror of a man burned to death for being wiser than his fellows. To die for a god unwillingly is to condemn a soul to the void. Sacrifice must always be willing and always pertinent. It was obvious to all our people that the potter should not have been sacrificed. Our gods would have been insulted by such behaviour, which confirmed Xiln's suggestion that the Sky Master of the strangers was foolish and petty.

'What you have to think about,' the stranger said, 'is that the story is only a symbol for what happens in real life. What it tells us is that to scorn the beliefs of the majority is to bring trouble upon oneself. To exist in harmony with each other, people must adhere to the common view. Then the love of the Sky Master can flow through us, without obstruction.'

'I see another message in your symbol,' Xiln said. 'To me, it suggests that, if a person wishes to diverge from the common view, as the potter did, he should keep quiet about it, or else go elsewhere to conduct his activities. Clearly, his neighbours were dolts with the minds of goats. The world is a celebration of variety. It is against nature and the will of the gods to cut the limbs from that variety.'

'You are a bright young man,' said the stranger to Xiln, although the currents beneath his words suggested otherwise.

'I am a priest,' said Xiln. The stranger raised his brows. 'Really. Tomorrow, we should talk again.'

The Research Complex had closed down over ten years ago. Workshops and laboratories surrounded the central building, in lines that radiated outwards to the living quarters, forming a perfect circle.

'Just like a big wheel,' Morton said, as Lady Coyote dipped towards the ground.

Judd peered down. People had come out of the buildings to wave up at the sky. He could see the blackened segment in the white outer ring of buildings. Rotten tooth. Rot. They landed on the roof of the centre building.

'Sure is pretty,' Morton said, putting the Coyote to rest. 'Like a vacation resort or something. Was this really just a research centre?'

'Yes.' Judd activated the side door which wrinkled

upwards with a sigh. He jumped out into the sunlight. Nearby, Cheyenna was disgorging her crew of two; the women. Mel was jumping up and down beside the bird, pumping some life into her blood, while Tammi fiddled with the med cases.

'I get so stiff flying,' Mel said as Judd sauntered over. 'Every time. Weird, huh?' She punched up at the sky. 'Lovely day.'

'Mmm. I think we should play cautious with these people.'

'Sure, Judd. You think they're dangerous or something?' Mel laughed at the suggestion, as if it might be more interesting if they were.

'No, not exactly, but they might be jumpy. Let's soothe nerves.'

'OK.'

'I could hand out a little cheer,' Tammi said, patting the case slung over her shoulder.

'If they'll take it - fine - but don't push it.' He turned to Morton who was swaggering bonelessly away from the Coyote. 'Is that bird secure?' Judd asked sharply. 'I mean really secure.'

'Yeah. Course.'

Judd noticed Morton exchange glances with the women; he was aware himself how he sounded so didactic at times. He couldn't curb it; a natural quirk. 'Well, let's go then. There's an elevator over there. Perhaps it's working.'

The elevator door slid open before they reached it. A welcoming committee stepped out. They were the sort of people generally associated with groups of this type - almost too typical. Underfed in appearance, apologetic, even fawning. There was a preponderance of denim and checks. Voices spoke all together; a depleted flock of nervous birds.

'OK, OK,' Judd said to them. 'Let's get on the ground. Let's talk there.' He touched shoulders, smiled a lot. Morton and Mel swapped glances, saying nothing, while Tammi spoke gently, asking people how they felt.

'It's just so awful,' one woman said. 'Just so bad. We had to tell someone. Our pathfinder is no longer with us. We didn't know what to do. The buildings are damaged. What about the lease? Are we liable? There's been a death. Horrible. We're so sorry...'

Judd interrupted her whining flow. 'That's OK. We're here to help. Just relax.'

Everyone crammed into the elevator, and Judd was aware of a sour smell; not sweat, just sourness, like the juice of living turned rancid.

Despite the traumatising loss of their 'pathfinder', the group had already elected new leaders, who were waiting by the lower elevator doors, surrounded by a protective court of followers. There were no weapons to be seen. The leading couple solemnly introduced themselves as Amos and Susie Lovelink, extending hands for ritual contact. Out of the corner of his eye, Judd noticed Mel slip her hands in her pockets. He thought it strange that such a young couple should have been chosen as figureheads for the group. The Lovelinks were nervous creatures, and if not still teenagers, then only recently past the milestone of twenty years. Susie Lovelink furiously twisted a lank strand of hair between her fingers as she stammered a greeting. Light's Fair Children had summoned Big People to help them out; now they obviously had no idea what to do with them.

'We got food for you,' Susie said. Perhaps this was seen as a peace offering.

'They'll want to wash first,' her husband reminded her.

Susie blushed. She had fluffed her lines. 'Course. Yeah.' She flapped a hand at the buildings. 'This way.'

Judd signalled for his people to follow. Everyone had recently eaten, and he doubted strongly whether any of his team felt in need of hygiene refreshment but, in cases like this, customs had to be observed. They must put these people at ease - then ask the questions. The air smelled of damp ashes.

In the morning, more strangers, both men and women, melted from the dawn forest and could be seen on all sides of the village. They carried heavy sticks made of iron, embellished with shiny clay, which, from the self-conscious way the strangers carried them, were clearly instruments of power. My mother and I peered through the window curtain of our dwelling, me holding the baby with my hand over her mouth to keep her quiet. 'I think this will be a hard time for us,' my mother said resignedly. I agreed. As always, we would become no-form in our heads until the strangers took what they wanted and left. I said this to my mother to comfort her, but she shook her head.

'I have a feeling these strangers will not want to leave,' she said. 'It is a different kind of treasure they're after this time.'

The whole village met in the sacred circle at the heart of the village to listen to what the strangers had to say. It was hoped they would present their demands and then depart. However, it was soon clear that they wanted our attention more than they wanted our treasures; their demands were for our ears alone. They had a leader - the man who had read to us the day before - and his name was Tarkus. He spoke, ignorantly, about our sacred rites, and told us it was wrong to kill; our noble offerings, in his eyes, were evil. Xiln brought up the subject of the potter's story and we were told that taking life to expunge evil was a different matter. We should not kill for pleasure. How little he knew of us. Our older priests, less hot-headed than Xiln and his peers, tried to explain our relationship with the mountains, and that the sloughing of flesh did not mean death as the strangers understood it. Tarkus would not listen. 'We have come to help you,' he said. 'You must change your ways.'

There is only one god for the strangers; their Sky Master. I hated this entity at once, as I'm sure everyone in my village did. I did not want to be this god's slave. Our older priests became increasingly troubled at the way things were developing, and offered the strangers metal and precious stones, promising to show them the secret pathways into the mountains where much more could be found. Everyone, including the priests, sensed that we were crouching beneath a cloud of sunless peril, and that unfamiliar artistry would be called for in dealing with these strangers. Behind their back, we called them Slaves of Misery, for, contradictory as it sounds, they were enthralled by the strictures they placed upon themselves in the name of their god, and in some bizarre way, enjoyed it. They shook their heads in the face of our most desperate offers. 'You should throw all your treasures into the lake,' they said. 'Or into your fire pit.' Now, there was a sacrifice they could understand. I realised then, that when they'd first arrived and I'd seen greed in their faces as they looked around the village, it had not been our treasures that excited them, but the people themselves. 'Live in simplicity to serve the Master,' they urged. They had come to steal souls.

I remember the day so clearly, the air hot and hard, the familiar faces around the sacred circle, bland but concealing their fear. We were all frightened. The strangers restlessly paced in the space we had left them, throwing their arms up against the sky, speaking nonsense in a hectic manner, supervised indulgently by Tarkus, who was obviously dangerously mad. What could we do?

Xiln leapt up from his place among the young priests. He was a totem of the fiercest mountain spirit brought to human form. 'Go away!' he cried. 'We don't want you or your god. You have your ways, we have ours. Leave us to what we know, the gods we love, who have shed flesh for us!'

He should have kept silent.

Like one great beast, the strangers gathered together, a beast the colour of dust. They poured over the ground towards the temple, driven by the wind from their hearts. Our beautiful temple of gentle stone, nourished by the sun's kiss, the moon's caress, sanctuary of the gods. I knew, in those moments, our holy ones were with us. Every icon in the annex would be throbbing with their presence, their love, their concern. Would they rout the strangers for us? Some of us tried to bar the strangers' way, but they pointed their metal and shiny clay sticks at the sky above our heads and made them scream thunder and flame. We were assured that if this power was directed at our bodies, it would destroy them. Helplessly, we clustered round the temple portal as the strangers went inside. We heard terrible sounds coming out; cries, and the sounds of breakage and ripping. Some of our number were incensed enough to want to take action, but they were forced to remain outside. Tarkus had directed a few of his followers to remain in the gateway to protect those that had rushed inside the temple. They carried long knives and the dangerous flame-makers. 'It is for your own good,' one of them said, his face creased in anguish. 'Everything will be all right. Soon.'

How could they say this? It was beyond us to understand their behaviour, the desperation they felt, the need to make us like them. Were they blind to our condition, our oneness with life and with the gods? We know that the Jaguar Woman cannot speak the language of men and that she lies down in the dappled grass to hunt the weakest creature that passes. Do we then go out into the trees and try to impress upon her that she must sow grain like ourselves? Would we take away her freedom or kill her when she did not understand our words? These strangers could not see the splendid blessing of variety; they worshipped sameness and the minimum of difference. Even their men and women looked alike. We had no defence because they were stronger than us in that they did not fear to kill for their beliefs. We could no more harm them than we could the jaguar or the wild dog who might prey upon our children. As they existed, they were part of the world, and therefore inviolable. We would need the power of our gods to be free of these strangers.

Then, even as I was thinking these thoughts, the most

horrible thing happened. All sounds within the temple had ceased, and now the strangers came out into the dust-filled sunlight, with smiles upon their faces. In their arms, they carried all of the god icons. We knew they would be full of spirits because of the trouble, and we began to moan in terror; a sound like the dark wind that hurries through the deepest mountain passes seeking stray souls. Some of us sank to the ground, hiding our faces against the fragrant dirt. I was standing near to Xiln. He turned to me and said, 'Temple-speaker, speak! Use your art! Tell them! Stop them!'

My mouth felt full of sand, but because Xiln had asked me to, I approached the strangers and said, 'You must not do this. These are the icons of our gods. If you harm them or take them away, we will no longer be able to speak with them and our people will be voiceless in the world. The rains will never come and the sun will burn itself out for it is the hound of the gods and needs a master. The moon will fall into the lake for she is the sacred mare of the spirits who, without a curb, will bolt from her celestial traces. I beg you, return the icons to their shelves. We will all suffer otherwise.'

'Your gods are not real,' the strangers replied. 'The sun, the moon and the elements obey nothing but the Sky Master. You have been deceived and must forget this nonsense. Embrace the Sky Master and he will reward you with bliss!'

I went back to Xiln. 'I tried,' I said. He put his long, brown hand on my shoulder. I was ashamed because I had failed him.

Our ways were so different. Perhaps we should have become as the Jaguar Woman and attacked the strangers, for they were like a pack of wild dogs threatening we who were the Jaguar's cubs. We should have become Her and torn them apart, but we did not. To us, the only deaths should be those of the noble way or those of accident, sickness and old age. We could not soil our hands with violence. Helplessly, we watched the strangers building a pyre in the sacred circle. We watched, powerless, as our gods were burned to ashes. It seemed to me that the air was full of wailing, and it did not come from human throats. I became utterly numb. All I could think of was my precious sister, Tila, toiling up the secret paths, deep in the rock, toiling up from darkness, expecting to be welcomed by the divine throng at the mountain's crown. She would come out of the rock to nothingness. She would be alone on the barren mountain, and she would not know what had happened. I wept for her, silently and desperately and Xiln offered me the delicious comfort of his warm arm across my back. Even in the centre of despair, I could derive pleasure from his touch.

The strangers immediately set about building their own temple on our land. They separated the men from the women and apportioned tasks to all. 'Do not look so glum, you have been saved,' one of them said. We were all too confused, shocked and terrified to do anything but obey them. All our gods had been murdered, leaving us defenceless. All of them, that is, but for Tila. I had told no one I still had her icon, and now sensibly kept it hidden against my body. She might be our only hope. I longed to tell my people she was still alive - their faces were so unhappy and desolate - but I knew it was important I kept this secret. There would come a time, I was sure, when I could use it.

Judd found Mel in the blackened ruins. She was collecting data with a scanning device, surreptitiously nibbling on a sweet fibregen biscuit she'd had in her holdall. Judd had noticed she'd barely touched the meal they'd been offered. A reticence he'd shared, even though the food had appeared wholesome.

'Hungry?' he said, and she jumped, pulling off her headset.

'Judd! You creep!' She rolled her eyes and clutched her throat.

'Jumpy?' He smiled.

'Yeah, well...'

'Picked anything up?'

She wrinkled her nose. 'No more than they told us. Yet. Still...' She shrugged. 'Seems an open and shut case to me. Some guy went loopy...'

'That much is obvious.' Judd kicked through the rubble.

The Lovelinks, as spokespeople, had double-acted their way through an explanation. Light's Fair Children were peace-loving; they didn't want to harm anyone. Didn't want any trouble. But something blasphemous had happened, and their pathfinder had reacted strongly, too strongly. 'He got fevered,' as Amos had put it. The Lovelinks evaded direct questioning and had vaguely referred to 'an accident', a fire, from which someone had ended up dead. Judd had thought it might have been their pathfinder who had died, but apparently this was not the case. There'd been no mention of a dispute among the community, but Judd had sensed its invisible presence at the meal table, all the same. Analysing what he'd heard, he'd already guessed that the group must have divided over some theological point. Things had got hot and out of control. Someone had died. He'd had to be quite blunt, demanding that the Lovelinks should explain why exactly they'd felt compelled to contact Central Arb. All eyes had become shifty at that point.

'Some of the brother and sisters have left us,' Amos had said. 'Our pathfinder took them away.'

'So?'

'So, they had weapons, so they were fired up!' Amos had gone scarlet, curling his fingers over Susie's timid hand, as she reached for his arm. 'We don't want trouble. It's nothing to do with us...'

Judd had pasted an avuncular smile over his face, but he felt weirdly sick. 'Wise move,' he said. 'Where'd these people head?'

'North,' Susie had replied. 'Towards the forests... you know the place.'

'Shit!' Morton had punched the table, ignoring protocol.

'Is this where we duck out, Judd?'

Judd had flicked him a reprimanding glance. 'We need the details,' he'd said. 'All of them.'

The Fair Children weren't eager to explain further, however. Perhaps a misguided sense of loyalty, perhaps natural aversion. Judd couldn't tell. He hoped the ruins would speak more eloquently.

'Well, whadda ya know!' Mel said suddenly. 'Take a look at this!'

Judd crunched his way through the wreckage. He whistled appreciatively. 'That, if I'm not mistaken, is the body of a Horus Five,' he said.

'State of the art,' Mel said. 'But dead.'

'The heat must've fused the bio-circuits,' Judd said, leaning forward to finger what remained of the machine. It was a miracle the thing was still recognisable, but then Horus Fives were acclaimed for being rugged. How had it got here, though? Surely, the Children hadn't brought it with them?

'Was this the murder they were talking about?' Mel asked. She was inclined to be romantic.

Judd shook his head. 'Doubt it. I can't see this lot looking on a machine as life.'

'Wonder why they didn't move it.'

'Superstition perhaps. It's clear this item is implicated. We'd better face them out with it.'

'You're the boss!'

'I'm a co-ordinator.'

'Same difference!' Mel sauntered out ahead of him. Judd looked back at the machine. Horus Fives were a conceit really; an expensive conceit. Artificial intelligence dressed up in a puppet that looked like a man. Plaything of the pale-faced techs to whom machines were more alive than people. Powerful, though, and rarely seen outside of a research park. Why here?

Tarkus could have been a handsome man, if his face had not

been so congested with all those things he tried to hold down inside himself. He had unusual green eyes and, most of the time, his hair was a furious thatch about his shoulders, though sometimes he groomed himself to speak with us. After a few days, the women of my tribe were handed over to the women of his and we saw little of him, but as our village was small, we could usually hear his voice and what he was saying. Everybody noticed he was most intent on converting Xiln to share his beliefs. 'A weak link,' my mother said, wisely, nodding her head.

Some of our people went wild, went against their beliefs. They fought back at the strangers, with their hands and teeth. It was a foolish, desperate thing to do. The strangers simply pointed their flame-makers, which spat a hole through the bodies of our people, so that their life ran out of them. At that point, everybody realised we were truly godless and helpless. We could do nothing but obey Tarkus' orders if we valued our lives. He wanted us to build him a temple for his Sky Master, upon the ruins of our own. Numbly, blindly, we followed his directions.

Xiln, however, refused to involve himself in the construction of the temple, and sat resolutely in the dirt of the sacred circle, looking very much like a statue of a god himself. I was afraid that Tarkus might point a fire-maker at him, and put holes in his body, but fortunately he did not. Tarkus squatted down beside Xiln, at first speaking gently, then quite harshly, then with exasperation. Xiln had evidently gone into no-form and ignored him. Eventually, Tarkus left him alone and went off to busy himself elsewhere. I took Xiln some refreshment, and he shook himself into the day and greeted me with a sigh. 'If they kill me for resisting them, will that be a noble death?' he asked me. I truly did not know, but was sure, if Xiln was to be sacrificed, it should be into the beautiful flame with due ceremony and not by being ground into the dirt by strangers. Still, if he offered himself, perhaps Tila would not be alone. Impulsively, I told Xiln about my sister's icon. His face bloomed. He gripped my hands. 'I give you my love,' he said. 'In this world and beyond. You are so wise.' He lifted my hands to his eyes and a tear squeezed out onto my fingers. My heart stopped with joy.

Then Tarkus noticed us together and came marching towards us. I had never seen his face so black, poor man. Again, I silently chastised his ignorant god for allowing him to wrap himself in such misery. 'Women to their own quarters!' he said. 'No interaction but for marriage duties.'

'Why?' I asked, braver because Xiln was watching me.

'Interaction between male and female weakens the soul of both,' Tarkus replied authoritatively. 'It is our burden we have to draw close to perpetuate our species. This should be recognised for the penance it is.'

'Your Sky Master has no mate,' Xiln observed. 'I suppose this is just another manifestation of his supernal jealousy is it? If he can't have the body-fire, then neither can we!'

Tarkus raised his hand as if to strike Xiln, but then collected himself and lowered it. 'You are an ignorant savage,' he said. 'Because of this, I forgive you. But soon, my young friend, you must relent and open your heart. If you do not, I can only assume there is a demon in you.' This was delivered dark with threat. He let the words hang there in the air for a moment and then gestured at me. 'On your way, young woman. There is much work to do.'

After the temple was built, we were directed to destroy our homes and construct long houses - two of them - where the men and woman would live apart. Our lives were to be dedicated to worship of the Master and we would work in the fields from dawn till dusk. The strangers spoke of the wonder of their lives, but I could see nothing pleasant about it. 'Where have they come from, do you think?' I asked my mother.

She made an angry sound. 'I feel they have been driven out of somewhere,' she replied. 'Is there a place on this good earth that would be comfortable letting them dwell upon it?'

I had to agree. It might explain something of the

desperation in the strangers' manner. They were running from something, and I suspected that something was themselves.

Every evening, the women gathered around their own fire and one of the female strangers would come to read to us. The men gathered a short distance away. The woman who came to us had a soft voice and, very often, could not be heard above the plangent tones of Tarkus who regaled the men with stories of terror nearby. I listened carefully for some instinct told me more could be learned to our advantage from Tarkus' ranting, than from whatever his female had to say, and especially so if his words were overheard by a woman. He did not speak for women, which is why it was so important to hear what he said. I was fascinated. He spoke with blood in his mouth, I felt. Words of being stalked by desire, having to hack away all vestiges of manhood, being pure and untainted by the thoughts of the flesh. He was, of course, a man in torment.

Xiln still sat in the dust, unmoving. Tarkus had him guarded, so that none of us could take him food and water. Soon, Xiln would die. I warmed Tila's icon with my breast and whispered to her not to be afraid. She must come for Xiln's spirit when the moment came and guide him into the mountains. Perhaps between them, they could think of a way to drive out the Sky Master. I imagined this god to be very like Tarkus; weak and watery inside. It should be easy to vanquish him.

The awful thing was, Xiln's beauty went quite away. I worried then that he would not be a fit candidate for the mountain throne. What would happen if he died and Tila could not take him? I did not want Xiln to die for nothing and took a great decision upon myself. I went to Tarkus and said, 'You must not let Xiln die. If he does, he will become a god.'

'He is a demon!' Tarkus declared, his tongue wrapping greedily around the words as if they were a ripe fruit.

'Perhaps so. But to my people, he will be a god and his

death will prove to them that the Sky Master has no power. Death is sacred to us. Especially a voluntary sacrifice.'

Tarkus looked at me beadily. 'You are right,' he said and then gave me a horrible smile. 'Thank you for coming to me.'

He went at once to the middle of the village with a flask of water, which he offered to Xiln. Xiln was lying curled up the dirt, covered with red dust. He looked like a dead thing, a weathered carving, and it was clear he could not drink. I watched anxiously in the shadow of a cottage. Several women came up behind me, putting their hands on my shoulders, asking questions. I shook my head to silence them. We watched. Gradually, everyone stopped what they were doing and gathered to investigate what Tarkus was up to. He tried to uncurl Xiln's stiff limbs, tried to force the lip of the flask between Xiln's cracked lips. *It is too late,* I thought. *He is dying.* 'Fetch water,' I whispered to a woman behind me. 'All of you.'

'Prevent the holy death?' she asked, suspiciously.

'It is not holy. Look. Xiln has wasted. Hurry!'

She understood and organised the others. Presently, a line of women filed into the square, carrying pitchers of water. These they laid in a row beside Tarkus. He looked up at them and, in his face, I saw his weakness. I walked calmly to his side. 'He has dried away,' I said. 'Yet his spirit still inhabits the flesh. Revive it and he will live.' I gestured towards the pitchers. Tarkus nodded, in a daze, and threw the first pitcher of water over Xiln's body, across his legs. The skin turned dark and gleaming. Tarkus threw another pitcher of water and Xiln's body jerked. One after another, he threw the pitchers, the last one over Xiln's head. Water flowed into Xiln's dry, open mouth. He coughed, and began to shiver. Shaking, Tarkus offered him the flask and he took a few sips. Presently, Tarkus helped Xiln to sit up.

'You have given life to this man of clay,' I said, and walked away, back to the women.

There was no temple now. In the darkness, I walked a

short way into the mountains and found a shallow cave. Here, I took Tila's icon from my shawl and placed it on a hidden ledge. How warm the wood felt beneath my fingers; it thrummed with life. I could not speak aloud for fear some stranger from the village would overhear me, but I communed with my sister as best I could, using silent speech. 'I feel I have triumphed in some way,' I told her, 'but I'm not sure how to use this triumph. If only the gods still lived. If only I could speak with them. You are new to the mountain, Tila, and I fear you do not have the wisdom to advise me.' I had told her everything that had happened, even down to the stories the strangers told us. Now, it seemed her quiet, lovely voice was in my head. She spoke clearly and I held my breath so as not to interrupt her. A few moments later, I piled stones before the icon to hide it and then went back to the village.

Xiln was no longer in the sacred circle, but had been moved to the men's long-house which was still half-complete at the opposite end of the village to the women's house. Using Tila's spirit I became the Jaguar Woman and padded silently over the ground to a place where the wooden walls of the long-house were still open to the night. I became no-form then and slithered inside. Xiln was lying some distance apart from where the other men slept, covered by a thin blanket on the floor. As a shadow I slipped to his side and bent low to whisper in his ear. I gave him a cake to eat which I had baked mixed with my own blood. It would give him strength. He nodded weakly as I spoke. Later, and for several days, I would bring him more blood-food as Tila had instructed. I was the temple-speaker, and the temple-speaker had become the Jaguar Woman. Hers is the spirit who rules the mountain passes and she is invincible.

'Macabee found the false man,' Amos Lovelink said.

'It was broken' Susie added.

'Macabee went back into the past,' Amos said. 'He remembered what he was before he became Fair. He wanted to fix the false man. We told him he shouldn't.'

Judd had cornered them in their house and, as he'd half suspected, they were willing to talk more openly, now he'd discovered the Horus Five himself.

'Just a minute,' Judd said, interrupting the disjointed explanation. 'Have I got this right? This guy - Macabee? - *found* the Horus Five here?'

Susie nodded vigorously. 'Sure did. It was under a stack of old crates in one of the store-rooms. Most of it, anyway, but Macabee thought he could fix up the missing parts himself.' Her eyes were round with excitement.

Judd couldn't help smiling. A Horus Five found dismantled in a store-room! Who the hell had left that behind, and where had their head been when they'd done it? He rubbed his face. 'This is... well, incredible,' he said. 'Didn't your friend Macabee realise what that machine was, how valuable it was?'

'It wasn't worth anything,' Susie said. 'I told you, it was broken.'

Judd shook his head. 'Machines like that are never just 'broken', believe me.'

Susie frowned. 'Then why was it left here? Everything else had been taken away.'

She had a point, Judd supposed. 'You'd better tell me the rest,' he said.

Later, he went out into the red evening and found Morton sitting with his back against one of the walls, swigging from a plastic container. Sunset dyed the sky improbably; behind them, in the building somewhere, the Fair Children were singing-in the night.

Morton offered Judd a drink, which he accepted silently. The pilot groaned and stretched his long legs out over the paving slabs. 'Well?' he said. 'Have you found out what we need to know?'

Judd slid down the wall to crouch beside him. 'Think so.'

Morton was still wearing his shades. Now, he raised them

from his eyes to communicate. 'And?'

'Where are we, Mort?' Judd murmured. 'Where are we?'

The pilot sighed. 'We're nowhere, Judd. What's the problem?'

'They've headed towards the Preservation Territories...' he said.

'Excuse me? May I attempt a translation here? By 'they', 'spose you mean the truant half of of the LFC's, right?'

'Yeah.'

'You think we should follow?'

'I've reported in already. We have no choice.'

Morton sucked in his breath with a whistle. 'I've never been there, never seen it. Guys like me can't afford the aerial tours over the place, either. The Territories: wow. We're talking major risk of contamination here, I take it?'

Judd made a gloomy sound. 'I hope it hasn't got that far.'

'I guess these people think they can hide in the Territories, huh?' Morton said.

Judd shrugged. 'Probably. I hope it's only that.' He sighed.

'What else could it be?'

'I learned a little about the guy we're looking for tonight, Mort. He's a catharsis waiting to happen.'

Morton laughed. 'Meaning?'

'Meaning the Territories is the last place he should be.'

'Preserve the sacred ground, huh? Don't worry, we'll find him.'

'I know we will, but it might not be soon enough.' Judd leaned his head back against the wall. 'I don't know what makes me more mad: the fact some fool left a Horus Five lying around - which is beyond belief in itself - or the fact that a bunch of crazies like these had to stumble across it.'

'The thing that makes me mad is that they destroyed it,' Morton said and laughed in a cruel tone. 'Boy, these religious nuts!' He shook his head.

Morton didn't know the details. Judd suspected he didn't

care. He'd just had to sit and listen to the most sickening story and keep a straight face.

Macabee had fixed the machine, and had been so proud of himself - rightly so, in Judd's opinion - he'd wanted to show off to the others. That had been when the previous pathfinder went crazy. In his eyes, Macabee had tried to create life; only their god could do that for the LFCs. Susie and Amos hadn't winced from telling the details. 'We were all looking at this weird man thing, when Tarkus, our pathfinder came along. He wasn't pleased at all. He was angry with us for looking at what Macabee had done. He had Macabee locked up inside his room. Tarkus' deputies did it. They threw gasoline over everything. Then, they burned it. They burned Macabee and his evil false man. We were there. We saw it. But we couldn't do anything.'

Judd wished there'd been a little more disgust in the Lovelinks' voices, a little less relish. He suspected that, in some ways, the Fair Children thought this Tarkus character had done the right thing. They were worried they might be charged for damaging the Facility though, and felt the fact that Tarkus intended to hide in the Territories was more serious than the murder. Nobody ever went into the Territories; it was an enclosed and uncontaminated world. The nearest a person could get - legally - was a flyover. There were only a couple of tours a year though, apart from regular surveillance sorties. The Fair Children, aware of the taboo nature of the Territories, were anxious to absolve themselves of blame for its violation.

'We'll fix up the place where the fire was,' Amos had said earnestly. 'We'll still be able to keep our lease, won't we?'

Judd wished Mel and Tam hadn't turned in for the night. He needed someone to confide in, and Morton was not really the person he would have chosen.

'There's something else, that bothers me,' he said.

'You're always bothered by something, Judd!' Morton said, and then pushed Judd's arm to defuse the rebuke in his voice. 'What is it?'

'These Fair Children: they can speak the Old Language.'

'You're kidding. All of them?'

Judd nodded. 'Yes, including those who've headed towards the Territories. It's...'

Morton joined in to finish the sentence: 'Part of their religion!' Morton exhaled noisily. 'Early start tomorrow then, is it?'

'Yes. Early start.'

I did not visit Tila again; it was too much of a risk. For three days, I walked in a daze, not least because I had to let so much of my blood to give to Xiln. I blessed Tila's spirit that she gave me the protection of invisibility, that I could walk among the men without the strangers seeing me. Naturally, as she had instructed me, I wore some of my uncle's clothes, which my mother had kept in a chest. Our house was still standing, although we were not allowed to live in it. The strangers had not yet demolished all the dwellings and, as we had lived on the edge of the village, for the time being our little house was safe. At night, I merged with the menfolk, keeping my no-form as much as possible, becoming a boy in the sight of the strangers. It was not that difficult. All of our people are slim and slight of build in comparison with the strangers. Both men and women wear their hair long. I could cover my face and slouch along. Nobody guessed I was a girl. Everyone was slouching because they were so miserable.

On the morning of the fourth day, I positioned myself to be near where Tarkus was working. By noon, I was frantic. Something should have happened. Then, I saw Xiln walking unsteadily out the men's house. He was radiant with the nourishment I had given him, his hair sleek as a wing, his eyes bright with sacred fire. *Tila must be with him,* I thought. He went straight to where Tarkus was working and, when everyone was watching, made an obeisance.

'What is this?' Tarkus asked, laughing and embarrassed,

looking round furtively at everyone.

Xiln spoke clearly. 'I was dead and you gave me life, master. I am your man of clay, and thus, you are a god. I give myself to you.'

Tarkus laughed again, with even less assurance. His companions were all looking rather troubled. 'I am glad you're well, my friend, but I am not a god, neither are you a man of clay.'

'You brought me back with water, like in the story you told us. You said it was a symbol for truth; well, I am the truth.'

'No, no; you were ill. You were alive, I didn't make you. There is no comparison.'

'In my head, I was dead. I had given myself to the noble death. Yet, I was brought back to this world and opened my eyes to your face. You gave me life and in your eyes, I saw that you knew this too. You wanted me to live, wanted to bring me back. So, here I am. A child of your god, and your god is you.'

Tarkus became angry. 'Get this boy out of here!' he snapped and hurried away.

Xiln stared after him with the eyes of fire. Soon they would burn more brightly.

We counted the days, one, two, three, four, five, six... I passed the secret knowledge of my sister's hiding place among my people and, at length, we felt Tila come down from the mountain and walk among us. Something was happening to the strangers. They looked around themselves, afraid, for even though they could not understand or speak of it to one another, they knew inside their hearts the power of their god was waning. Tarkus had become a haunted man; he could no longer fire their hearts with his loud words. Thunderheads brooded over the mountains, waiting, waiting. The woman who spoke to us beside the fire sometimes forgot what she was saying. She would glance around herself, as if looking for enemies, and shiver. I felt sorry for her. On the fifth day, I approached her with a cake, which she took gratefully. Her face was dirty and smeared with the cleaner lines of tears. 'Who are you?' I asked her. 'Where do you come from?'

'The world is a terrible place,' she answered, her brow creased into a frown. 'We try to bring purity back to the hearts of humanity, we try to drive out the badness, and bring enlightenment to the benighted - such as yourselves - but it is so hard. We are misunderstood.'

'Would it be so terrible to take your lives to a place where you could live them as you pleased - alone? Do you really need to enslave us in this way?'

She put her hand on my arm. 'My dear girl, we are not enslaving, but freeing you. You don't realise how enslaved you are; that's the trouble. Anyway...' Another frown. 'We have tried what you suggested. We have tried it.'

'I do not understand what you mean by purity,' I said. 'Is Tarkus pure?'

She gave me a strange look as if she suspected I was laughing at her in some way.

'Where do you come from?' I repeated.

'A long way away,' she replied, 'an evil place. Very evil. I wish we could communicate what we have seen, but I can't. Tarkus thinks you should never know, because here, you have a chance. Here, the people are uncontaminated.'

'If you have seen this evil, it has attached itself to you and you have brought it with you,' I said. 'You have crippled our tribe-soul and murdered our gods. Are these pure acts?'

'Oh, I don't know! I don't know!' she snapped irritably.

Once, she would have smiled gently and spoken earnestly about the love of her Sky Master. Things were changing.

On the sixth day, a finger of lightning poked the dirt in the centre of our sacred circle and the sky went black. Fumes from the holy fire filled the air with incomprehensible perfumes. I thought I saw a beautiful girl walk through the murky air towards the dwellings of the strangers. Her hair was lifted from her back like an inky flag. It was Tila; I knew it. At this point, I went inside the women's long-house and told everyone to lie down and cover their faces with their blankets. I alone slipped out into the hot wind and went to the sacred fire pit. It seemed I was the only person alive in the whole world and this made me strangely happy. I sang a little and then danced on the lip of the stone, as my sister had once done. The fire pit growled beneath me and I blew kisses into its steam. My whole being was filled with a sense of freedom and, although I mourned the death of our gods, I knew a new time was coming, when there would be different gods to aid us. From the place where the strangers slept came a terrible cry, more terrible than anything I have ever heard. I squatted down on the stone and waited. Soon, Tila came out to me. She was but a vague shape in the steam of the fire pit; all I could see was her slimness and her flying hair. I put my forehead against the rock in a gesture of respect. She spoke quietly. 'Carve an icon for the man who will come here,' she said.

'What have you done to him?' I asked, not raising my head.

There was no reply. I looked up and there was only a lumbering shape coming through the steam, its arms held out in front of it. Maybe he spoke to me, or maybe he thought he was alone and spoke only to his own soul. 'Everything has gone,' he said. 'It has been taken from me. Everything. The demon took it.' He shook his fists at the boiling sky. 'Lord, where are you?' he screamed. Even the thunder was silent. The man, who was Tarkus, lowered his arms, his head, bowed his shoulders. 'I tried to do your work, but I was weak,' he said in a voice so low I could barely hear it, even though I was crouched so close to him, I could have touched his feet. 'Now, I am tainted.' With no further words, he walked confidently to the lip of the fire pit and kept on walking. No cry, no hesitation, just pure, unstinting sacrifice. I sang a song for him immediately, and, after a while went back to the village to find a piece of wood to carve an icon.

Tila had enticed Tarkus into the sacred fire, and he had gone willingly. The strangers, some of whom had witnessed what had happened at their dwellings, panicked like a herd of oxen plagued by stinging flies. They gathered up their belongings and fled into the mountains, where, if they were lucky, Tarkus would come to guide them. Xiln helped me make the icon for Tarkus because he had remembered to gather the right substances. After this was done, he and I placed the icons of Tila and Tarkus in the temple annex. Xiln went out into the storm and danced until the rain had washed him thoroughly. Then, I took him to my old home and we made the body-fire together. He will always be mine now, because he is part of Tila, and she is part of me. This is a holy wheel.

Lady Coyote picked up an interpreter from the perimeter station. There had been reports of a fence violation some clicks east. A foray team had gone in-territory, as far as the zone marker allowed, but had seen nothing unusual. They'd reported back to the Preservation Committee, who'd passed on the information to Central Arb. The station officers were curious about what was going on.

'Who's on the run in there?' they asked.

'A screwball,' Morton had replied.

'A sick man and a bunch of fools,' Judd had corrected.

Two settlements had been infiltrated. Both had driven the strangers out, but not without incurring casualties. One had been burned virtually to the ground. Mel and Tammi circulated id graphics of the LFC people and, with the help of the interpreter, soon confirmed that they were behind the devastation. Inhabitants of both settlements spoke of how Tarkus claimed to have come to help them, to build a new civilisation.

'This guy has flipped,' Mel said to Judd. 'He's on a conversion spree.'

'We're closing in,' Tammi said. 'We've got to be!' Her face was bleak. Judd guessed she had never faced madness, or death, before.

The mysteries of the mountains run so deep. Tarkus toiled inside the rock, ever upwards, and Tila would be at the summit to greet him, where he would emerge reborn and cleansed of misery. We had smeared his icon with a powder of herbs and his own seed, mixed with my spit. He took part of our people with him, but only a small part.

When the rains came again, all evidence of the strangers' passing was washed clean into the river and away.

Some time later, the spinning spirits appeared over the forest, but low this time, so low. Everyone hurried out into the fields, for we feared the god-carts were going to throw themselves to earth, for they had never come so close before, but our anxieties were unfounded. Like graceful birds, the spirits settled themselves on the flattened corn, and their whirring wings slowed and drooped so that we could see there were four for each cart, rather like a river fly's. Then, miraculously, living men and women came out from the bellies of these carts. For a while, we were afraid a terrible thing had come to us again, but these strangers were different to Tarkus and his kind. Our faith had been so shaken recently, we could no longer recognise the servants of gods when we saw them. Only one of them could speak our language, and he spoke for all of them. They showed images to us, wonderfully accurate representations of Tarkus and some of the people closest to him. Only gods could have made such images. Had we seen this man? they asked. At these words, a single thought passed from mind to mind throughout the tribe. Had Tarkus been a holy man after all? We thought it best to say we hadn't seen him, just in case. The strangers said they'd been trying to find Tarkus and had learned he had headed this way some time ago. Were we sure we hadn't seen him? 'Why are you searching for him so hard?' Xiln asked them. 'Is he your holy man too?'

At this, the stranger who could speak to us gave the others a strange glance and laughed uneasily. 'No,' he replied, and then, in a gentle voice, 'You have seen him, haven't you.'

'He went into the mountains,' Xiln said. 'Yes, we did see him.'

'Did you give him anything?' the man asked. 'Did he take anything from you?'

Xiln stared at him steadily, but said nothing.

'He can be dangerous,' the man said. 'We have to find him, to take him back. He has caused a lot of damage to other river tribes further south.'

'He is no longer dangerous,' Xiln said.

The interpreter sucked his lip and nodded, frowning. He turned to Judd, who was close behind him, and repeated the information. 'Well, you want to go on?' he asked.

Judd hardly heard him. He was paying more attention to the language of these people, the Old Language, like a breath of history, their wild appearance. He sensed power, of a kind, and innate nobility. This boy, this girl, in their simple clothes were holy people, uncontaminated, in spite of everything, and he was convinced quite a lot had happened here. Beyond the fields, he could see the wreckage of the village, and he could feel the proud and wounded indignation of these very special people. He nodded. 'Tarkus and his followers are interlopers here. They're not sanctioned to enter the preservation area, and they have caused damage. We can't go back without... proof that they're no longer here. Ask some more questions.'

The interpreter sighed and turned back to the boy. He knew the interrogation was pointless. Something had happened here, but the reconstructees weren't going to spill anything. He tried just one more time. 'Did this Tarkus character leave nothing behind?' he asked. 'It's very important. What about his followers? Did any of them... stay behind?'

The boy tossed back his hair, eyes glittering. 'We did not kill any of them!' he said indignantly, obviously divining the implications. These people were no fools, but the interpreter had known that for a long time. These people were the centre of the Territories, its heart, its soul.

He nodded at the boy. 'Very well, but if you see them again, will you send someone down south to Rivermouth and make sure they tell the ranger there about it?'

'That is a long way. There is also a barrier that the vine people made.'

'I know.' The interpreter wrinkled his nose and turned, once more, to Judd, relayed the information, such as it was.

'We have to fly over the mountain, then,' Judd said.

'You can, but I'll tell you one thing for certain,' said the interpreter, 'you won't find this guy. Never.' He spat into the corn.

The reconstructees were clearly impressed by this gesture, which must have been significant in their tribal code, for they immediately clustered around the interpreter, grabbing hold of his clothes, offering refreshment.

'We can't stay,' Judd said. 'Contact has to be kept to a minimum. Enough damage has been done as it is.'

He looked at the bland faces, the flying hair, against the backdrop of the mountains. He needed to get away. Quickly. 'Let's go,' he said.

'Who are you?' I asked, as they began to climb back into their god-carts. 'Who are all the people who come to us? Where do you come from?'

'Beauty,' said the man, patting my face, 'we kind of look after you and sometimes other people, who ain't so caring, get past us. You are very special, like the memory of something good. Understand?'

'Are you gods?' I asked. 'Or the ghosts of gods?'

The man laughed, but he did not answer.

Xiln and I knew the answer. Some strange new beings,

powerful spirits, had come to avenge the death of our gods. They would hunt down the people of Tarkus and kill them for us, because we could not. We all stood in the fields and watched the spinning spirits rise up and away over the mountains. We stretched out our arms to the sky in their direction. Everything was complete. Everything was good. We would never be alone.

Priest of Hands

The flying city is unthinkably ancient. As its tidal shadow dapples the land beneath in a groping, amoebic procession, the city too is always reshaping. As an *idea*, it is pursued by diverse minds. As a form, it is burgeoning with diverse bodies; inhabitant and visitors. Ground-dwellers cluster like abscesses on the hempen ladders hanging down like entrails from the city's belly. Many make the climb. What they find in the city depends entirely on what they have recognised within themselves. Some see only the weaponry - long abandoned - and they speculate. Some see the maps on alleyway walls; the maps don't tell them where they are, but simply indicate somewhere for them to go to. Some gravitate to the humid forest that flourishes beneath a range of glass domes. Hidden among the trees, there is a lake. It has flooded only once; during a storm, when the highest panes of the domes shattered. Market stalls surround the forest in a hectic ring. The hub of hot leaves and noise and animal smells is surrounded by wide radials, slanting upwards, away from the city centre. These are the avenues of commerce, lined by businesses; some with buildings of their own, some without. The avenues are crossed by a warren of narrower streets; the habitat of performance, ideas, experiences and knowledge. The higher the street, the loftier and more abstract its creativity. On the next tier up, the family homes and civic buildings are to be found. The highest building is lair to an unconscious militia of social valuers, and from here a soul might rise to the stars, into dreams. Wide-winged birds soar frenziedly around this building - indistinct scraps of white among the rusting iron scaffolding - as though startled by a threatening sound. The only sound that startles anyone in this city, however, is the whirr and chirring of the birds.

Within a tiny room of one of the dwellings, halfway up
the second tier of the city, the glimmering light of tiny floor-
lamps blossoms gently around the silhouettes of two people;
one a young priest, kneeling; one a dead man, flat on his
back. The priest is tired - his shoulders are slumped. He has
been working hard.

Whenever the priest concludes a piece of work, he is
often asked a question by a disembodied voice in his memory,
someone who never really asked that question, of whom he
cannot gather up the pieces and recognise. The voice is too
close, as if a whispering mouth is pressed up to his ear. He
can almost remember the warmth of breath pouring along the
nape of his neck, and a fragrance of birdwine in the air.

'What do *you* get from this?' The question seems to
assume he has to have some kind of intense motivation, or be
party to an agreement. His lips echo the question but he
never has an answer.

The job done, the question done, he packs away his
trappings; neatly and without haste. He turns off the music
maker, hanging on the wavy pound of the skin-bell, the
delicate rapid chime and hum, as it fades on the memory of a
harmonic. He picks up the sleepy-jar that contains a blue
powder as light as dust, as fibrous as thick hair that has been
finely diced. The music-maker and jar go into the bag he
hangs over his shoulder. Then the rest of his equipment goes
into a silk scarf; plain black with a fringe. These things are a
glove made out of fur and a glove made out of snakeskin. The
snakeskin is always wearing thin; its scales shed themselves
too quickly. He is always having to order a new one, because
people like that glove a lot. He leaves the tiny lamps behind; a
gift, for remembrance. The scarf is stuffed into a pocket of his
trousers. Tidied, and ready to leave, he then draws the sheet
up over the body on the bed. The dead face is usually smiling.

Relatives and loved ones tend to sidle into the room some
minutes after his music has faded to the silence of death. 'May
we give you something?' they ask, through white lips. Their

eyes are reddened, but from the effects of intoxicants rather than grief. They will contain their grief until he goes away. The relatives often want to give him some kind of payment, as if to appease the limbs and fingers of the Death Woman, keep her far from their doors for a while.

He smiles at them gently when they ask him this. 'Not now,' he says, reaching out to touch an arm, a shoulder. Then, he walks out of the house. He is never part of the mourning process. His name is Ays. He is seventeen years old, he is a Priest of Hands, and he lives in a city named Min; a city that always flies.

What *does* he get out of this? Sometimes, Ays asks himself that question again as he saunters back to his own community, in the honeycomb warren near the Temple itself. That he should receive some kind of gratification seems absurd. A job is a job. Each to their own crack in the stone. Death does not frighten him, of course; perhaps that is one of the rewards. Nobody has to pay for his services because the talents of Temple priests and priestesses are part of the community amenities.

Ays has been indentured to the Temple all his life. He does not know who his parents are, but likes to believe they were city-hoppers who, having stayed in Min for a while, had fulfilled their fiscal obligations by delivering a child to public service. Not many people who have been born in Min ever abandon it, because they would miss the sensation of flight. They know that relocating to a passing ground city would leave them feeling empty. Sometimes, nagged by the receding effects of the drug in his blood, Ays has experienced an urge to travel, but it is always slight. He and Min are part of each other; its wood, clay and iron seem like his own flesh in another form: his sensory organs are extensions of the city's heart: his work is a manifestation of nurturing concern for its inhabitants. He believes that to be apart from Min would be like dying for him, and no gloves of fur and snakeskin could stroke away the pain.

Ays lives on the second tier of Min and his chain of narrow rooms snakes rockwards towards the city's warm heart. The main room, in which he relaxes, eats and entertains friends is at the front of the chain, and has round windows that let in a clear natural light. His kitchen area is small, a curtained niche in the main room, but also boasts a window. His bedroom and bathroom, further back, are lit by gas lamps; he never lets the lights go out. The walls of these rooms are of rough-cut rock, the porous morphacite of which Min is constructed. Ays has hung coloured rugs on his walls, except for the one where a pale and sparkling vein of thremite runs through the rock. This, he has lit to best effect. At night, when the lamps are low and starlight comes like a spear through the window, the vein of thremite seems to move. Ays likes to watch it with half-closed eyes.

Back in his own setting, he removes his pale ritual clothing, and dresses himself more comfortably. Not that his uniform is uncomfortable in itself, but he would feel odd doing mundane things while wearing it; not sacrilegious or heretical, just insignificant, as though he wasn't really there at all.

There might be messages waiting in the chute of his auroscope; news of another commission, a few words from a friend. The chute is connected to the city network, a tangle of tubes through which the voices of the people whisper and hum, relayed by the passeteers, invisible presences stationed in hanging cubbies along the network. A system of mirrors relays the image of the caller, but the voice is never theirs; they are a gesturing ghost ahead of their stolen words.

Ays keeps his auroscope mirror in his living space, balanced in a long-legged dish. Other people fix theirs to the wall for safety, but Ays likes to see it standing there, poised on the edge of destruction. Light from the window comes in behind it, entering the silvered scales that make up its deceptively smooth surface. It directs splayed beams of light into the room, which look as if they are searching for something hidden within the walls that Ays has never found. If there are no messages in the chute, he blows into the tube hanging down from the wall, to open a passage to the Temple. 'All finished,' he says to whichever Brother or Sister appears in the mirror, half obscured by a disjointed window view.

'Another commission just came in. Can you take it?' they might say, or 'Nothing else for you today.'

If there is no further work, He always says, 'Not *yet*.'

And the Brother or Sister might smile thinly. 'It is, of course, impossible to predict... We'll call you.'

'Till then.' His communication finished, he closes the tube to break the connection and flicks the mirror with his nails to tilt it around a little. He doesn't want any bored passeteer spying on his privacy. After this, he goes to wash his hands. He takes his snakeskin glove out of its wrap and holds it up to the light for inspection. Sometimes, if it has reached that state where it is as transparent as a soul, he tosses it into the waste channel straight away, (where small scavenging mammals will drag it off for tidy consumption), and orders another. 'Skin me a snake,' he says to the auroscope. It usually arrives within an hour, delivered by chute.

Min flies low over the yellow land, and Ays is out walking after his work is done. Above his head, the city is an abstract pattern of angular metal skeletons, clutching at gentler wooden shapes that look like the silhouettes of vast, mechanical devices. The high buildings are all connected by a branching network of covered bridgeways that hang their shadows over the lesser roofs of stone and clay below. Winds whistle in the suspension ropes overhead as he walks the narrow streets. The skyline ahead is dominated by a cluster of huddling glass domes, around which a mass of birds are soaring and diving. Amongst the ragged flocks, cagekites bob and dip. They are the skycraft of small, agile children who, windblasted with nets, are poised to capture the birds.

Ays strolls down a steep rampway, out of the natural light, into the intestinal stone labyrinths of the inner and under city. He is fond of walking there, following the rise and fall of the circling paths. He descends a throat-like tunnel of orange light that leads him out into one of the cold, blue-white crystal chambers, where Min's water is stored. Towering, pale ranks of moist, fleshy fungus grow quickly in the breathing dark amidst the patter of scurrying claws. Despite the whispers of furtive activity in the shadow, Ays finds these chambers very tranquil, and he has need of tranquillity today. He cannot dispel the image of a young boy he had to visit earlier. The boy was only fifteen years old, his sickness pernicious. Ays has had to burn both of his gloves. Still, his work was necessary. The boy would have died whether Ays had visited him or not and had at least been eased into death in the proper manner. Ays tells himself this calmly, several times, but it's difficult to dispel a nagging uneasiness. After a few moments' quiet meditation, he leaves the Heartplace of the city and directs his steps rimward.

Ays is often drawn irresistibly to the city's rim, where he can watch the dark shadow of Min crawl hungrily over the ground beneath. The rim has its own community. Some people sit along the rails, telling stories to the passers-by; others paint or write, inspired by the vertiginous view, while others merely stand against the rail, staring silently at the ground below. Ays has his own rim ritual. People know who he is and allow him a few moment's solitary privacy when he arrives. Eventually, when they judge the time is right, the rim-watchers - young and old alike - come to lean against the rail beside him. They might share their food with him, if they have any with them, and then ask him jaunty questions about his work, even though they know he is honour-bound not to answer them. Ays remembers their faces; he likes their company.

As he mounts the wide worn steps that lead to the observation rails, he becomes aware of a strange, fluttery feeling in his belly. At first, he thinks this must be yet another unwelcome reaction to his most recent work. Then, just as he has found a comfortable space for himself along the rail, the youngest rim-watchers all start jumping around, pointing out over the rim. Ays recognises the disturbance in his body for what it is; precognition of displacement. He squints his eyes against the blood-and-daffodil light of the sinking sun, and can see that, down below, one of the ambulatory ground cities has become static, a diamond-shaped leviathan, balanced on its apex. It has been travelling along a long, deep valley between softly undulating hills that are misted with lavender flowers and dark green shrubs. Steaming waste fluids are spattering down from the motionless city's pipe-coiled underbelly, puddling in the torn and muddied earth. People can be seen slipping down rope ladders hanging from beneath the city; others are already scurrying around in the valley, gathering whatever plants and animals they can find before their city recommences its lumbering journey. Ays peers through one of the many public telescopes situated along the rail, and notices a cluster of dark brown canopies on the slope of one of the hills that advertise the presence of a terranaut camp. Terranauts are a secretive, nomadic race, who cause the cities to move by planting lines of crystalline pilot-stones in the ground, which the cities are mysteriously compelled to follow. By arranging the stones in a significant pattern, the terranauts can also cause the cities to halt. The mysteries of the pilot-stones are guarded fiercely, so that only the terranauts understand how and why the cities obey the stones' invisible power. Ays can see that there is a thick ring of pilot-stones around the city beneath, which has clearly caused the stoppage. As he scans the landscape with his telescope, Min is drawn towards the panting city beneath and hovers over it, smothering the distant streets and towers with its shadow. Min has no option but to pause for a while as well. Everyone that Ays knows takes these conditions for granted, even though, when the cities stop moving, strange things can happen. Displacements occur - distortions of things, time, or people. Some people think that during a displacement terranauts travel unseen between the cities, but no one knows for sure. A few Minnians, like Ays, have the ability to predict displacements, rather like others can predict the coming of storms. The Temple is pleased Ays has this ability; it is as a much part of the regalia of his work as the music box, the jar of blue and gloves.

Ays returns home to await the displacement. As usual, he sits down in a chair to prepare himself for it. He feels the tug when it comes, a crystalline gurgling in the flesh - it is the only way he can describe it to himself. It reminds him of the thremite; he feels like a vein of brightness in starlight. Afterwards, just a few moments later, Ays blinks, and finds the shade over the gas lamp opposite is now in the shape of a glass lizard. Before, it was a simple globe. He approves of this change. The furniture has altered its colour slightly, but has undergone no drastic modifications. The rugs beneath his feet feel a little softer perhaps, and the quality of the light is different; faintly pink.

In the bathroom, it is a different story. The bath is full of baby lemurs, a softly undulating foam of fur. Ays smiles and puts his fingers against his mouth, wondering whether he should strip off his clothes and climb in among them. A bath of fur might feel quite agreeable.

He ponders, quite wistfully, how he would feel if one day, after a displacement, his bath was full of terranaut; a lean, young male with long, black hair. Ays is intrigued by terranauts, even though he has never seen one close to.

During his meal, the auroscope chimes, not only to advertise the arrival of a new glove through the chute, but also to indicate an incoming call from the Temple. He flicks the mirror into position and uncaps the tube, taking his new glove from the delivery slot as he does so. He is not annoyed at being disturbed. The very nature of his work means that his days can never be planned.

'Here,' he says to the Sister in the mirror.

'Brother Ays, a commission,' she answers, her mouth moving ahead of the words. On this occasion, the passeteer speaking is male.

'Location?'

'A transient's hostel... Thoroughfare Steep Steps. The hostel is called Resting on the Hop.'

'Oh.' Ays raises his brows at her image, to show her that more information is required. 'A transient? That's unusual.'

'They came in with the displacement.'

This is more unusual than Ays thought. 'What, climbed up to us?'

The Sister shakes her head. 'From the report of their condition, it would seem unlikely. We can only assume they were caught in the displacement unwittingly and transferred here, perhaps from the city we're over. I expect it's a traveller.'

Ays walks around to face the mirror squarely, trying on his new glove for size. 'And they're dying? How odd!'

The Sister nods. 'An unexpected failing, true, but the hostel patron feels that we should offer his guest all of the city services, yours included.'

Ays looks at his fingers in their new snakeskin glove and flexes them slightly, watching the scales glimmer. 'I'll go right there,' he says. 'Oh, I need food for tonight. Any chance of a shrinee slipping out for me? Seeing as I'm working...'

When the message reaches her, the Sister raises her eyes for a moment, manifesting wry patience. This is not an uncommon request from Ays. He makes no secret of the fact that he is impatient with the market. Lesser minions can shop for him; he is a prestigious person, after all.

'Leave a list out,' says the Sister, *'and* the wafers. I'll see what I can do.'

Ays blows a kiss at her image to show appreciation. 'Blessings, Sister.'

The Sister shakes her head, smiling. 'I hope it will be

some time before I need *your* blessings, Brother.'

So does Ays. He quite likes her.

Evening is coming down. Ays puts on a thick coat of hempweave before going outside, because there is a chill breeze squirming through the streets of Min. He puts as many of the baby lemurs as he can comfortably carry into a large embroidered bag, which he carries over his shoulder. Mounting the steps to the third tier, he pauses for a moment to let the wind snag his hair and gazes out towards the rim and the dark horizon. Min has moved on. There are no cities near, no sign of life at all, other than a few root bladders, half deflated and empty of passengers, drifting on the air currents to a final, distant landing and decay.

Ays feels excited and intrigued by this new commission. Wanderers, travellers, transients - whatever name they are known by - are always mentally abnormal in some way, because as the cities themselves travel constantly, to leave home for a while and find your way back again is a difficult task. If being unconcerned about that isn't abnormal, what is? Generally, transients are individuals following bizarre and esoteric quests that most people could not even begin to understand, never mind be sympathetic towards. They have forgotten their homes, their origins, and even if they haven't, are ignorant of where their homes might actually be. Some are mystics - a category Ays prefers to think his own parents must belong to - and some have important, but mysterious, purposes. Terranauts, of course, are eternal wanderers, like the cities they lead, but no one thinks of them as abnormal. However, barring unforeseen accidents, visitors to Min rarely need the attentions of the Temple. Transients who are ill generally migrate instinctively towards the special sanatoriums where they can be properly cared for. If they are lucky, their feet will lead them to a suitable place before it is too late. These sanatoriums are found in ground cities having a reputation for inordinately frequent displacements. Quite often, after a displacement, a person might find they are no longer ill. True, it is also possible for such people to disappear completely from their current location's reality, but most invalids think this a slight risk worth taking. Ays thinks his new commission must involve someone who has fallen sick unawares, or perhaps he'll find they are one of those extreme crazies who simply doesn't care what happens to them. He also considers that it might also be possible he'll have a real live terranaut on his hands. Do terranauts ever have accidents, he wonders.

Resting on the Hop, a narrow wafer of stone, nestles between two more imposing hostelries whose facades are clay-scaped with concealed amenity-pipes. As a contrast, the Hop's wall is braided, almost carelessly, with rubbery heat conduits that sprout from the pavement, breathing the warmth of Min's heart to the water tanks and cosy-stones of the inn.

Inside, the proprietor is waiting for him, and after a formal greeting, offers him a biscuit and a mug of curds to augment his strength. Ays' stomach is already full, but he respects the ritual and takes a single bite and a single sip. He offers the man the baby lemurs, for which he is grateful. All of his mantises have disappeared with the displacement.

'How urgently is my attention required here?' Ays asks.

The man frowns. He doesn't know. 'Retching,' he replies and makes a harried gesture with his hands. 'Blood. Foam. Refuses a physick. Says no one can help.'

'I see. Perhaps you had better introduce me right away.'

The proprietor nods and precedes Ays into a shadowy, upward-sloping passageway. Lighted bowls of oil set into the wall do very little to dispel the gloom, but the atmosphere is oddly homely.

'Came in with the displacement, I've heard...' Ays says to the broad back ahead of him.

The proprietor grunts an affirmative. 'Found on the street outside. No currency and no indication of a name.'

'The sickness could be infectious,' Ays says, a slight note of censure in his voice. The inn really should have called in a physick, whatever protests had been made.

'No, the rats were already trying to get at the meat. They know whether flesh is bad or not.'

Ays cannot contest that. 'Are you sure he's dying?' He has to ask.

The man turns round. 'He? It's a woman. As to the rest, you'll see.'

The proprietor takes Ays into a room that is hardly more than a cell, and was perhaps once a bone-cupboard, but it is warm and the oil-bowl is freshly fragranced. The bed is extremely narrow, because of the confined space, but the sheets are glaring white and the downy-sack plump. Within it lies a dying woman, her breath liquid in her chest, her face yellow and damp. Ays has not come too soon, it seems. He becomes aware of the proprietor standing just behind him in the doorway, the man's deliberate silence. He is hoping Ays will forget he is there, because he wants to watch the priest at work. People always want to watch. Ays has no personal aversion to this, yet somehow feels instinctively that his work should remain secret, like the moment beyond death itself. He looks over his shoulder at the spectator until the man closes the door and goes away. Then, Ays unpacks his equipment.

He opens the lid of the music maker and a thin sound comes out like a question. He puts it on the floor. He takes out the sleepy-jar, the picture on its lid long worn away. When the lid comes off, a thick scent spills out into the room and he pokes his fingers into the swirling blue dust within. Next, he unwraps his gloves. Snakeskin for immortality, of the soul, the essence, the invisible bird of spirit. Snakeskin for the place beyond life. Fur for protection by winter beasts, earthy reality; the luxury of fur, its sensuality. Ays knows his symbols. He puts some of the sleepy mix inside a sticky tissue, and rolls it into a narrow cylinder, which he lights with a flare-pin. He takes the first lungful of smoke, sucking it down into his body, closing his eyes, visualising the silvery-purple haze sinking into his blood. The effect is instantaneous; the world flexes around him. The thin sound from the music-maker becomes briefly strident; an insect din. Expelling smoke through his nose, he draws on his glove of fur, over the fingers of his left hand.

'I am Ays,' he says to the woman lying on the bed. Her eyes are closed, her face expressing no pain, although fluid leaks between her lax, yet bitten, lips. For a brief moment, Ays wonders whether she is already dead and reaches out to touch her with his ungloved hand. She looks at him. The eyes are surprisingly clear. What is she dying of?

'I am from the Temple of Mother Darkness,' he says.

'They sent for you.' Her face is that of a mature woman, perhaps someone fifteen years older than himself, but the voice is young. Ays feels as if, even though he is staring right at her, he cannot exactly *see* her. What does she look like? He does not know. He only hears her voice.

'Yes,' he answers. 'I am here to travel with you for a while.'

She sighs and her mouth smiles. 'Then I must be dying.'

Ays squats down beside the bed. He can see she is looking at his gloved hand. 'What is your sickness?' he asks.

The woman screws up her eyes. 'It is... a fading,' she says, in a soft voice, and then a flicker of panic twists in her eyes. 'Where am I? Why am I here? What is this place?'

'Hush,' he says, putting his ungloved hand on her shoulder. He can feel, he thinks, a fever heat. 'You are in the flying city of Min. Are you a traveller?'

'I don't want to die in an unknown place,' she says. 'I don't want to die at all.'

'That is why I am here,' he murmurs gently, 'to help you die. That is my function. I soothe away the terrors of it.'

The woman laughs weakly. 'You cannot do that. I am a stranger.'

'It makes no difference,' he says. 'Lie back. Be still.'

He draws the downy-sack away from her. Beneath it, her

thin, damp body has been dressed in a clean, woollen nightshirt, which he guesses has been donated by the Hop's proprietor. As is the custom, the body has been bathed and oiled, ready for his attention. The dying woman's hair has been tied neatly back behind her head. As a priest, he is not to be bothered with such sordid tasks.

Before he touches her further, he offers her the burning sleepy-mix. She stares at it for a moment, forcing him to say, 'Go on.' Then, she smiles and takes it from his hand with thin, shaking fingers. With some clients, he has to put the smoke stick in their mouths himself, they are so far gone, but not with this one. She screws up her eyes as she inhales. She inhales very deeply, almost with gusto.

'You are kind,' she says. 'You cannot imagine how thankful I am for this.'

An unusual remark. 'Part of it,' he says. 'That's all.' He gently pulls the smoke stick from her mouth. 'Not too much. Not yet.'

'You are a beautiful boy,' she says. People often say that.

He smiles. 'Part of it, that's all,' he says.

She lies back, blinking, and he presses the glove of fur against her belly. It will feel like a cat rolling over and over. His animal hand traces the line of ribs, the hollow, the torso's throat, beneath them, the rippling landscape of stomach and loins.

'A city that flies,' she says. 'Yes, I have heard of it.'

'Mmm,' he says, 'be still.' It is uncommon for them to want to talk. He does not like them talking.

'There are stories too of the Sisters of Midnight who live there,' she says, ignoring him. 'Those that come with the hands of a beast, a snake, to lift the spirits from the weak.'

It is time to give her more sleepy-mix, clearly. She takes the smoke from him; her eyes are dark now, the darkness of midnight. She watches him as he strokes her, as he strokes her further away from life. He is full of a sleepy haze. He is a body of smoke. The music maker hums upon the floor, curtains at the tiny window tremble in a breeze and he is empowered by the stillness of his art, called up from the core of him. He sways, lets his hair fall upon her, stroking away her life. *Listen to me, beloved, listen to the rhythm of my blood, my calling.*

It is time for the glove of snakeskin.

The moment is stillness itself, as he peels away the glove of fur. It falls to the floor; a beast sucked of life. A skin without quickening. His left hand squirms into the scales, and the air is full of curling smoke. She is watching him, watching him, the essence of her condensed into her eyes.

As he touches her lightly with his fingers, she makes an unexpected sound. It is a crystal sound that cracks across the sound of breath, of the music, of the infinitesimal hiss of the smoke.

It is the sound of laughter.

Ays feels as if he is made of glass, some brittle substance, and her laughter cracks him. He feels the power of his skill drain out from his body, out like thin, rancid liquor, down through the cracks in the floor.

He cannot even ask a question.

'I am sorry,' she says.

Sorry? Sorry? She speaks! She should not speak. He realises he can no longer work; she has made him a thing of comedy, of bathos. The snakeskin glove is resting on her belly. When he looks at it, he has to snatch his hand away, because he cannot bear to see it lying there. It looks ridiculous.

He sees her glance at the smoking stick where it rests against the lid of the tin, its glowing tip held away from the floor. 'The herb of Mara Hela,' she says, with some reverence. 'I should have known I squeezed out into reality here for a reason. My god self must have been with me, if not my thinking mind.'

'Who are you?' Ays asks sharply. She knows. She is a terranaut; she must be. Lean and dark, long black hair, talking of bizarre ways of travel. She does not look so haggard now. Perhaps this is the realisation of his dreams. He had not expected it to manifest as female though.

The woman puts her arms behind her head and smiles at him, but she does not answer his question. From her mocking expression Ays has to accept that she is no dream creature of his. 'The herb is fatally toxic, but of course you know that, don't you. And the little helping hands of Mother Darkness train themselves to resist its effects. They are addicts. You are an addict. How quaint.'

Ays is shattered. Doesn't she know that? What is this creature? Why is she doing this? Why isn't she dying, like she should be, held in the arms of Hela's cloud? How is she different from other people?

'You were never ill,' he says.

Now he is angry. Somehow, the anger helps restore his dignity. He stands up, kicks the music-maker with his left foot, stops it singing. He scrunches up the gloves and roughly stuffs them into his pocket along with the black, silk scarf. He takes the smoking stick and sucks from it himself. The effects are no longer tranquillising and dreamy, but disorientating. He feels sick and dizzy, but he won't give any more of it to her.

'Are you a terranaut?' he asks her. The question seems silly, as if he'd asked her whether she was a ghost.

She grins. 'I'm a traveller,' she says. 'I have knowledge which enables me to move around in ways you'd find unusual, I suppose.'

'What knowledge?'

'Secret.'

'Are you a priestess?'

'No.'

Ays cannot contain his humiliation. 'You let me work on you! You weren't dying! You mocked me!' He feels absurdly violated.

She shakes her head. 'No. I *was* dying. Really. I am a toxicate. The most unlikely events stranded me in a no-city place. There was no sustenance in that wilderness, no Hela. Only death, because I need Hela to live - like you do.'

Ays stares at her. This cannot be true. The smoking mix is the secret of the Temple of Mother Darkness. Its herb grows only in the garden of the outer shrines. This is impossible. 'You are lying,' he says. 'The herb only grows in Min. It was created here.'

She shakes her head slowly, still smiling. 'No,' she says. 'Before Min flew, it must have taken its herb stock from the ground below. There is a place, pretty Ays, called the Womb of Hela, where the herbs grow high. I lived in that place and thought I learned to control the bitter lady. Now, she controls me, but life can be sweet in her kingdom.'

What she says might well be true. Ays has no way of proving it, one way or the other. He realises he might as well give her more of the smoke. She is not going to pass from this world today, that is certain. As she inhales, he wonders what he should do now. This is unprecedented in Min. No one survives a visit from the Priest of Hands; no one. Ays almost suspects she's manipulated the displacement to reach here deliberately, but that too is impossible. No one can manipulate the displacement; it is all random. No one except a terranaut perhaps.

He narrows his eyes at her. 'So, what's your name?'

'Eleanore,' she says, around a circle of smoke.

Later, because he has no other option, because, by surviving his attentions, she has surrendered her soul into his care, he takes her away from the hostel with him. The inn people are afraid of her; she has conquered death, in their eyes.

Back in his rooms, Ays gives Eleanore a pallet on the floor as a bed. The remaining baby lemurs have taken over in his absence, stealing what was left of his food, blinking, round-eyed from behind the furniture. 'Stay there,' Ays says to Eleanore, pointing at the pallet. It feels as if he has yet another animal to stay. Like a slim, elegant dog, Eleanore curls obligingly into a posture of meditation and then watches him unblinkingly as he calls the Temple. Will they help him? No. Are they embarrassed by this exemplary failure? No. They are simply not interested. It is his problem, they say, and the mirror goes dull before he can protest. He is rudely reminded of the freelance nature of his work.

Eleanore makes his home feel small and self-conscious, although she is happy to sit on the pallet and smoke her way through the contents of his sleepy-jar, while playing with the lemurs. She is a wiry, strong-looking creature, swathed in a veil of thick black hair, which she shakes about often. The Temple, avoiding confrontation, does not balk at Ays' terse order for extra supplies of currency wafers and Hela. He sends them a dozen lemurs in return.

Eleanore will not answer questions with any sense, and sometimes pretends to have lost her memory. She has been with Ays for a whole day and he cannot sleep with her so close. No woman has ever slept in his home-space. He suggests she might like to be lowered to the ground in a passenger basket to resume her travels. She frowns and does not answer. What can he do? She is his responsibility now. She has attached herself to him like an infection. Surviving the call of Mother Darkness, she has become part of him, the Mother's erring son. Ays knows this and it does not please him at all. The extent of his displeasure is illustrated by his sense of relief when the unavoidable inventorian comes to call.

Madam Abey is accompanied by a pillar of ledgers, which are held together by a leather strap and transported upon the head of an acolyte. She carries a rolled bundle of parchment charts beneath her arm.

'A miracle...' she begins, as Ays lets her in and indicates his guest.

'Not a miracle,' Ays replies, 'but *that*. I suppose you have an interest.'

The inventorian nods and minces up to inspect the exotic specimen Ays has acquired. She is a grand figure, in elaborate robes of green and yellow linen. Eleanore watches her blandly. Ays realises she is not like a dog at all. 'I am Hagar Abey,' the inventorian announces, as if the name should mean something to Eleanore. Eleanore smiles but does not speak. Madam Abey turns to Ays. 'We have consulted the records,' she says, in a lowered voice, 'and there is no information to compare with this.'

'I am not surprised.'

Madam Abey snaps an order at her acolyte, who withdraws a notebook and pen from a jacket pocket; very carefully, so as not to upset his cargo. The inventorian puts down her charts on Ays' table, and then, lacing her fingers before her, begins to dictate some notes in a strident voice. She gazes at the ceiling as she pronounces, defining Eleanore as a lean-bodied female, whose eyes and general physique correspond to the celestial house of the Dusk Dancer. Her posture, she supposes, suggests a natal moon position in the house of the Cowled Snake, but she might be mistaken. Reluctantly, Ays concurs with Madam Abey's diagnosis, although his knowledge of the heavens is confined to the public predictions and character listings posted in the markets every three days.

Next, Madam Abey clicks her fingers and her acolyte produces a complex instrument of metal bands, bone vanes and struts, with which his mistress can measure the circumference and diameter of Eleanore's head. She feels Eleanore's skull for reprehensible lumps, signifying psychosis, and prods in her mouth to inspect her teeth. She pulls down Eleanore's eyelids and pinches her cheeks and sweetly-tilted snub nose. Eleanore submits to all of this quite passively, although she refuses to stand up for any more measurements, so Madam Abey is forced to make a shrewd guess.

The inspection over, Madam Abey unrolls her charts, chooses one representing the human body, and marks it with various glyphs, thereby transforming the anonymous chart into a depiction of Ays' unwanted guest. Very soon, it will be filed away in the Inventory and probably never looked at again.

'You have to accept responsibility for this person,' Madam Abey says.

Ays sighs. 'I have already done so. Haven't you noticed?'

'Tradition dictates that should you save a soul, the soul becomes yours.' The Inventorian peers at Ays intently.

Ays shrugs. Eleanore's soul is not a commodity he desires to own particularly. 'She was doing something before she came here,' he says, 'perhaps we should be assisting her to resume that, whatever it was.'

'I wasn't doing anything,' Eleanore says, speaking for the first time since the inventorian arrived.

Madam Abey gives Ays a significant glance.

'Have some lemurs,' Ays says, putting a couple on the acolyte's shoulders.

Madam Abey shakes her head. 'I have two bears in my solar that came in with the displacement,' she says.

After the inventorian has left, Eleanore asks Ays who the visitor was. It is the first question she has asked him about Min since he brought her home, and he is strangely encouraged by this new development. Perhaps she will also rediscover an interest in her former life if he indulges her. He tries to explain about Madam Abey, but it is difficult for foreigners to understand the Inventory and its minions. It doesn't really have a function; it just *is*. The inventorians are always hurrying around collecting information. Ays tells Eleanore they are like lice, or fleas, but he thinks this conveys the wrong picture.

'Min is lunatic,' she decides. 'It was founded by lunatics.'

She is quite wrong, so much so, Ays has to sit down and talk to her about it. 'No, Min was built by a coven of philosophers,' he says. 'They wanted to withdraw from the world and see the world at the same time. It's quite simple.

They were astrologers too and over the years they evolved into the Inventory.'

'And where did you evolve from?' she asks, grinning.

'Well, people came in with the displacements I expect, or else mystics just came visiting. The city was called something different in the beginning.'

'And what will happen to you when your crazy city falls from the sky?'

Ays stands up. 'It will never fall from the sky!' he says. 'Are you really so stupid?' When he's not actually working, he has difficulty being patient and tolerant with people.

'So how do *you* think it stays up, then?' she asks, taking a generous pinch from his sadly-depleted sleepy-jar and rolling it into a smoking stick.

Ays has the impression she is attempting to mock him; she with her smoke-scrawled grin and Dusk Dancer eyes. 'If you know anything at all, you will realise that only the terranauts really know the answer to that,' he says. It is very difficult to keep his voice pliable; it sounds as stiff as his clenched jaws.

Ays can't take Eleanore with him when he's working, but neither does he feel comfortable about leaving her alone in his rooms. Compromising, he decides she can sit with the relatives of any clients he visits. This is not very kind of him, he knows, because Eleanore has a tendency to stare at people too long; a habit which might be a prickly deterrent to spontaneous grief. Perhaps someone will complain about her to the Temple, thereby forcing them to acknowledge his problem. He does not feel particularly desperate, only rather stunned. How can his life ever settle itself with this large Eleanore-shaped absurdity in it?

They are walking to Ays' first commission since Eleanore intruded into his life. She seems to be taking an interest in Min, as Ays feels she should, because to him it is a very interesting place.

'Where do you get your water from?' she asks. 'Do you lower a vast appendage to the ground below and suck from the lakes?'

'No, we take water from the clouds,' he tells her. 'There is a reservoir within the city and when there are clouds in the sky, we fly up to milk them of moisture.'

'And you trawl the sky for seeds with enormous nets, no doubt, for food,' she says.

'We have hanging gardens,' he says. 'And farms within the heart itself where fungus grows.'

'Such an efficient community!'

'Here is the house where I have to work,' he says, wishing Eleanore did not grate on his nerves so much.

The family are surprised by Ays' companion. He does not attempt to explain her presence but simply tells them she will be sitting with them while he works. Eleanore cheerfully makes herself at home in the most comfortable chair and announces, 'Death! Who needs it?' She rolls her eyes and tosses her head; the family do not respond, but they glance at Ays anxiously. He makes a careless gesture with his hands. Perhaps they will think Eleanore is part of some new ritual being tested by the Temple.

A mature woman leads Ays to the room of his client, where the air is hot and stale with sickness. He finds an ancient male, withered and yellow, quite worn out with life, who is calmly ready to die. It soothes him to work. He can forget his dilemmas in the haze of Hela, performing so brilliantly that the old dog's flame is extinguished, not with the habitual sigh or faint gurgle, but with a loud and ecstatic whimper. Ays hears the relatives gasp outside the door. Then there is another sound: laughter. Eleanore is laughing - loudly and without restraint. Ays cannot bear to look at the dead face on the bed and throws the sheet over it hastily.

There is no offer of gifts, not even a question about his work. The family are glad to see him leave the house. They do not even thank him for the lemurs he has given them.

So begins the undermining of Ays' vocation. When he mentions to Eleanore that laughter is perhaps inappropriate in the presence of the dead, she only shrugs. 'I have to bring you with me on commissions,' he says, 'so at least have the courtesy to contain your offensive mirth.'

'You don't *have* to bring me,' she says. 'I could stay in the cave.' She always refers to his home as a cave.

'No, you can't,' he says.

'Why?'

'You just can't.'

She pulls a face. 'Oh well.'

The next time he is working, Eleanore whistles a tune between her teeth in the adjoining room. Ays is astounded at how loud and piercing a whistle can be. It is a sound quite at variance with the haunting serenade of his music-maker. The grieving wife is plainly angry at Eleanore's intrusion. Ays attempts to explain, but the woman's face is stone, her mouth a thin crack. It is obviously better just to leave quickly.

'No laughter, no whistling!' he says to Eleanore as they walk back home. 'No harsh noises at all. I mean it! Or else...'

'Or else what?' she asks, striding jauntily along beside him, a smoke-stick hanging from the corner of her mouth. She is about an inch or two taller than him.

Inspired, Ays takes his sleepy-jar out of his bag. 'You don't want to know,' he says and shakes the jar under her nose. The message sinks through her blithe mood.

'Oh, I see. No harsh noises,' she says.

Feeling somewhat less anxious, Ays takes Eleanore without qualm to his next commission. Now, he has the edge over her. She will fear him withholding the sleepy-mix. He feels almost warm towards her as she sits herself cross-legged on the floor and adopts a pious pose. The family will think she is augmenting his work through performing some serious contemplation. He should have known better. Just as he is changing gloves, a reverberant hum vibrates through the house. It is a sonorous meditation mantra, resonated so well, it sets his teeth on edge. He has little doubt that the teeth of the resident family are similarly discomforted. He dare not imagine their accompanying mood. Although sacred, the humming is not a suitable sound to accompany the extinction of life.

The first complaint to the temple is made.

'Ays, we humbly request you leave your guest at home when you work.'

'Brother, I will not leave her at home. She is unfamiliar with the customs of Min. I am attempting to rectify that.'

'Ays, we realise your predicament, but must stress that this transient's place is not at your side while you're working. You must steel yourself to leaving her behind, no matter how attached you are to her.'

Attached! How dare they! 'I see your point, Brother,' he says coldly, 'but as you know, this person is now my responsibility. I am concerned she might damage herself if left alone.... Perhaps I should leave her at the Temple with you?'

There is a pause, followed by a terse response. 'We will adjust your work schedule to accommodate your responsibilities.'

Ays' commissions become fewer. All his clients are people who live alone. Consequently, he begins to spend more time at the rim, Eleanore in tow.

'Where do you come from?' he asks her, a nonsense question, but he feels she has a definite origin somewhere; she is not just a feather blown upon the winds of displacement. She is something else.

'I am part of infinity,' she says, 'like you', and smokes his sleepy-mix.

'Why are you doing this to me?'

'Just tell me to leave and I will,' she says.

She must know he cannot do that. Why can't he? Is it merely superstition? 'Do you want to stay here?' he asks her.

She shrugs. He hadn't really expected an answer.

'What do you get out of this weird job of yours?' she asks. 'How can you put your hand down the trousers of all those decrepit old goats? It's disgusting!' She is laughing, of course. How dare she insult his art! He does not even bother to answer, but walks away along the rim-rail.

She follows and stands humming behind him; he has turned his back on her. 'Look, I have to work,' he says, in a low voice, punctuating his words by slapping the rail.

'Why?' she asks.

He is unsure how to answer. Nobody *has* to work if they don't want to. Min supports everybody. 'It's my life,' he says, lamely.

'Your life is other peoples' deaths,' she says, and laughs.

'Look at it like that if you want to, it's none of your business!'

'Your life is a perversity! And you enjoy it!'

He turns on her then. 'I've had enough of your insults! You've barged into my life, you've upset my living pattern and have deeply offended the relatives of my clients! Have you no sense of decency?'

'No,' she says, 'only of the grotesque. Tell me to fall over the rail of Min, and I will. Why don't you? What is this stupid idea you have that you own my soul, or whatever it is you think? You're crazy, and I'll stay until you tell me to go. It will do you good. Stupid belief system!' She laughs again and hops up onto the rail, holding out her arms to balance herself. Ays' flesh freezes. She raises one foot and wobbles. 'Well, Priest Ays, do you condemn me to death, or not? There are ways to die other than by the smoke of lovely Hela. If you're quick, you could give me a short fondle before I fall.'

'Get down!' he screeches, without dignity of any sort. Other rim-walkers are looking at them. He can see astonished faces, and hands clutching throats, out of the corners of his eyes.

'Ah, you don't want me to die, is that it?' she says.

'No, of course I don't want you to die!' It is not exactly

the truth, but he is grateful when she jumps back to the walkway.

'Neither do I.' She has the audacity to take his arm. 'The air in this city of madness is surprisingly good for the soul,' she says and inhales deeply. 'Break out your sleepy-jar, Ays, it is a time for euphoria!'

He could withhold it from her. He could. But he doesn't.

He feels as if his bones are made of the same stone as the bones of Min. He feels them groaning inside his flesh as if they are being stretched. He is still working - just - but there is something missing now. Something has been taken from him. He's not sure what it is. He keeps hoping he will wake up one day and find Eleanore gone. And yet, her face, which from the first instant he saw it seemed oddly familiar, has become significant in his life, a part of daily routine.

'What do you do with the dead?' she asks him. 'When your job is finished? Is there a burial ground in Min?'

'No,' he says. 'The bodies are wrapped in a membrane of fungus skin and lowered over the side of the city. We believe they sink into the ground. Perhaps they do.'

'Or perhaps scavengers take them,' Eleanore says. 'That can happen you know. Some people get very hungry, and will eat anything.'

'You are absurd!' He should hate her, and has been trying to, but whatever disruption she has caused, he enjoys looking at her expressive face, her long, mobile hands. With so little work, there is plenty of time for him to talk with Eleanore now. She tells him about the cities she has visited, and he can see and smell them through her voice. She is bored with Min; he is sure of it. Her world is far bigger than his. He wonders if she dislikes him. Perhaps she has no feelings at all.

One evening, they are sitting upon a stone bench at the rim, surrounded by wilting telescopes, watching the sunset.

Eleanore deftly prepares a smoking-stick as Ays kicks the bench and sniffs the cool, fragrant air. 'Don't you see how you encourage death?' Eleanore announces into the comfortable silence.

Ays feels weary, and cannot summon the energy to argue fiercely. 'Our ways of dealing with death are civilised,' he says. 'That's all.'

Eleanore lights the smoking-stock. 'Oh, yes, very civilized! So, tell me how you think death works here on Min, then.'

Ays shrugs. 'People just die, Eleanore, like you nearly did.'

'Oh, that was only fear!' she announces airily. 'I don't actually believe in death. None of my people do. Of course, intense pain mixed with fear, or fatal injury, would very likely kill me, but that episode in the hostel was simply a ritual, an imitation.' She raises one eyebrow and glances at him sideways through a tangle of hair. 'Perhaps I might have died if you had not been so beautiful or, even more likely, if you hadn't given me some blue.'

'You have unusual beliefs,' he says. 'Anyway, who are your people?'

Eleanore grins sheepishly. 'I'm not supposed to tell, but it has a lot to do with stones.'

'Then you are a terranaut! I knew it!' He swiftly attempts to smother his rather joyous expression. 'Why didn't you tell me?'

'It wasn't important.'

'Wasn't important?' Ays laughs at that. He realises Eleanore has bestowed a privilege upon him. It must mean she trusts him. 'Don't any of your people die of old age?' he asks.

Eleanore shakes her head. 'No. But tedium has claimed a few. As long as we displace ourselves regularly, we stay fairly youthful. In the cities, people convince themselves that one day they will die. Death is a way of preventing overpopulation, I suppose, but we have found that people tend to breed less if they free themselves from their personal death sentences.'

Ays frowns. 'It can't be as simple as that.'

'Well, no, I suppose it isn't,' Eleanore agrees. 'However, examine your role in Min for a moment. You bring death to those who expect it. Why do they expect death? Because some physick has told them to? Has life itself driven them to desire it, or has someone else been courteous enough to inflict that desire upon them? Whatever the reason, the result is that *you* are called in. In my eyes, that makes you nothing more than a cold-blooded killer whose activities are sanctioned by the citizens.'

'I've never thought about like that,' Ays says. He is listening to her unorthodox ideas simply because she is a terranaut. If she hadn't confessed her identity, he knows he would have been arguing hotly with her by now.

'I don't believe it,' Eleanore says gently. 'You must have dreamed about the principles behind your work, at least. Anyway, do *you* expect to die?'

Ays squirms uncomfortably on the bench. 'I'm not sure. I can't help feeling different from the people I work for, but then all of us indentured to the Temple feel we are different. We are encouraged to feel that way.'

'Is that an answer?'

Ays stands up and rubs his chilly arms. 'I don't want to think about it.'

Back in Ays' rooms, they sit down to eat their evening meal. Ays feels numb and exhausted. He knows that, in the light of what Eleanore has told him, he should be experiencing slightly more impassioned feelings. His desire to meet a terranaut, now that it has happened, appears to have become lost within the fog in his mind. He looks up as Eleanore speaks his name.

'What?'

'You look tired,' she says.

'I *am* tired. Tired of this situation! I want my life back. I don't feel real.'

Eleanore rests her chin in her hands and stares at him steadily for a few moments. 'The game was good,' she says, 'but I'm tiring of it too, now. Tell me, what was it that made you take me in like this? Are you really so dedicated to your beliefs? Do you really think you are responsible for my soul?'

Ays sighs. 'No... yes... I don't know.'

'I *am* going to leave,' she says.

'I thought so.' He knows that, despite the disruption she has brought into his life, he will miss having her around. It's as if some opportunity he couldn't recognise has slipped past him like a shadow.

'There is somewhere I have to go,' Eleanore says. She puts her hand in her pocket and rolls something onto the table. It is a piece of stone, a strange mineral; it looks burnt and it is veined with a glittering, metallic substance.

'A pilot stone?' Ays asks, amazed. 'You have one with you! Surely, that's not allowed?'

Eleanore places her open palm over the stone and rolls it around beneath her hand. 'Look, you don't have to believe all the myths associated with my people. As a privilege, and because you are a friend who saved my life, I'll let you into a secret; most of the stories are lies.'

She is not laughing. There is not even a hint of a grin on her face. Ays realises she is serious, for perhaps the first time since he met her. A shiver ripples down his body from head to toe.

Eleanore reaches out and touches his hand. 'We could hitch a ride from the next city we pass over. I could fix it so we displace together. We could go anywhere. What do you say?'

'No! Min, my work, my home, the Hela...' She is asking him to go with her. She really is - isn't she?

'The first three are irrelevant. The fourth is easily catered for. I told you it was unusual circumstances that caused me to end up in the middle of nowhere. It was an accident. All I had was this' - she tapped the pilot stone - 'and a withdrawal problem. I had to displace blind, from nowhere to somewhere. It wasn't easy. Luck brought me here...' She sighs and smiles in a charming, melting way. 'I like you Ays, and I think you'd like me, if I let you get to know me.'

'You are an arrogant, conniving nuisance,' he says.

She shrugs. 'I know, but think of what you could see with me. You don't have to be one of the little people now. You could ride the cities like I do, even slip in and out of a billion universes if you wish. This is a serious offer, Ays, and a rare one. The probability of it being made to a boy like you is unfathomable. Whatever you think of me, consider the opportunity I'm giving you. Wake up.'

Wake up? He is a part of Min, a part of the stone. Has Eleanore succeeded in chipping him away from it? He cannot tell. If he goes with her, it will not be for the wonders she can show him. It will be for the eyes of a Dusk Dancer; nothing else.

Before he goes to sleep, he lies in his bed listening to the noises of the city. He feels as if he has never heard them before. Does this mean he has somehow slipped outside the organism of Min? Or is that simply an excuse for his decision? He dreams of pilot stones, rows and rows of them, marching into infinity. They glitter fiercely in the sun, and a hundred cities, like little motes of dust, tumble round them in the air. Now he is among the colliding cities, jumping from one to another, feeling the tug of displacement with each leap. It is intoxicating. He looks behind him, and there is Eleanore juggling pilot stones. She throws one to him and it flies into his open mouth. He swallows. 'Wake up,' she says, and the world turns over.

Gasping to wakefulness, Ays immediately senses her presence in his room. He turns his head to the wall and closes his eyes. No woman has ever shared his bed. But then, he has never met a woman like Eleanore before. He throws back the downy-sack in invitation.

Ays' gloves flap on the wind like little birds; one of fur, one of snakeskin. They fly away from the passenger basket, heading out into the wilderness. Ays has released them to the wind. Min is a monstrous shadow overhead; he looks up at its receding bulk with streaming eyes. Eleanore puts her hand upon his arm, and he reaches to touch her fingers. Everything has changed. Yesterday, they would never have touched one another.

'Adventure, Ays,' she says, 'Life.'

He makes a noise, unsure. He's still confused as to why he's doing this. It feels as if he has no choice. He holds out his hands in front of him and examines them carefully. What will they do now? What will their purpose be?

'Don't think about it,' Eleanore says, misinterpreting his thought, or perhaps not.

'I cannot think at all,' he says.

'You should be glad,' she says. 'Experience your new freedom. I can't understand why you did that *work*. It's bizarre. What did you get out of it? There must have been something. Tell me. I want to know. I want to understand.'

'Distance,' he answers. 'That's all, and sleep.'

'You're awake now,' she says, and with a final squeeze of his arm, turns around to look down over the side of the basket.

He became responsible for her soul. He became part of her, and there was not enough room inside him for Min as well. Is he really awake? He doesn't know. Maybe he has just exchanged one crazy dream for another. Maybe he can never wake up.

'I thought we would travel by using the pilot-stone,' he says.

'Not yet,' Eleanore replies. 'There is a secret to the stone, a secret you must learn before we use it. I cannot tell it to you; you must discover it for yourself.'

'If we are together, then we should have no secrets,' Ays says. He feels uneasy.

Eleanore reaches out to touch him again. 'Sometimes there are secrets that we don't know we have, Ays. The secret of the pilot-stones is one of those.'

'But how will I find it? I don't know how or where to begin. This just isn't fair, after everything I've done for you.'

'Well, precisely. What have you done for me?'

'Brought you back from the death.'

'Bought me, or brought me, you also did something else, something that anyone can do.'

'How can I know?'

'What is your question, your personal question. Everyone has one and, more importantly, what is your answer to that question?'

Ays remembers. A memory that was never real, a fantasy, an intimate dream thrown at his by his profession. The question never concerned his job at all, he can see that now. It was the fantasy itself being questioned.

'Well, Ays?'

'Desire is my question. My answer, desire.'

Eleanore smiles and places her hand in his. Ays feels the pilot-stone, held in her palm, linking their flesh.

Joy in Desire

In the village of Lionsmount, more rain fell than in living memory. People began to think that all their recollections of blue skies and sunshine were faulty and this was the way it had always been: the province of a damp, brooding god whose frown filled the sky. Whole houses floated off, people went mad, and those who killed themselves in despair melted away before their bodies were found. The land did not feel right. The river was angry. Old superstitions rose like boils in the psyches of those who believed themselves more civilised than that. But then, one day, the miserable god moved on to harass another realm, and the sun came back.

Now, the river has begun to withdraw into itself once more, but the landscape it reveals somehow doesn't the look the same as it did before. It's a damaged thing, like a person who has suffered a nervous breakdown, gone into hospital, only to re-emerge as someone unfamiliar and strange. It's delicate, easily hurt, somehow unpredictable. In a strange way, it has woken up.

Melissa Kershaw lives alone in a cottage halfway up a hill to the north of the village. She inherited the house from her mother, Ella, who died young but managed to outlive two dissolute husbands. Melissa knows she is not at all like her mother, perhaps because Ella died before she could have a great effect on her daughter. Ella enjoyed a wild bohemian life, full of lovers and parties and scandal, whereas Melissa works quietly for the local council offices, in nearby Brockhampton, and looks older than her thirty six years. She has never had lovers or dyed her hair, but she is not discontent. She loves the cottage and the village and wants for nothing.

In her childhood, Melissa was always farmed out at weekends to older aunts and a grandmother, who tutted their disapproval of their sister/daughter, and spoke in whispers when they thought young ears were listening. When Melissa returned home, the cottage always seemed pained and exhausted, as did Ella, who was generally to be found semi-conscious on the sofa, a gin and tonic listing in her hands, her abundant hair spread out over the cushions like hanks of wet grass, ash trays spilled on the carpet around her.

She died accidentally, when Melissa was only seven years old. The story went that Ella was out for a walk, drunk, and fell into the river, where she drowned. After this tragic event, which occurred while Melissa was at her grandmother's, Aunt Susan moved in to the cottage at once: a capable woman of no nonsense and firm hair. She remained obligingly alive until Melissa was old enough to look after herself.

Ella had been a fey sort, who believed in fairies and ghosts. Strangely, women from the village had not appeared to disapprove of her as her own relatives had, which might be seen as odd, given that most of the villagers were well to do and appeared quite prim. On the surface, at any rate. Melissa can remember these women coming to the cottage in summer evenings, and how she would be shooed out into the garden to play. Sometimes, she heard weeping coming from the kitchen and the clink of the gin bottle against glass.

As an adult, Melissa realises that her mother used to perform services for the village women. No one ever used the word witch, including Melissa herself, but it has always hung unspoken in her mind, like a black dress at the back of the wardrobe. It was not a hereditary occupation, however, for Ella's sisters and mother had been god-fearing women, who'd thought Ella strayed too far from the path. 'Look what happens when you do that,' they'd muttered together. 'The Lord takes his vengeance.'

Melissa doesn't believe that. Ella's death had been a sad

waste, as had most of her life. There is nothing else to think.

Melissa always has more holiday than she knows what to do
with, because she spends so many hours at work clocking up
flexitime. Now, in this strange June, which follows even
stranger preceding months, she is at home, looking out at her
suffering garden, where there is nothing to be done, because
Melissa has already done it. The house is spotless too. Five
more days of the holiday stretch before her. And now the
heat is creeping in.

It comes like a sultry demoness, crawling over the land,
making everything steam and smoulder. The waterlogged
ground gives up its vapours, so that everything seems misty
and unreal. So much heat after so much rain. Melissa doesn't
like the way it makes her perspire, as if she too is
waterlogged. Her clothes stick to her skin. Her shoulder-
length, unstyled hair hangs lank. She feels listless and nothing
can hold her attention. The thought of even reading a book is
too exhausting for words.

She has just taken a couple of Paracetamol to throw off a
dull headache, and now drinks a glass of ice-cold lemonade
that she made herself from plump lemons with waxy skins.
She's so bored it feels like an illness.

Melissa has local friends, affluent men's wives, who don't
go out to work. Some of them had been friends of Ella, or
their mothers had. Melissa isn't blind to the fact that she's
treated with a peculiar sort of respect, as if these women
think that one day she might decide to take on the mantle
that floated down the river on the day that Ella died, but
there's no chance of that. Ella had been a one-off, a naughty
but spirited creature, who'd never grown old, whose light had
burned brightly and briefly. Melissa does not feel she has the
same light. She's a good listener, but that's as far as it goes.
Now, despite her boredom, she lacks the energy to walk
down the hill to visit any of her friends. The baked interior of
her car will be unbearable, so she can't stomach the prospect

of driving either. Perhaps later, once the sun begins to set, she might be able to throw a cardigan around her shoulders without feeling suffocated, and stroll down to the village. People meet in the pub, which has only just reopened following disastrous flooding, being situated next to the river. Mindful of what excess drinking can do a person, Melissa does not over-indulge, but enjoys a cold glass of dry white wine in the evenings, especially during the summer, when she can sit in the pub garden and chat to whoever comes by. She longs for the balm of dusk, when even if the heat won't abate exactly, breezes might arise to soothe the skin.

Through the open window, she can see the narrow lane that curls around the hill, where two children are cycling slowly to the top. Their voices sound shrill and desperate. At the bottom of the hill, fields, and then marshes, stretch towards the river. Only weeks before, it had been a furious bloated torrent, bent on destruction. It had gushed nearer and nearer to the road that led to the hill, and Melissa had often feared being cut off. Fortunately, she'd fared better than most of her neighbours and hadn't missed a single day's work. Now, the river is a sluggish lazy thing, shawled in steam. Ancient willows, of several varieties, droop along its banks. Their leaves have been damaged by rain, now they are shrivelling. The heat has made hags of them. Through the ground mist, they seem to lean towards one another, gossiping maliciously. The whole landscape feels alive and sentient, and to an impressionable mind - which Melissa tells herself hers is *certainly* not - on the brink of rising up in rebellion against those who sought to tame it.

What is happening? Melissa thinks. *Has the earth gone mad? I don't know this eerie place. I don't want to.*

She purses her lips and sighs through her nose, placing her glass down precisely on the windowsill. She brushes a hand through her hair; finds both sticky. She'll take a cold bath, lie down for a while. But then something catches her eye in the distant marsh, an image so unlikely and preposterous, she has to stare at it to make it disappear. And so it does, after a moment, but not before Melissa realises what it is. A sort of lion, a great gilded thing, but then not a lion at all. It's difficult to tell through the mist, but it seemed, for all the world, to have had more than one head. Someone was riding it too. Melissa puts both hands against her lips and utters a short laugh out loud. 'Now, *I'm* going mad,' she says. 'Whatever next?' She dismisses the vision at once, as the product of heat and exhaustion, even though, for a delusion, it took more seconds to vanish than were surely necessary.

The cold bath water doesn't stay cold for long, but quickly warms up from contact with Melissa's fevered skin. She has to keep turning on the cold tap, which is a hideous and unnatural departure from the usual routine of bathing, in fact a complete reversal. Still, despite this, Melissa emerges from the water somewhat refreshed, dresses herself in a loose bath-robe and winds up her hair in a towel. She pads into the bedroom, which is fortunately in shade and therefore moderately cool, but before she lies down, feels compelled to open the wardrobe and remove from its deep recess a cardboard box done up with Sellotape.

This box contains all that is left of Ella Kershaw. Melissa looked through it a lot as a teenager, searching for blurry photographs of her father. She kept a few of her mother's floaty embroidered scarves, because they were so pretty, her wedding rings, and a few other bits of jewellery that had been handed down from grandmothers. She kept a pair of shoes: Indian slippers made of dark red silk and covered with designs fashioned of gilt wire and tarnished sequins. There is also some of Ella's make-up, which appealed to a younger Melissa, even though she never tried wearing it. Now the garish red lipsticks will be gummy and rancid, and the beautiful sparkly nail-varnish set like glue. There's mascara in a compact with a caked little brush, and powder that smells of old houses. But Melissa doesn't reach for any of these things. She takes instead an item wrapped in black chiffon, bigger than the size of her hands. For a while, she kneels before the wardrobe and gazes at her lap. In her heart, she's slightly afraid of unwrapping the bundle, but eventually she does so, and a scent of old incense spills out. She holds her mother's Tarot cards, of which her grandmother and aunts heartily disapproved, but agreed Melissa should keep them, because of their value. It is a rare first edition of an unusual deck. Melissa wants to examine the cards now because of what she saw on the marsh. Their edges are tattered and they feel thick in her fingers, indicating how much they've been used. Ella didn't care for them very well, and some of them have clearly been wet at some point in their history, no doubt from when Ella spread them out sloppily over sodden pub tables. Melissa doesn't believe you can predict the future from cards, but she acknowledges that each illustration conjures a certain mood with colour and image. She finds the card she's looking for, the major arcarnum numbered XI and named 'Lust'. As she remembered, dimly, it depicts a strange beast with several heads being ridden by a naked woman, whose face is turned away from the viewer.

Lust on the marsh, Melissa thinks with a smile. *Sounds like a romantic novel.*

It's not the sort of image she'd expect her mind to conjure, no matter how much affected by heat.

Purposefully, she puts the cards on the floor and goes through into what was once Ella's boudoir. Here, there's a case full of Ella's books. Almost annoyed with herself for doing so, Melissa finds the right volume and looks up the meaning of the card. It means joy in desire and the reins held by the woman riding the beast represent the passion that binds her to it. Sounds very Ella. But Melissa doesn't believe in omens.

That evening, she decides to make light of her 'vision', make an amusing anecdote out of it. Mary Heath, Elizabeth Smith and their respective husbands are out in the pub garden, and when the men go indoors to replenish the drinks,

Melissa tells her tale. 'You'll never guess what happened today!'

The other women, both older than Melissa, listen quietly, but the only laughter at the end of the story is Melissa's. She realises, with a sinking heart, she should have known better. But then she hasn't mentioned the Tarot card. 'It wasn't *real*,' Melissa says.

Elizabeth makes a strange little sound and shakes her head, while Mary says, 'Do you often see things like that?'

'No!' Melissa says firmly.

Ella is a ghost at the table, hanging in the dusk like a pale moth. Melissa knows her mother is on everyone's mind. She wants to say, 'I'm *me*. I won't be her,' but keeps quiet, realising, with a sickening jolt, that perhaps her friends have been waiting for a moment like this for many years.

'She was the light of the land,' Mary says to Elizabeth. 'The passion of it.' Neither of them glance at Melissa. She knows that, even though she's staring at the table.

Walking back through the humid night, Melissa listens to the unfathomable prophecies of owls, their white wings shrouds on the dark blue air. The moon is almost full and wears a nimbus. Midges are out in their thousands, battalions drunk on human blood. Curls of hair lie wet against the nape of Melissa's neck, the skin of her arms is burning. Three glasses of wine have gone to her head; it's more than she usually drinks. She breathes deeply and can identify a host of different scents. Beautiful place, but injured. The land is a seeping wound.

Where the road to the hill turns away from the hedged lane, a young man leans against an old wooden gate, apparently staring out over the fields at the marsh. Melissa recognises him as the son of a local farmer: she can't remember his name. His body is long and rangy, his hair pale over his shoulders, his shirt loose and white. He is the sort of boy who might very well have once scuttled from Ella's cottage in the early hours of the morning, his boots in his hand, and his flies undone, but this one wouldn't have been born then. He could be Melissa's own son, if she'd had him when she was sixteen. Or he could be running from her cottage in the dark, worried about his mother finding out. For the briefest moment, Melissa wonders what it had been like, for Ella. What had she thought when the lusty boys had left and she was alone with the overflowing ash-trays, the smell of stale tobacco and the spilled drink? She had died alone, her fringed shawl swept down-stream and caught up in the arms of a willow.

The farmer's son has heard Melissa coming and turns from the gate. 'Evening,' he says, clearly not remembering her name either.

'Humid, isn't it?' she says in a brittle glassy voice, batting a hand before her face. Her cardigan has slipped off her shoulders and now she holds it in one hand. 'Dreadful midges.'

'A lot've come out,' he says in a measured, deliberate way, and she gets the impression he means more than flies, but perhaps that's just the effect of the wine: strange fancies.

'Reckon we need your Ma again,' he says.

She smiles. 'Ah well.' The road to the cottage suddenly looks incredibly inviting. She waves a farewell. 'Have a nice evening.'

He says nothing as she moves away from him, but she feels his eyes upon her.

The cottage smells musty and a gang of flies are circling in the middle of the living room. Melissa opens the window again, spies the slender form of the boy still leaning on the old gate. She wishes there was a bottle of ice cold wine in the fridge, but there is only lemonade, and the milk for her tea in the morning. She feels restless, as if she should be doing something. It is not an unpleasant feeling.

The upper floor of the cottage breathes softly in blue

darkness. It is hot up there, and a warm draught that has snuck in from the marsh makes a window rattle. Melissa kicks off her shoes and the thin carpet of the landing feels gritty against her bare feet. If she strains her senses, she can imagine the scratchy sound of her mother's old record player, the music that used to drift up the stairs on summer evenings. She can imagine muted laughter, quickly silenced. Perfume on the air, the sharp tang of cocktail onions. Perhaps time doesn't exist anywhere but in the imagination, and layers of thought are laid over events that continually repeat themselves, disguising them. Endless moments of now.

In her bedroom, Melissa can hear the restless tinkle of a metal wind chime, even though she doesn't possess one. The sound seems to come from beyond the window. She can hear her clock ticking on the table beside the bed, marking away her life. She wants to stop its cruel relentless march.

The box of her mother's things still stands before the wardrobe, where the door hangs open slightly. The floaty scarves drift over the sides of the box as if they've been trying to escape, waiting for the breeze to carry them. Melissa picks up the scarves, holds them to her nose and the scent that fills her head seems to come from beyond the fabric, from her own wrists. She feels delirious with joy. She is laughing. But maybe this too is an illusion, and the real Melissa is downstairs, drinking cold lemonade, flicking through the TV channels, trying to find some late night news.

The real Melissa wouldn't throw herself to her knees like a careless girl and start rummaging through the cardboard box. She wouldn't go 'Ah!' and sit back on her heels, pushing her hair behind her ears, before picking up her mother's red slippers. Neither would she slip those slippers onto her feet and wiggle her toes in them, so that the moonlight flowing through the window conjures sparks in the sequins. Would she get to her feet with unaccustomed grace and twirl slowly around the room, dancing in and out of the moonlight? Would she stretch out a hand before her to admire its pale slimness? No. But the Melissa in the moonlight feels quite happy to leave her old self downstairs, poring through tragedy. This is not a night when the outside world should intrude.

Her heart is beating strong and true and she has never felt more alive. She kneels before the box again, her summer skirt pooling around her. She ties a scarf around her neck and a longer one around her hair, so that the tasselled ends dangle down her back. She picks out a metal tube of lipstick and when she turns the base, the oily crimson pigment that emerges looks black in the fairy light of the room. She holds it to her nose, inhales, and thinks of old theatres, of panstick and dazzling lights. Slowly, deliberately, she takes up the powder compact, opens it and looks at herself in the cloudy mirror. Her nose is shiny, so she powders it, surrounding herself with the scent of old summers, of a locked room in a dark warm house, where the sun barely penetrates, and someone beautiful has died in there.

What is she doing? Why is she compelled to smear Ella's lipstick over her mouth? It feels good, though. Comforting. And the lipstick isn't as rancid as she thought it would be. It glides on in a thick, slippery slick. She spits on the worn black cake of mascara and brushes it onto her eyelashes. She is someone else now: nearly. Before she leaves the room, she opens the one bottle of nail varnish that isn't glued shut and paints her fingernails. For some minutes she sits staring at her splayed hands, waiting for the polish to dry. It does so, very quickly. Dark red with sparkles in it, but it all looks black to Melissa. The colour red doesn't exist very easily in the world of night.

As she tiptoes down the stairs, and into the corridor below, Melissa feels she has to creep past another woman who's sitting in the living room, watching the TV. But the cottage is in darkness and there is no sound. The now she inhabits has overlaid the other one, where dreary news soaks the room in harsh blue light. Melissa is drawn to the outdoors, to the embrace of the scented night.

The temperature of the air is just right, like the temperature of blood. It is neither hot nor cool against her skin. It is her element. Moonlight and the scent of grass, the cries of owls and the lowing of cows in distant meadows, ripple through the leaves of the apple trees in her garden. The lane is a pale ribbon down to the road that moats the hill. Mist hangs over the fields like a veil between the worlds of reality and dreams. It would be dangerous to walk out onto the marsh, and Melissa, even though intoxicated by *something*, is still too sensible to take such a risk. But she can walk in the fields, through the damp grass, and listen to the slow coil of the river.

The farmer's son is no longer leaning against the gate, but as she climbs over it, Melissa wonders whether, in another now that she cannot perceive, he's still there, and he feels a ghost move through him, smells her scent.

Mist tumbles around her thighs. It's like walking in the sea, but in water you cannot feel. There is a slight resistance against her body. Was it a night like this when Ella went down to the river? Melissa remembers, with a small shock, that it was indeed this time of year when her mother died. She remembers drought, the parched land cracked, but not bleeding, like the skin of worn, overworked hands.

They need her again, Melissa thinks, recalling the comments of her friends and the farmer's son. *They want me to do it. Ella went down to the river and died in it. Did it rain again afterwards?*

Melissa can't remember, but feels it must have done. Must she too give herself to the land to heal it? A brief image splashes across her inner eye: her workplace, her computer, the insistent phone. She belongs to that world, it's waiting for her. But tonight, she's not there, and it cannot help her. Another place has claimed her, lured her in. She has crossed its threshold willingly.

Melissa glances over her shoulder towards the road, sure

she will retrace her steps at once. But the pale-haired boy is there again, leaning on the gate, clearly visible in the moonlight. He is waving to her and she waves back. Strange fancies. There is nothing to fear. She can hear the viscous voice of the river.

Last year's bulrushes rise from the mist, their cigar-shaped pods gone to seed. The ground sucks at her feet now and twice she has lost one of the red slippers and had to retrieve it from a muddy pool. It is not far to the water. Her skirt is soaked, and a wicked hawthorn with spiky fingers has stolen one of her scarves. Something is moving towards her through the mist, and she is sure it will be a golden lion with seven heads, ridden by a naked woman. She can hear it, the suck of its paws in the sodden ground. Lust. The Whore of Babylon. All that Melissa is not, but she can do this. She can do *this* thing. There is no point to anything but the land itself. She has been grown for this moment from a seed, a dark, hard little seed, but now she has broken the shell of it and can feel the air against her being, perhaps for the first time.

Melissa stumbles and falls to her knees, breaking her fall with her hands. It's difficult to get up, but she must go on. It's taking too long now. She must complete the cycle. On her feet, swaying, her clothes sticking to her body, she sees the shape ahead: a shadowy female silhouette cutting through the mist. She does not ride the lion, she is on foot, but it must be her. Lust. The land is a terrible, pagan thing. It bleeds and kills and copulates without morality. It is a beast and humans want to be angels of rarefied essence and lofty thoughts.

What Ella and I do, Melissa thought, *we do alone and in secret, because it is vile, an abomination. But the land is needful, and that is our burden.*

She holds out her arms to the vision, waiting to see the face set in a wicked lascivious smile, the scent from the whore's body that will smell of men's seed and corn. But when the woman emerges from her cloak of vapour, it is Ella standing there. Ella in her favourite shawl, her hair pinned up with glossy Spanish combs.

'Lissy, what are you doing?' she says. 'Look at you.'

'I'm following you, Mum,' Melissa says. 'I know it now. I know what we do.'

Ella appears perplexed for a moment, then says sharply. 'You don't have a daughter. You can't follow me.'

'That doesn't matter,' Melissa says, aware, even in these dreamlike circumstances, how bizarre it is to be arguing with her dead mother. 'Gran wasn't like you. It's just you and me.'

Ella shakes her head vigorously. 'It's my fault,' she says, apparently to herself. 'I wasn't good with you, was I? I thought you'd just grow up and *know*. It's not our blood, Lissy. It's the land. This place. The women who live here.'

'It suffers,' Melissa says, 'and I will end it as you did.'

'He never told, did he,' Ella says, and doesn't wait for an answer. 'What I did was something else, but no one could find out because, well, because of who he was. I lost my skin because I was drunk, Lissy. I was too drunk for sense. He left me alone and I lost my way, or maybe I was looking for a quick way home.'

Melissa only stares at her mother, whose outline is shimmering faintly. She might not be there at all. This could be a voice from her own head.

'You only know half of it,' Ella says. 'Turn around.'

'Are you always here?' Melissa asks.

Ella laughs. 'Oh, I think you know about *that*,' she says. 'Tonight, you stopped the clock. Now turn around.'

The beast is there as if it stepped from the card, shining golden, full of colour in the black and white realm of the moon. The heads are turned in her direction: each stares intently, but with a strange kind of hesitancy. Melissa walks forward, feeling as if she glides across the surface of the marsh. She kisses each of the heads in turn: the poet, the bacchante, the warrior, the saint, the angel, the satyr, and the head on the end of the tail, which arcs over its back, the head of the lion-serpent. She grasps the thick fur above its shoulders and swings herself onto its back. A shawl of scent envelops her: the musk of warm fur.

The beast walks away from the marsh, and for a time Ella strolls beside it, one hand in its mane. Mother and daughter do not speak, but a wealth of knowledge passes between them. The mist over the fields is clearing slowly, being drawn back into the marsh. The river is inhaling it.

'There,' says Ella, pointing.

Melissa sees the young man at the gate, his pale hair, his dark arms, the aching white of his loose shirt. He is the one, the one she must use.

Ella utters a cry and slaps the side of the beast. 'Be free!' she shouts. 'Give yourself to the forces of life!'

At once, the beast leaps forward and Melissa is galloping, galloping towards the future. She can feel the mighty muscles of the creature working beneath her legs, between her thighs. Her hair streams back from her face and the boy is so close now, not moving at all. Just waiting.

When Melissa reaches the gate, she finds she has been running. She's lost both her slippers and the scarves, and her skirt is wet and torn. There is no beast, not on the outside. It's in her now, alive and hot and powerful. The boy still does not move, but he's watching her closely. 'What's chasing you?' he asks.

Melissa climbs over the gate and jumps down beside him. She feels sixteen again. Her body is lighter because her soul is lighter. She is beautiful, as Ella was. 'Nothing,' she says. 'I just got hungry.' She holds out her hand. 'Feed?'

For a moment, he hesitates and then takes her hand. She will lead him to the cottage, through the darkness, up the stairs, to her own empty room. She will make her sacrifice to the land there, in all its glorious wantonness. She will take him and ride him and life force will pour out of her like steam. It will plump the corn and make the cows' milk sweet. One day, there will be a wind-chime at her window and she will listen to it with her lovers. She will offer lemonade, not gin, to the women who come to her door. She is Melissa Kershaw, a woman of the land. She is lust, she is strength, she is power, lady of the crossroads, heiress to the ancient ways. She knows how to ride the beast.

The Fool's Path

The night Carlotta challenged the Fool began with laughter. There she was, mock sober, one foot up on the table in the spilled wine, bangles clanking, looking for all the world as if she'd been invented solely to fit her gypsy name.

'I'm not afraid of anything,' she said.

I remember the heat of the night and the way the slow-moving river below the theatre bar gave off a summer smell that was half of flowers and half of rot. The wall of windows over the river was open to the air and it was like being on a high boat, drifting through the season. Looking out, you could see all the lights burning on the theatre roof reflected like fireflies in the water. We were all too hot, fanning ourselves with anything that would lend itself to the job. And the heat had lured the magician out of his cave, or whatever place he lived in.

He came to the theatre bar often, although it was impossible to predict his movements, but we all knew that was the way he wanted it. Older than all of us, he'd come in and do card tricks at the round corner table, drinking beer because he said spirits or wine made him see things he'd rather not see. He told us about phantom drinkers, the ghosts who'd stand behind the living as they drank, make-believing they could still do it too. Apparently, the theatre bar had quite a few of those. It was impossible to put an age on the magician – he could have been anywhere between thirty-five and sixty. He was the sort of man that hardly ever changed and had probably looked mature, in a freakish kind of way, when he'd still been a child. Handsome? Yes, in a bizarre manner. He took girls away with him when he wanted to, at the end of the night, through the smoke and the fruity smell of stale beer. They went to hotels, never to his home, and nobody ever complained, even if they didn't say much about what happened. I think he told them to be secretive, just to wind people up. He probably taught them the smug smile too.

The magician would always come in late, and then the theatre staff, when they'd finished work, would drift into the bar and sit down to let him entertain them. Sometimes, a few of the minor actors would join them. Carlotta, the other bar staff and myself would flit about all night, waiting and yearning to join the raucous party in the corner.

I'd worked in the bar for five seasons, but Carlotta was new. Most people liked her, even though she made no secret of knowing she was gorgeous and could be a bit full of herself. She was a dare-devil with a loud, almost masculine laugh. She could rake her hands through her thick black hair and flutter her eyes, and a thousand empires might fall. I'm not sure why she ended up working in a bar – even a bar with high kudos like the theatre's – but I guessed she'd had a rough time of one kind or another and was down on her luck.

So, on this night, the devil was in Carlotta. She was hot and high, full of mischief. She'd told me earlier in the night that she had her eye on one of the actors, and that she was sure he had his eye on her. The actor in question was my friend, Jack. He was not destined to be a leading man, but took fairly prominent parts in the productions on a regular basis. He was too lazy ever to be a huge success in life, but while his looks lasted, he intended to make the most of it. I had no doubt his eye had noticed Carlotta, as it noticed any attractive female. During my five seasons, I had counselled over half a dozen Jack-broken hearts and now wondered whether I was due for another or whether Jack had met his match.

The magician came in at just before eleven and Jack was one of the first to join his party. Weirdly enough, given what happened, Jack was playing the Fool in the play – a court jester in actual fact. The following night would be the last performance of the current production.

When the last of the customers had been shooed from the premises, Hugh, the bar manager locked up and gestured for Carlotta and I refill the empty glasses at the corner table. It was Friday. We could tell Hugh was looking forward to a long night.

The magician already had his cards out and a young, pretty actress called Mel was in debate with him. She'd come in with Jack, and none of us really knew her. I'd heard what she had to say before, from other sceptical mouths.

'It's just sleight of hand, tricks,' she said. 'That's all it is.'

'Did I say otherwise?' said the magician.

'It *is* otherwise,' Jack said sternly. 'You've taught us that.'

The actress pulled a face. 'Oh, come on! Magic doesn't exist, not real magic. If it did, the world would be a different place.'

'It's the Cosmic Joker,' Jack said. 'The Fool. He governs it all.'

'What?' The actress laughed in the most convincing manner of her profession.

Carlotta and I sat down, and I sensed Carlotta's engine begin to rev beside me. I wondered if we were heading into dangerous territory. The magician hardly ever talked about the Fool – his obsession – unless it was with people he had known for a long time.

Jack leaned forward earnestly. 'The Fool exists. We've heard him.'

'Heard him?' said Carlotta.

Jack nodded. 'Yes. He's spoken through this guy here,' (indicating the magician). 'It's a different voice. Isn't that so, Haze?'

This last demand was addressed to me. I looked into the magician's eyes. He was squinting, drawing on a cigarette. I wasn't sure what to say. He might have been a trickster, but I respected the man. He blinked at me slowly, as a cat might, to signify approval.

'Yes,' I said. 'Some nights we've done séances and he's come through.'

Both Carlotta and the actress laughed, but not together. Neither noticed they were the only two laughing. 'Seances!' exclaimed Carlotta. 'It's like being at school!'

Now these women were attacking one of our traditions. I'm not sure how many of us actually believed in the séances or the card tricks, but in a way they belonged to us and were part of our culture. We moved in the magical world of theatre, the world of illusion, lights and glamour, and the magician was part of it, a character, a fixture. He had become the shaman of our tribe.

'Don't mock,' Hugh said. 'You don't tangle with the Fool. Treat him with extreme caution.'

'Huh!' Mel said. 'And what is he exactly? Mr Punch?'

I noticed she and Carlotta actually exchanged a conspiratorial glance and grinned together. Wonders will never cease.

'I'm not afraid of anything,' Carlotta said.

'Mr Punch is one of his masks,' said the magician.

'Right, I'm really scared now!' cawed Mel. 'A big scary kid's puppet. Has he got your hand up his ass?'

Carlotta snorted loudly.

'I would say,' said the magician, fastidiously knocking ash from his cigarette, 'that the Fool's hand is firmly up mine!'

Again, whoops of laughter.

The magician was quiet, serious, but I couldn't believe he was offended. No, there was another reason for it. He was playing to the house.

'The Fool,' said the magician, 'is one of the oldest archetypes. His is the path between Chokmah and Kether, from the realm of ideas to the divine and vice versa. It is the raw energy of creativity, without rules, without boundaries.'

Mel shook her head. 'Well, that makes a lot of sense.'

'That is a remark the Fool would make,' said the magician, 'seeing as you mean exactly the opposite.'

There was a sting in his voice that hooked right into Mel. 'I just don't believe in this hocus pocus crap,' she said.

'You should,' said Jack.

'Make him come through then,' Carlotta said, clearly having been waiting for this perfect cue. 'Do it now.'

The magician smiled to himself. 'Oh, I don't think you would like that.'

'Prove it to us,' Carlotta said. 'Come on. Prove he exists.'

I didn't like it one little bit and I could tell not many of the others did either, but Jack was fired up with wanting to convert the sceptics into believers, especially two attractive women, who he no doubt believed were his for the taking. Well, they probably were. 'We could,' he said.

'I want you to,' said Carlotta, with one of her best artillery fire glances.

Perhaps Mel sensed Jack was drifting away from her, and became more acutely aware of Carlotta's exotic, heady charm, because she said, 'Yeah, let's. I want it to be proved. I want to believe!'

She laughed alone that time, even though she'd made an effort to make the laugh sound pretty rather than cruel.

'Well?' said Jack to the magician.

He sucked a long draw off his cigarette and took some time carefully stubbing it out. Then he frowned. 'Perhaps,' he said.

'A séance!' Carlotta exclaimed. 'Dim the lights!'

We shouldn't have done it, not with Carlotta and Mel there, for the simple reason we should have known that the Fool would relish the situation. People thought of jesters' hats, goggling eyes and stupid antics, but the Cosmic Joker was a far darker character than that. The greatest darkness being that he hid behind this pantomime façade. The magician had taught us tricks, but he had also spoken long into the night of the secrets of the universe. Not to all of us, but a select few:

Jack, Hugh and myself among them. In the strange hours before dawn, anything seems possible and anything can happen. We had seen things happen that, later, in the light of day had seemed ridiculous. With his quiet, whimsical voice, the magician had led us – willing apprentices – along the paths of magic. In the cold twilight before the sun rises, he had made us psychic. After many hours of fortune-telling play and guessing games with the dog-eared old bridge cards, when coincidence seemed to be aligning in our favour, the cards would be put aside and the magician's Tarot pack would come out. He'd unwrap it with reverence from a grey silk handkerchief. 'Chokmah's colour,' he'd tell us, 'silvery mist.'

Without the magician even touching the deck, we could pull any card we named from it. It had started as fun and ended up serious. We had gambled our lives and our happiness on it.

'This game exists,' we would say ponderously, our palms upon the cards, and then, 'If the Priestess comes to me, I'll get all that I want. I will cross the abyss of Da'ath to the source of creation. I will become my own god. If she turns her face away from me, I lose everything.'

And with that we made our pact with the universe. We meant it. Then, came that moment, when the hand is on the cards and anything is possible, even though the top card of the shuffled deck has already been chosen by random chance. It's already lying there, face down. Or is it? That is what the magician taught us to question.

'That is the secret of magic,' he told us. '*You* must become the randomiser.'

And how many times had I taken that card in my hand, sweating all over, only to turn it face up and see the one I had named, be it the Priestess, the Empress or the Devil, gazing back at me from the picture. I never believed I could do it. Never. And yet, when the magician fired us up and prepared us over a long night, we *could* do it. If we didn't win, we'd play again, until we did, until we'd promised our very souls to the Fool. Seances were an intrinsic part of the proceedings. We'd talk to the Fool time and again throughout the night. Dangerous games. Occult Russian roulette. But at least we knew the rules.

Hugh looked at me and I shrugged. We could have stopped it perhaps. The magician himself was in two minds, I could tell, perhaps because he already knew the outcome. But he was the avatar of the Fool, his greatest detractor and his most faithful servant. We had already invoked him. The circumstances and dynamics of the evening were his. The dice had been rolled, the cards dealt.

Someone went to dim the lights, while someone else got the candles stuck in old wine bottles. We kept a plank of Formica behind the bar that, years ago, someone had inscribed with the letters of the alphabet and the words 'yes' and 'no' – our ouija board. Not exactly decorative, but it did the job.

'Will the Fool speak through you?' Carlotta asked the magician as we arranged the table.

The magician glanced at Jack. 'Well, seeing as our young friend here is playing the court jester at present, I think it should be him.'

'Me?' said Jack.

No one but the magician had ever tried to channel the Fool before.

'Why not?' said the magician. He had some more tricks up his sleeve.

An upturned wine glass went onto the board, and in the flickering light, we all put a finger on it.

'Is there any presence here that wishes to communicate?' said the magician, his finger lightly on the glass. With his free hand, he lit another cigarette.

The glass began to move almost at once.

'Someone's pushing it!' cried Mel.

The magician ignored the remark and exhaled silvery smoke. 'Is there someone here who wishes to communicate?'

The glass sped towards the word 'yes' on the left of the board.

'No!' said Carlotta.

The magician withdrew his hand, folded his arms, hunched forward.

'Will you tell us your name?' he asked.

The glass sped crazily around the board, jabbing at random letters.

'Are you the Fool?' the magician asked.

The glass shot towards 'yes' again.

'Someone's definitely pushing it,' Mel said and removed her finger from the glass. 'This is stupid.'

The glass skidded towards the letter 'C', then 'V'. 'Me,' said Carlotta. 'It's talking to me. Those are my initials.'

The magician leaned back and delved into the pocket of his jacket. The Tarot cards came out, wrapped in their silk. We all took our fingers from the glass and watched the magician shuffle his cards. He then handed them to Carlotta. 'Shuffle and cut them,' he said.

Carlotta raised an eyebrow but did as he asked. She set the cards down on the table and cut them into two piles. 'Turn over the top card,' said the magician, 'the one from the middle of the deck.'

She did so. It was the Two of Swords.

'Demon of Chokmah,' said the magician. 'Turn over the other half of the deck.'

Carlotta did so and uttered a delighted squeak. The card revealed was the Fool.

'You did that,' said Mel to the magician. 'You fixed it.' She was so annoyed at no longer being the centre of attention, she was definitely not playing any more.

The magician shrugged. He didn't care.

'Put your fingers back,' Jack said. 'Come on. We're on to something.'

'No, wait,' Carlotta said. 'The Fool came to me, so I want to ask him something. I challenge him now to prove he exists.' She turned to the magician. 'Can he grant wishes?'

'Anything is within his power,' said the magician. 'That is the game. Gamble with him.'

'What if she loses?' Mel asked sourly.

The magician gestured elegantly. 'Then she can win back whatever she loses.'

'I don't intend to lose,' Carlotta said. 'There's no deal and this isn't a game. If he's so powerful, I don't have to gamble.' She put her finger on the glass. 'Fool, if you're real, then make me beautiful for ever. Grant me eternal beauty.'

'What a strange request,' drawled Mel, arms folded defensively. 'Worried about your looks, honey?' It was as if she wasn't there.

The glass began to move slowly around the board, again towards letters that made no sense. Then Jack said, in a strange high-pitched, Mr Punch voice, 'I'll make you as beautiful as I am!'

'Jack! Carlotta exclaimed. 'Cut it out!'

'Cut what out?' Jack said.

'That voice. Come on. We're supposed to be doing this for real.'

'I didn't say anything,' Jack said.

'Yeah, that's right.' Carlotta took her hand from the glass. She looked slightly unnerved. 'This is weird. I don't know why I'm doing it.'

'You just did,' said Jack.

No one wanted to continue that night. The working had been accomplished, although we didn't know it.

The following evening, the cast of the play planned a party after the show, in the apartment reserved for their use at the top of the theatre. I was feeling lousy, and in no mood for celebration, having drunk too much the night before, but Carlotta was determined to go. 'Oh come on,' she said to me in the afternoon as we began work. 'Come with me. We can share a cab home afterwards.'

'You go,' I said. 'I'm not in the mood.'

'Well, see how you feel later,' Carlotta said, disgruntled.

I realised she wanted support because Mel would be there.

Before the audience moved over from the hotel gardens along the river, Carlotta took some refreshments to the actors backstage. She was gone for ages, and I was starting to get annoyed by the time she bounced – or rather floated – back into the bar. 'For God's sake,' I said. 'Where have you been? There's going to be a riot in here soon.'

She took hold of my hands and waltzed me round the limited space behind the bar. 'Guess what? Guess what?' she sang.

'Something to do with Jack,' I said, dead pan.

'He said something really – *intriguing*,' Mel said.

I sighed. 'I bet.'

'He said, "there's something on the cards for you tonight, my lady".'

'How eminently flattering.'

'It was. He was all in costume and did the Fool voice and everything.'

'A game, that's all.'

'You weren't there. You didn't see his eyes.'

I could imagine them vividly. 'He's a flirt, Carly. You must know that.'

'So am I,' she said.

The night, as I'd predicted, was busy. It was even hotter than the previous evening if that was possible, and all I could think of was the balcony of my apartment and the bottle of Chardonnay chilling in the fridge. I yearned for it. I yearned for solitude and no babbling voices, my favourite CDs and communion with the stars above the city. Carlotta tried in many different ways to persuade me to go to the actors' party: threats, wheedling, flattery, you name it. I realised she was actually nervous of going alone, mainly because few of the bar staff, or theatre crew she knew fairly well, were going.

Could it be possible that brazen Carlotta had a shy streak? I felt really mean saying 'no', but I just wasn't up to it. Sometimes, I enjoy the company of actors, with their fervid, peacock insecurities, but I knew that tonight they would have the same effect on my equilibrium as fingernails down a blackboard. 'Just go,' I said. 'They'll all be drunk. You can talk to anyone.'

'Fuck you!' Carlotta hissed. 'Just fuck you, Hazel.'

'Don't fall out with me over this,' I said. 'I'm not here just to accommodate you.'

'I thought we were friends.'

Were we? I realised I didn't really look upon Carlotta as a friend. She was a work acquaintance. None of my friends were going to the party, not even the magician, who was visiting friends out of town. Jack didn't count, because I knew what he was like when he was on the prowl with women.

'Look,' I said. 'If it's Jack you're after, he'll be in the thick of things tonight. You might not get near him. If it's so important, I'll call him and we'll go out for lunch or dinner tomorrow. Just the three of us. OK?'

'He likes you well enough to do that?' Her tone was slightly acid.

I sighed. 'We're friends, Carly, old time friends. Yes, he'll do lunch if I ask him.'

That mollified her. 'I'll share your cab home, then,' she said. 'Do you think you should ask him before we leave in case – like – he makes alternative arrangements?'

'Sundays, to Jack, are sacred,' I said. 'Trust me. I'll call him late tomorrow morning.'

The fact I had to ask for her phone number shows just how big friends Carlotta and I really were.

We didn't finish clearing up until nearly midnight and the last drinkers were forcibly ejected from the premises. I locked up because it was Hugh's night off. The cab was purring outside as Carlotta and I went down the steps to the street. Behind us the theatre was in darkness, but for the yellow lights on the high top floor. We could hear their music, their laughter. Now, I felt even more mean. Should we just go up for a while? Perhaps I could introduce her to some folk, then leave.

But Carlotta took my arm and opened the cab door. She didn't seem to care now, so I said nothing.

It was quite a ride out to where I lived, and some distance on from that for Carlotta. We talked in the cab about Jack, and I felt mellow enough to offer Carlotta a few crumbs from the table. He was probably quite lonely, really. Probably needed a woman he respected.

We were near to my street, when Carlotta started to get restless. 'I think I'll go back,' she said.

'What? But we're almost home.'

'I know, but I keep thinking about it, and Jack might think I'm not bothered if I don't turn up.'

Too many crumbs, clearly. I should have kept my mouth shut. 'Carly...'

'No, it's OK, really. I have to do this. I have to do it alone. A test, maybe.'

The cab came to a halt by my door. 'Well, if you're sure.'

'Absolutely. Still call me tomorrow though.' She laughed. 'If I'm at home, of course.'

It was only once the cab had driven away that I realised I hadn't given her the code to open the fire exit door or the actors' apartment phone number. There's no way they'd hear her at the front of the building. Oh well. Too late now. If her liaison with Jack was meant to be, she'd find a way in.

I waited until nearly mid-day to call Jack, but he sounded fairly spritely when he answered the phone. Perhaps a good sign. 'How was last night?' I asked, injecting a slightly lascivious tone into my voice.

He yawned down the line. 'Actually, quite dull,' he said. 'I went home at two.'

'Oh dear,' I said. 'What about your fan club?'

'Meaning?'

'Carlotta and Mel. Any cat fights?'

'Mel was busy networking with more incandescent guys than me, and Carlotta wasn't there,' he said.

'Oh damn, my fault! She went back to the party after we left the theatre, but I forgot to give her the door code.'

'Now that's a shame.'

'Yeah. Sorry. Look, I'll call her and perhaps we can all go out for lunch.'

'OK. Give me an hour and I'll pick you up.'

He sounded really keen, I thought.

I rang and rang, but there was no answer from Carlotta's phone. The stupid creature obviously hadn't turned on her answerphone either. If she missed this, she'd kick herself. Perhaps she was a heavy sleeper. Fortunately, I knew where she lived, because it was in one of the apartment blocks that a lot of the theatre staff lived in. It was recommended to new employees who came from out of town. When Jack arrived, I suggested we went there and tried to wake her up. He only crossed one red light on the way there, which was good, considering his clear enthusiasm to reach our destination.

But Carlotta was not at home. Her apartment intercom at the main door was clearly marked with her name, but we could get no response. I eventually roused someone else I knew in the building and got them to knock on her door. 'She's not in,' they said. 'Go away. I was sleeping.'

'Now I'm worried,' I said. 'Where the hell did she go last night?'

'I should have arranged something with her,' Jack said. 'I did think about it, but didn't get the chance.'

'Then what was that flirty remark all about?'

He frowned. 'What?'

I told him what Carlotta had said.

'I didn't say that,' he said. 'I'm sure I didn't.'

'In costume,' I said. 'The Fool.' We stared at each other for a moment, and were in complete and utter empathy. We had shared strange evenings with the magician. We had a link. We knew.

'Fuck,' I said.

'Come on.' Jack took my arm and dragged me back to his car.

He drove like a maniac to the theatre. I don't know what we thought we'd find, or why we even went there, but we did. The back of theatre faced a small yard, and was approached by a couple of alleys. We parked the car out front, and I half expected to see a forlorn Carlotta curled up before the theatre doors. No chance.

We went round the back. Nothing.

'Why are we here?' I asked.

Jack went over to a pile of rubbish sacks. I watched him paw through them, feeling sick to my stomach. He went to the fire escape, looked up, towards the door on the top floor. No one was there. 'Perhaps she's inside,' I said. 'We should look. You might not have noticed her.'

'I would,' he said. He turned away from the steps and stared at the ground.

'Haze,' he said.

I went over. 'What is it?'

'Blood,' he said, pointing at the ground. 'I think it is. What do you think?'

'It looks like blood,' I said, swallowing hard. 'Someone could have had a fight.'

Jack hunkered down and picked something up, then another: small things, white like pearls. I watched him turn his head to the side jerkily, press the back of one hand against his mouth.

'What is it?' I asked. 'Bone?'

'No,' he answered. 'Teeth.'

I looked up the alley ahead of us, and could see, in the shadows, the vague trail of blood that led to it. I felt faint but I walked towards it. It was me who found her. I recognised her by her clothes. She must have crawled there, seeking help. At the time, I thanked God she wasn't dead. But that was more for me than for her.

The official report said that Carlotta Visconti, aged twenty-two, had fallen from the fire escape of the theatre and smashed her face on the ground below. She had escaped life threatening injury through sheer luck, although would require extensive reconstructive surgery on her face. It was assumed the effects of alcohol had caused her to fall while banging on the top floor apartment door. What the report didn't account for was the fact that the railings around the fire escape platform were intact and Carlotta wasn't drunk. But Carlotta herself, when she was able to give a statement, said that was what had happened.

I steeled myself to go and visit her in hospital, long before Jack did. I hadn't realised he was so squeamish. As I saw her lying there in the bed, unrecognisable but for her hair, one thought looped through my mind: you got your wish. You got your wish. Nose bashed in, cheekbones shattered, jaw ruined, a hideous caricature like Mr Punch. I will make you as beautiful as I am. The worst thing was she realised it herself.

That first time I visited, she took my hand and tried to weep, which was difficult because it hurt her so much. She wanted to thank me for coming, for facing her, I know, and I just squeezed her hand and said, 'hey, no problem. That's what friends are for.' It broke my heart to see the way that dreadful cliché comforted her.

Perhaps the best that can be said is that the whole experience made her a better person, because whenever I visited her, I sensed a deeper, more contemplative being within the skin. But who wants to get better that way, when your beauty was so important to you and no matter what the surgeons did, or how well they did it, some precious essence was lost forever? Lesson one: do not challenge the Fool. Lesson two: magic takes the path of least resistance.

Jack and I had dinner with the magician a couple of weeks after it happened. I said to him, 'You knew, didn't you?'

'Not exactly,' the magician answered. 'What kind of monster would that make me? They invoked it. I had no control over it. She was warned.'

'Not enough,' I said. 'Not nearly enough. By any of us.'

'She didn't say, "this game exists"', Jack said. 'If you don't say that, then you're not really playing. What happened could just be coincidence.'

'You don't believe that,' I said.

Carlotta herself was strangely sanguine about the whole affair. I'd expected suicidal grief, bitterness, anger or resentment, but it just wasn't there. I admired her strength, her ability to have faith that all would be well. But then, there was yesterday.

I visited her in the evening and she brought the subject of the séance up for the first time. 'It's real, Haze, isn't it,' said. 'People have no idea.' The only tone in her voice was a kind of wonder.

I took Jack's stance. 'We have no proof of that. Life just is. Believing in all that stuff is fine for late at night, but we can't live by it, Carly. It would all get too insane. You had an accident, that's all.'

'It's real, Hazel,' Carlotta said. 'It's me who was the Fool.'

'Just clumsy,' I said with a hopeful smile.

'No.' She was emphatic. 'I didn't play properly. I mocked. I tried to trick him.'

'You shouldn't think like that...'

She fixed me with a stare. 'Bring him here, Haze.'

'Bring who? Jack?'

She shook her head. 'No, the magician. I want to see him.'

I cocked my head to one side. 'Er... why?'

Her smile, in her ruined face, was scary. 'Because I have

to play him at his own game,' she said. 'I have to win it all back.'

The Fool's path. Once trodden, it is difficult to find the way back. Riches pour from the trickster's sleeves and not all of them are fairy gold. I'm standing at my own cross-roads. To join her game or not. In Carlotta's place, would I risk the same? This game exists.

The Time She Became

We were sitting on the kerb edge of Celestial Alley just watching the night go by, when the girl out of time walked past, looking for a moment to keep.

'Well, lookit that!' Sax declared, thinking twice about handing me back the smoking-globe in the excitement of the moment. All I saw was a twitch of something not-quite-real swiftly skimming between the carcass-poles of the meat-traders, a buzzing brightness, whiter than the vine-bulbs. People stepped back and looked, traders and browsers alike, then leaned in to talk together about it. We'd all seen things like that before, but such events were hardly regular. The no-time people came to taste our hard world and swim in the tides of consecutive events. It was rumoured this was a danger sport in their reality, that they risked being trapped in the relentless time-stream, where they become solid and then grow old and die. We could not communicate too well with the visitors, but I had an envious admiration for their courage.

Sax got to his feet, shaking the alley dust from his hard toenails and twisting the smoke-globe until it shrank and fell in upon itself. I did not mind. Nearly all the smoke had gone anyway, but I still made a disgruntled noise out of habit. 'Tick tick,' said Sax, 'don't be wearing me thin, Zeeb, my stripling. Wet your tongue on the smoke of time, no less.' He had a habit of slipping into market-pole slang whenever he was smoke-steeped enough to get his tongue round it. I shrugged.

'If you mean, follow the bright thing, it's been done,' I said, 'and no-one has ever been any the wiser for it.' Trying to get close to one of those people was like trying to remember a fading dream. Always just out of reach, just a hint, just a fragment of memory. Sax would not be deterred.

'But we are on Celestial Alley, my loveling, bathing in the pretty moon,' he argued, 'and this is a night for timeless things. Come on.' We had nothing better to do and I'd been about to suggest we went for a walk to explore the alleys anyway, seeing how they always tended to twist into new patterns at such a rare moontime, so I stood up and went after him, into the caper of markets and yodelling street-rogues. He didn't even wait to take my hand.

It wasn't hard to follow her trail. There was a luminous, confused mist hanging around wondering what it should do with itself; fall to the ground or vanish gracefully. Passing through it put my teeth on edge. Already some of the more enterprising hawkers were catching it in bottles, which tomorrow would be on sale as 'measures of timeless vapour for those who seek euphoria'. I'm not sure whether what was experienced in the sizzling nothingness of that stuff could ever be termed euphoria - friends have told me about the stretch-writhe effect - but people like to buy expensive nonsense and the mist does sparkle so. I expect there are hundreds of bottles of it in hundreds of homes throughout Jubilee Garter town, just sitting on shelves as amusing ornaments, never to be opened or sniffed.

Sax skipped along the mist, squawking and high-stepping enough to make me embarrassed. I walked alongside, avoiding the glances of subtle whores and trying to look as if I had a destination. Spiky, black buildings, barnacled with balconies and walkways, towered into the night around us, silent and unlit above the melee of the market, the sky huge and majestic above them, the court of the pregnant moon. I wondered about those timeless people and whether they had a sky like ours where they came from. Did they have such things as skies at all? No-one had ever been able to find out.

We followed the trail right out to the edge of town where everything declines into a tumbled wasteland of broken walls and discarded lives, the rubbish our advancing community drags behind it as it crawls across the land. Jubilee Garter is a voracious beast. In the last fifty moon-cycles the used and useless ground had increased beyond all proportion. Sax once joked about what would we do when we'd crawled all over the face of the world and ended up right where we started. I pointed out that must have happened a dozen times in our history. The world repaired itself eventually, but he rightly added that progress had speeded up in our lifetime. We might live to see the day Jubilee Garter met itself coming back. Would we then have to re-think our existence and pop away into the no-time place where the visitors came from? I hoped not. I liked the day and night of our reality.

There she was; a fizzing flame of uncertainty, wearing a familiar form that didn't look at all natural or comfortable, pacing carefully like a drunkard over the big stones of the Great Dead. What did she want here? Why had she come? Sax and I stood right on the edge of the town-life. If I moved my toes forward, I could feel the cold, the utter stasis of the Dead. It was not a shunned place however. Many people came here to pick over the past, looking for treasures that might have been left behind. Our shunned places were locked in the heart of the Jubilee Garter and they were the centre of things always.

'Hallooo!' Sax cried, waving his arms at the girl. He is such a fool. Most times, those people don't even seem to see us. I don't think he was expecting a response. It was simply a gesture to show me what a strong- blood he was, undaunted as the shadows, and worthy of my attention. Little did he know these were attributes I often doubted. Both of us sucked in our breath and made the Safe Sigh when the girl jerked like she'd been surprised and turned what could only be a face in our direction. She was like a picture on a scry-screen which wasn't tuned in too well. Something solid at the centre, yes, but wavery on the edges. Like all of her kind, she was wearing clothes that looked as if they were only holograms projected to cover the essential She. I don't know why I thought it was a girl. There is no way of knowing really if they have that kind of distinction. Perhaps because they are more 'Essence' than anything, they appear only as an assumption of elemental polarity; the she-ness of female, the he-ness of male. This may be something they can choose at whim. Do such creatures have whims? Sax clutched at my arm, panting with stimulating fear. 'Does she see us?'

Yes, she saw us. I have no doubt of that. I was looking through water it seemed, deep water, and she was struggling through it towards us, slipping to grasp at stone and splintered wood. Both Sax and I were stepping back. This was unforeseen.

'Maybe she's not one of them,' Sax whispered urgently. 'A trick. A game. Maybe.'

Maybe. She was close enough for me to see her smoky-white face, the dark bruise of eyes. We were not the followers now. I knew that. She had seen us and fixed on us and could not, would not break away. A fix. A point. A moment in time.

'What do you want?' I said because I truly did not want her, this thing, getting too close. The smoke-globe and Celestial Alley might never have happened now. This gave me a nano-glance of the concept of time itself but it was too brief to be grasped at. The sting of a strange,sharp aroma made me blink. I saw her mouth working. It was black inside. It seemed she knew how to talk but had perhaps never actually done it.

'Here,' she said, as if invoking all the gods of everwhen and everhow, the greatest word of power. She raised her arms, leaving a scintillating stream of after-images behind them, saying, 'Now.'

How I fought with the urge to run, run, run, back into the living night of Jubilee Garter, even though I knew one of the most important things in my life must be happening. I'm sure it was the same for Sax. I was thinking about how I would have to be changed forever after this meeting and the world would be a different place. It was hard to discern between excitement and instinctual terror at such a moment.

'Here? Now?' croaked Sax. Such simple harmless words. The girl from no-time had invested them with a power we'd never encountered before.

'Is!' she insisted and then made a wallowing, helpless gesture, lurching, stumbling backwards over the stones, as if we hadn't understood her. Of course, we hadn't - how could we? - and it must have been so important that we should. I was filled with a sharp sense of sympathy, of grief. In an instant I was seeing Profound Lostness - a religious experience rarely encountered outside of a moon-rite. She had given me that. I blundered forward.

'What is it? How can we help you?' She looked confused, failing, ephemeral, yet it was apparent, in hindsight, that she was becoming more real with every instant. She ignored me, peering close at the ground, this way and that, a maddening swirl of images and light vapour.

'Let's go!' Sax urged, pulling at my arm. Such a sentiment appalled me.

'There's something wrong,' I said. 'Can't you see that?'

'Nothing of ours to care to fret,' Sax replied in an unconvincing surly voice. He had wanted her to remain a ghost, a vision on the edge of vision, tantalising and mysterious, a moon-time transient pleasure. His phantom girl had become an animal, real and grubbing at the ground. I could see she was kneeling there now. I could see the flesh of her thighs through torn, thin fabric; dirty skin. She was crying, real enough. Light, wispy hair falling over her face like feather-down, the trembling, sharp shoulders of a bird. She kept patting the rocks around her, and then touching her face, smudging it with the grey, ash-like dust of the Great Dead. I pulled away from Sax and clambered through the ruins, just a little way, till I was standing right over her. No vapour out of time now. She was just an earthly creature 'Who are you?' I asked, simply because I'd always wanted to know. 'Where have you really come from?' It is only assumed the ghostly visitors come from no-time. We do not know for sure, only that they have always been passing through our world, creating legends. Some, who have the knowledge, glean information from deep-thought and say they have proof the visitors are exactly what the stories say they are. Perhaps they are right. It is more exciting to think so. Looking down on that girl, I was beginning to wonder whether her origins were not rather more mundane. Perhaps she was a snooper from a town travelling crossways to our own, spinning a vapour disguise about herself to see the ways of our lives. Perhaps it was all a lie and she came from a Shunned Place, existing only to deceive our senses. At that time, I did not consider she might be a victim of her own adventure, trapped in the time-stream she had wantonly dared to sample. I reached out to touch to her shoulder and said, 'Well, will you answer me or not?'

'I will,' she said, setting her strange, bony face in an expression of courage, and at first I thought she meant to answer me, but it was a different kind of will she spoke of. 'I. Will,' she said again, an began to struggle to her feet, groping out to touch me for support. Her costume had fallen apart; she'd grown so quick she'd burst it. The nipples of her small breasts were tensed with cold but it did not seem to concern her; neither the temperature or the revelation of her body secrets. This person could only be human; female. She had become solid; a creature of space and time.

I think the trouble was we had too much time; it was haphazard, all over the place, in and out, fast and slow, sometimes looping just for fun - and, where she came from, they had none at all. Be too fast, too much and you get kind of used to it, part of it. It was a Wondering Moon we were in then, rare and beautiful, a lust-time of sensual pleasures; smoke- globe and skin-in-the-dust. It was a bad time for her to come. I led her to the crust of the town-life and could tell every step was pain and hurting to her. 'Cannot will,' she said miserably as our feet touched the warmth and she looked back over her shoulder at the Great Dead, a smokeless vista of worn-out living. In the distance everything turned into mountains, but it was a long way away and even in daylight no greening of vegetation could be seen in that direction. Jubilee Garter devours life in its forward creep, leaving very little behind, but it is only a temporary death.

We took her back to the room over Helot's Inn, where Sax and I lived our two-life, though Sax was grudging about having her there. I was thinking what a treasure she was, even soiled and torn. Much more of a treasure than a flask of sparkling vapour, though she no more sparkled than the dust of the Dead. I fed her soup, which she ate without sickness, though with little pleasure. Then I peeled off the rest of her ruined body-sheath, sponging down her skin with milk-water and a song. She touched her tired eyes, dragging her thin, white fingers over her face and asked, 'What?' in a bewildered voice, her eyes telling me she hadn't the words to explain what she really wanted to know. I told her she needed to sleep and lit a green lamp to help her. Sax had gone out onto the street again, waspish and ready to sting. I did not go after him because I feared my find would disappear if I turned my eyes away from her.

'You are my little ghost,' I told her as she began to drowse.

'I am,' she murmured dismally in reply.

Nobody believed she was a no-time girl. Why should they? They thought I'd found a burned-out whore and brought her home to fuss over.

Sax's friends from the ore-shop where he worked came to stare and smile uncomfortably, hoping for a pretty distraction, finding something weirdly crippled that made them feel awkward. She did not look at them much. Me, I paid no heed to their words and brought her presents from the markets; beads to wear and scarves for skirts. She accepted these wistfully and filled my breast with love as she tried inexpertly to fix herself as decently dressed. I tried to tell her about myself, that I was a stone scryer. When I threw the stones for her, they fell in all the wrong places on my painted cloth, telling me nothing. I had not expected more really.

Gram'ma Pangelo, the big woman from the Inn below, to whom we paid our gratitude for shelter, stopped me in the passage one day and said with a hand on my arm, 'That girl's got a sickness, Zeeb. She ain't a rightness that's for surely.'

'She's confused,' I answered patiently. 'She doesn't really feel comfortable in this world.'

'Poffle!' Pangelo spat, stamping in emphasis. 'World or no world, she's seen or been something that's knocked her head two spits left of her shoulders!' The Gram'ma didn't like my no-time girl being in the building, I could tell, but didn't go further than hints or gestures to make that known. The next day I saw her solemnly draping the barrels in the bar with benign ale-berry. Courting risk, I offered to help, but Pangelo only looked carefully at my hands before shaking her head.

Jubilee Garter was moving so fast at that time, we could hear the inn groaning in distress at night. I'm sure Sax suspected our visitor was somehow to blame, and perhaps she was, though I wouldn't admit it even to myself. Twice Pangelo came panting up our dull, narrow stairs, asking us to help her straighten the wall struts at ground level. She said she feared we'd have to abandon the building and find a new one to make into Helot's Inn. No wonder she was upset. Everyone knew Pangelo had grown fond of the angles and crannies of the existing Inn. I sympathised. It was a good place, and one which I felt sure had enough character to creep soundly forward for a long time to come. Some buildings were so weak and vapid they simply sighed into dust without anyone really noticing they'd gone. Helot's Inn wasn't like that, too full of life and merriment every evening to fade without struggle. Pangelo wasn't comforted by my reassurances. She merely looked wordlessly at the ground where backbones of earth flexed and wriggled, testament to her insecurity.

Even through such times of domestic panic, my visitor didn't take to speaking much, though one day she shouted, 'You are!' at Sax, which I guessed was some kind of insult in her reality. Sax kept teetering between interest in the girl and outright hostility. I suppose it was unfair I'd brought her to our nest, our one-place, where we were he and me and no-one else, but it was beyond me to turn her out. She was so lost, so helpless and when I reminded Sax of this, he had to shrug and agree, though I suspect he harboured desires to steal her away and propel her into a Shunned Place so we'd be rid of her. He was wary of making the heart-signs in her presence, but even when we touched she didn't appear to notice. Flesh to flesh, it had no more impact on her than if Sax and I were just eating from the same plate. I can't say she was beautiful because she wasn't really like anything or anyone we set such standard by, but I enjoyed looking at her because she saw the world as perpetually new, unnamed and had no way to name it. I tried to teach her about how to live in our reality but she was revolted by it. I think the crudest, most animal, of human bodily functions were less sickening for her than making things real by defining them. What a horror our world was to her, huge and overpowering and rushing. She could not stand up for long without becoming dizzy and sometimes it overwhelmed her so much she cried out in pain and terror. I wanted so much to know her as a person but it was impossible. All I could do was hold her hands when she felt worse than usual and sing to her. I think she liked that, although even singing involves time because you have to begin and end it somewhere.

One day Sax said, 'Do you think she's dying?' which was more of a hope than a question. It would have been better for her if the answer had been yes, I'm sure, but I knew it wasn't. Her body had become human; she ate and slept and woke up again like anybody else, but the soul in her mind was in an alien place. She had the physical ability to adapt, I think, but not the acquired knowledge to do so. I lived in a cycle of time.

I knew about changes, about how nothing remains the same and that things always have to begin and end. Even Helot's Inn would have to disappear eventually, no matter how strong it was now.

For a full turn of the moon, she stayed as a guest in our room, silent and undemanding. Daytime, I led her to my booth, a light, manoeuvrable construct I'd set up in a market alley close to the Inn. It was no bother to shuffle it about if necessary and I enjoyed rearranging things inside afterwards. My no-time girl would sit, shrinking against the canopy while I threw bright, polished stones for profit. I'd collected a sackful of glittering chips, rockeyes, bloodmarbles, moonstar- mirror-straws and a host of others from the most scarred places of the Great Dead, all exciting to touch and full of the past. Often, I pressed a bagful of them into my visitor's hands, making her feel their hard, smooth or spiky heaviness. There was this dream in my head that one day, she'd lean forward to the table, cast the stones and pronounce some Marvel Scry. It would have seemed natural. Everyone would be surprised and respect her for the power she possessed. This never happened of course. She just sat there, blank-eyed as a moony-blind, her fingers lax and open, unimpelled to curl around the stones. People wondered why I didn't take her somewhere she could be cared for, out of my sight, estranged from my income and privacy. I never even tried to explain how I was waiting, just waiting, for a glimmer of light in her eyes telling me she had woken up in my world and was ready to live in it. I never stopped hoping.

One day, I took her to the prowling, forward edge of Jubilee Garter town, where the fingers of civilisation creep into the lush meadows of the future and people harvest the retreating fields. I jabbered on, as I always did, not telling her things exactly because I'd learned that was a fruitless exercise, but just making pictures with words to help ease her progress. She smiled at me sometimes and hung onto my arm like any ordinary girl. It lifted my heart. I thought we were friends at last and that she could understand me. When we reached the meadows, rolling strong and powerful to meet the far sky, she stopped abruptly, swayed, and gasped. Never had I seen her react so definitely 'Like?' I asked. It was a question she'd quickly come to understand. Now she made a sweeping, urgent gesture with her arm. 'There!' she exclaimed proudly. I realised she'd grasped some concept or another. I shook my head and grinned. She was so lovely in her innocence. She bent down and pressed her hands against the first stone of the town and then the shrinking grass beyond it. She nodded to herself vigorously like a child at play, lost in some make-believe world. She stood up and touched my face lightly with her fingers.

'Zeeb,' she said tenderly, naming me utterly. I felt faint at the compliment. And then she was running, running out into the hazy meadow, past the gatherers who lifted their heads from their work as she scampered by. I called out and began to hurry after, but she was fast, so fast, a blur in time. I had no name to call. I'd never done that to her, stripped her of the last of her being and chained her to the earth; given her a word to be. So all I could do was shout,

'Here! Here!' She did not look back, just ran and ran into the future, speeding like a comet, faster and faster until she was all fire and steam. Soon I was running into a trail of sparkling vapour, knowing before she even blinked out of existence, that I had lost her from my time, my space, my heart. Forever.

How could I grieve for long? How could I grieve for something, someone, who was essentially nothing in the nowness I occupied. Sax was sympathetic, stroking my skin with a satisfied grin on his face, full of a relief of which he was thankfully too polite to speak. Now she had gone, I could name her. She became Ephemeralia, a wraith chained briefly by the heaviness of time. Sax laughed indulgently at this and eventually recovered enough to speak fondly of her memory, but he never followed such a visitor again. Now I stand at the future of the world, looking forward, and wonder, if we keep on moving faster, if we'll eventually stop moving forever and come to be in the world where there is no time at all.

Where the Vampires Live

Zenna knew where the vampires gathered after sundown. She could climb out of the attic window, jump onto a limb of the ironwood tree outside and be free of the house, unheard and unseen, in minutes. She would run like a white hind between the dappled shadows of night, perhaps shape-shifting as she ran; hind to girl to hind. Her feet seemed barely to touch the ground. Her hair would be full of moths, drawn to it as if to a white flame.

Ariel would watch secretly from her own window, further down the house, full of envy, wistfulness and other aches she could not identify.

Ariel was Zenna's cousin, and she had come to live in the Green House in the spring, right at the edge of the forest, far from town. Ariel's father had died many years before and recently her mother had suffered some kind of disgrace that had affected her ability to be a mother – apparently. Ariel did not know what had happened; all she knew was that her mother had seemed to become someone else, a stranger in familiar skin. This troubled her so much she couldn't bear to think about it, so it came as rather a relief when her uncle and aunt had offered to take her in for a while.

It quickly became clear to Ariel, who was well-mannered and prudent, that she was the kind of daughter that Maeve and Darn would have liked to have had. They tried very hard not to show it, but Ariel was aware of the irrepressible leaps in their spirit when she asked for things politely, or did chores without being asked. Zenna was a wild creature; wilful, often bad-tempered, but seductively fascinating. When she turned on her light, none could fail to be blinded by it, hypnotised into adoration. Getting her own way was a trait inbuilt into her being. She had magic in her that made it happen. No one could dislike her, because it is impossible to dislike a beautiful wild thing, a rare spirit of nature, just because it is naturally wild. But sometimes, watching her cousin, Ariel could not help but remember something her maternal grandmother had once said. 'Some people are cursed in life, darlin'. Watch out for them. When a soul touches you on the inside, so that the whole world goes black but for them, take care. For they can take you to a doom.'

There had been more to this conversation, one of many lectures Granny gave on the potential horrors of life, but Ariel had forgotten the rest now. All she could think about, remembering those words, was what it would be like to be black on the inside, as if a hooked finger had poked through your skin and bone and had touched your heart, leaving a dark spot that grew and grew.

'Do you believe in vampires?' Zenna asked Ariel that one summer afternoon, as the girls sat by the pond in the garden. The day was hot.. The air smelled green.

Ariel laughed politely. She always did that when she didn't have an answer.

'Well, do you?'

'I don't know... Do you?'

Now it was Zenna's turn to laugh, and this was a very different sound from Ariel's. 'Do you know,' she said, 'people always say "you can't be too careful". But the fact is: you can.' She jumped to her feet. 'Come on,' she said.

Come where? Down to the greenwood, where the shadows are brown and gold. Down to where the earth breathes so loudly you can hear it with human ears. Step through a barrier from here to there. It's where otherness comes alive.

Zenna took Ariel to a place deep in the forest. They passed a tumbledown wooden shack covered in ivy. Zenna said the body of the woman who had lived there was still lying on the floor behind the door. No one knew that she had died. She had become mostly ivy. Ariel shuddered and ran on. When she held Zenna's hand it was as if her feet too barely touched the ground. If they ran fast enough the world became a blur and it was possible to see another world beyond this one - . always there, but you can't see it normally.

Zenna's destination was a dragonbark grove. The trees there were ancient; they were tall yet they stooped beneath the weight of their own age. Five of these trees were still alive; three dead, lying on the ground and riddled with insect nests. Zenna sat down on the spongy wood of one of the dead trees. There was a dampness to this grove, even though the sun was hot and high summer reigned in the greenwood. It was the breath of the earth, oozing out through mulch and mold. The canopies of the living trees were immense, the wings of dragons. Despite the absence of breeze, the leaves fluttered high overhead as if impulses from the roots shivered through them; impulses to fly.

Zenna swung her legs, leaning back on stiff arms.

'Are they here?' Ariel whispered. She wondered whether ithis was a game, and whether she was playing it right.

'At this time of day? Are you kidding?' Zenna sighed. 'I wonder if they sleep beneath the dead leaves, but of course you'd never find them, even if they did. They would just become part of the soil, or would look like soil anyway. They are not what you think.'

Ariel wasn't sure what she thought vampires to be. In her mind, all she saw was a flash of red eyes, some fangs glinting, a hiss of silk. 'What are they?' she dared to ask.

'Very much creatures of earth,' Zenna replied. 'They are not about death, nor come from death. They are the greatest example of life. They live on life itself.'

'Blood...'

'Well yes, everyone knows that.' Zenna stood up.

'Have you actually seen them?' Ariel asked.

Zenna glanced at her cousin over her shoulder. 'It is actually very difficult to see them. They are camouflaged. At night they must be clustered on the roofs of houses, standing beneath the trees in gardens, watching and waiting for a place of entry.'

'That's horrible.'

'Why?' Zenna pulled a scornful face. 'They don't kill people, you know. That's just made up, because people are scared of what they don't understand. But if you are bitten, you are never the same again.'

'You become like them?'

Zenna paused. 'No. You are never the same again because you don't become like them.'

'But have you seen them?' Ariel persisted.

Behind Zenna's silence, Ariel could hear the cracklings and rustlings of the forest. It was never silent. It seemed to be quiet but was full of noise. Things moved unseen.

At last Zenna said, 'You can only see them for yourself. This isn't something that can be told.'

Perhaps it was just a game, the wild fancy of a girl at the cusp of womanhood, seeking romance and danger in the breathing forest. If Zenna had come across a strange creature in this place, it might not be a vampire, but something else, far less mysterious and far more dangerous.

'I would like to see for myself,' Ariel said.

'Then wish for it,' Zenna said. She held out her arms and turned slowly in a circle, head thrown back. 'Wish for it with all your might. But you will never know when it might come true.' She was clearly in love: with the place, with an idea, with life itself.

Ariel did what she thought people were supposed to do when making a wish. She closed her eyes, very tight, and thought hard. I want to see the vampires. Even as she thought this, half of her was playing a girlish game, but the other half was standing at the brink of fear, holding out a tiny flickering candle into the dark. This half was actually a very old part of herself, who was wise enough to know even the most outlandish wishes can come true.

Two days later, Zenna shook her cousin awake in her bed, in the dead hours of the night. Ariel awoke from a dream of red flowers, something to do with a white dog, a star that could speak. She blinked at the pale vision of Zenna, whose eyes were wide and dark. 'What? What?' she hissed, suddenly afraid. Was the house on fire?

'I need you to come with me,' Zenna said.

'Why? Where?'

Zenna pursed her lips, screwed up her eyes and shook her head briefly. 'It's your wish,' was all she'd say. 'Please hurry.'

Ariel got out of bed and put on her clothes. Were there vampires on the roof now? If she listened carefully enough, would she hear them scratching at the slates? Part of her was lecturing the rest of her many parts with a quiet and patient voice. Don't go with her. Whatever she's found, whatever she wants to show you, it won't be what she thinks it is. A good girl now would say 'no'. Why are you putting on your shoes?

'Don't put on your shoes,' Zenna said. Perhaps she could read minds and could hear the measured voice of Ariel's inner good girl. But her reasons were different. 'We must go barefoot. It's quicker that way.'

At night, the forest dares to speak aloud. As Ariel ran with her cousin, she could hear the immense cracks and groans of the trees, as if they were flexing their stiff ancient spines, pulling painfully their twisted roots from the possessive soil. The breath of the forest was now loud in Ariel's ears. All manner of creatures might lurk in the darkness; humans were interlopers in this particular time and space. But when Ariel held Zenna's hand and ran so fast, she felt she became something other than human and that this would protect her. She would not let go of Zenna's hand, whatever happened.

The dragonbark grove felt as if something had just finished there; it had the air of a room where twenty people had just walked out of the door. All that is left is the smoke of their conversations, wisps that will eventually fade away. The bright moonlight made it possible to see almost as clearly as if the sun were in the sky.

'The vampires were here,' Ariel whispered. It was clear to her now that Zenna had wanted to share this experience and had come for her quickly. A pang of affection went through Ariel's heart. It felt like a long, white-hot pin.

'It's not just that,' Zenna said. She let go of Ariel's hand and immediately Ariel felt fear, not affection. The pin was cold in her heart; it made her breathless. Zenna was already walking away through the dappled moonlight; she was like a white hind again, lifting her feet delicately. Ariel blinked. She ran after her cousin.

Zenna had come to a halt before the greatest of the dragonbark trees; it must be their queen. 'Here,' she said. 'Look.' A pause, and then, with the slightest tremor of doubt: 'Can you see?'

Ariel came to stand beside her cousin, and Zenna took her hand again, lacing their fingers lightly. With her free hand, Zenna pointed gracefully at the foot of the queen tree.

For a time Ariel could see nothing. She realised she didn't believe, and that in itself was quite shocking to her. But then she could see: there was someone curled up among the knuckles of the roots. As she looked closer, she could see that this someone was trembling. They were half covered with leaves, perhaps their shadowy garments were actually made from leaves. Zenna dragged Ariel nearer, her fingers had closed tightly about Ariel's own.

'It's a boy,' Ariel said, half relieved, half disappointed.

Zenna glanced at her, said nothing. Again she let go of her cousin's hand and hunkered down. 'He's hurt,' she said. 'They left him behind.'

'He's a boy,' Ariel said, in a voice that sounded to her

like her aunt's. Maybe she was shattering magic, but if the boy really was hurt, fairy tales were no good for him.

You can't be too careful... you can...

Ariel went to the boy and touched him. He uttered a sigh and shuddered. He reminded her of a wounded dog, but it was too dark here to look for injuries. 'We should take him back,' she said.

'Into our house?' Zenna sounded afraid, and for once Ariel felt older and more confident and capable than her cousin.

'We can't just leave him here. He needs to be looked at... a doctor...'

'We shouldn't do that. They'll come back for him. It would be stealing...'

'Zenna!' Ariel sighed heavily. 'Stop it. I don't know what he's doing here, but this lad is very much flesh and blood like us. Help me get him to his feet.'

Ariel put her arms about the boy and tried to lift him. It surprised her how light he was, almost insubstantial. 'He's half starved,' she said.

With clear reluctance, Zenna came to help. He didn't resist them. He uttered soft whines, like a puppy. All the other sounds of the forest had faded away. For the briefest moment, Ariel thought how they might just have dragged this boy into the mundane world. Perhaps he didn't belong in it. But it was just a fleeting thought.

Maeve and Darn, and the doctor who came to inspect the boy, decided he must be a traveller lad, somehow separated from his people. He did have an injury, yes. He'd been shot in the thigh.

'No doubt caught stealing from some farm,' the doctor said as she put away her things.

Everyone was gathered in the small spare room at the top of the house; an attic full of light that remained golden-brown even when the sun shone right through the window.

The boy lay on a narrow bed. He was dark of skin and hair, slight of form, more like an elf than a boy. No wonder Ariel and Zenna had been able to carry him home as if he were no more than a handful of leaves.

'We'll call the police,' Darn said.

But Maeve said, 'No.' She was Zenna's mother after all, and perhaps the sight of this fey, dark creature affected parts of her that had been asleep for many years. 'There's no need for that. Not yet. Let him speak first.'

The doctor had cleaned the boy's wound and stitched him up. There was no bullet. It had gone right through him. No one spoke again of official things, such as hospitals and authorities. They lived right on the edge of the forest and things were different here.

The boy slept for two whole days, and Maeve stayed with him, sitting by the narrow bed reading a book, or else curled up on the mattress that Darn had carried to the attic room. Zenna was often there too, frowning at the boy on the bed. No one really spoke about things, not even Zenna, although Ariel guessed her cousin's head was full of unspoken thoughts. It was as if they were all waiting for something. The weather became hotter and all around the Green House was a narcotic humid atmosphere that slowed movement, that stilled voices.

Ariel found sleep difficult during that time. At night, she lay awake breathing quickly, listening to the soft pound of her heart, her ears straining for other sounds. In particular, her senses extended upwards, out through wood and slate, to the roof. I am too many people, she thought. She wasn't sure what was real; the sort of world where common sense held sway or the sort where you could run so fast you could flash into another world. She sensed nothing on the roof, and in some ways that worried her more than if she'd felt the opposite.

On the morning of the third day, the boy opened his dark

eyes and for some time lay staring at the ceiling. Maeve heard him sigh and put down her book. It was as if an invisible call shuddered through the Green House and everyone who lived there was drawn to the attic so that by the time Maeve murmured softly, 'Who are you?' Zenna, Ariel and Darn were in the room also.

The boy looked at Maeve and there was no expression in his eyes that Ariel could interpret. If anything, he just looked resigned.

'Water,' Maeve said and Darn brought a cup of it to the boy. They held his head so that he could drink, and he did so.

Zenna flicked a glance at her cousin, and Ariel was able interpret what it meant. Maybe we shouldn't be giving him that. But both girls remained silent. He was drinking. Perhaps he needed it after all.

'Can you remember anything?' Maeve asked the boy.

He shook his head very slightly, still looking at her.

Maeve smiled at her husband. At least the boy could understand them. 'You were hurt,' she said. 'Everything will be all right. Don't worry. We'll help you.'

'What's your name?' Darn asked.

The boy shook his head.

'Where are your people?' Darn continued, voice firm. 'We'll need to find them.'

Now the boy looked cornered, eyes wider, gaze flicking from the window to the door.

'Stop that,' Maeve said. 'He's only just woken up. Give him time, Darn.' She stroked the boy's hair, hushed him as you would a baby. 'It's all right. Nothing to fear. I'll bring you some soup.' She stood up. 'Help me, Zenna.'

The family left the room, leaving only Ariel behind. No one had noticed she'd stayed back or that she hadn't been given her a job to do. She wanted to tell the boy she was only a visitor too, but what was the point of speaking? She could sense it displeased him. So she sat down on the chair where Maeve had sat for the past few days and began to hum a tune. She closed her eyes and made the tune green and cool, like the forest depths.

She heard a soft sound, like water running over stones. It was the boy's laugh. 'We can speak,' he said, hardly more than whisper, 'but only when it's needed. And we rarely answer questions.'

Ariel opened her eyes and stared at him. 'This is a question you must answer,' she said. 'Will your people come for you?'

'I'm not lost,' he replied. He would not speak again that day.

Everyone knows that if you bring a changeling child into your home, or some creature of the otherworld, the otherness rubs off. It drifts like pollen through the still, summer rooms, and what were once just shadows take on feet and walk.

It was inevitable that Zenna was most affected by what had happened. Ariel felt she was destined only to be a witness to whatever transpired, nor would she affect the inevitable outcome in any way. She told herself firmly not to lie awake listening for sounds on the roof, because there wouldn't be any. She must not be infected by Zenna's feyness. The boy himself was like the summer light of the forest, sometimes green-gold sunlight, sometimes almost invisible in shadow. They named him Jack, because he would not tell them any other name. Most of the time it was easy to believe he was just a boy, separated from his family, but then his wound healed so quickly. After only a couple more days he was back on his feet. He did the chores that Maeve asked him to do without hesitation. He whistled to the geese that strutted around the pond, and they came to him, wings held out like arms. Maeve watched him from the kitchen window, smiling.

Jack was quiet, inhumanly so, but no trouble. He kept himself busy, and did not interact with the girls particularly, other than to nod his head in greeting should he come across them. Zenna could not keep her eyes off him. She speculated about him continually; it was naturally the topic that consumed her, and Ariel mostly played along because Jack interested her also. She just didn't want to think he was anything but a stray, albeit an intriguing one.

Every afternoon, they would sit by the pond and Zenna would talk about Jack. 'He walks in daylight, he eats the food we eat,' she said one day, clearly perplexed. 'I had thought they would be white as ghosts, like moon people, but he is dark like the trees.'

'Maybe that's because he isn't a vampire,' Ariel had to say.

Zenna tossed her an annoyed glance. 'I don't know why I bother telling you things. You just strip the magic out of everything, so the world will never be like that for you. How can you possibly think he's just a normal boy? Look at him.'

Jack was stacking logs he had just chopped in the shadow of a shed attached to the house. Ariel could see nothing abnormal in his behaviour or movements. 'He's a gypsy boy,' she said.

'But what does he want with us?' Zenna continued, ignoring that response. 'He's not spoken of his people or even questioned what he's doing here. He simply is, part of our lives now, living here amongst us. I wonder if we're foolish.'

'He's fed well, he's got new clothes, and probably has a better life,' Ariel said. 'If he was thieving when he got shot, he's not going to tell us about that, is he?'

'He could steal from us, but he hasn't,' Zenna said. 'He could take everything we own and run away and sell it. But he stays, and chops logs, and does what Ma asks him.'

'Then it's because that's what he wants. Perhaps he likes it here.'

'No, he's just waiting,' Zenna said firmly.

'Then why don't you just ask him what for?' Ariel asked, somewhat tartly, because she was feeling impatient with her cousin. She didn't think Zenna would do any such thing because Jack had an air about him that turned questions to stones in your throat. Even if you wanted to speak to him, and imagined it vividly, actually doing so was another matter.

Zenna gave her cousin an arch glance and jumped to her feet. The geese were startled and bustled off, honking. Ariel watched Zenna walk to the shadow of the shed. She was a girl in a fairytale about to reach out to a wolf, about to prick herself on a deadly thorn, about to change the future. Ariel also got to her feet. She didn't want to miss what might be said.

She was still some feet away from the shed when Zenna said to Jack, 'What are you waiting for?'

Jack didn't pause in his work; there wasn't the slightest hesitation.

'Well?' Zenna persisted. 'It's not that you can't speak, it's that you won't. But you're living here in our house, eating our food, sleeping in our attic, and I demand that you answer me.'

Still there was no response. Zenna grabbed hold of Jack's right arm and shook him. Ariel fully expected him to retaliate then, to bare his teeth in a snarl, to show a darker nature. All he did was cease working. He let Zenna shake him and when she had finished he turned to face her. He reached out with the arm she had grabbed and touched her, very lightly, with one finger just above the heart.

Zenna shot backwards a couple of feet as if he had punched her. She staggered a little then fell on her back.

Ariel couldn't help uttering a cry. Jack looked at her for a moment, then carried on stacking the logs. 'Tell her she cannot come,' he said.

'What?' Ariel had heard the words very clearly. She didn't know why she queried them.

He walked away, round the side of the house.

Zenna had scrambled to her feet. She ran past Ariel in the direction Jack had taken, but presently returned. 'He's gone,' she said. 'What did he say to you?'

'Are you all right, Zenna?' Ariel felt light-headed. The day no longer seemed quite so real.

'Never mind that. What did he say?' Zenna rubbed her chest in the place where Jack had touched her.

'He said to tell you that you cannot come. I don't know what he meant.'

Zenna frowned and pulled down the neck of her dress. 'Did he mark me?' she asked.

Ariel leaned forward. 'Yes,' she said. There was a small mark on Zenna's pale skin, in the shape of a crescent moon. He must have dug his fingernail into her, and yet the touch had appeared to be so light. 'It's just a scratch, I think. Not even that. What did it feel like?'

'I can't remember. I simply found myself on the ground.' Zenna shook her head. She didn't appear to be upset about the incident, just puzzled. 'Tell me now you think he's just a boy,' she said.

That night, very late, a wind came up from the east. The moon was nearly full, but the clouds rushed past her, didn't pause to carry her like they sometimes did, edged in silver. The Green House creaked in the arms of the wind.

Sitting sleepless by her bedroom window, looking out, Ariel realised that everything had a voice; houses, forests, wind, even, impossibly enough, silence. The wind was singing and Ariel knew what it meant. It was a song of searching, for the wind never stops, always going forward, asking: Who? Where? When? There were feathers in the wind, glowing white. It had its own wings. And in that moment, Ariel realised her true nature. Stubbornly refusing to believe in something did not make it go away. The world had a secret life and some people could see it. Perhaps her mother had.

Then she saw them. Four of them. Down in the garden, among the rhododendrons, shapes in the dark. There were no glowing eyes, no vivid flash of white teeth, just shapes. They looked like beasts, crouched and waiting. They had come for Jack. He would leave now.

In an instant, Ariel was on her feet. She ran out of her room and down the stairs and her feet made no sound. They didn't even touch the stairs. Sure enough, Jack was in the kitchen and no one else was there. She had to ask a question. She couldn't help herself. 'Who are they?'

'My father and his brothers,' Jack said. He opened the door to the garden, where the wind was hurrying past. 'Will you come?'

'Yes,' Ariel said. She took the hand he offered her.

'It will be just this once,' Jack said. 'Do you understand that?'

'Yes.'

Walking across the wind was difficult because it wanted them to go the way it was going. It seemed to take a long time to reach the other side of the garden. Jack's hand was hot and dry. He was speaking in a language Ariel did not know, a constant sibilant murmur; 'ah kaya, hala, hala, mah kah nay.'

Jack's kin came out from the foliage, huge and sinuous. They were cats and yet not. They had golden hoops in their tufted ears, and manes that were plaited with feathers and beads. They stretched and groaned and rubbed around Jack. One of them looked at Ariel, and breathed upon her. Its breath was hot and moist. Ariel reached out and laid a hand upon the enormous dark head. It smelled of the earth. The animal raised a paw and then, with a swift and unexpected movement, slashed Ariel with its claws across the chest, above the heart, tearing right through her shirt. Ariel did not stagger back, nor felt any pain, but saw she was bleeding. Her blood looked black. She looked at the beast and let the questions fall from her eyes: Why? Had she not trusted? Had she not believed and so allowed the true sight to come to her?

The cat reared up and then it was a man standing before her, dark and wild, a creature of the hidden places. 'You can't be too careful,' he said.

Jack put a hand upon her shoulder. 'It's all right,' he said.

'Let me, not him. His tongue is too rough.'

So Ariel let him lick up her blood, which he did neatly, as a cat would savour a saucer of cream. These things were really happening to her, there might be no future, but she didn't care. She was dreaming on her feet. Jack's voice brought her out of her reverie.

'You see, you're fine. Now we can run.' He took her hand again.

'Where?'

'With the wind.'

When she awoke in her bed, Ariel knew she was supposed to believe it had been all a dream. Then she would get out of bed and her feet would have soil between the toes, her legs would be scratched from brambles, there would be a wound above her heart from where a vampire had supped her blood. She lay in bed, breathing quickly. Above her, the ceiling was covered in sparkling motes that did not disappear when she blinked. She heard Maeve call her name. So she slipped from between the white sheets and looked down at her feet. They were clean. Perhaps he had licked them clean after he'd carried her to her bed, exhausted. It hadn't been a dream. There were her clothes, thrown over a chair, and the shirt was torn and bloody. Ariel picked the shirt up and stuffed it into the back of the wardrobe, among dozens of pairs of old shoes that perhaps Maeve had worn, many years before. Ariel looked at her wounds; they were nearly healed. She hoped the scars would not vanish.

The first words Maeve said to her downstairs were: 'Have you seen Jack?'

This was ridiculous. How could she? She'd been in bed. Ariel shook her head.

Zenna came in from outside. She looked like someone lost. 'He's gone,' she said. 'I know it. They came for him.'

Ariel could not look at her cousin. She was thinking of fast paws, galloping along the wind, of hot moist breath, of the time when true sight came to her and made it so that she could never be the same again.

'You must be glad,' Zenna said to her. 'Everything can be all normal again now.'

'Stop it,' Maeve said. 'He might be taking a walk.' But the tone in her voice showed she didn't really believe that.

How can you love someone who is so beyond all that is real it is impossible even to give them a name? If a person stands up in his real skin and shows you his real self, and you see it is not human, but something more beautiful and wondrous, even though it is potentially deadly, is that enough to change a life forever? But it is a fairy-tale, just words in the dark. How can you feel grief when that is taken from you?

The women of the Green House were struck down by grief. Even the geese by the pond lay down and stretched out their necks, spread out their white wings in the grass.

For a week Ariel was not entirely in the real world. The east wind had brought rain, dark and heavy, so that every day felt as if it was weeping. Ariel didn't think about whether Jack and his people might come back for her or not. It was impossible to think about anything. She lived in memory alone, like walking through a gallery of pictures, studying each one, experiencing it, but without having any opinion. Her memories brought her great pleasure; her secrets. No one knew. No one suspected. Ariel was the sensible one. It was Zenna who would have strange things happen to her; be taken under the hill by the faery folk, and be allowed home for only six months of the year.

Ariel drifted through the weeping days, while Maeve and Zenna comforted each other. They drew closer in a way they never had before. They were changed too. But the spell over Ariel eventually began to melt away. She could feel the real world coming back. She could not turn into a beast and walk the wind. She could not drink blood and become 'other'. That was the tragedy of it. She would never be the same again because she couldn't be like them. Zenna had been right about that. But at the same time she was not how she'd used to be. She was marked, lines down her torso the colour of mulberries.

On the night of the next full moon, Ariel climbed onto the roof of the house. Summer was ending, already the air smelled of decaying fruit and smoke. Autumn air would always smell that way, even if there were no fires, no fruit trees. There were no vampires on the roof, or down in the garden. How cruel they were. And how stupid was she to have believed that once would be enough. Of course it wouldn't, but even so she had consented.

It was no surprise to her that Zenna wriggled out of her window and used the limbs of the ironwood tree to reach the roof. She did not speak to Ariel at first, but just stood beside her, hands on hips, gazing at the forest behind the house. Eventually she said, 'Are you going to tell me or not?'

There seemed no point in being arch and saying, 'What do you mean?' Ariel sighed. 'I will show you,' she said.

Zenna turned round. Ariel could see she was full of pain and jealousy. She had guessed, no doubt, because Ariel's secrets were written all over her; she smelled of them. Ariel took off her shirt. In the moonlight her skin was parchment and the claw marks looked like burns.

'Claws, not teeth,' Zenna said.

Ariel nodded. 'When they take your blood, perhaps it is something in their saliva that makes things happen. But it doesn't last. You were right about that. It does change you, though; enough to feel a stranger in this world, but not enough to belong in theirs.'

'Tell me what happened,' Zenna said. 'Please.'

Ariel did so. She spoke the words of a story so unlikely, she could hardly believe it herself, yet it had happened.

'I should hate you,' Zenna said, 'because it feels like you took something that was mine. But I'm glad it changed you.

We are similar now.'

Ariel tried to smile. 'We can outrun time.'

'For now.' Zenna held out her hand. 'Come on. Maybe we are not as stupid as they think.'

Hand in hand, two girls run through the moonlit forest. They run so fast they are merely blurs of light. They run so fast they cause cracks in the bark of trees that leak a green-yellow radiance. It is the were-light of seeing.

.

The Deliveress

According to fantastical tradition, there are many ways a person might find themselves transported to another world. Car crashes are popular; one moment of terror and noise, the next finding yourself sprawled out on an alien turf, awaiting the unimaginable. Sometimes, you might simply wake up in the morning to a new sky, wearing a new skin, or else an inadvisable investigation of bizarre mists might lead you, unsuspecting, into an alternate reality.

Jenni (short for Jennifer) Brampton did not experience any of these. She was not pushed under a car, did not trip over, or walk through an imposing ancient gateway. She *did* have a piece of grit in her eye which, given that she wore contact lenses, caused her a momentary problem, but other than that, there were no bizarre circumstances. She simply rubbed her eye, blinked a few times and went suddenly, inexplicably freezing cold.

One moment she'd been standing outside Tesco's on a warm June afternoon, the next she was being buffeted by an icy wind in utter darkness. It was not absolutely dark, you understand, but because of the abrupt change, and the fact her eye was still a bit sore, Jenni thought it was. She did not scream and run, but simply made a small distressed sound and dropped to the floor, curling up into what her instincts told her might be a safe position. She thought, naturally, that she had gone blind and that the weather had changed rather abruptly for the worse. That was not impossible, given all the dire warnings about ecological calamity, was it? It was certainly more probable than finding yourself transported to a different reality.

After a few moments, Jenni groped her way to her knees and said, 'Help, I can't see.' It was unusual that her words were snatched so wildly from her mouth by the wind, and a deep part of her mind could actually discern the dark shapes of bushes around her, but her conscious self edited out this information and told her to ask for help again. By now, the right hand side of her brain was banging frantically on the interface with the rational left, insisting there were no people around and that something very strange indeed had happened. Left brain, ignoring such unwelcome news, firmly assured the body that nothing of the kind had occurred; a conviction destined to brief life.

'Help. I can't see.' Jenni blinked rapidly; her eyes were streaming with water from the stinging wind that blew her hair across her face. As her eyes got used to the light, Jenni could see that where the glass frontage of Boots the Chemist should have been was a lone, wild landscape of desolate heathland. Thick clouds, the like of which she'd never seen other than on a cinema screen, boiled across the moonlit sky above. It didn't make sense. Couldn't make sense. Whimpering, disorientated, cold, and going rapidly into shock, Jenni crawled instinctively towards cover; a tangle of bony shrubs some feet away. Here, she curled into a foetal position with her hands over her head, shutting herself away from whatever world was outside.

Primula, the High Priestess of Kaynah, led her band of intimate followers across the heath. She held aloft the Staff of Power, which emitted a dim, ghostly light. It looked impressive, but was not much use as regards lighting the way. Primula's followers held onto each other's robes and shuffled after the striding Priestess, who was admonishing them in a fearless voice.

'Hurry now, oh Children of Kaynah, for the night has come when the shape of our destiny is formed, when the fate of our oppressed people will be forged upon the anvil of heaven!' She repeated this statement regularly to keep up the spirits of her followers; all pampered acolytes of the temple who never went out, as a rule, when it was wet or windy. They passed by a lonely outcropping of rock, where Primula took shelter for a few moments. The wind was now accompanied by icy rain. Not betraying the slightest hint of unease to her followers, she wondered whether she'd read the oracle correctly. It had been quite emphatic about which direction she should take, how far she should travel and what she would find at the end. Still, she could not discern any irregularity in the rhythm of the night, other than that of the weather. Was it possible she could be <u>wrong</u>? No, surely not. If the oracle had told her the Deliverer would be found in this place, then she would find him. Simple as that. Doubting herself was nothing but the insidious work of the Dark One. She must ignore it.

'When are we going home?' asked one of the priests.

Primula raised a commanding hand. 'Silence! Have you no faith?' There was no answer. Primula drew herself up to her full height. 'Follow!' she snapped and strode out into the rain.

'This is the place!' Primula boomed, throwing out her arms. The followers all looked around themselves dismally. It was a dreadful, empty place, just uneven peaty ground with a few miserable shrubs dotted about. There was no sign of a Deliverer. Primula had assured them he would be of heroic stance, handsome, tall and suitably armed with magical weapons. Not even a sheep moved over the heath. It was, but for themselves, completely devoid of life.

'Where is he?' asked a priestess through chattering teeth. Primula fixed her with a stern glance.

'Well, we might be early,' she said. 'Here, hold this!' She thrust her Staff into the priestess' hands, and pulled out a rolled parchment from her robe, a sketched map of the area which she'd drawn up after consulting the oracle. 'No! Hold it here! Stupid girl!' She held the parchment up to the dim, fluctuating light of the Staff. 'Hmm, this is definitely the place.

I knew it was.'

'I can't see any heroes though,' one of her followers said, unhelpfully.

'Listen, wretch! If the Deliverer has been promised to us, he will come from another world to aid us. There can be no argument. Do you doubt the word of the spirits?'

'No, no, definitely not,' muttered the followers.

'Well, then, be quiet. We'll wait.' Primula sat down in a cross-legged position on the wet ground, her back as straight as her Staff. Grumbling to themselves, the followers did likewise.

Nearby, Jenni Brampton shivered senselessly under the cover of a bush.

The Children of Kaynah waited until morning. No hero came. Then, they went home.

The woman did not *look* like a nurse, because nurses wore white uniforms and this person had a long woollen dress on. The room did not *look* like a hospital ward because, instead of squeaky clean floors and metal-framed beds, there was straw on the ground, only a smoky kind of light, and too many dirty shadows. But, waking up like this in a strange place, feeling weak and feverish, where else could Jenni be but a hospital? She squirmed where she lay; a revolting smell filled her throat and something unpleasantly hairy scratched against her bare flesh. She realised, with horror, it was an animal skin.

'Where am I?' She attempted to sit up, but couldn't. Any movement made her feel sick and her head whirl. The strange woman put a big, rough hand on her shoulder.

'Hush now, pretty. Lie you there. You're safe.'

'I am?' Jenni pressed her fingers over her eyes. They felt dry; her lenses were very uncomfortable. It must be the smoke. What had happened? She'd fallen over in the street. Yes, that was it. A headache? Of course. Possibly a migraine. Where the hell was she though? She peered through her fingers at the smiling face of the woman, then quickly assessed the roughspun dress, the enveloping shawl, the long, greasy-looking hair. A hippy. Must be. Had she been kidnapped and taken to some appalling convoy encampment?

'How did I get here?' Jenni asked.

'Krak found you on the heath. The dogs sniffed you out. Wet through you were, poor lass, wet and fevered. Brought you back here, Krak did. You been sick, pretty, very sick.'

'What heath?' Jenni asked in a tiny voice. She was afraid something disgusting might have happened to her after her blackout. Perhaps these hippies weren't the first people to have found her. How had she got to a heath? The nearest one to Eddlewick, her home town, was fifteen miles away, Minsley Moor. Murders had happened there. Jenni shuddered and swallowed a ball of bile that rose in her throat. No, don't even think about it.

'*The* heath,' the woman said. 'Corcanrac Wild, we call it. Lost your way, pretty, did you, out there in the weather?'

'Lost my way! God!' Jenni tried to sit up again. Where the hell was Cor... whatever it was? Did the hippies have their own name for Minsley? 'I have to get to a telephone,' she said.

The woman frowned. 'No-one of that stature here,' she said. 'We got a priest. You want to see the priest?'

Jenni groaned. 'No telephone! God! Yes, a priest then, bring him here. Perhaps he has a phone in the vicarage.'

The woman, obviously an imbecile, nodded and bustled out of the room, a puzzled expression on her face. It was as if she'd hardly understood a word Jenni had said.

The priest was a young man, with dirt in the lines of his face. He would have been good-looking but for his neglect of hygiene, Jenni thought. Another hippy. Must be defrocked or something. The conversation did not progress well. They seemed to be talking about completely different things. The priest hadn't even heard of Eddlewick and genuinely appeared to be ignorant of what a telephone was. Neither did he respond favourably to queries about cars and buses. He told

Jenni she was in a village called Brayness. When she asked if that was in Scotland, he hadn't heard of that either, and insisted the country was called Kaynahmia. 'Look, one of us is mad,' Jenni said, flopping back on the unsavoury bed for the fifth time. 'I don't suppose you have any saline, do you?'

'What is that?'

She gestured towards her eyes. 'For my lenses. I need to take them out, soak them? Yes?' She sighed. 'Don't tell me, you don't know what I mean. Salt-water, salt and *boiled* water will do. Can you manage that?'

He stood up. 'Of course. Your eyes are injured?'

'They will be!'

He hesitated. 'Your skin, your strange, fine clothes... You are a lady of stature from a foreign land, aren't you.'

'I'm a receptionist for an estate agent from Eddlewick,' Jenni said. 'And very confused. Perhaps I'm hallucinating... Oh, God, I was supposed to meet Kevin... how many days ago? What's happened to me?' She began to cry, from frustration and post-fever weakness, more than helplessness. It at least eased the soreness of her eyes.

Targ was a warrior. He rode about virtually naked, even in the coldest of weathers, on a massive horse, surrounded by his massive weapons, which hung from the saddle. He was handsome, fearless, impervious to pain, noble, honourable and a skilled fighter. Songs had been composed about his brave exploits in the world; the monsters he had hacked to pieces, the various Dark Ones he had coolly despatched, the ladies he had rescued from unfortunate circumstances. He was, in anybody's mythology, a hero. He was not, however *the* hero, the one that Primula had summoned to aid the country in its war with the current Dark One. But, because of his reputation, Targ had been selected to seek out the Deliverer. By now, it was assumed that the oracle had got its bearings wrong. The Deliverer must have arrived *somewhere* at the appointed time; Targ would just have to find out where. It was even possible, however unlikely, that the Dark One had somehow intercepted the Deliverer and had magically incarcerated him. Targ, dimly, hoped so. He liked to fight and flex his muscles. He did not want to discover the Deliverer just in a tavern somewhere, lost. Also, although he would not (in fact could not) admit it consciously, he was rather put out that he had not been chosen as *the* hero himself. He rather fancied the idea of having an excuse to dispatch the Dark One, before this other person could, whatever Primula might think.

He rode into the ancient forest of Sithe, and interrogated a charcoal-burner he found there. The old man could not remember having seen any lost heroes wandering about, and the best information he could come up with was that, in Brayness, a few leagues north, a foreign princess had been stranded away from her caravan. She was the only stranger the charcoal-burner had heard about, but perhaps, being foreign and reputedly rather mysterious, she might be of interest to Targ. Targ did consider whether the lady might need rescuing. He enjoyed quests of that sort, but did wonder whether now was an appropriate time to deviate from his mission. Primula would not be pleased if he failed her, and as she was so adept at humiliating people in public, Targ was very wary of upsetting her. The Dark One's filthy hordes massed in the evil mountains of Theng. Soon, unless something was done, the whole land would be subjected to the Dark One's terrible rule. A time of famine, pestilence, misery and despair would come to pass. Still, Brayness was more or less on Targ's route. Surely an extra day's travelling wouldn't make that much difference to the fate of the land, and maybe the princess would be enchanted or something, and able to give information about the Deliverer. It was worth a look, at least. Targ thanked the charcoal-burner and rode deeper into the forest.

Jenni Brampton was not a happy young woman. Once she was strong enough to get up and totter around, she had to face the grim reality that she was not in a land she knew.

The possibility that she had been magically transported to another world didn't occur to her at first. Why should it? Such things were not a common occurrence outside Boots, after all. She fluctuated between believing she'd gone completely insane, or that her previous life, as she remembered it, was a dream. Only the fact that her watch, her lenses, and her clothes, were so alien to the people around her allowed her to keep a tenuous grip on her true history, but it was difficult. The people of Brayness were pleasant, if uncouth. They seemed to appreciate their rude way of life was rather unfamiliar to Jenni and tried to do what they could to alleviate her distress. They called her a princess, and after having argued about it a few times to no avail, Jenni let them believe that. At least it meant she could keep a certain distance between herself and the terrible place she was in. If only she still had her handbag with her. She'd had a travel-size bottle of saline in there and a few tampons, some makeup and a comb. All of these things, once taken for granted by Jenni, were unknown to the people of Brayness. Jenni knew that her lenses would only last so long without being cleaned properly. Once they were gone, she'd be virtually blind. Mercifully, the shock of her situation had interfered with her menstrual cycle; she could not bear to think about what it would be like once her body went back to normal, if it did at all.

Jenni was more or less adopted by the woman called Silsa, whose son, Krak, had found her out on the heath. Silsa was convinced that Jenni had been travelling across the heath with a rich caravan (perhaps her father's) and had somehow become estranged from her companions. The weather had been awful that night, after all. Silsa had never heard of the country called England, which Jenni talked about, but then she was only aware of a small portion of the world. 'When you're really well, you must go to Kaynahria, the city,' Silsa said. 'Someone there will help you home, no doubt.' She liked looking after Jenni though, because she was so helpless, and admitted to her friends she would be sad to see Jenni go. 'So small, so fragile,' she said, shaking her head with benevolent concern. 'A wee thing alone in the world.' It was clear to Silsa that Jenni was of noble birth, because she was so concerned about trivial things like whether her skin and hair were clean. Any clothes that Silsa lent to her, even her best dress, brought Jenni's fair, delicate skin out in an angry rash. Jenni's own clothes were too flimsy for the robust climate of Kaynahmia. It was also obvious to Silsa that Jenni was a bit touched in the head. She came out with such nonsense, sometimes. Still, it made for good stories around the fire when the community had a gathering. Jenni spoke of a magical carriage called a Minnymetrow, in which she was used to riding, and mysterious artefacts of great power that could carry a person's voice around the world. Yet despite this familiarity with the weird and fantastic, she was frightened of the placid ponies tethered outside Silsa's cottage, as if she'd never touched one before, and had a peculiar, almost obsessive, concern about where the sun was in the sky. When Silsa woke Jenni in the morning, she would ask 'What time is it?' And Silsa would always laugh and reply, 'Why *now*, pretty!'

On the day when Targ came to Brayness, Jenni had wandered out to the pool at the edge of the forest, where the villagers washed their clothes and, on rare occasions, their bodies. Washing had become a compulsive ritual to her, although the lye and ashes she had to use on her hair had ruined its condition. As she rinsed her head with the freezing water, she thought wistfully about the bottle of split-ends treatment that stood on the shelf above the sink in her old bathroom. What had happened to her apartment? Had it ever existed at all? She'd been in Kaynahmia for nearly a month now. How she'd got there, she still didn't know, and now suspected she never would. Perhaps it had happened to other people. Perhaps she would meet them one day. Perhaps they could find a way home together. No, that was just wishful thinking. She knew that someone else was doing her job back home, someone else dating the desirable Kevin, and that the chances were she'd never have an opportunity to reclaim either. She sighed. Here, the men were all filthy and, as she didn't have her contraceptive pills with her, any dalliance with them, even should she be able to stomach the stink, was out of the question. The possible consequences were too dreadful. There were no doctors around, only smelly old women clutching herbs and muttering spells. There was no electricity, no real heating, and the food was appalling. She didn't even have a book to read. As for the toilet facilities - well, they were beyond words. Jenni felt she could kill for a roll of Andrex, never mind a little privacy. The people of Brayness were frank about bodily functions and clearly could not understand Jenni's fastidiousness. Still, there were perhaps some compensations. Her skin had definitely improved, despite the rough living. And, perhaps because the food was so unappetising, she had lost some weight. Jenni did not consider this might be because her diet had improved, free as it was of additives and excessive sugars and fats.

Being a person who naturally needed to keep busy, Jenni had soon tired of playing the stranded princess, mooning around the cottage, sighing. There was nothing to do there except stare at the walls, so she had offered to help Silsa with her animals and the garden plot behind the cottage. Silsa had seemed surprised, but had also appeared grateful for the extra pair of hands. For the first few days, Jenni's back and arms had ached horribly, what with the hoeing, the bending and stretching, and carrying heavy bales of hay on her shoulders. But now, her muscles had strengthened, and she woke up in the morning able to function in a spritely manner, even without a few cups of coffee. But, however hard she tried to make the most of her situation, Jenni felt she had to face facts. The people of Brayness were not on her wavelength, she could not really communicate with them. There was no-one like her former best friend, Karen, with whom she could share her thoughts. She would never spend another day out on a shopping trip with Karen, returning back to the flat, exhausted but excited by the clothes and makeup they had bought, sinking down to an evening of Liebfraumilch, videos and cosy conversation. All that was gone forever. Even should she become used to the comparative discomfort, Jenni felt she was doomed to a life of inner loneliness and eventual blindness. That was too much to bear.

Dwelling on her unhappy thoughts, Jenni was nontheless alert, and jumped to her feet, ready to flee, when she heard the sound of hooves coming towards her through the trees. She had swiftly learned there were many dangers to be encountered in Kaynahmia, and although she didn't believe the stories about dragons, had heard the wolves with her own ears several times. Krak, Silsa's unsavoury son, had given her a knife with which to defend herself, should the occasion arise, and now, with dripping hair hanging over her face, her long, homespun dress hooked up into her belt, she dropped into the crouch Krak had taught her and brandished the weapon. At that moment, not even her mother would have recognised her as the demure young receptionist from Eels and Allen, Estate Agents.

'Ho! Wench!' yelled the man on the horse. He looked like a barbarian warrior - all long hair and muscles - and was grinning from ear to ear. A bizarre thought crossed Jenni's mind: well I never, they really do wear hardly anything at all. Just like in the films!

Her experience with such films (and she'd only watched two, at Kevin's insistence) also reminded her that barbarians were either noble loners with a heritage problem, or potential rapers and looters. At first glance, it was impossible to determine which category this character fell into.

'Hold it right there!' Jenni said, gripping the knife firmly, and aware that her script-writing was perhaps a little hackneyed.

The man leapt down from his horse and held out his

hands in a gesture of goodwill. 'Put away your blade, woman. I'll not harm you.'

'Don't come any nearer,' Jenni said, backing away along the pool-side, towards the village.

The man shrugged. 'As you will. I'm looking for Brayness.'

'Well, you've found it. There. What there is of it.'

'And a foreign princess...?

Uh oh, Jenni thought. 'What do you want with her?'

The man folded his arms. 'That's between me and her. Can you take me to her?'

She thought for a moment and then said, 'Mmm, alright. Come on then. Follow me.'

She left him outside Silsa's cottage and hurried inside, to where Silsa was stirring a pot of something unpleasant, which would have to be eaten later, over the fire. The older woman, after hearing Jenni's story, seemed to think the warrior must be from the city. 'Perhaps your family have asked about you there. He might have come to take you home,' she said, looking a little disappointed.

'There's no chance of that!' Jenni said. 'Where are my old clothes?'

To preserve her original clothes, Jenni hardly ever wore them. It seemed she only had to step outside the cottage to get completely filthy, and she wasn't sure how long Miss Selfridge garments would hold out against lye and ashes. She dressed herself in the wonderful soft fabrics. The long skirt swept sensuously round her ankles, the silky blouse felt like a caress against her breasts and arms, and it seemed that, even though she'd had to wash both garments after her night out on the heath, a fragrance of deodorant and Lou-Lou still lingered in the cloth. Now, she really felt like a princess. Strange, how quickly she'd become used to Silsa's scratchy garments, and she had to admit her arms felt a little constrained in the blouse. She tied back her damp hair and said, 'Show him in, Silsa, but don't leave me alone with him. We don't know what he wants.'

The barbarian lumbered into the cottage and bowed. 'I am Targ!' he said.

'And I'm Jenni Brampton,' Jenni replied. 'Yes, it's me, from the pool, don't bother commenting on it. What do you want?'

Targ looked a little non-plussed. 'I am looking for a man who is the Deliverer,' he said, sounding unconvinced by the statement himself.

'Oh yeah? What has that to do with me?'

'You are a stranger. I am alert for symbols, for clues to follow. I followed the clues to you. Madam, we need the Deliverer, for if he is not found, the Dark One's hordes will overtake the land with their shadow of death and all will be lost...'

'Oh, which Dark One is this?' Silsa interrupted. 'I thought the Dark One was dead, killed in the Battle of the Two Spires, eight years ago.'

'This,' said Targ ponderously, 'is *another* Dark One, more terrible than the last and twice as evil.'

'They always say that,' Silsa said.

'Wait a minute!' Jenni raised her hands. She was quite pleased at the way she'd become so assertive since everyone had started treating her like a princess. 'Are you telling me there's a war on?'

Targ bowed his head. 'Sadly, madam, there will be. It will be the war to end all wars when the filthy hordes of...'

'I've yet to see one of these wars,' Silsa said. She turned to Jenni. 'Don't you worry, lovey. There's always talk of war and Dark Ones, and there's always a hero to sort it out. It don't bother the likes of us. Tch, if people like this one here didn't come blabbing about it, we'd never know about these things at all. And...' She glared at Targ. '.... I'm thinking we don't need to know either.'

'You may scoff, woman!' Targ said coldly. 'But if the

Deliverer is not found, I believe you *will* see one of these wars, and in the most horrible, painful manner! The blight will come, the leaves fall from the trees though it is High Summer, the beasts fall in the fields, the children die weeping blood...'

'Bloody hell!' Jenni said. 'This is all I need. Is nowhere safe?'

'Madam, it would be my privilege to escort you to the safety of the city,' said Targ, primly. 'I am renowned for my valour.'

'So, who is this Deliverer you talked about?' Jenni asked. She was perched behind Targ on his horse, carrying only a bag with her original clothes in it and a supply of salt and water for her lens care. She had been surprised by how sad she'd felt at leaving Silsa, but had steeled herself against such sentiment. After all, if she travelled, there might be a chance, however slim, of getting home.

'The Deliverer will smite the Dark One,' said Targ, with a note of bitterness. 'But first, he has to be found.'

'How did you manage to lose him, then?'

'You don't understand, madam. The Deliverer was due to arrive in our world a moon hence. The High Priestess of Kaynah summoned him from another world. The Children of Kaynah walked to the heath, to the sacred place where he would appear to them, on a night of wind and rain, but he never came.'

'A month ago? Strange, that was when I arrived...' Well, that's a coincidence! Jenni thought, and then felt a chill pass through her. Or is it...?

'You have gone rather quiet madam.'

'Mmm. Where was this Deliverer supposed to come from?'

'It is the custom in this land that, in times of hardship so severe even the bravest and strongest cannot allay it, a summoning is made to the world beyond, and a hero steps forth to aid us.'

'They come from another world, you say?'

'Indeed.'

'Just sort of... *snatched* from another world, by any chance?'

'They are called, they are the only ones, they are the chosen.'

'I see...' Jenni wriggled uncomfortably on the saddle. 'Er, you've never had a Deliver*ess*, I take it?'

Targ was quite emphatic about that, which Jenni found slightly offensive. '*Most* unlikely, unless she was a sorceress,' he said, 'but generally, the Deliverer has to be a fighting man of proud brow and rippling thews.'

'Yes, I can see that would be better....' Jenni said, but her sarcastic tone was obviously wasted on the barbarian. From what she had seen in Brayness, it was the women who carried the community: wise women, healers, spell-binders. And wasn't the local deity female? It did not seem unlikely to her that, should there be a need for a Deliverer, it could be a heroine rather than a hero. 'Targ?'

'Madam?'

'Can we stop for a second? I'm a bit sore, a bit thirsty.'

'With pleasure.'

Targ gallantly helped Jenni down from the horse. She felt a little shaky, and not just because she was still nervous of large animals. It was so bizarre, but could it be possible *she* was the Deliverer Targ was talking about? Perhaps she'd been summoned by mistake, instead of someone who was the *real* Deliverer. After all, she had come from another world, or what appeared to be another world, and she'd arrived a month ago, on the heath. She wondered whether it would be wise to confide in Targ about this. He might insist she go and fight this Dark person, or else be terribly disappointed. Good God, it might be that, because of this hideous mistake, Kaynahmia would be destroyed! She wasn't a warrior; she couldn't even see properly. Still, it might be a coincidence. Perhaps people were continually blipping out of existence in her world, and finding themselves here. She was just going to have to tell Targ though, because if she <u>was</u> the one he was looking for, his people would just have to find themselves another Deliverer to go waving weapons about. Jenni abhorred violence of any kind. God, what a mess.

'What?!' Primula's voice shook cobwebs from the rafters of the temple. 'Are you insane?'

Targ withered before her rage. 'Milady, I repeat only what I have heard. I would not presume to conjecture...'

Primula stalked up and down beside the altar, her dark robes flapping, her hands gripping each other tightly, as if to prevent themselves from gripping some part of Targ in an unfriendly way. 'A slip of a girl, the *Deliverer*?' She laughed, a forced, unpleasant sound. 'I can't believe you'd think such a thing, Targ!'

'But the evidence...'

'Evidence! Evidence? Where are her weapons, her physical power? Where was she when we waited on the heath?'

'Under a bush,' Targ said awkwardly.

'Under a bush?! The Deliverer? Under a bush!? Hah!'

'That was where the peasant's dogs found her, milady. She was very cold and wet, quite ill, I believe.'

'The Deliverer would never be ill!' shouted Primula. 'He would shrug off the most piercing of wind and rain as if they were the breath and tears of a baby! He is crowned by bolts of thunder and holds the storm in his eyes!'

'Yes, but, she does claim to come from another world...'

Primula narrowed her eyes. '*Claim*, yes, claim. She could be a creature of the Dark One!' Primula paused. '*Pretty*, I suppose.' Her voice was scathing.

'Well... a bit,' Targ conceded, blushing. 'But I don't think she is a Dark denizen, milady. She is too innocent and trusting a soul. Perhaps her power lies in a direction other than that of the sword.'

Primula tapped her cheek with her fingers. 'Hmm. A

sorceress?'

'Could be. There is no definite specification that the Deliverer should be male, is there? Perhaps Kaynah has deliberately chosen a woman.'

Primula considered this suggestion carefully. Targ was right, of course. The legends spoke of how Kaynah had handled any number of difficult situations in the days when She had walked the land. Primula glanced at the statue of the goddess behind the altar. Was this a message of some kind? Blinking, Primula turned back to Targ, and shook her head. 'I don't like it! I need to know what I'm dealing with. You can always trust a warrior, they have their souls written all over their faces, like dogs. Women are complicated creatures, sneaky. I don't like it.' She took a pinch of incense from a bowl on the altar and sprinkled it over a metal dish of smouldering coals. Pungent smoke billowed past her, forcing Targ to step backwards, coughing.

'We'll see,' Primula said, folding her arms, and assuming her most dangerous expression. 'Have this girl brought to my rooms in an hour. I will assess her myself.' She waved Targ away from her, who gratefully strode off between the temple columns. Primula steepled her fingers beneath her chin, staring up at the stern features of Kaynah's statue before her. The Deliverer, a girl? Was such a thing possible? 'Lady, I am Your vessel,' Primula silently said to her goddess. 'But would You please try to be a little clearer in this matter?'

No answer was immediately forthcoming.

High Priestess Primula reminded Jenni of an old schoolteacher she'd had. Handsome, in a severe sort of way, and difficult to please. The two women eyed each other with mutual suspicion, across the marble and tapestried splendour of Primula's reception chamber. A representation of the goddess lurked in a curtained alcove, looking on with cold, ruby eyes. Priests and priestesses were ranked behind Primula's throne-like chair, oppressed, but with curious faces.

'Look, this is not my fault,' Jenni said, into the silence

which had followed her story. 'I don't like it any more than you do.'

Primula did not even look at Jenni. 'She's not even a sorceress!' the Priestess snapped at Targ, who was standing nervously by the door.

Targ shrugged helplessly.

'I never claimed to be!' Jenni cried. 'What's wrong with you all? I'm the one who's been snatched from home. I'm the one...'

'There is only one thing we can do,' Primula said, interrupting Jenni's outburst. 'The girl must be tested. Only the Deliverer can pass the test.' She smiled at Jenni, in a manner devoid of reassurance. 'Do you agree to undertake it?'

Jenni shrugged. 'Well, will it hurt?'

'Only if you are not the Deliverer!'

'Oh, hang on!' Jenni said. 'This isn't fair! I was only trying to help by telling Targ how I got here. Why are you being so negative?'

'What do you mean?' Primula said. 'Negative?'

'Oh forget it!' Jenni said. 'I'll take the test. I'll do whatever you want. Just get on with it.'

Primula drew a small, carved wooden box out of the sleeve of her robe. She opened it. 'In here, are Biting Spiders of the Oracle,' she said. 'They will recognise the Deliverer if they touch him... or (she raised a sneering nostril) her.'

'Touch?' Jenni said, in a small voice, realising the box was not quite as small as she'd thought. 'Look, maybe this isn't a good idea. I'm not your Deliverer. I think I should just leave now.'

'Too late! You consented!' Primula cried, standing up, and pointing imperiously at Jenni. 'Seize her!'

'It's alright, she's waking up.'

Jenni recognised Targ's voice, and opened her eyes to his concerned face hanging over her. He gently lifted her to a sitting position, and Jenni was appalled to find her nose was bleeding, all over her original clothes, which she'd worn to try and impress the High Priestess. 'You fainted,' Targ said. 'Hit the floor with your nose.'

Mercifully, and perhaps sensibly, the memory of where Primula had put the spiders had not been retained by Jenni's mind.

'Congratulations,' said the High Priestess. 'The spiders took to you like a kitten to the mother-cat's teat. They positively flocked to nestle round your neck.' She bowed her head stiffly. 'I have no alternative but to conclude you are the Deliverer.'

Jenni let her head flop back against Targ's chest. 'Oh no,' she groaned. 'I would be.'

Control of Jenni's life seemed to have been whipped from her grasp. One moment she'd been viewed with dark suspicion and virtually tortured by Primula, the next she was being shepherded around by the High Priestess, and introduced to the Duke of Kaynahria as a woman of power and status. Jenni found it all a bit overwhelming, and was still bewildered about how she had come to be in this position. True, the comforts of the palace were far preferable to life in Brayness. She had access now, at least, to cosmetics and proper soap, and some primitive feminine toiletries of a more intimate nature. She had a maid to brush her hair and the food was surprisingly good. She liked the sweeping halls and terraces of the palace, the coloured birds that lived upon the balconies, the long, gauzy drapes that wafted in the breeze at every huge window. Kaynahria was just like her idea of a fairy-tale city; she loved the architecture and the fact that there were no junk-food establishments around. The people were certainly colourful and could be forgiven their rather uncivilised habits. She even had to admit she rather liked Targ, but refused to dwell on that. It was a purely physical attraction, because he was so obviously dense in the upstairs department. His loincloth was pleasingly filled, but Jenni knew it was unlikely anyone in Kaynahria used condoms, and she had no intention of risking pregnancy. However, it might be worth consulting one of these sorceress people about that; women must do *something* to look after themselves here.

What really troubled her though was that everyone would be looking to her for an answer to their problems. She knew nothing about politics or warmongering. The nearest she'd come to it was the weekly staff meetings at Eels and Allen.

One morning, very soon after she'd been installed in the ducal palace, Jenni was summoned to the governmental chambers on the first floor. She sensed the time had come when the Kaynahmians expected her to prove herself.

'I don't suppose you've thought of negotiating with this Dark One, have you?' Jenni asked. She was sitting with Primula, the Duke of the City, several of his staff and Targ, round a large table. So far, she had only been regaled with the past exploits of previous heroes and Deliverers. None of their actions seemed really her style.

'Abramoth is not to be reasoned with,' said the Duke, who was a kindly, if rather non-descript elderly man. 'He is beyond reasoning, pure evil.'

'Oh dear.'

'Perhaps you can appreciate now why we were so concerned about you being the Deliverer,' Primula said.

Jenni disliked the woman's smug, self-congratulatory tone. 'Look,' she said, directing her remarks to the Duke. 'For whatever reason, I have apparently been summoned here to help you. My talents do not lie in the realms of sorcery or sword-fighting, but I am a very good receptionist. I'm trained at calming people down and, when you work for an estate agent, that's very important. Maybe I should just speak to this Abramoth.'

'The girl's demented,' Primula said, throwing up her hands.

'Has anyone ever tried that, though?' Jenni asked. 'You know, just walked up to the Dark One's door and asked to talk to him about all this?'

'She has no concept of evil!' Primula said. 'She's a child!'

'Exactly,' the Duke replied calmly, and smiled at Jenni. She realised, with satisfaction she had an ally in him.

The Duke turned to Primula. 'Nobody <u>has</u> tried to do that before. Nobody would dare. But a Deliverer might.' He turned back to Jenni, leaving the stone-faced Priestess to digest his comments. 'What do your instincts say to you, my dear?'

'They say I'm up to my neck in it,' Jenni replied. 'But I've been thinking. All your other Deliverers have been fighting men, soldiers and generals plucked from their lives in my world to help you. I'm not a fighting person, but like them, I do have a speciality. I'm a communicator. So, it seems to me, we should be thinking of how we can use my talent. It's the only conclusion I can draw.'

'And you are prepared to face the Dark One?'

Jenni sighed. 'If I am prepared to face Mrs Watling-Smith when she believed she'd been gazumped, I can face anything. When do I leave?'

The castle was made of black, wet stone, rearing between sharp, obsidian cliffs, where lightning played and thunder growled. A narrow, twisting path led up to the castle. The drawbridge was down, and there seemed to be no guards on duty. Jenni shivered in her thick cloak. Appearances were deceptive. On the occasions when she'd provided holiday relief in the Rent Department of Eels and Allen, she'd had to visit truculent tenants with a colleague. Those houses had appeared very much like this, deserted, and had been impossible to enter, locked and barred so tight a flea couldn't get in. Targ, and the armies of Kaynah, waited further down the mountain. She had insisted on making the last stage of this journey alone. For a moment, she paused and looked back. The green, fertile plains of the city were invisible from here, but, oh, the power of the elements, the soaring splendour of the cliffs, with not even a single Coke can to spoil it. The air, though tinged with sulphur in this locale, was still purer than any air she had breathed back home. She had assumed the natives of this tiny country to be dirty and savage, because they were not obsessed with the rituals of over-civilisation, but in reality, there was very little disease. The land itself was clean, the soil untainted, the rainwater itself fit to drink untreated. Mountains, hills, forests, rolling fields: all stretched to a horizon unblighted by ugly industrial plants or monstrous hyper-markets. Whenever the natural line of the landscape was broken, it was by small, rural villages or the graceful spires of Kaynahria itself. Real beauty.

Jenni realised, with a wry tug of humour, that she had not only got used to life in Kaynahmia, but was beginning to take pleasure in it. She had status, she had respect; things a lowly receptionist could only dream of. People called her beautiful, and bowed as she passed. Although she did miss the comforts of central heating and a ready supply of paracetamol for those annoying stress headaches she was still prone to, she had to admit the career prospects here were certainly more *challenging* than those offered by Eels and Allen. She felt far healthier than she ever had back home, and because of the lack of technological communications, which at first had seemed an isolating and terrifying thing, the world felt so *big*, so full of promise. She had found, to her surprise, that it *was* possible to live happily without television and duvets, toothpaste and chicken tikka sandwiches. Was it also possible that, deep inside, this translocation was something she'd always yearned for?

Jenni turned and faced the castle of the Dark One. Flame belched from a crack in the rock wall nearby. What would the Dark One be like? Would he be a monster? Well, I'm ready for him, Jenni thought. I've handled enough monsters in my time.

She straightened her spine. She felt powerful, unstoppable. She walked to the castle gate.

'Hello!' Jenni called through the looming arch of the gate, into the echoing yard beyond. She was not terribly keen on venturing beneath the shadow of the gate-arch unless somebody, however foul and misshapen, appeared. She also began to question the wisdom of her decision. She was only a girl of flesh and blood. If someone dropped down behind her from the castle walls, they could easily cut her throat before she could even squeak. The yard, flagged in wet stone, streaked with slime, rank grasses growing weakly from cracks, looked as if it had not been occupied by a living creature for centuries. Jenni felt a little spooked. Unpleasant images of walking dead, ghouls and ghosts began to trickle into her mind (Damn those films of Kevin's!). Perhaps she should go back for Targ and the others. Yes, there was obviously nobody around; she would go back for the others.

'Tell them I came,' she couldn't resist saying, before she turned away. She'd always loved that poem, 'The Listeners'.

'Wait!'

Jenni froze. Steeling herself, she turned round slowly, glad she'd taken the steeling precaution, because what faced her was horrible. She supposed it was a troll, or an orc, or something like that. Whatever it was, she couldn't help feeling a little sorry for it. Fancy being born so ugly! Tusks protruded from the overshot lower jaw over the cheeks. The nose was non-existent, the eyes small and rheumy. The skin was warty and grey. It wasn't even as tall as she was, but looked rather like a bull terrier; all muscle. Some people loved bull terriers, though. She shouldn't let appearances sway her judgement of this individual.

'Hello,' she said, holding out her hand. 'My name's Jenni Brampton. I'd like to see Abramoth, if he's at home.'

The creature twitched its face like a puzzled ape, squinting at her offered hand. 'We thought you were the alchemist,' it said. 'Are you? Her name was Evilia, though.'

Jenni shook her head, withdrawing her hand. 'No, I'm from the city. I'm their Deliverer. Do you think Abramoth will see me? I'd appreciate you asking him.'

The creature blinked. 'No-one from the city climbs this path,' it said, clearly not believing her. 'Are you a performer?

The party's not till next week, after we've won the war.'

'Well, I suppose I *am* a performer in a way, but it's very important I speak to Abramoth. Please? I'd be very grateful.'

The creature shuffled on its short legs, rubbed its nose cavity and then said, 'I'll ask. You'd better come in.' It kept shooting suspicious backward glances at Jenni, and she liked to think it was because no-one had been civil to it before, no-one human, that is.

'Awful day, isn't it?' she said brightly, as they climbed some slime-covered steps to the main entrance.

'Oh, I like a bit of bluff,' said the monster, 'some savoury sulphur on the air. It's good for you, you know.'

'Really? I must say it seems to work for you. You look very healthy and strong.'

'Oh I am,' said the thing, 'very strong, very healthy. This way. Mind the mess.'

Jenni stepped inside a dark and cavernous hall. Seemingly hundreds of squat, ugly creatures were dozing on the floor, all making obscene noises from one end or the other.

'You just can't get the staff nowadays, can you,' said Jenni, lifting up her skirts a little to step over the indescribable mounds of filth covering the dirty straw on the ground.

'Yes, it is a problem,' said the thing. 'We think it's because they don't like the climb. Steep path from the nearest village, you know.'

'Perhaps you should offer accommodation.'

'Tried it. Doesn't seem to help.'

They climbed an enormous stone staircase to an upper level of the castle, where conditions, though bleak, seemed slightly less disgusting. Jenni patted her hair. 'Place needs a good airing,' she said.

'Wait here,' said the creature. 'I'll speak to the guv'nor.'

'I would appreciate a swift reply,' Jenni said. She didn't really want to spend any time in this place alone. There was no telling what might lurk in the shadows. Resisting an impulse to stalk nervously up and down on the bare flags, Jenni tried to calm herself by taking deep, even breaths. If the Dark One's staff were so ugly, what would he be like? What if he was so hideous she fainted? She tried to keep the whiskered jowls of Mrs Watling-Smith in mind; that had been a pretty terrifying countenance when enraged, and she'd stomached that.

Fairly soon, the creature came waddling towards her again. 'He'll see you,' it said. 'You're lucky. He's in a fairly good mood today. Has been known to wither people on sight for disturbing him.'

'How antisocial,' Jenni said. 'No wonder he's not very popular in this country.'

The creature tapped its nose cavity and lowered its voice. 'Trouble is, folk just don't *understand* him, you know. He's a very sensitive person.'

'I can believe it,' Jenni said, thinking that the Dark One's sensitivities couldn't possibly extend to his immediate environment.

She followed her ugly guide up a dark passageway, lined with tapestries and animal skulls. Naked torches spluttered on the walls, emitting an oily smoke. That couldn't be doing the tapestries much good, Jenni thought. What the Dark One needed was a good housekeeper, or perhaps complete refurbishment of the castle. It was probably living here that gave him such an unpleasant character. More light, pastel shades on the walls, could do wonders for the spirit. She made a mental note to suggest it.

The creature paused before an iron-studded door and knocked respectfully. A dour voice came from the other side. 'Enter!' The creature opened the door, and gestured for Jenni to go in.

'Aren't you coming?' she asked, quite scared, at this final moment, of facing the Dark One alone.

The creature shook its head. 'Not invited,' it said. 'Hope he spares you. It's been nice meeting you.'

'Same to you,' Jenni said, and taking a deep breath, stepped over the threshold.

Her first thought was 'Wow!' and that was even before she took in the room. The man himself was enough to prompt her unspoken exclamation. Abramoth had just risen out of a chair, one hand still resting on its carved back. He was tall, slender, pale of skin, with enormous dark eyes and a wealth of jet black hair. In short, magnificent.

'So, *you're* the Dark One,' she said, hoping she didn't sound too surprised.

The man drew himself up to his full height. 'I am Abramoth, son of Elamoth, Lord of the Fiery Pits, Wielder of Unholy Flame, Despoiler of the Pure, known to the lesser beings of this world as the Dark One, yes.' He stalked towards her a few paces. 'And you are?'

'Jenni Brampton. But you may call me the Deliverer.' Jenni turned away from the compelling, paralysing stare of the Dark One. 'Well, this is quite a place you have here!'

'The *Deliverer*?' Abramoth enquired delicately. 'You are a woman!'

Jenni glanced back at him, and could tell he was suppressing a smile that clearly didn't belong in his repertoire of dark mystical expressions.

'So they tell me,' she replied coldly. 'There's no need to look so surprised. It is obviously about time a feminine touch was brought to the organisation of this country. Wars, really! You're just like a gang of little boys!'

Abramoth appeared to be sticking to his own script, because Jenni's observations were clearly not penetrating. 'The *Deliverer*? Scourge of the family Dangkurst: *my* family! At last, my powers have waxed to their full, and you are drawn, against your will, to my domain!'

'Well, I wouldn't put it exactly like that,' Jenni contradicted. 'I had to insist on coming here actually. The Kaynahmians just wanted to surround you with an army and attack the castle.'

This, at least, the Dark One paid attention to. 'The Deliverer *dares* to tread this dark path alone?'

'Yes, she does. As you can see...'

'Then you come to your death!' Abramoth cried victoriously. 'I have had enough of sword-wielding numskulls splitting the heads of my ancestors. This time, there will be no mistake! The Dark shall triumph!'

'Please, there's no need to shout,' Jenni said, pulling a sour face. 'I don't wield a sword. And there'll be no head-splitting. I've come to negotiate. War is uncivilised and wasteful. There is always a better way.'

'No, there isn't!' Abramoth said. 'Blood must run black in the fields, children must grieve the death of their mothers. Mothers must grieve the...'

'Be quiet!' Jenni said. 'This is real life, you know. How would you like *your* children's blood to mess up the fields? Really! Fighting hurts people, your people included. And it's such a waste of money, too.'

The Dark One appeared to consider these words, and then blinked rapidly. He pointed a long, white finger at Jenni. 'Enough of your sorceress charms! I am invulnerable to your ploys! Prepare to die, woman, most horribly.' He raised his hands in a threatening manner, purple sparks sizzling round his fingers.

'Now, look here,' Jenni said, marching towards him, her hands planted firmly on her hips. 'If you must know, I'm feeling a little pre-menstrual today, and I don't want to lose my temper! Stop acting like a naughty child, sit down, and listen to what I have to say!'

The Dark One raised his eyebrows a little, but lowered his hands. 'Feisty, aren't you!' he said.

'When I have to be. Now, tell me, what exactly do you hope to gain by turning Kaynahmia into a wasteland?'

The Dark One sat down and shrugged. 'It's my profession,' he said. 'That's what I do; lay waste. It's hereditary.'

'But what's the point? It always ends in the Dark One being vanquished, you know that.'

'Well, so far, the cycle has tended to end that way,' he agreed. 'But I intend to change that.'

'As did your father, no doubt, and your father's father, etc.'

The Dark One pulled a peevish face. 'There has to be a first time,' he said, defensively.

'Precisely!' Jenni said. 'A first time to change things completely. Why not make your peace with Kaynahmia? Live to a ripe old age. You could do with some help renovating this place. It's a mess.'

'You forget, sweet lady. If I kill you, the Kaynahmians won't have a Deliverer. I'll be able to conquer them immediately.'

'Ah,' Jenni said, thinking wildly, 'what you haven't realised is that I am a *martyr* Deliverer. If you kill me, my blood will turn into a poison storm that will destroy you instantly, and, incidentally, any heirs you might having hanging around.'

'Oh, there's no worry about that. My heirs just spring into being when I'm dead,' Abramoth said, 'but I must admit, this is a new angle. What a quandary! You could be lying, of course.'

'Deliverers never lie!' Jenni announced grandly, and added, 'you should know that.'

The Dark One nodded glumly and sighed. 'Yes. Oh, damn! All my life I've been working towards this moment, ransacking nearby communities, spreading a bit of pestilence. I don't think I could go on living, if I couldn't do that. What would I do to pass the time? This is dreadful, absolute hell. Perhaps you should just split my head after all.'

'You could move,' Jenni said. 'You're obviously rich, so go somewhere warm and sunny. Buy a villa by the coast or something. Leave this place to the trolls.'

'They're orcs,' he said, and sighed again. 'Oh, I don't

know, sun isn't really my thing. I need darkness and dankness, fiery pits and sulphur lakes.'

'But it's so miserable here. It can't do anything for your depression.'

'Who says I'm depressed?' the Dark One said sharply. 'I revel in my depravity and evil, I am content!'

'Oh, come on,' Jenni said, sitting down on the arm of his chair. 'You're obviously depressed. Depressed people don't clean up around themselves and, well, just look around *you*! I'm sure you'd feel differently if you changed your environment.'

'You don't understand,' said the Dark One, mournfully. 'I am hated and despised in every corner of the world. Wherever I tried to run, the people would want to destroy me. This is the only place where I am safe.'

'Oh, rubbish,' Jenni said. 'If you have a peace conference with Kaynahmia, blame everything on your parents, and say you've always disliked the situation, people's opinions will change. You look like a real star to me. People like stars, especially when they're reformed criminals. Trust me. I know what I'm talking about.'

Abramoth rested his chin on his fist and gazed up at her. 'I wish I could believe you. I also wish I'd attacked Kaynahmia before you got here.'

'Look, Abramoth, if you must know, my reputation rests on being able to deal with this problem my way. The other side are as keen on this war as you are. You're as bad as each other. Do me a favour, and let me prove them wrong, will you?'

The Dark One smiled. 'Well, seeing as you put it that way...' he said.

'Shake on it!' Jenni said.

The Dark One nodded uneasily and tentatively put his long-fingered white hand into her own.

Jenni was convinced the people of Kaynahmia weren't too pleased that her negotiations with Abramoth had been successful. As she had suspected, they rather liked wars themselves. Still, they had to face the fact that when they had asked their goddess for help, Jenni Brampton had been given to them. Perhaps Kaynah Herself was getting a bit sick of the tedious cycle of Dark Ones, wars and heroes. Through Jenni's arbitration, an arrangement had been made between Abramoth and the Duke of the City. In return for minerals from the mountains of Theng, Kaynahmia would provide various comforts for the Dark One, including a team of interior designers, and domestic staff. The orcs had been worried about their position in the new order, but Jenni had dissuaded them from emigrating en masse to seek a new Dark master abroad, encouraging them instead to better themselves, and seek employment in the new mines that were being dug.

Now that all the fuss was over, Jenni didn't really know what to do with herself. She'd half expected to be sucked back to her old world, but nothing like that had occurred. Upon being questioned, Primula told her that all previous heroes had retired to the coast, once their quests had been completed. Jenni thought the same thing was expected of her. A pity. She felt she had somehow woken up, come alive, found herself, in Kaynahmia. She felt restless, eager for more adventure. The prospect of joining the colony of ex-heroes on the coast, even if they were people from home, did not excite her particularly. She was also still worried about her eyesight. Her lenses hadn't been cleaned of protein build-up for two months, and were getting more and more uncomfortable. Targ, after his clumsy wooing of Jenni had failed to produce tangible results, had moved on, seeking new quests. Jenni was lonely. She could not communicate with the Kaynahmians very well, and had more in common with the ugly orcs, who at least seemed to possess a fairly down-to-earth view of life. Abramoth, while his castle was being refurbished, had gone off on a world tour, which Jenni herself had suggested. Now, she wished she'd pressed for him to take her with him.

One day, she walked to the hills beyond the city, sat down on one of the grassy summits, and took out her lenses. She held them in her palm and watched them curl up and dry out. She blinked at the horizon, which was nothing but a blur of green and blue to her. How long would it take for her to get a headache? She heard the beat of hooves, the clink of harness, and a black horse crested the hill. Jenni squinted at it, as someone dismounted.

'They said you'd come this way,' said a male voice.

'Abramoth, you're back!' Jenni tried not to sound too pleased. 'What about the world tour?'

He sat down beside her on the grass, letting his horse wander around to eat. 'I got bored. There are too many Dark Ones about. I found it embarrassing really.' He groaned. 'Look at all this brightness! It's revolting. Makes my eyes ache!'

'At least you can see it,' Jenni said. She explained to him about her eyesight and showed him her lenses, which were nothing more than two wizened bits of plastic by then.

'Fascinating,' said Abramoth, 'but nowhere near as ingenious as the optical fluid my father invented. The Kaynahmians aren't quite as scientifically advanced as my family, of course. I wouldn't have expected them to come up with anything better than those pathetic things!'

'Hang on,' Jenni said. 'I didn't get these lenses from Kaynahmia. There's nothing here to correct bad sight. No-one seems to have bad sight, as it happens.'

'Really? Perhaps you'd better come to Theng with me then, if those dratted designers you inflicted on me haven't wrecked the laboratories.'

'You mean you can fix my sight?'

He shrugged, made a careless gesture. 'No problem. I'm as blind as a bat myself, without the fluid.'

Jenni leaned over and hugged him. 'Great! That's wonderful.' She was encouraged by the fact that Abramoth didn't try to pull away. 'Now, there is one other problem I have,' she said. 'And seeing as you appear to have some kind of medical knowledge...'

'What problem?' he asked.

'Well, it's a bit personal... I - er - well, I'm not that keen on having children, you see...'

'Oh, that!' Abramoth interrupted. 'Even simpler. You simply find yourself a lover who can't make you pregnant, who because of his racial make-up, is quite capable of amorous behaviour, but who is infertile and merely self-regenerates when appropriate.'

'Oh. And how do I recognise such a man?' Jenni asked.

'Easily. Usually, they're very short-sighted, and fond of the dark.'

'Mmm,' Jenni said. There was a slight pause. 'Well, you're right, it is terribly bright out here. I think I fancy a few days locked in a dark, dank castle. Can you suggest anywhere?'

'I've already asked you to Theng, haven't I?'

Jenni smiled and unwound her arms from Abramoth, stretching out on the grass. 'Well,' she said, 'this *has* been an interesting day. I feel as if another adventure has just started!'

Jenni and Abramoth lived a full and happy life together in Theng. When Abramoth died, an old, contented man, a youth stepped forth from the husk of his body. The Kaynahmians wanted him to carry on the tradition of his grandfathers, and enquired whether he would consider becoming Dark. Nothing ever seemed to happen in Kaynahmia now, and they missed the old ways. 'Life is too predictable and safe,' they said. 'We need a Dark One to keep things balanced.'

The son of Abramoth, however, had much of Jenni's common sense, for although she was not his mother, her opinions had influenced his father considerably. He suggested that, every couple of months, he would create a few haunted fogs and cast them over the land, he would spawn pit-monsters and make them prowl through the village, and also send out the orcs on raids, with mock weapons. The

Kaynahmians could destroy all the haunts and monsters, because they would not be real creatures exactly, and fight off the orcs, but also with mock weapons.

The project proved very successful, and has been continued to this day. It keeps everybody happy.

Candle Magic

The candle was already lit when Felicia came home with the intention of enjoying her Friday afternoon off in peace. She hadn't realised her flat-mate, Emma, was off work as well. A scorching day, too hot for May, and Emma was sitting on the floor lighting candles.

'Oh, you're here,' Emma said, looking up. She sounded as disappointed as Felicia to find she'd have company for the day. The air in the room was thick with pungent fruity incense.

'Hmm. Had time in lieu. What are you doing?' Felicia went to open the windows.

Emma glanced at the candle. 'Thinking...'

'Thinking...' Felicia nodded. There was a suppressed excitement in Emma's expression she was familiar with. 'Anyone I know?'

Emma smiled secretively. 'You know what's going on...'

Felicia shook her head and dragged her handbag, which was more like a satchel, over to the sofa. She slumped down and delved for her cigarettes in the depths of the bag. 'I don't think either of us know what's going on,' she said, lighting up and inhaling with gusto.

Emma laughed again. 'Poor Fliss, you're just too practical!'

Felicia disliked the implication in Emma's words. She knew Emma often thought her a dull, unimaginative creature. She took a deep breath. 'Look, Em, I'm a friend, so I have to say it: you're obsessed!' She waved her arm emphatically, scattering cigarette ash over the sofa and Emma's lap.

Emma brushed the grey powder from her curled legs as if without thinking. Her expression had soured. 'So grateful for your support!'

'Em, *please!*' Felicia groped behind the sofa for an ashtray. 'What am I supposed to think?' She laughed nervously. 'Next, it'll be eye of newt and wing of bat; you're crazy!'

Emma drew up her knees gracefully, pushing back her auburn hair. She reached towards the single blue candle standing in a congealing pool of wax on the coffee-table. Her fingers were a fan against the flame. 'It can be done,' she murmured.

A week previously, Emma had announced that she was in love. Felicia had known Emma for a long time and recognised immediately that her friend had fallen victim to yet another of the intense romantic fantasies, to which she seemed particularly vulnerable in the spring. Outside the window, even in the heart of the city, there was a thrumming vitality to the air. It was possible to feel the thrust of growth, and to be carried with it. Emma's imagination certainly seemed drawn to greater extravagances. Felicia was used to this ritual behaviour. Sometimes she became impatient with it, at other times she was prepared to be understanding. For all Emma's peculiar habits, she and Felicia got on together well, and Felicia had shared accommodation with too many people to undervalue that fact. Still, she and Emma were very different. Felicia had been in love three times in her life, and had once been engaged, but all her affairs had ended in infidelities and unpleasant scenes. Now, she was being cautious, and kept her few suitors at arm's length, allowing them the occasional privilege of her company in a restaurant or club, and even more rarely the odd night of sex in the flat. To Emma, however, love seemed to mean spending endless hours alone, locked in desperate reverie, a condition encouraged by periodic sightings of the object of her desires. It seemed almost like a sickness, a ravaging fever that burned her out. Actual relationships had occasionally sprung from her obsessions, but they had possessed the life-span of a plucked poppy. Felicia doubted Emma had ever been out with anyone that she wasn't obsessed with. Any other man who had the temerity to approach her was rebuffed instantly. Since Felicia and Emma had lived together in the flat - nearly four years now - Felicia had seen several beautiful young men go in and out of Emma's room, and a couple of those had wanted to become permanent fixtures. It had always been Emma who'd sent them packing. Felicia had even been out for a drink with one of them afterwards, to listen to his woeful rantings of unrequited love. Once Emma had decided she no longer liked them, they might as well not exist for her. Still, until the moment they cut their own throats with an unwise remark or behaviour Emma found disappointing, her regard for them was merciless in its intensity. No wonder they felt so bewildered once they'd been rejected. Felicia often felt very sorry for them, but she stood by her friend's determination not to stick with a relationship she was not happy with.

'You'll never learn, will you!' Felicia said, shaking her head, the remark softened by a smile.

Emma refused to be drawn into a sisterly spirit. She frowned. 'I know what you're thinking. "Not this again." I don't expect you to understand, but...' She hesitated. 'This time, it's different.' Before Felicia could respond, Emma uncurled from the floor and began to prowl about the room.

Felicia didn't know what to say, wary of encouraging Emma's fixations, but nervous of upsetting her too much. Emma was touching things in a slow, deliberate manner; her beads hanging across the mirror, her crystal in its nest of velvet on the sideboard, her own throat. She and Felicia were the same age - twenty-seven - although Felicia always felt so much older than Emma.

'Perhaps we should talk about it,' Felicia said, aware that her voice sounded too shrill. Even though she'd opened the windows, the air in the room was hot; hot and damp and dark. The flat only got the sun in the morning. Later, there might be thunder.

'Talk? There is little to say. I know what I want.' Emma

turned and smiled a cat's smile, lifting her thick hair in both hands. It appeared to be a studied pose, but Felicia had never quite convinced herself that Emma struck her regular dramatic postures consciously.

'Then, why bother telling me about it at all?'

Emma shrugged. 'I thought it best to, in case anything happened.'

'What do you mean by that?' Felicia became aware of tension across her forehead, a frown forming. Perhaps it was caused by the humid atmosphere. 'Sometimes, you frighten me, Em.' She stubbed out her cigarette with swift, sharp prods. 'What you need is a good time. Less mooning around, more real life.'

Emma ignored the advice. 'There's nothing to be afraid of. I *will* have him, Fliss...'

Felicia shook her head and gestured at the candle. 'And is that what this is all about? Sitting here being witchy and dreaming dreams? Oh, Em, I can't decide whether you want to be the Lady of Shalott or Cleopatra!'

'You always laugh,' Emma said nonchalantly, apparently unembarrassed. She came back to squat before the coffee table, her pale hand hovering over the candle flame, her eyes intent. 'This candle, it is exactly the right colour...' Her voice sounded portentous and full of intent.

Felicia sighed. Emma's mystical leanings occasionally bothered her; mostly, they could be ignored. 'It's just a candle,' she said, and then jumped up too quickly from the sofa. Emma's image seemed to vibrate before her eyes. She rubbed her face, finding her upper lip wet. 'Can't bear this heat! Want a drink?'

Emma shook her head. 'I'm ok, thanks.'

Left alone in the room, Emma cupped her hands around the flame. She took a deep breath, held it, breathed out slowly. 'Listen to me...,' she said to the flame. 'Help me...' She closed her eyes and threw back her head, clasping her crossed ankles. The image of The Man was difficult to conjure, because she was distracted by the sound of Felicia humming loudly to herself in the small kitchen off the sitting-room. She couldn't visualise his face properly. Traffic outside, the sound of children across the street as they played in the school playground; the clatter from builders working on the house next door: all mundane intrusions.

'I believe in what I want,' she whispered fervently, 'And to believe is to *make* it true.'

'What did you say?' Felicia's voice asked from the doorway.

At night, alone with the moon, it was easier for Emma to direct her thoughts. Arms by her side or across her breast, it didn't matter; she visualised. Felicia had argued: 'O.k. so he's good-looking, but that doesn't mean he's a nice person.' Felicia *would* say something like that. She was attracted to men who were like herself; dependable and direct, scrubbed and neatly dressed.

Emma undressed in the dark and spread out her Tarot cards face down on the rugs in the pale light that came in through the shivering, gauzy curtains. Silvery incense smoke filled the room with the scent of jasmine. She picked a card and held it to her chest for a while, without looking at it. Then, she examined the picture. It was The Moon; signifying secrecy and delusion. *No*, Emma thought. *It is mystery and magic.* She scooped the cards up into their silk wrap and lit a cigarette, leaning back against the end of her bed. She felt the flat was aware of her, its walls listening to the beat of her heart, her thoughts. Felicia was out with all her secretary friends, drinking in wine bars, no doubt being chatted up by dull men. Emma always felt the flat manifested a different personality when she was in it alone. In her opinion, people like Felicia, for all their good intentions, killed any subtle atmosphere that did not fit into their narrow view of reality. Their presence suffocated mystery. They were like rotor-scythes ploughing through an overgrown garden, restoring order to something that had been precious and beautiful in its wilderness.

Tonight, Emma felt powerful and it burned within her like hate. If she stood up, her head would brush the ceiling. Her heart was projecting a net of luminous beams, each of which pulsed like a star at its tip.

She couldn't remember where she had first seen The Man. She was aware Felicia privately scorned what she saw as Emma's regular crushes on people, but Emma couldn't convey to her friend how, this time, the invasion of her thoughts had been not only unwelcome, but somehow threatening. She was torn two ways by the yelping dogs of Resentment and Yearning. The last time she'd fallen in love had been devastating. The man had shattered all her dreams by being not only insensitive and coarse, but unintelligent. He'd confessed he'd not read a book since childhood, and the mirror of Emma's hopes had cracked from side to side. He had been beautiful, but the beauty had been a scale on his skin, easily scratched off. Since then, Emma had vowed not to fall into the same emotional state again. She would retain her common sense and snuff out any mad desires before they took hold of her. She was too old now for childish passions. Felicia was always saying she should go for personality rather than looks in a man, but for Emma the two had to be intertwined. She had very precise standards. Still, this did not mean the right person wasn't waiting for her somewhere. She must not make another mistake. Surely the intensity of her feelings now meant she might have found her soul-mate at last?

Felicia did not know to what extent the current infatuation had affected Emma, because Emma had kept the details quiet. She could not confess to how she had become a fevered, feral thing; spending whole evenings following The Man from bar to bar, skulking in shadows, awed and sickened by what she saw as his unbearable loveliness. His face looked intelligent, his bearing was aloof yet intriguing. He was like a well-bred animal; graceful and aware of his own beauty without seeming arrogant. All this, Emma had discerned from a distance. For some reason, she could not employ her usual tactics and approach him. It was not fear of rejection exactly, but perhaps a fear of being disappointed again. She'd seen him looking at her sometimes.

'Where have you been?' Felicia would say when Emma came in late alone.

'Out.' A shrug.

'Who with?'

Emma would lie. 'Pat, Alison... you know.' She didn't want Felicia to know she'd been on her own. Solitude was part of the condition. The pain conjured by the aching desire for The Man was companioned by an exquisite melancholy. She had to be alone, in order to surrender herself to the daydreams that filled her mind. At work, it was easy, because she could fantasise as she was hunched over her drawing-board. Nobody would bother her because she seemed so busy. In her mind, she lived out a hundred scenarios of actually speaking to The Man, different ways in which they could meet. She knew the best nights for locating him: Saturdays, Sundays, and occasionally on Wednesdays. He always seemed to be with people, but she couldn't remember their faces. She didn't know any of them. They were nobodies, eclipsed by his flame. At night, she dreamed of cards falling like leaves, twisting before her face, but she could never see their symbols. During the day, she would sometimes get angry with herself and say aloud, beneath her breath, 'This is stupid! I'm going to forget it. It's pathetic!' And she would straighten her spine, empty her mind of wandering thoughts, apply herself to a mundane task, and imagine the yearning had gone. But then the night would come again and that strange magic would start stirring within her and she would say to herself, 'I have to see him,' and find herself on the street, pulling on her jacket, her face hot, walking quickly.

Sometimes, she couldn't find him, and then she'd become a demented thing, knocking back drinks too swiftly, going into places that normally, she'd never dare enter alone. It was as if he <u>knew</u>. At the end of the evening, almost out of her mind, she would catch a glimpse of him; his tawny hair, his dark eyes, and that would be enough. Then she could go home again and light the candles. Sometimes, she wondered whether she really had seen him or not.

On Saturday, Felicia thought Emma looked listless and depressed. The fizzing euphoria, so typical of her infatuations, was absent. Could it really be different this time? She knew so little about Emma's latest crush. She resolved to be sympathetic, and made them a pot of tea so they could sit down to a chat. 'How many times have you spoken to this man?' she began, intent on building a dossier of facts about him.

Emma's eyes skittered away from Felicia's own. Felicia made a mental note.

'Well.... Once. He passed me in the pub. Put his hand on my arm.'

'Is that all?' Felicia tried to keep her voice low. 'What did he say?'

'He said "excuse me".'

Felicia took a sip of tea to smother an involuntary smile. Then she put down her mug. 'Emma... how can I say this? You can't be in love with someone you don't know.'

Emma jumped up angrily. 'Then it isn't love! Something else!' She clawed her hair.

The outburst surprised Felicia. 'What else?'

Emma stared at her fiercely with eyes that seemed to burn within. 'I've been looking for something,' she said quickly, 'looking for years. Now I think I've found it. I have to have him, Fliss. We have to have each other. I know it's right. I feel it. I...'

'Hold on!' Felicia held up her hands. 'Does he ever look

at you, make any signal he's interested in you?'

Emma swung around and began to play with her beads hanging over the mirror. 'Of course he does.'

'Then perhaps you should simply make the first move. Go up to him. Speak. It can't be that difficult. Pat or Ally would be with you.'

Emma was silent.

'Shall we go out together tonight?' Felicia suggested brightly. 'We haven't been out together for weeks! You've been seeing so much of Pat and...'

'I need some of his hair!' Emma interrupted hotly. 'Then it would work better. I'd have a focus. I need to bring him to me.'

'Emma,' Felicia began carefully, 'if you got close enough to him to pull his hair out, you could also say hello...'

Emma suddenly threw back her head and laughed loudly, causing Felicia to visibly wince. She saw something ancient standing there, something primeval yet essentially female. Emma thought Felicia lacked imagination, but she did not.

Although Felicia hadn't seen The Man, Emma had described him in such detail, she felt she'd recognise him if she saw him. Tall, long hair, and, like Emma, a lover of the colours black and purple. Emma had found paintings in books with which to illustrate her descriptions. 'His nose is like this, his mouth like this...' Felicia indulgently paid attention, inwardly rather appalled that a woman of Emma's age could act so immaturely. This man might as well be a famous musician or a film star, seeing as Emma had built up her love for him on appearances alone. Still, Felicia comforted herself that Emma would soon tire of this paragon, once she got to know him. So far, all her infatuations had burned themselves out quickly, once the object of desire proved themselves to be disappointingly human and therefore unworthy of Emma's attention. Therefore, in Felicia's opinion, Emma must introduce herself to this new idol as soon as possible. What

Emma expected from a man was, in Felicia's opinion, virtually supernatural, and nobody could live up to that.

'Emma, tonight, you are going to speak to your fancy man, even if I have to drag you over to him myself!'

'Perhaps you're right,' said Emma.

Felicia sighed. How could a grown woman be such a child?

Emma dressed herself in a long black dress that swirled like smoke around her ankles, and wore her rich, dark red hair loose down her back, almost as if it was a symbol of her own power. Felicia dressed in a short dress that hugged her figure and shouted at the night in tropical colours. Both wore jackets - Emma, leather, and Felicia something expensive in cashmere she'd picked up in town. She and Emma walked along an avenue that was fragrant with spring, an unlikely-looking pair of companions. Above them, the moon rose full and heavy. Felicia chattered on aimlessly about people at work, mostly because she could think of nothing else to say. Inside, she felt quite nervous.

Emma appeared serene, nodding vaguely at Felicia's remarks, a slight smile on her face. She was imagining that a black panther walked on either side of her, and her hands were touching each one lightly between the ears.

They went from bar to bar, drinking, Felicia talking, an occasional friend pausing to chat; the evening stretched before them. Emma looked feverish, as if she was about to go into battle, and her eyes were never still, scanning faces. Looking at her friend's strained expression and darting eyes, Felicia thought, 'I don't really know this woman; she is a stranger.' And bought them both another drink.

Emma raised her glass, smiled. 'The elixir of life!' she said.

It was late, nearly closing time in the bar that had an extension until two, when Emma eventually spotted The Man.

She hissed and grabbed Felicia's arm savagely. 'There!'

Bodies milled around them, obstructing sight. There was high laughter, the offence of conflicting perfumes.

Felicia peered. 'Where?' Her face had gone shiny. She was beginning to grin back at the shaved-neck office boys lurking at the boundary of her and Emma's space.

'Over there.'

Felicia giggled, and stood up. 'Right, this is it. Come on!'

Emma pulled her back down onto her stool. 'No!' For a moment, she sat silent, her head bowed, and then she looked. up. 'I'll go alone. I have to.' She swallowed the last of her drink, stood up and smiled shakily. 'Well, this is it! Now or never!'

Felicia raised her glass. 'Good hunting, then!.'

Felicia let herself into the flat alone. All the rooms were in darkness. Felicia didn't like the way the flat felt when it was dark. She turned on lights everywhere, and picked up the remains of Emma's candle, which was nothing more than a blue puddle in an old saucer on the coffee-table. Kicking off her shoes, Felicia padded into the kitchen and turned on the kettle. She felt light-headed, but not drunk. The night had been fun. Pity Emma had walked out on her. Hardly a sensible thing to do. No woman should walk the streets alone in the early hours of the morning. Luckily, Felicia had had enough cash left to get a cab.

The kettle thumped and groaned to itself. Felicia put instant coffee and sugar into a mug. There was a click, followed by a disgruntled whine as the kettle switched itself off. As she picked it up, Felicia became aware of the intense silence of the flat beyond the kitchen. It seemed as if time had stopped.

Then the sounds came.

It was like flapping, something huge and dark, flapping. Felicia ran out into the living-room, convinced an owl, or some other large bird, had got in and was rampaging round the flat. The noises stopped the instant she walked into the room. For a moment, there was silence, and then she heard a muffled crash from the hallway, followed by an abrupt mew or stifled cry. Felicia stood in the living-room doorway, perplexed, the kettle still held in one hand. The hall beyond looked endless. Emma's door was closed.

'Em!' Felicia called. The silence had come back, that thick silence she hated. The walls seemed vigilant, waiting. Felicia crept forward.

Suddenly, a great sound, a trumpeting, like a siren going off, blasted right through her. She realised it was a scream. Rapid, frantic sounds, like something beating itself against the door, came from Emma's room. Then, again, silence.

'Em!' Felicia ran to the door, but was reluctant to open it, afraid. She knocked on it loudly. 'Em, are you all right?' She put her ear against the door. She thought she could hear Emma's voice. No words, just inarticulate sound; distress.

Are you brave? Felicia asked herself. Is someone in there with her? Is someone hurting her? She gripped the kettle more firmly, and put her hand upon the door handle. She expected the door to be locked, but it wasn't.

Emma was alone, sitting awkwardly on the floor beneath the window, which was slightly open. The lamps were off, but the street-lights outside shone right into the room. Emma's possessions, which she treasured so highly, had been strewn about the room, as if in fury. And over everything were shining droplets of a dark liquid; the walls, the floor, the bed. Near Emma, by the window, a large, dark puddle covered the carpet. Felicia's gorge rose; at first she thought it was blood. But the smell in the room, the overwhelming stink of burnt wax, of a hundred candles recently extinguished, quickly advised her sensible mind otherwise. Still, she was aghast. 'Em, what's happened?' She glanced around herself, afraid some man would leap from the shadows.

Emma stared at her without expression. Her feet were bare; spattered with droplets of wax. It looked as if she'd been scratched.

Felicia advanced cautiously into the room, stepping over the mess. Emma owned over a dozen Tarot packs, and they seemed to have been scattered at random around the room. Many of the cards were torn. 'What the hell have you done? Em... Em?' Felicia put down the kettle and squatted beside her friend. She attempted to pull Emma into a comforting embrace, but Emma struggled away.

'Get off me!' Her voice was unnaturally gruff. She seemed to have no whites to her eyes.

Felicia felt nauseous. The smell rising from the huge puddle of congealing wax at Emma's feet was too cloying; sweet, but somehow meaty as well. Some cheap scented candles? No, surely not. How many would Emma have had to burn to produce such a pool? There were feathers stuck in it; feathers and unidentifiable dark lumps. Felicia looked away. She did not want to think about it. 'Emma, where did you get to? You shouldn't have come home alone. Why are you upset? What did he say? Wasn't he interested?'

Emma blinked slowly and crawled along the wall on hands and knees. Then she squatted with her knees up by her ears, her mouth stretched into a grin. There was a dark oily crust around her nostrils, as if she'd been bleeding wax. 'I went to him. I spoke...'

'What did he say?'

Emma sighed, her head rolling from side to side. 'Everything. Everything that I wanted to hear.'

'Then why did you walk out like that?'

'We walked out together....'

Felicia stood up, brushed down her dress. 'Emma, don't lie! I saw you. You went out of that place like a hurricane! In fact, you knocked one girl's drink all over her. I thought he'd told you where to go!'

Emma threw back her head. It looked as if she was laughing, but there was no sound. 'We were together,' she said, in the same dull, low voice. 'We are together now, and he is with me always.'

'Emma... Emma!'

Emma had clasped her knees, and began to rock gently. She sang an insistent refrain: 'Together, forever, together, forever...'

Outside, the moon hung low in the sky like a bag of blood, mottled with cloud. A full moon, a lunatic's moon. Felicia heard a dog whine in the yard next door.

Look into the candle flame, Emma. Make a wish...

Of a Cat, but her Skin...

She ran into the shadows of the trees, down hill, down the worn paths. He called after her 'Nina! Nina!' She ignored it. Her sandalled feet hit the bare earth. Another afternoon ruined, another scene. Am I mad? Am I? Only anger, exasperation, gave her the strength and the freedom to run away. And that too would be brief. Still, the experience while it lasted was exhilarating. He did not run after her, knowing she would return eventually, contrite.

Soon, her chest began to ache and she slowed her pace to a walk, panting heavily. She felt shaky at the exertion, but tingling too. For minutes, maybe an hour, she was free. Free of him, her weakness. This was a deserted part of the garden, far from the restored Victorian tea-rooms, the landscaped formal pleasances, the slowly-moving river. Nina preferred this kind of scenery, with its great old trees, hugged by lush grass, too green to be real, perhaps nurtured by unhealthy secrets buried deep. Woody nightshade tumbled across the path, bearing dark purple velvety flowers, with spears of shocking yellow at their hearts. Amaradulcis; the bittersweet poison. It seemed no-one had walked here for years. Sunlight came down through the high canopy of oak and beech, stroking raw perfume from the herbs and grasses. Nina paused and took a deep breath. In such an idyll as this, could the real world with all its terrors, cruelties and abuses ever intrude? She felt protected, tranquil, as if the path had closed behind her. Scott would call this yet another symptom of her 'dreaminess', as he referred to it. 'You're too dreamy; that's your trouble.' Perhaps it was true, but if so, why should that be seen as a flaw?

The trees receded and revealed a small glade, ceilinged by ancient branches. A green room. The path seemed to end here. At the centre of the clearing was a weathered black monument: there were many of them scattered around the grounds of the old house. Some had been defaced over the years, others restored. This one appeared unmarked by human vandalism, but neither had it recently been cleaned. A stone dais of two steps supported a wide, four-sided obelisk. Crouched on the apex, was the statue of a lean cat. It was frozen in a pose of alertness, a hunter's stoop, forever gazing back along the path, as if waiting to pounce. Nina sat down on the steps and put her hot face into her hands. What am I going to do? She had asked herself this question many times. The constant arguments with Scott, the groundless accusations, the pestilent silences that gnawed away at her resolve would never go away; she knew that. And yet she felt so powerless; in a financial and emotional sense. She had some money of her own, but not much. She was an illustrator of children's books, but was neither well-known nor well-paid. Scott, a successful designer, held the reins of her life; she was trapped in the traces. But there were good days, weren't there? And she did love him, despite his jealousies, which were fretful and anxious, and therefore cruel. She knew the problem was his, and that it ran very deep. Sometimes, in dark moments of bare honesty, he would weep like a child in fear and frustration. Because of this, she could never leave him. He was a casualty of his own life.

The argument that afternoon had been senseless, as usual. They were taking a couple of well-earned weeks off work, renting out a cottage in the country only a short distance from the city where they lived. So far, they had spent every day exploring local historical sights. Both of them were interested in the past. Admittedly, things had been fine until today, no arguments at all. But something had ignited his temper. The paintings in the hall of Elwood Grange. Nina had admired them: fading reminders of a past age; Lords and

Ladies of haughty mien, long dead, staring down at the milling masses for eternity, disdainful of those who came to pick over their remains. Without thinking, she had remarked that one of the couples portrayed were very striking for their time. 'They have an almost twentieth century look,' she'd said. 'They look like a couple of rock stars, or perhaps people who run a dodgy religion!' Her light comments were a grave mistake.

Scott said nothing at first and then, outside on the wide, sweeping steps, with the heat of summer baking the arms and bare heads of the tourists, he'd presented his sulk to her. Nina had been confused at first. What had she done? She could think of nothing. Nina was used to living her life by walking on eggshells, and had become very adept at doing so. If the fragile shells broke nowadays, it was rarely because of anything she'd actually said or done, but something generated in the hot, aching nest of Scott's fecund paranoia.

'What is it?' she'd asked, wondering if someone else inside the Grange had upset him.

He'd walked off, between a stand of yews, towards the river. She'd followed. 'What is it?'

Eventually, the time came for him to wheel round on her. 'You always like men who are nothing like me! I don't know why you're with me! You're just sponging off me!'

Nina was aghast. Weariness was invoked immediately as her body reacted in its accustomed manner to verbal attack. 'I don't know what you mean,' she said.

Scott made an explosive sound. 'That pretty fucker in the painting!' He strode off.

Nina followed. 'Scott! Don't be absurd!'

They had argued all the way to the river, along the gravel path, past the gazebo and the folly Grecian temple. Eventually, like a chemical flooding her system, something clicked on in Nina's mind. Enough! She almost felt the physical change.

Uttering a wordless cry, she'd fled, prompting curious

stares from other tourists.

What now? Nina leaned back against the cool stone. It was so peaceful here. She wondered at the significance of the place. Why the narrow path through the trees to this glade, why the monument dominated by a cat? Scott had the guidebook in his jacket pocket. She wished she'd kept it in her shoulder bag. There was a definite presence to this place, something brooding, and yet she did not feel discomforted by it. If anything, it echoed her mood. She felt strongly that she would not be pursued here, and even doubted whether any other tourists would appear along the path. This was her time and, for these scant moments, her place. It happened to her sometimes. Just when she needed them, she found sanctuaries. It could be an empty car park, a deserted alley, a wooden bench in a park. But whenever she found them, she experienced an encompassing feeling of security, and apartness. Had this only happened to her since she'd lived with Scott? She couldn't remember.

Nina stood up and jumped off the steps, walked around the clearing, looking up at the monument. She'd always wanted a cat, but Scott didn't like them. She felt unable to persevere, sure that if she acquired a kitten, it would suffer at Scott's hands. He wouldn't be overtly cruel, but she envisaged it would not be allowed in at night, and most of the house would be off-limits to it. There would be complaints about mess and smells and hairs. Might as well not have one. She realised, with bitter regret, that was her answer to everything. Easier to give in, to let him have his way. The tense atmosphere in the house when she defied him seemed to burn her skin. She could not bear it.

Behind the monument, the stone was lichened and damp, and it seemed to be less weathered. Details of carvings could easily be discerned. Nina mounted the steps again, slippery here with moss, and put her fingers against the stone. A legend written there. Message from the past. She traced the word "mau". There was a carving of the sun and moon, and the words, "who shall play with a wounded prey". Perhaps the person who built the monument had not liked cats. Nina examined the other sides of the obelisk, but all the engravings were in Greek or Latin. On the most deteriorated side, that facing the path, she thought she discerned Egyptian hieroglyphics. An eclectic arcarnum. Nina smiled. She had already read in the guide book about how one of the nineteenth century earls of the estate had dabbled in the dark arts. Who, in the aristocracy, hadn't done at that time? she wondered. It seemed to have been fairly prevalent then. Gleeful tourist pamphlets sermonised about the mysterious trips abroad, the exposure to exotic belief systems, the desire to transcend the mundane in lives shorn by wealth of petty worries. Nina and Scott had visited many estates in order to search for the folly clues left by past incumbents who'd not been able to resist leaving proof of their obsessions behind, for those who chose to look for them. Nina had rarely felt anything unusual in these places, and she was sensitive to atmospheres.

Now, she stroked the damp, cool stone of the monument, and wondered. Her imagination supplied a history for it. The obelisk would have been commissioned by the woman in painting, she of the petrol blue gown, the heavy brows, the modern features. She had been a witch, of course, a co-celebrant with her partner of arcane delights. The guide-book spoke of earls and scholarly mysticism; the true sorcery remained secret. Nina smiled. Here, the cat, symbol of woman in her most terrifying aspect. Not she of claw and fang and raised cry, nor of motherhood and nurturing, but she of the night, of treachery sheathed with eloquence, of the ability to torture without compassion, of stealth, hidden beauty and disdain, the allure that could wither men's hearts, destroy them. Nina was sure that these were the things men feared existed unseen in women. Although they could never witness the true witcheries of female kind, which Nina thought were intensely personal and impossible to articulate, men found the potential of their existence all the more fascinating and terrifying. She felt that men were always trying to guess what went on in the secret selves of women. Groping to understand a virtually alien species, they imagined they knew the hearts of women, but they could never actually be sure whether the secrets existed or not. And yet, even as they feared, and struck out in every way at the object of their terror, they yearned for their dark suppositions to be realised. The Goddess beneath the skin. The potent, unspoken strangeness that separated women from men was, Nina believed, the very thing that bound men to them. The cat, the familiar of darkness was perhaps the most enduring symbol of this secret power. Nina wondered if that was why she was so drawn to the animal. She herself felt very much in tune with all that the cat represented. The dark, vengeful sibling of the bright, yielding girl. She Who Must Not Be Unleashed. Nina wondered whether she was alone in feeling the presence of this coiled inner self, an aspect of her being she had to control with a firm hand, or whether all women felt her crouching there inside. Nina had never unleashed the cruel one, and never wanted to, fearful she'd be unable to hide it inside herself again afterwards. But in moments of emotional crisis, she was always conscious of the coiled one's presence, her voice.

She smiled and patted the stone, said, 'Mau!' The feline: a symbol of liberty, because no animal is as opposed to restraint as a cat. Let any unwelcome intruder tread the path to her grove with caution.

He was still waiting for her, sitting on the bank of the lazy river, throwing stones into the central current. Nina walked up behind him. She felt excoriated, yet vigorous. Her weariness was not rekindled by the sight of his back, rigid with misery. She experienced, in a moment of blinding clarity, a supreme yet serene pity for the man. He would not, and could not, ever grow up emotionally, and yet the strengths of childhood had died in him. She sat down beside him. He turned to look at her, censure in his face. She could not care about it. 'Are you hungry?' she asked. 'Let's go eat.'

He did not mention the argument, which was unusual. She thought he looked at her with wary puzzlement throughout the rest of the day.

The following morning, they drove back to the city. Nina felt removed from reality; she could not stop day-dreaming. Scott, as if sensing her mood, was temperate. They addressed one another across a tidy boundary. They were supposed to have stayed in the cottage for another day, but rain had come - a downpour - too heavy to walk out in. And the rooms of the cottage were gloomy; too small for people with sensitive skins to occupy together.

Nina was relieved to get home - she always was - but regretted not being able to investigate the cat monument further. That evening, she browsed through the guidebook to Elwood Grange. The house itself was not that remarkable, she thought, and the grounds predictable, but for the hidden place where the monument stood. The obelisk was not listed in the index of follies to be found at Elwood, but a map of the gardens showed that the book was out of date, and that the glade with the monument had not been open to the public when it had been published. Flicking through the pages, Nina noticed a photograph of the painting that had caused her argument with Scott. Lady Sydelle and Rufus, Earl of Thurlow. They had been young when the portrait had been painted. Dark garments, dashing, almost foreign-looking features, glossy black hair. They had to be brother and sister, of course, not husband and wife as she'd first thought. The background, like their clothes, was dark; a dusky landscape. Only their white faces and hands glowed from the picture. Lady Sydelle's fingers were curled over something on her lap. Nina lifted the book to hold the photograph close to her table-lamp. Her heart contracted. There was a cat on the Lady's lap. Nina lowered the book. She had to see the picture again, and the monument. She felt as if she had discovered something marvellous. She glanced across at Scott, who was reading yesterday's paper, a can of beer open by his chair. He was back at work next week. So was Nina, although she didn't have to leave the house for it. She had a children's book to illustrate, and the deadline had almost crept up on her. Still, she could justify a trip out to make sketches. The book was about a witch and her cat.

She mentioned it to Scott in bed. 'I'm thinking of going back to Elwood Grange. I'm so behind with my work. Lack of inspiration, I think, and I saw some great places at Elwood to use in my illos.'

'It's a long way for you to drive alone,' he said, which was a mild complaint for him.

'I'll take a friend with me,' Nina lied.

After Scott had left for work, Nina telephoned Elwood Grange and spoke to the tourist office. Would they be open that day? No. On Mondays, the Grange was closed to the public. Nina expressed disappointment, mentioned her work. The woman on the other end of the phone hesitated for only a moment. 'Ah, well perhaps we can make an exception, in that case,' she said.

Nina told her she could be at the Grange in two hours, perhaps sooner if the traffic wasn't bad. The only companion she took with her was the guide-book to the Grange, which lay on the passenger seat beside her. She wanted to be home before Scott got back from work, as she hadn't mentioned her trip to him again this morning. Seemed best not to.

The woman Nina had spoken to on the phone was called Lydia Hunt, and had apparently appointed herself as Nina's personal guide for the visit. Nina was disappointed. She'd wanted to roam around alone, but perhaps that had been too much to hope for. Before looking round the house, they had a cup of coffee in Lydia's office, and Nina talked about her work. Lydia thought one of her children might own a book that Nina had illustrated. 'People have come here before to research material for books,' Lydia said.

Nina nodded. 'These old places have their histories, don't they? It's fascinating. A wealth of material to be plundered!'

Lydia smiled. 'Mmm. A lot of the old stories are exaggerated for publicity purposes, I think.'

'So tell me about Lady Sydelle,' Nina prompted, smiling in complicity over her coffee cup.

Lydia laughed. 'Ah yes! Of course you would be interested in her!' She gestured with one hand; a confident, attractive woman, Nina thought. 'Lady Sydelle is my favourite character as well. She never married, even though she was a very beautiful woman, and I imagine local gallants must have thronged her threshold. The money too, would have been attractive to them.'

'And what were her secrets? I suppose she had some, or they were invented for her?'

'Her brother, the Earl, was rumoured to be rather a rake-hell. Well, to put it bluntly, he was an occultist.' Lydia pulled a sour face. 'Misguided boy! It was he who commissioned the zodiac ceiling in the music room, and the two Eleusinian folly shrines in the grounds. Lady Sydelle is not associated with her brother's rather insalubrious pursuits, but she did erect the tantalisingly obscure obelisk in the gardens after his death.'

'The cat monument,' Nina hurriedly interrupted. She felt breathless, almost faint.

Lydia nodded. 'It's actually called the Cat Stane. We only opened up that part of the gardens last season, and there's still work to be done there. Scholars presume the Stane's a bitter joke about Rufus' exploits - the melding of mystical symbols from several ancient cultures, none of them making much sense. It's supposed Sydelle was sceptical about the whole thing. She was very fond of Rufus, naturally, and took his death badly. Still, it's an odd memorial.'

'How did he die?' The atmosphere in the room seemed

to have become tense. Nina found herself thinking that at one time, the servants of Lady Sydelle had occupied this area of the house, whispers would have been exchanged here in times of crisis. Perhaps they still bled from the walls.

Lydia shrugged. 'Accounts vary, I'm afraid. His neck was broken. Some say it was caused by a hunting accident, others that he tumbled headlong down the main stairs in a drunken stupor. Whatever happened, he lived for nearly a week after the incident. Sydelle nursed him herself apparently.'

'No other legends?'

Lydia narrowed her eyes. 'You're looking for mysteries!'

Nina forced a laugh. 'Of course I am!'

'Lady Sydelle never divulged her secrets, I'm afraid! After Rufus died, she lived alone here to an advanced age, and died peacefully in her sleep. There are no diaries, no local legends. Nothing. She was a respectable woman.'

'But the Stane...'

Lydia stood up. 'Would you like to see it again?'

'Yes.' Nina put down her coffee cup and followed Lydia to the door. 'Could I see Sydelle's rooms?'

'If you wish, although she left little mark on them. The furniture is late Jacobean, and other people lived there after she died. Her bedroom is part of the guided tour - you've undoubtedly already seen it - but I can show you her parlour, if you like. It's only available for view by appointment.'

'Why?'

'The wife of the present Earl uses it as an office. But the family are never in residence when the Grange is open to the public.'

Nina felt downhearted by the time she and Lydia went out into the gardens. It was a dull day but the lush verdure of high summer was unsuppressed by the louring sky. The green was startling, acidic. The gardens held far more presence than the house itself. Nina had felt nothing in the rooms Lydia had shown her. No shade of Sydelle persisted there.

The two women took a slow stroll down to the obelisk.

Nina had collected her sketching pad from the car, intent on making a few quick drawings, even though it seemed her impressions of the monument might have been misguided. Lydia talked about how there was debate whether this untamed area of the gardens should be cleared or not.

'No, it shouldn't be touched!' Nina said.

'I agree,' Lydia replied. 'It's a pleasant walk.'

A cool breeze fretted the leaves of the trees overhead; there was a sense of agitation in the air. Then, the monument became visible around a corner.

It is here! Nina thought. *The spirit of the place! I wasn't wrong.*

'The monument will be cleaned in the autumn, restored,' Lydia said.

Nina mounted the steps, wondering whether her guide would approve of that, and touched the stone. 'I like it the way it is.'

Lydia peered at the hieroglyphics. 'It's a shame some of the inscriptions are damaged. This one was perhaps the most intriguing.'

'What did it say? Do you know?'

'It is still readable, just, if you can translate the symbols. I understand it says something like "what can you own of a cat but her skin".'

'How true,' Nina murmured, holding the words in her mind. 'How true.'

Lydia gave her an odd glance. Perhaps she was beginning to think her visitor was a little too intense. 'Well, shall I leave you to your drawing? Call back into the office before you leave and have another drink.' She glanced at the sky. 'Don't stay out here if it rains!'

'Thank you,' Nina said.

Lydia hesitated, as if she was about to say something, and then retreated up the path without speaking. Nina did not move for a few moments, so that the atmosphere could close behind Lydia's departing figure. Then, she moved back from the monument, so that she could look up at the cat. Perhaps she should have brought a camera with her. The animal looked as if it was waiting for something. Nina's hand moved quickly over the pages of her sketch pad. She meant to draw faithful representations of the obelisk, but was continually drawn to depict the sombre figure of a woman standing just behind the stone. Her skin prickled. She felt that soon the figure would manifest before her. Lady Sydelle; her hand against the cold stone of her private statement. 'What is your secret, what?' Nina whispered. 'Tell me.' She felt the answer was relevant to her own life. It was no coincidence she'd found this place.

Nina basked in the atmosphere of the glade; it was like rolling over and over in fur. When the rain came, she covered her sketch pad with her jacket and threw out her arms to the sky, let the fast, heavy drops fall onto her. Rain pattered against the foliage around her. She heard distant thunder. Nina shivered, glanced at her watch. What was she doing? If she didn't leave quickly, Scott would be home before her. Where had the afternoon gone?

There was no time to share another coffee with Lydia Hunt, but Nina briefly put her head round the door of the woman's office and thanked her for her help.

'My pleasure,' said Lydia. There was no offer of a repeat visit. She seemed affronted by the sight of Nina's soaked clothes and hair.

Nina raced down the country lanes, away from Elwood Grange. She felt excited, as if she was going to meet a new lover, which of course she was not. Sad to be so excited about nothing. She pushed a cassette into the tape player, but the music was intrusive. She turned it off. Lady Sydelle, what happened in your life? Nina felt that she knew. The Lady had never married, and the brother had been a rogue. Women of that time had little freedom, bound by convention, by financial dependence. Even the privileged were subject to such restraints. The closeness of the two figures in the portrait was surely unnatural for brother and sister? Was that it, then? Incest? But how could she murder a man she loved? The thought came into Nina's head so forcefully, she had to slow down.

Oh my God...

Nina pulled into the next passing place, and stopped the car. She leaned her forehead against the steering wheel. It seemed so obvious to her. Sydelle had both loved and hated her brother Rufus. Her emotions had been complex, beyond simple understanding. Magic. Darkness. A cat upon the stairs. A fall. Nina heard the cry; echoing. The footsteps of servants and a tall, slim figure in the shadows at the top of the stairs; a white face, watchful. The figure turned away from the chaotic scene of yelling servants, of blood upon the marble floor below. Something small ran ahead of her up the dimly-lit corridor. A black shape, a cat. Of course she nursed him. Of course. "Who shall play with a wounded prey?" She would have kissed his paralysed body. Her cat would have sat upon his chest, tasted his breath. Her soul was her own; dark and potent, full of repressed power, a power that had been repressed in women for centuries. He could direct her physical body, but her soul, her mind, no! What could he own of her, but her skin?

The sky was so dark, it was like twilight. Nina started the car, switched on the windscreen wipers, resumed her journey. On the motor way, she turned on the cassette tape. Faster cars hissed by her. She felt relaxed, at ease. The story might be the product of her own imagination, or not, but the effect was the same.

Scott was already home by the time Nina let herself into the house. 'Hi!' she called, brightly.

Scott appeared in the hall, wiping his hands on a towel.

'My God, what happened?' Nina cried. His face was bleeding, scratched.

'Where the hell have you been?' Scott demanded,

ignoring her question.

'I told you: Elwood.' Nina went to look at his cuts. 'You look like you've been attacked!'

Scott pulled away from her. 'I have! How many times do I have to tell you to check all doors and windows are locked before you go out? You left the kitchen window wide open. It's lucky we have anything left in the house! Anyone could have got in. As it was, we did have a visitor. I found them making themselves at home in my chair. Bloody animal!'

'A cat!' Nina said. She wanted to laugh, but managed to repress the urge.

'I don't know what you're grinning at. Damn thing nearly took my eye out when I tried to get rid of it.'

'I'm sorry; you're right. I should have checked the windows. I always forget!' Nina breezed past him into the kitchen, noticing his expression of surprise. Normally, she would have curled in on herself, refused to apologise, cringed away from his angry words, which would, of course, have invoked more of them. 'Have you started dinner?'

Scott trailed into the kitchen behind her. 'No...' He knew Nina sometimes bitterly resented doing all the cooking, but she would never say so. He went out to work; she worked at home. It only seemed fair she should cook the meals. She didn't have an hour's drive home through heavy traffic. 'What's wrong?' he asked.

Nina shrugged. 'Nothing. I feel fine.'

'You seem... hyped up about something.'

'No. I'm not. Shall we order a pizza?'

'If you like.' Scott felt uneasy. Buried anxieties patted at their grilles in the depths of his mind.

Nina went to the phone. 'What did you do with the cat?'

'It went out the way it came in. Knocked two plants off. I cleared up the mess.'

Nina ordered dinner. She felt as if she was about to burst. As she put down the phone, she said, 'Scott, I want a cat.'

He looked confused. 'What?'

'You heard. I was going to mention it tonight. I've always wanted one.'

Scott shook his head. 'Nina, don't be ridiculous. Who would look after it when we go away? It's such a responsibility. And what about the smell, the...'

'Scott, I want a cat.'

'I don't think...'

'And I'm going to have one.' She wondered why she had ever given in so easily to Scott's wishes. What had she been frightened of? It seemed ridiculous now. Scott's strategies involved attack; he was powerless when she attacked first. She marched into the lounge and threw herself down on the sofa.

'You're in a weird mood,' Scott said, following her into the room. 'Where have you really been? Who were you with?'

Nina threw up her hands and uttered an inarticulate sound of outrage. 'I've been to Elwood Grange, alone!'

'I don't believe you! Someone's been saying something to you! You're not yourself.'

'Oh shut up!' Nina's voice was low with contempt. 'Do you know, I'm sick of the way things are! I'm sick of your jealousy, and your pompous behaviour. Do you really think if I had a lover, I'd put up with you? Do me a favour! Things have got to change.'

Meekly, Scott sat down, staring at her with round, shocked eyes. Nina was staggered by his submissive posture; he was like a dog fearing a slap. She had expected a thunderous row, and had braced herself for it. Scott's reaction was the last thing she'd anticipated.

'You're not going to leave me, are you?' he said. It was a child's fear of abandonment.

Nina didn't answer immediately. Was she? She realised she'd always had the choice of walking out. She didn't have to put up with things she didn't like. Lady Sydelle had perhaps not had that choice. Nina had an income, albeit small, but she was not totally dependent. She had become used to a certain standard of living, that was all. 'I hope we can sort things out,' she said eventually.

The rain came down all night, but the air was hot. Nina opened the bedroom windows wide, and water came into to puddle on the window-sills. Scott made a complaint. Nina told him she'd wipe the water up in the morning. He said nothing more. She decided to make love to him, and let him cling to her afterwards. 'I love you,' he said. 'I love you so much.' She stroked his hair. Began to doze.

Something jolted her awake. In the darkness, with the sound of rain persistent against the night, the scent of it coming into the room, Nina saw a dark shape on the bed. She was frightened for only a moment. The dark shape stretched out, advanced towards her slowly. So long and lean. Then she heard it purring. Nina pulled the cat towards her, hugged its wet fur against her naked breasts, inhaled its musky perfume. The animal continued to purr rapturously, limp in her arms.

Scott woke up, turned on the lamp, looked at her. Her face was buried in the black pelt. It was an enormous cat. *I don't know her*, he thought, *I don't know anything about her.* He felt that she, like the cat, could leap away from him, out through the window into the wet darkness, knocking things over, breaking things as she went.

She turned her head and smiled at him. 'Here's my cat!'

'It's the same one,' Scott said in distaste. 'The one that scratched me.'

'I know. You threw her out, but she's come back.' Nina kissed the cat's brow.

Scott risked a strained grin. 'It must belong to someone. It's in such good condition. You can't just... keep it.'

Nina laughed. 'No, I can't. No-one can own a cat. But she'll stay with me. I know she will.'

Scott looked at the muddy paw-marks on the pale duvet. He said nothing. Something seemed to have come into the house, something more than a cat.

'She'll stay with me because she wants to,' Nina said in a low voice. 'And that is the only reason why any two creatures should stay together.'

Scott experienced a stab of panic. 'Are we all right?' he asked. 'Are we?'

Nina stared at him for a few moments, stroking the cat's head. Then she nodded. 'I think so. Go back to sleep.' The cat curled up beside her, and presently she leaned over Scott and turned off the lamp. Rich purrs filled the darkness.

Nina thought of the glade at Elwood Grange, the monument, the shadow of a long-dead woman against the stone. Was the obelisk bare of its guardian now? She wondered whether she should go back and see, but perhaps that would be disrespectful towards the power blossoming within her. It was a stupid thought, anyway. The stone cat would still be crouched upon the stone, staring back along the lonely path. The statue was still there, but the spirit wasn't. The spirit had moved on to seek another hearth. Had found it.

The Silver Paladin

with Sian Kingstone

'Run, Mariana, run!'

It wasn't a voice that called to her, but the beat of her own heart. Mariana ran away from the keep, through the windings of the herb garden - all that was left of her mother now - towards the gate in the outer wall, beyond which lay the darkness of the forest.

'My lady, wait!' Her maid-in-waiting, Sarah, came puffing behind, her round cheeks red with exertion.

Mariana glanced back over her shoulder, laughed with all the breath in the world, and ran into the shadow of the huge archway. The guards inclined their heads to her, but made no comment. Her excursions into the forest were common knowledge, but no one believed she strayed far, not with sensible Sarah at her side. The girls crossed the drawbridge and stepped onto the steep road that led down to the trees. The greenness called to Mariana, the verdure of high summer, with the trees as tall as cathedrals, peering down. She had to run again.

At the bottom of the hill, Mariana waited a few minutes for Sarah, who could not run so fast. While she waited, she spun around in a circle upon the deer-cropped sward. Her heart sang. She did not know why. Life, that day, was thrilling. She felt that she was on her way to an assignation, and in a way, she was.

Presently, Sarah caught up with her, a hand pressed to her side. 'Don't go far, my lady, don't go far.'

Mariana took hold of her maid's hand and hauled her towards the reaching toes of the forest, the carbuncled roots that sidled towards the hill. 'Be quiet, Sarah. Look around. We'll go as far as far can be.'

Sarah groaned, dragging her feet. She cast mournful glances back up at the imposing silhouette of the keep. 'We shouldn't.'

'Shouldn't, mustn't,' said Lady Mariana. 'I don't care. Come on!'

'But bears! And boars!'

Mariana laughed again. Bears were just shadows in the undergrowth, and boars a furtive, snuffling rustle in the distance. On a day such as this, they were her servants, her subjects. She had no fear of them. Fear was something else, and resided in walls of dark stone. It was heavy words, black looks, the sound of locks turning. Out here, she was free.

The girls passed beneath the first of the soaring sycamores. The air breathed moistly here, exhaling a scent of loam and cut leaves. Tiny, bright flowers sequinned the springy grass that looked too green to be real. 'Words have a weight,' Mariana said. 'Have you ever noticed that, Sarah?'

Sarah grunted, her eyes sliding to left and right, as if seeking the first tusked boar that would accost them. 'The only weight I can think of is that of Mistress Talbot's hand across my head when she finds out I've let you do this again.'

Mariana could not be bothered to pursue this topic. '"Do not" are heavy words and so is "chamber". "Sun" and "air" are light words. Can't you see that?'

'You're fey!' said Sarah, a common saying of hers.

'I hope so,' Mariana sighed. 'Fey is such a light word.'

'Wife is light,' observed Sarah.

Mariana's brow wrinkled into a frown. 'Perhaps so, but it is the lightness of a whip.'

Whip: she winced invisibly at the sudden, unwelcome memory. Her father did not beat her, but his words stripped and bit and pummelled her continuously. Light or heavy, they were his armoury. Mariana took a deep breath and banished the memory, at least for now. At this precise moment, she was free of it. She must look forward to the treasure of the forest that had been revealed to her. Coming to this place was a compulsion she could no longer ignore.

Sarah shook her head. Mariana knew that she was a puzzle to her maid, and that her actions often made stolid Sarah feel uncomfortable. Sometimes, Mariana couldn't help exploiting that. A mischief would come into her and she'd say things on purpose that she knew would make Sarah feel as pained as if a needle was being threaded through her skin. Mariana sensed a lot of what the servants thought of her. They believed her strangeness came from her mother. It was no secret that the Lady Ylaine had been the feyest of fey, although exactly what this might have entailed had never been revealed to Mariana. She had been told her mother had died in child-birth, even though Mariana was sure she could recall vague memories of a beautiful red-haired woman bending over her crib. Perhaps it had been a ghost.

They came to a natural clearing in the forest, where a stream chuckled out from an undergrowth of ferns and low-growing briars. The mud around its narrow banks was pocked with the spoor of deer. Mariana again twirled around on the spot, her eyes cast upwards, her green skirts flying. Presently, she collapsed in a giggling heap on a mossy mound. The sun-laced canopy of the forest around her still seemed to circle above her head. Soon, she would approach the mantle of the trees and open herself up to what would come.

She rolled onto her stomach and kicked up her heels. Sarah sat down demurely beside her, skirts carefully tucked, and began to pluck some tiny purple flowers from the grass.

'There's so much life out here,' Mariana said, breathing hard. 'Can't you feel it leaping from blade to blade, leaf to leaf? It's a kind of fire.'

Sarah shifted uneasily, one suspicious eye on the shadowed undergrowth. 'There's far too much life out here, if you ask me!'

Mariana laughed. Sarah could always be relied upon to state what was most expected of her. 'Oh, Sarah, do relax. There's nothing to fear. The forest will look after us.' She rolled onto her back, her arms flung above her head, her hair spread out around her in a coppery, silky fan.

Sarah paused a moment - a time during which Mariana anticipated what would come next - then spoke primly. 'What you need, my lady, is a nice young gentleman to look after you.'

Mariana fought the incomprehensible lance of annoyance - or what it anger? - that shivered through her. 'You are talking, of course, of Sir Henri de Grisaille.'

Sarah was impervious to her mistress' tone. 'Exactly. When you are married...'

'Ugh! Don't!' Mariana sat up quickly. She felt as if she didn't want someone, or something, to hear Sarah's words.

Sarah's eyes were round, her thin eyebrows high. 'You are a strange one! All the ladies of the shire would give their eyes to be the bride of De Grisaille.'

'If I gave my eyes, the prospect might not seem so bleak, seeing as I wouldn't have to look upon him,' Mariana said, unable to suppress a smile.

'He is very fine to look upon!'

'Without doubt,' Mariana said smoothly, casting a sidelong glance at her maid. 'I dare say you imagine his face quite often!'

'Oh, be quiet!' Sarah said, flushing. 'I can't understand you. Whenever he visits, you're winter's first ice in his presence. It upsets Lord Arroby, you know it does. Your father only wants the best for you.'

Mariana sighed, and briefly put her hands against her eyes. 'How could he possibly know what is best for me?'

'He's your father,' Sarah said.

Mariana studied her maid, then pursed her lips. 'Do you ever have thoughts of love, Sarah?'

The girl looked wary. 'Well...'

'I do,' Mariana said flatly, 'and strangely enough, the image of De Grisaille is not compatible with them.' Her expression took on a dreamy cast. 'I know the one for me.'

'Who? Don't be daft!' Sarah said.

Mariana looked away, her eyes drawn to the murmuring depths of the forest. 'Listen,' she murmured. 'I will tell you a secret.'

She could sense that Sarah felt greatly disturbed now, no doubt dreading some terrible revelation. Maybe she should remain quiet, but she couldn't. She had to speak. The words were a pain inside her, bursting to be released. 'I see him,' Mariana said, 'whenever I come to this place.'

'When?' squeaked Sarah. 'Do you come here alone, my lady? Oh no! It cannot be!' She looked terrified.

'Oh, don't fret,' Mariana said irritably. 'I see him *in my mind*, even when you are here with me. His stealth is in the shadows beneath the canopy, his laughter in the gurgle of the brook, his blood the sap in every bough.'

She glanced back at Sarah, who now appeared appalled, in a prim kind of way. 'What are you talking of? A fetch?'

Mariana shrugged. 'I cannot tell. He is as real to my heart as a friend, yet I have never seen him with my eyes.'

Sarah wriggled her shoulders uncomfortably. 'You shouldn't dwell in such dark reverie, my lady. There's danger enough in the world as it is.'

Mariana knew she could never confide in Sarah, not properly. The poor maid would either fall into a fit or run screaming from the forest should she discover the true contents of her mistress' heart. Sighing, Mariana stood up and wandered beneath the shadow of an elm, her hand upon its green-stained bark. It was time. All she had to do was concentrate hard enough and he was there, out amid the shifting veils of leaf and shadow.

Today, she could see him clearly between the branches, his antlered helm glittering in the sunlight. His face was mostly in shadow, but she could perceive a smile upon his thin, well-shaped lips. His armour flashed like quicksilver as he came towards her; an evanescent ghost or the desire of a girl made flesh. Was he real, or just a rapture conjured from her imagination? She'd always been able to imagine things so well, maybe too well. Perhaps thinking of something with such concentration was enough to bring it into being. Hadn't God done that? Mariana smiled to herself. Such blasphemy! The priest would go white at the thought of it. Just for a moment, Mariana closed her eyes, and swore she could feel breath upon her neck. Her skin blushed from the sparks of that near touch. But perhaps it was just the summer breeze that snaked through the leafage. In her mind, words whispered, but maybe she imagined them because she wanted to hear them. *'Have you no faith, my lady?'*

'Perhaps not enough,' she murmured. Surely his hands hovered above her shoulders now. Strange foxfire lights would be shifting in his shadowed eyes. He had never spoken to her before, nor seemed to come so close.

At night, Mariana had laid awake many times, fantasising about how he might storm the keep and claim her. He would ride up the great stairs on his silver horse and break down her door. He haunted her dreams too. In dreams, they would walk through an ancient landscape, where the power of the trees pressed down upon them, and flakes of white blossom filled the air. Glistering forms would pulse in and out of being around them, and she would experience an utter completeness and contentment that was beyond the human language to describe. Always, she awoke to find the grey stone of the keep hard around her, and later, her day would be greyer still. In her dreams, he seemed so real, she could not understand why he never came for her.

Sarah's voice broke Mariana's reverie. 'Are you all right, my lady?'

Mariana started, as if coming out of a trance. 'Quite so.' He was gone now, her dream knight, her silver paladin of the forest.

'Perhaps we should be making our way back,' Sarah said.

'In a while. Just a few more moments.'

The sunlight had begun to fade, conjuring wolf shadows amid the undergrowth. Time had passed so quickly. Mariana became aware of Sarah's increased agitation. The maid did not like to wait for the dusk in this place, craving the sanctuary of the keep, where everything was solid and known. For a while, Mariana tortured the girl, standing silently beneath the elm, gazing mournfully at the bronze-tinted sky. She would give in soon, even though she often dreamed of discovering what the forest felt like when it was swathed in velvet night. What creatures would come forth, unseen by day? Would her dream knight take on more substance from the ash light of the moon?

Eventually, Sarah could stand it no longer and got to her feet. 'Please, mistress, let's be getting back now. We must have been here hours, you've been standing there dreaming for so long! If we don't start off now, the dark'll be upon us afore we get home.'

Mariana felt as if hardly any time had passed at all. 'Oh, very well.' She sighed and held out her hand. 'Come, Sarah, let's run, before the faeries come, and take us beneath their hill.'

Sarah uttered a little shriek, half in delight. Together, the two girls scampered back towards the keep. Mariana felt invigorated, as she always did after spending time beneath the forest canopy, and what was more, she was sure her phantom paladin had spoken to her. Not even her father's black moods could overshadow her joy today.

It was almost dusk by the time the keep loomed ahead of them, its squat, solid tower uncompromising against the first of the evening stars that glittered in the red and turquoise sky. Just for a moment, Mariana felt a wildness tug within her, and had to fight the urge to run back into the whispering darkness of the trees, seek out the glade once more and wait for the moon to rise. Instead, she put the temptation firmly from her head and marched purposefully to the gate. She paused to wave at the guard who stood to attention directly above the portcullis, but he barely even acknowledged her. His attention seemed focused on something that was taking place within the walls of the enclosure.

The skin at the base of Mariana's skull began to prickle. Instinctively, she lifted her skirts a little and increased her pace, Sarah following. The fire in Mariana's skin told her something was wrong.

Merchants and soldiers alike milled around the outer bailey. Mariana pushed her way through them with perhaps unbecoming urgency, ignoring Sarah's protests. Once in the inner bailey, the keep rose menacingly above them. It dwarfed the Great Hall that lay beneath it, like the oaks in the forest dwarfed the hawthorn. The Hall was not a mean building either, its long stone structure comprising several rooms on two floors, the main hall itself being the central room. The top floor was reserved mostly for guests, while the lower rooms were used for stores.

Mariana hurried across the yard, which was already lit by torch-light. Ramshackle out-buildings clung to the inner defensive wall like ivy. The stables were situated fairly close to the Hall, and here Mariana espied a knot of people clustered around a prancing black stallion. Mariana recognised the beast at once. It was Lightfoot, the mount of her Uncle Edmund. Was this the cause of her misgiving, but if so, why?

'Uncle?' she murmured under her breath. What was he doing here? Generally, his visits were announced well in advance, so that a suitable feast could be prepared and a bed made ready.

An ashen-haired man swung himself into the saddle; undeniably her uncle, the brother of her dead mother. He wore a cobalt blue cloak carelessly across his shoulders. His features were somewhat hawk-like, and he carried his maturity like a banner, rather than a millstone. He was renowned for the control he maintained over his expressions, revealing nothing that might give an enemy the upper hand. People often joked that not even a cannon blast could crack that imperious visage. To Mariana, as indeed to anyone who sought her uncle's protection, that face represented more security than any keep could provide. But today, she sensed a change in him, a difference. A discomfort played around his features.

Mariana struggled to his side, pushing past those who still shuffled around him. The smell of dirt and stale sweat filled her nostrils. One of the guards recognised her and pushed the rest of the crowd aside. 'Make way for the Lady Mariana!'

Edmund turned his head, gathering up the reins. It seemed that, until the guard had called Mariana's name, he'd been unaware of her presence. This in itself was unusual, for he often sensed her coming, long before he saw her.

Mariana put a hand against Lightfoot's quivering neck and looked up at her uncle. 'I did not know you would be visiting,' she said.

Despite the cloud in his expression, Edmund still managed a smile, albeit tinged with weariness. 'Ah, my little Mariana,' he said, 'it is a joy to see you.'

Somehow, his words carried little conviction. Mariana grabbed hold of Lightfoot's reins. 'When did you arrive? Are you leaving? Why so soon? What has happened?'

'Nothing of import,' he answered. 'I had business with your father. That is all.'

'But surely you can stay for supper? I haven't seen you since Candlemas.'

'Alas, I must leave immediately. I have matters to attend to.'

He seemed distant from her, a stranger. Mariana adopted a different tack. She set her face into an expression of coquettish pleading. 'Oh, come now, what of your promise? Did you not tell me that the next time you visited, you'd teach me the trick of the vanishing coin?'

Edmund twisted his mouth to the side wryly. 'So I did.' Then his expression became hard once more. 'There were many things I'd planned to show you, but it is not to be, at least not for the present. Perhaps when you are old enough to visit me...'

His words were full of endings. A strange panic welled in Mariana's heart. 'But I can't wait that long!' She narrowed her eyes. 'If you must leave so quickly, then on your next visit you must show me the trick. I insist.'

Edmund's glance skimmed upwards towards her father's chambers. For a moment, she glimpsed a flash of fiery waters within his dark eyes. 'Child,' he said, 'there won't be another visit. Sadly, this is my last, for I am forbidden ever to return.'

Mariana couldn't help laughing. The idea was preposterous. 'You're speaking folly! Have you argued with my father again? Oh, this is ridiculous. I won't hear such talk.'

Edmund shook his head. 'This is no joke, Mariana, and no slight matter. Your father is set upon it, and it would be easier for a child to rein in an ox that has decided its own path than for any of us to change his mind.'

Mariana stared at her uncle for a moment, speechless, then spoke in a low angry voice. 'If this is true, then you sought to leave before bidding me farewell? I cannot believe it. What have you said to my father? How have you angered him?'

'It is an old conflict, child, that would make little sense to you now.' He gathered up the reins once more, lifting Lightfoot's head. 'Remember it was never my doing, and remember this also: you are fortunate to have your mother's blood in your veins, despite whatever it might bring you.'

'What is that supposed to mean?'

He would not smile. 'No matter. Come to me if and when you can. My doors are always open for you, my dear, but don't upset your father. He has reasons for his decisions, and even though they are misguided, you should respect them.'

Before Mariana could question him further, he urged Lightfoot forward and headed for the gate. He did not look back. Mariana stared after him, her mind in turmoil. How long would it take until this fact sank in? It was inconceivable she should not see Edmund again. The gate swung shut. Night was on the keep now, the forest kept at bay.

Lord Arroby's study was situated high in the tower so that he could keep a better eye on his domain, inside and out, but occasionally he favoured the open space of the hall itself. Today, he sat at the long eating table in this capacious chamber, hunched over a pile of parchments. Mariana did not need to see his treasurer nearby to know that the estate accounts held her father's attention.

She paused at the doorway, and her courage suddenly dissolved. Despite the warmth of its oak walls, the Great Hall seemed a depthless, cold place that threatened to swallow her. Above her stretched the whale bone rafters of the ceiling, browned with age. A fire crackled in the great hearth, although its voice spoke of malevolence rather than cheer. Mariana did not often defy her father, let alone challenge him outright. Sometimes, she felt sorry for him, imagining it was grief or shame that drove him to shout at her. After all, she was not the boy-child he had wanted, and her mother had died in birthing her. For some reason, Lord Arroby had not taken another wife, even though he had no son to follow him. Ah, a son: all that a man craved, a bonny lad with whom to spar, to teach the secrets of the hunt. Daughters: they were a different thing, especially a daughter who preferred the company of animals to men. As a very young child, she had wept openly for the quarry of the hunt, when the limp bodies had been carried into the keep strung out on the gamekeepers' poles. Now, when he had found her a suitable match in De Grisaille, she was being awkward. Mariana knew his thoughts about her, because he often spoke them aloud.

She still wasn't sure whether he did it deliberately or not. The other thoughts, that he kept silent, she felt in her heart.

Arroby looked up from his papers, perhaps sensing her scrutiny from the doorway. He frowned at her - a furrowing, bristling frown - but she would not be discouraged. He set his hands upon the table slowly, palms down. 'Daughter,' he said. He would know why she was there. 'I am busy, and resentful of intrusion.'

Mariana straightened herself, as if by stiffening her spine she could somehow withstand the blows of her father's words. 'I would speak with you, sir' she said, pleased at the sound of her voice; not commanding, but firm enough to catch his attention.

Arroby sighed through his nose. 'What is it, then? Speak quickly, for I have no time to waste.'

'I...' She hesitated. 'I just saw Uncle Edmond in the yard. Is he well?' Slowly, she ventured into the hall; her gown a small green flame in the shadowed hollows of the room.

Her father's frown deepened. 'Is this all you've interrupted me for?'

Mariana touched the scarred table-top gently, attempting to keep her voice light yet firm. 'I haven't seen Edmund since Candlemas, and his visits are precious to me. We have visitors so rarely. He galloped away so quickly I did not even have time to thank him for the present he sent me last month. I would have liked to have done that, sir.'

When she finished speaking, she dared to raise her eyes and saw the familiar bleak expression on her father's face. His voice was low and clear, yet as darkly threatening as thunder. 'It would please me if you never mentioned that man's name in this house again. Do you hear?'

'But father...'

'Do you hear?' His voice was louder now.

'Yes, sir.'

'Good.' He directed his attention towards his papers once more, picked up a quill. 'Now, take your leave.'

'But Father, I want to know...'

'*You* want to know? You want to know what?' A fleck of spittle seeped from the corner of his mouth. 'There is nothing for you to know. Go, before I take a stick to you!'

'I apologise, sir.' Mariana curtsied to him, and left the hall swiftly. She was not really surprised at this turn of events. Her father rarely talked freely with her, except on occasion when an excess of ale loosened his tongue enough to bring forth reminiscences about her mother. Mariana realised she had acted too impulsively. If she had approached the subject when he was in a better mood, he might have talked to her. Now she'd stirred his anger and would have to employ other means to discover what had transpired between her male relatives.

She made her way directly to her chambers in the tower, the stone corridor echoing to the sound of her light footsteps. In her bedroom, threads of sunset light shone dimly through the narrow casement. All the furnishings, even the dour walls, were seen through a red cast. Mariana had heard that some of the grander castles boasted casements so wide you could step through them, although the apertures were filled with panes of glass. Her father was scathing of this extravagance, claiming that lords who favoured such wanton excesses knew little of the art of defence. Mariana, however, wished she lived in such a place. Perhaps then she would have a better view of the outside world. Her favourite spot in her chambers was on top of the chest which she kept right by the casement. The box was covered in cushions and furs, making it a luxurious seat, where she commanded a view, however slight, of the forest to the south. Mariana spent many hours there, gazing out through the narrow chink of stone, day-dreaming. Disconsolately, she now curled up there, and stared down into the courtyard below. She saw the farrier examining the hooves of her father's new bay steed, Windrush. Nervous stable-hands restrained his powerful, snaking head. Mariana could feel the young stallion's pent-up energy. He was eager to escape, and had already done so three times since her father had brought him up from Shrewsbury. If she could, she'd turn herself into a wren and flit through the crack in the stone. She would alight upon Windrush's broad back and there transform herself into a follet, whose magical presence would whip the steed into a fury, so he'd break free of his grooms and flee the keep. His polished hooves would crash through the great gate, splintering wood, and then they'd be off into the darkness, she a glimmering, flame-haired nymph clinging to his wild mane.

Take me with you, she whispered, pressing her face against the slit in the stone. The horse shuffled nervously below, conjuring complaints from the grooms. *What am I thinking of?* she wondered. She was a lady of the land and her high born status was to be treasured. Every Monday, she saw some of the horror that might await her in the outside world, when beggars in rags queued at the alms-house to partake of the lord's meagre generosity. Poverty waited outside, and disease. The first time she had seen a man with only half a face, she had fled, sickened. The smell was so terrible. No, she was safer here, away from dirt and decay. Every woman should marry; was it so bad? She would be lady of her own keep, with daughters to raise, and sons. It was what she'd been born for.

The great gates to the inner bailey creaked open slowly, and horses came curvetting into the yard, like wild elementals in the torch-light. Mariana recognised the grey stallion of Henri De Grisaille among the troupe, and her heart sank. He was without doubt a handsome man, and did not seem unkind, but there was something missing in him, something that her heart craved. She felt that once his golden ring was upon her finger, and the Bishop had bound them with words, some part of her would be forever in chains, or would die completely. Did other girls ever feel this way? She had no way of knowing, having no noble-born friends her own age. Servants seemed to wed whom they chose, but then they were common people. The lot of the nobility was different.

Sarah came in just then to prepare her mistress for the evening meal. 'Sitting there dreaming again, my lady?' she said with a smile. 'Sir Henri has just arrived, I believe.'

'I saw,' said Mariana, uncurling from her seat. 'Dress me in red tonight, Sarah.'

Perhaps it was the wearing of the red gown that caused the trouble. Mariana reacted to colours with great sensitivity, and whereas her habitual green tempered her spirits and imbued her with calm, red tended to inflame a wilder aspect. The gown was trimmed with dark fox fur and the tickle of it against her breast and shoulders did nothing to contain Mariana's feelings. She made an entrance into the hall, and saw that the Sheriff of Shrewsbury was present, along with the Abbot of St Bede's, a local friary and Sir Henri De Grisaille. No other women graced the gathering, but this was not unusual.

'Good evening, daughter,' said her father, bowing.

She inclined her head and sat down at the table, prompting the men to take their seats as well.

The conversation, which Mariana's entrance had clearly curtailed, started up again. She was not interested in the discussion of horses and distanced herself from it, sipping from a tankard of ale. De Grisaille kept his earnest attention upon her father, occasionally indulging himself with a covert glance at her face. She wished he wasn't so eager to please Lord Arroby; his manoeuvres were too obvious.

After the meat had been brought in, Mariana felt a quiver of mischief start up in her belly. She wanted sport, believing her father would always maintain a facade in front of his friends. 'I wish you would speak to my father, Sir Richard,' she said to the Sheriff in a clear voice. 'He has been quarrelling with my uncle again.'

Her remark invoked a brief if stony silence as all eyes turned to Lord Arroby. He expelled a short laugh. 'What is this, daughter?'

She shrugged. 'Your friends should explain to you that family quarrels are best mended as soon as possible. Is this not right, Father Castell?'

The Abbot stuck out his lower lip, nodded thoughtfully. 'Under God's law, we should love our neighbour, and relatives can be seen as our closest neighbours, I suppose.'

'There you are, sir,' Mariana said to her father. She smiled at the company of gentlemen. 'In truth, I have no idea what they quarrelled about, only that my uncle either now refuses to, or has been forbidden from, visiting our home ever again. Is this not the most absurd thing to hear?'

'This must be Edmund Spenser,' said the Sheriff, pouring himself more ale.

Lord Arroby's face was a curious mixture of contained fury and exasperation. 'The same. Blackguard that he is.'

'He is the only remaining blood of my mother,' Mariana said. 'This conflict grieves me.'

'Grieves you?' Arroby's two words were spoken in a vibrant undertone.

De Grisaille attempted to defuse the situation. 'My lady, you should not be grieved by the politics of men. Stick to your charming tapestries and...'

'Charming tapestries?' Mariana interrupted, in an arch, glacial voice. She was conscious of the red fabric around her, its colour bleeding into her soul.

'Guard your tongue!' Arroby snapped. 'Do not speak to your future husband in such a shrew's tone!'

'I see no one in this hall who fits that description,' Mariana said, regretting the words even as they left her lips.

Lord Arroby got to his feet and pointed at his daughter with a rigid finger. 'You dare to speak to me in such a manner? Apologise at once!'

Mariana got to her feet. She felt mortified, unsure of how and why she had spoken so freely. 'Excuse me, gentlemen,' she said and began to run from the hall. Behind her, she heard the heavy scrape of chairs against the stone floor.

Out in the dark corridor, she leaned against the cold wall to catch her breath. Her father would punish her now. What had possessed her? And she'd still learned nothing. Should she return and apologise? She didn't know what to do. Before she could make any decision, the doors to the hall banged open. Mariana cringed, seeing her father at the threshold, limned against the glow of the fire from the great hearth.

'My lord,' she began, as he advanced towards her. She held out her hands to him in appeal.

The blow exploded silver sparks behind her eyes. She fell back against the wall, dazed. He had never struck her before. Then came another, and another. Mariana felt like a rag doll beneath this attack. She was powerless.

'Spenser would turn you into a demon and more!' he hissed. 'He is the devil's man, girl, seeking to ensorcel you.'

'No!' Mariana managed to moan, inviting a further blow. After that, she kept her silence.

Presently, her father's rage was spent. Mariana drooped against the wall, her head spinning and full of pain.

'If you would live a gentle life, daughter,' Arroby said quietly, 'attend this. Be all the things a good woman should be; silent, demure and modest. Do not succumb to the devil's call. I beat you only to purge you of evil. Your mother, God bless her soul, fought it all her life and with her life. I pray she did not die in vain. Honour her memory in humility and grace.'

Mariana's lips and the left side of her face felt numb. She put her fingers to her mouth, found blood there. 'I hear you sir,' she whispered.

'Good.' He retreated into the hall and the great doors slammed shut. Presently, she heard the sound of male laughter within.

Somehow, Mariana struggled to her room, where she rinsed out her mouth with cold water. In her glass, she saw the damage her father had inflicted upon her. Her eyes were swollen, but fortunately he'd only drawn blood from her lips.

He talked of the devil in her, yet what other agency could have possessed him to provoke such an attack? Had her words really been so bad? And what was this talk of devil's work connected with her uncle and her mother?

Mariana flopped fully-clothed onto her bed. She could not weep, and strangely did not feel the need to. If anything, she felt inspired, but could not fathom how to make this work in her favour. She was aware of grief and a sense of injustice within her, but these seemed only superficial, needless emotions. She had learned something momentous today, and soon would understand its import.

Shortly, Sarah came in to prepare her lady for bed. From her stern and troubled countenance, Mariana guessed the servants had already disseminated the information about the altercation she'd had with her father. No mention was made of the wounds, although Sarah did bring a herbal balm which she applied silently to Mariana's face. Once in her night-gown, Mariana climbed into bed. Sarah stood at its foot, her hands on her hips. She shook her head. 'I worry for you, my lady.' The words were blurted out, as if she couldn't prevent their escape, despite their impropriety.

Mariana managed a painful smile. 'I bring it upon myself, Sarah.' She paused. 'Will you tell me one thing?'

Sarah looked uneasy. 'I'll try.'

'What do you know of my mother?'

'She was a fine and gentle lady...'

Mariana interrupted her. 'I know this. I've been told a hundred times. What I want to know is what was different about her? There was something, wasn't there?'

Sarah sighed, hesitating. 'Folk talk,' she said at last. 'You know how it is. Lady Ylaine was a strange little body when she came here. This was in my mother's time, of course. Like you, she was a one for the forests and the animals, always flitting about. And she used to sing to the beasts. Folk say she could tame a wild stallion with her voice. They say she had a witching way, which was not so, because she was a good

Christian woman. But, as I said, folk will talk.' She paused. 'Is that all, my lady?'

'Is that all you know?'

Sarah nodded, frowning miserably.

'What of my uncle?'

'I know nothing of him,' Sarah said, 'other than he loved his sister, as a good man should.'

Mariana sensed the reserve in her maid's words. Sarah knew more, of this she was sure, but wouldn't speak, because it was gossip. The gulf in status between them meant she could not speak her heart. Mariana had no doubt Sarah talked freely with the other servants. 'You may go,' she said. 'Thank you, Sarah.'

For a while, Mariana lay awake in the darkness, aware of each hurt upon her face and shoulders. So, her father thought she had witch's blood. It was absurd. She wanted no truck with evil. She loved the world and all who lived within it. How could she be a bad person when she felt that?

When Mariana awoke abruptly, her heart racing, she wasn't aware of having gone to sleep. Something had awoken her, but what? There were no echoes of sounds in the room. Warily, she sat up in bed and searched the darkness. It must be near morning, for the moon had set. But no, wasn't that moonlight striking the corner of her room? A radiance seemed to hover there, as if someone was holding a candle aloft. Mariana's first thought was that her father had come into her room to punish her further, but she quickly realised this was not so. The strange glow was too bright for a candle or even a lantern. Also, its colour was bluish white. As she watched, it approached her bed with a bobbing motion. It emitted a feeling of power and truth, as if it was an angel hovering there.

God's wrath, Mariana thought in terror. *He has sent a seraph to purge me of my tainted blood.*

She wanted to duck back down beneath the covers or, preferably, leap from her bed and run from the room, but fear, or something else, kept her immobile. Her eyes were fixed on the ball of light, which presently began to spin, increasing in pace with every moment. Gradually, in its heart, a figure seemed to take on form and solidify. Mariana had an impression of spreading horns rising from its head. No angel then, but perhaps a demon. A small sound of distress fell from her lips. Her paralysed limbs ached with cold.

The room was filled with a silver radiance now, and the figure stood tall at the end of her bed. It took only a few moments for her to realise what she was looking at. The silver armour, the tall antlered helm: it was her dream knight from the woods, but here in the keep, real and terrifying. She had yearned for him to come for her, but now she was afraid. This was no human thing. What had she summoned to her?

'No!' she cried and found the strength to put her hands over her eyes and bend her forehead to her raised knees. 'Go away! In God's name, go away!'

Presently, as nothing untoward occurred, she dared to raise her head and lower her hands. The room was in darkness. The knight had vanished. Mariana panted upon the bed, feeling disappointed and relieved all at once. Had she imagined him again? Had she been dreaming? Her head reeling with a hundred mordant aches, she got from her bed and struggled to the window, her vision briefly occluded by motes of light. There, she collapsed upon her cushioned chest, and peered out through the casement.

Out in the courtyard, all was still. On the southern wall, a guard rested in a crenel, fighting the slumber that dragged at his head. All seemed normal, and yet... Mariana caught her breath.

Beyond the castle perimeter, beyond the sward and the rummaging of night creatures, a luminous sphere rose up and hung over the forest. It flared brightly in a surge of radiance, then died almost immediately.

Mariana stared unblinking at the dark forest, until her eyes were watering with strain. The strange light did not return. It had been her paladin, returning to his realm. She had banished him.

Oh you fool! She chided herself. *Fear has turned away your dreams!*

He had looked at her with concern, she was sure of that. Had her pain called him to her? He might have done something to help her. But wasn't he part of what was wrong with her? She saw things and felt things that other people didn't. Only now, after the day's revelations, did it occur to her this might estrange her from what remained of her family and indeed humanity itself. Witch, outcast, devil's spawn. Mariana slapped her hand against the cold stone of the wall. Oh, what did it matter what others thought? They had already cast their judgement upon her. Where would it end? Must she prove herself to be good until the day she died?

She sighed, and rested her hot cheek against the wall. The sky was greyed with dawn and soon the sun would rise. If only she knew where to reach him. But of course she did know; the light in the forest had been his signal.

The Farmer's Bride

A Poem by Charlotte Mew, 1916

Three Summers since I chose a maid,
Too young maybe - but more's to do
At harvest-time than bide and woo.
When us was wed she turned afraid
Of love and me and all things human;
Like the shut of a winter's day.
Her smile went out, and 'twasn't a woman—
More like a little, frightened fay.
One night, in the Fall, she runned away.

"Out 'mong the sheep, her be," they said,
Should properly have been abed;
But sure enough she wasn't there
Lying awake with her wide brown stare.
So over seven-acre field and up-along across the down
We chased her, flying like a hare
Before our lanterns. To Church-Town
All in a shiver and a scare
We caught her, fetched her home at last
And turned the key upon her, fast.

She does the work about the house
As well as most, but like a mouse:
Happy enough to chat and play
With birds and rabbits and such as they,
So long as men-folk stay away.
"Not near, not near!" her eyes beseech
When one of us comes within reach.
The women say that beasts in stall
Look round like children at her call.
I've hardly heard her speak at all.

Shy as a leveret, swift as he,
Straight and slight as a young larch tree,
Sweet as the first wild violets, she,
To her wild self. But what to me?

The short days shorten and the oaks are brown,
The blue smoke rises to the low gray sky,
One leaf in the still air falls slowly down,
A magpie's spotted feathers lie
On the black earth spread white with rime,
The berries redden up to Christmas-time.
What's Christmas-time without there be
Some other in the house than we!

She sleeps up in the attic there
Alone, poor maid. 'Tis but a stair
Betwixt us. Oh, my God! - the down,
The soft young down of her; the brown,
The brown of her - her eyes, her hair, her hair!

The Farmer's Bride

As the Yuletide holly bared its bloody poppets in the lane, she'd been married only a four-month. Thomas Gifford, a gentleman farmer, ten years older than she, had wed her in the simmering high summer, taken her tiny, sun-gilded hand in his among the corn, where the regal poppies had shed their crimson gowns like fragile brides. Her parents had been pleased. It was a good match, and they'd feared their fey Melusine would never catch the eye of a man - she being what she was.

The priest had bound their union in the old grey church hidden by yews. The sun had pressed itself through the high coloured windows, and the blood of Christus had flushed her skin, her pale linen gown. Red: that was the colour she saw most of all in this land of green and earth.

She hardly ever spoke, which was one of the reasons her father had feared for her future. His own mother had sometimes whispered that Melusine, with her fey, faintly inhuman beauty, might be a changeling child, but the old woman had a love of gossip more than any true suspicion, and love had never thrived between her and her daughter-in-law. 'She's no changeling,' Melusine's mother would declare. 'Put the holy cross on her tongue and see the truth of it. She's but a babe, and a little touched. She'll make a good wife for a man.'

True, Melusine was a strong girl, despite appearances, and had a way with the beasts of the field. She would work from sunrise till the twilight. Yet there was a strangeness about her, some affliction must have struck her in the womb. Not simple, no, but a stranger among her kind. Poor little Melusine. She was fair enough and obedient enough not to invite fiercer censure.

At first, as Mistress Gifford, the girl had been resigned

to her fate. Thomas was not a cruel man, and she imagined that life with him would be good for her. She tried to be personable, and murmur words appropriate for a wife, but something sealed her tongue in the presence of others, and had always done so. In private, she chattered to the animals, unaware that sometimes others heard her and puzzled about it. In fact, she loved language; to her each word possessed its own magic and wonder. It was not that she did not want to speak to people, but that she could not. Mostly, she had nothing to say to them anyway. Perhaps they did not speak her language.

She had her own room, at the top of a narrow, twisting stair, and each night, she would listen for the creak of the boards which would advise her of her husband's approach. This too she bore in patient silence. She knew the way of the animals, and what must be between a man and a maid. She kept his house for him, and he called her his little mouse. Yet she knew he was disappointed. Perhaps he thought her strangeness would hide a passion. If it did, she did not offer it to him. Before Yule, she ran away.

All her life, she had been haunted. The feeling would come to her in the evenings, in the summer fields, with the shadows of clouds dappling the hills. It was as if the world was a far larger place than it seemed, and something immense and unimaginable would be revealed to her. At these times, the landscape became still, almost unreal. Her lungs would squeeze shut, and the air would shimmer before her scalding eyes. She would have to sit down where she stood, afraid yet full of a strange desire.

Other times, this feeling would come to her in the yard as she worked the pump or fed the chickens. It was as if thunder had boomed over the landscape, and yet the sky was clear. Looking up, she would expect to see tongues of lightning split the clear blue. Only a bird would be wheeling high on the ocean of air. She might hear a piercing cry, and the feeling would crash over her like a wave, like a deluge of rain. Again, she would crouch down, grip hold of whatever solid was near, gasping and drowning.

These episodes she put down to what her mother called her 'difference'. There was something wrong with her. Her mother had advised her to conceal these convulsions, and she always had. They might fade away as she grew older, or had a child of her own. Melusine knew she would not have a child, not with Thomas. The idea felt wrong, and she had learned that when things felt a certain way to her, she was generally correct about them. This too, she kept a secret.

When Melusine was five, the priest had spoken out against Mistress Mathen, a woman of the parish. Living alone, she too had been good with the animals, and also with people. Many a body trod the violet path to her cottage by the lee, and she would offer possets to cure an ague, sweet leaves to press against a burn. Then the Aitken child had been struck with a spasm of the heart and Mistress Mathen had offered up her posy balms. The only outcome had been that the Aitkin cow offered sour milk and its calf was born with two heads. The child had died, writhing. Mistress Mathen was a witch, said the priest with flecks of spit at the corners of his mouth. She must be burned. Melusine's mother had whispered to her daughter in the dark. It was not necessary actually to be a witch to be identified as one and then disposed of. The priest was a good man, but he saw the shadows in everything. 'Go to church regularly, my little flower,' her mother murmured. 'Have your lips shape the words, if not your tongue. Look to Christus and he will protect you.'

Mistress Mathen had died upon a pyre, and the smell of her burning meat had stolen like a curse across the landscape. Even so young, Melusine had decided that day she would never die in such a manner. She would fold in on herself and forget things, and she did.

On the night she saw the angel, four months after her marriage, she knew her strangeness had slipped over into something more terrible. This was no holy creature like the statues with sad faces and drooping wings that stood guard in the church-yard. This was a being of fire and storms, whose eyes were the smoking flames of madness, whose voice was a howl that broke men's hearts. It manifested from the shadows in her high, narrow room in the farmhouse. She awoke from a dream she could not recall and her eyes searched the darkness. Thomas could be heard snoring in his chamber below. She felt afraid - almost - certainly not alone. Then she saw the blue glow in the corner of the room, and the being had stepped forth as if coming through a door. Behind it, if she could but see, there would be another world of light. The angel, however, cast shadows of radiance that eclipsed everything but the immensity of itself. It hissed to her in a language she could not fathom. It raised its right hand and pointed at her heart, all the while silver tongues of fire falling from its lips, its hair. To Melusine's eyes, it was an effulgent creature, yet her heart knew that it was, in reality, black. She scrabbled her way backwards in the bed, until her body was pressed against the rough head-board. She uttered little grunts of horror, her breath puffing on the cold air. Outside the stars shone like unwinking eyes, as God beheld her unholy transaction. All her life, when the episodes of strangeness had overtaken her, she had sensed a far-off presence in the fields, like a shadow she could not see. Now it was manifest before her in all its dark glory. It had come for her soul, which all these years had been leading a stolen life in the world of men. Thomas knew not what he had married. She would bring a blight upon his house, and the wrath of the Church. What could she do but run?

Thomas, waking from a libidinous dream, stumbled up the stairs to his wife's room, and found the door hanging open. Winter had invaded the room with its cold breath, and a frost had formed over the furniture, the blankets of the bed that lolled onto the floor. She was not lying there awake with her wide brown stare, as he was accustomed to find her. Through the open window, he saw a slight black shadow rippling over his fields and knew that it was she. Something cold, hard and hungry stole into Thomas' heart. He was a good man, but he was a man denied. He sensed the 'otherness' in Melusine and wanted to taste it, yet lacked the knowledge and the words to frame this desire.

'She is out among the sheep,' they told him as he ran out into the yard, pulling on his coat. His people had been awakened by the crashing of the great front door, by the babble of the disturbed hens and the alarmed honking of the geese. She had left chaos in her wake, and a sense of herself like a perfume, lingering on the chill air.

They chased her across the seven acre field, dark and ploughed, and over the spreading downs, where the heather bunched fibrous and unyielding. She flew like a hare before their flaming brands, her feet bare and pale against the crackling, frost-rimed soil. She ran all the way into the village, and here they cornered her in the churchyard. It was old Mag found her, crouched behind a crumbling tomb, her hair hanging over her wild eyes, all in a shiver and a scare. Then, they brought her home, Thomas a silent presence behind the company. He watched his girl-wife struggle in the hold of the women, heard her strange mutterings. What had possessed her? He shuddered. In the house, they dragged her up to her room, closed the window tight, and turned the lock upon her, fast.

Trembling on her bed, Melusine heard them leave the house, saw the yellow lights wink out one by one in the cottages around the fields. She heard Thomas' heavy movements in the kitchen far below, and then the more subtle sounds, of the beetles crawling over the hearth, of the cracking of the last embers in the fire, and finally, his breath, his weeping.

She did not want to be cruel, but now this room filled her with terror. She was marked, and her fate was inescapable. In this colourless world of midnight, even her blood would be black. She leaned her face against the cold window, and whined beneath her breath.

Down the winding road, on the other side of the village, there was a modest castle of three stories. In this place lived Sir Renaud Aquinas, lord of the district. Renaud had inherited his estates at a young age - his father had only died a few months before in a hunting accident, while his mother had succumbed to a mysterious palsy three years previously. Renaud was regarded as a handsome man, yet insular. Books meant more to him than social gatherings. Women might cut their eyes at him to no avail, despite the machinations of local dowagers and matrons, seeking to foist nubile relatives onto the house of Aquinas.

On the night Melusine fled across the fields, Renaud was sitting before a roaring hearth in his hall, drinking mellow foreign liquor with the priest, Father Rathford, the two men having recently completed a game of chess after a sumptuous supper. They had heard the yelping of the dogs as Thomas' company brought Melusine to earth in the nearby church-yard, but paid it little heed. Father Rathford was holding forth on the superstitious nature of the villagers, and Renaud, only half listening, nodded and smiled at appropriate moments. 'I despair of them,' Rathford said. 'They are little more than barbarians.'

'Surely, that is a harsh judgement,' Renaud responded softly, pouring more golden liquor into the priest's goblet. He knew that Rathford wished he'd been given a parish in a more enlightened area, a larger town, perhaps, or somewhere in London.

Rathford laughed. 'It is the wine speaking, my friend, exquisite as always, yet...' he sighed. 'I do not lie. The pagan creed lies in a shallow grave in these parts. It takes little for them to go scrabbling at the mould to dig it up again.'

'You have a hard task,' Renaud said politely.

Father Rathford nodded gravely, and took a sip of liquor, rolling the fiery liquid pleasurably around his mouth. His heavy grey robes still seemed to steam in the heat of the fire. 'I give thanks for enlightened men, such as yourself, milord. It brings me comfort.'

Renaud smiled into his goblet, thinking that perhaps the hospitality of the castle provided greater comfort than mere companionship.

After the priest had gone, red-cheeked and reluctant back to his parsonage, Renaud climbed to the highest room of his castle. The hour was late, yet he felt languid and at peace. In the great hall, his servants snuffed out the candles one by one and the old stones of the walls cooled themselves to sleep. In one of the circular turrets, Renaud had his work-room. It was approached by a precarious, winding stair, where ancient dust, fragments of neglected birds' nest and bat droppings made the climb more perilous. Only one other person apart from Renaud possessed a key to the thick, iron-studded door that garrisoned the bottom of the stair.

The work-room was decorated in a fashion very different to the rest of Renaud's domain. Colourful rugs from Persia hung upon the walls and adorned the floors, and the chair and divan were plump with cushions encrusted with gold embroidery. The air itself smelled perfumed with a scent which partially eclipsed a certain sulphurous aroma. Artefacts gathered by his ancestors from every hidden corner of the world reposed in dusty alcoves or crowded upon sagging shelves. The dying fire-light glimmered off yellow brass and iridescent jewels. This was a Sultan's den.

Renaud lit the tapers and replenished the fire himself. No servant stepped across the threshold here. Although monied, Renaud preferred people to think of him as an astronomer and scholar rather than a rich man of leisure. These pursuits gave ample cover to his true interests. He was a man of secrets, who held court with his enemy, the orthodox Church, in the hall below. Now, he stood before the great desk where a hide-bound book looted from a German monastery lay open, and flexed his fingers against one another. *Soror mystica, my sacred sister, how she eludes me. Must I continue in this? It pains me.* He sighed, and a vapour purled from his lips. In a world where all occult knowledge is feared, and therefore persecuted, a man like Renaud must be circumspect. He had long ago woken to his calling, felt the beat of the Great Work course through the channels of his body.

As a child of eleven, out riding his pony on an autumn morning, he had suddenly experienced an epiphany. The world had bleached of colour before his eyes and when his vision cleared, it seemed he was in a different place. He could see the life force pulsing through the earth, sucked up by trees and ferns and forest grass. He could see coloured lights high up in the leafy canopy, the living energy of squirrels and birds. And most importantly, he felt his own connection with the world around him, with every leaf, and beast, fragment of mould and drop of water. The same energy that gave them life surged through him. A web of shining strands pushed out from his body and made union with other strands coming towards him. He knew the secret of life and it was simply this hidden light. One day, he would control it as he controlled his pony. At once, he rode home and told his father.

If Renaud had expected surprise and acclaim, he was disappointed. His father was pleased, but told his son he had been expecting such an event to occur in any case. 'You have the wyrding way within you, my boy,' he had said, 'as do I, and of course, your mother. You have awakened to one of the great truths of the universe and you shall never sleep again.'

The family of Aquinas were magi, and it seemed always had been. Renaud felt slightly annoyed he hadn't been told this before. His special event seemed somehow lessened by it. However, once it was clear their son followed in their calling, Renaud's parents set themselves diligently about raising their child to the arcane arts. Their pace was measured, because they felt too swift an advancement would rob the boy of his youth. Unfortunately, their early deaths left him alone too young, vulnerable to older members of their Hermetic Order who might take advantage of his estates, his father's priceless books. The world was no easy place for the philosophers of the hidden spirit, persecuted by the sleeping and awake alike. It was hard to place trust in any but the most simple, ignorant souls, such as Father Rathford, who knew nothing and could comprehend nothing, and was therefore no threat.

I am the King of my domain, Renaud thought, and a freak breeze snaked through the chamber, lifting his dark red hair. He searched for a Queen, canicula, bitch of the moon, his tormentress and Guardian Angel, but found none. He could not advance any further until he had established a link with this primal spark of his being, and no matter what rituals he had recited, what elixirs he had scattered and burned, what desperate entreaties he breathed into the aether, he remained alone. Sometimes, he sensed a far off presence, almost teasing him with its distance, but he could not be sure whether this was an illusion or not. Fortunately, he now had help in his quest, but even that seemed ambiguous.

The pages of the book turned slowly before him. His eyes paused at the words of Leonardo 'It should not be hard for you to stop sometimes and look into the stains of walls, or ashes of a fire, or clouds, or mud, or places in which you may find marvellous ideas.' Dreams and phantasms resided in the instruments of his art arrayed around the book: the mercurial serpent with its winding glass pipe, the Hermetic vessel, in whose womb were visions to be sought more than scripture; the dangerous vessel of the dancing bear, an aspect of the dark mother; the basin of the tortoise and the pelican of circular distillation, representing the bird who pecks its own breast to nourish its young with blood. The instruments were but a reflection of the true work that took place within Renaud's soul and his most recent knowledge had come from the east.

'The hour is late, my friend. Will you begin work now?'

Renaud looked up. His mentor, Kalid, - the only other to possess a key to the tower - sat among the shadows in a high-backed chair near the fire. Renaud could not recall noticing the man as he'd replenished the flames. Kalid could melt in and out of shadows with ease, it seemed. He had taken the place of Renaud's own father, following his mysterious arrival at the castle gate some weeks after the old lord had died. Renaud had been suspicious of this taciturn, hooded man, although Kalid had been quick to assure him, in mellifluous, soothing tones, that he had worked with Renaud's parents, and had in fact trained alongside them somewhere in the Orient. On the exact location of this establishment, Kalid seemed vague. He claimed that Renaud's father had appeared to him in spirit and requested him to assist his orphaned son. He had travelled long, through many dangerous places, but now was ready to begin work. Renaud could not advertise Kalid's presence in the castle, although the servants obviously knew about him, and had doubtlessly talked in the village. Kalid's presence in this land was precarious at best, for he was a Saracen, whose kinsmen had been slaughtered by Soldiers of Christ. Yet in the Order, boundaries of culture and belief did not exist. Kalid was an adept; it was his duty to instruct the needy student.

Renaud had learned much already, but Kalid was a hard, relentless teacher, who seemed never to weary. They worked at night, once the other occupants of the castle were asleep, and on many occasions worked through till dawn. Kalid's instruction varied from endless lectures on occult practice, to the performance of complicated rituals, to the telling of tales.

'Tonight, we shall again walk the world of spirit, and you will call to your anima,' Kalid decided. He was smoking from an absurdly tall water pipe, its stem held lightly between his long, agile fingers.

Renaud sighed. He felt immediately tired. 'Am I being tested, Kalid, or do we have to face an unpleasant reality? Perhaps I shall never find this creature. Perhaps I am blighted in some way.'

There was a rustle, then Kalid was beside him, bending low to whisper in his protégé's ear. 'You must not lose heart, my friend. Who knows what events transpired in your previous lives? Perhaps there are more than the usual barriers to cross. We shall partake of the *vinum nostrum*, and you must look within yourself once more. Enter the shadows of your heart.'

Renaud steeled himself at the thought. He had partaken of the mercurial wine on several occasions. Each time, he had been swamped by dreams of hideous clarity. The angels of the corners had released into his mind the four demons, Azazel, Azael, Mahazael and Samael, along with all their poisonous insects and beasts. This is what Kalid had told him to explain the terrifying sights of death, horror and cruelty which had assailed his psyche. Now, as an awakened adept, it was essential he make contact with his Guardian Angel, his connection with divine source of creation, the higher self. In the beliefs of his kind, this was always of the opposite gender, the lost half of the self, in Renaud's case, his anima. But in searching for her, he could not break through the battalions of demons who wheeled around him on horses of fire that breathed the smoke of brimstone.

'Face the shadow of chaos in all its repugnance,' Kalid had said. 'For within lies the gold of your soul.'

Renaud could not imagine ever finding it. Now, he rubbed his forehead, where an ache had begun. He wanted to work, yet did not. 'The anima resists me. I will not find her.'

'Once the Deluge of the initial chaos recedes, she will be there,' Kalid said. His fingers rubbed together quickly, making a papery sound.

It occurred to Renaud that the Arab enjoyed the effects of the *vinum nostrum* on more than one level. Perhaps, one day, when Renaud himself could control the experience, he would find joy in it too. The elixir was said to be composed of the mercurial waters of the *prima materia* - the virgin's milk, the fountain's vinegar and the water of life - yet Renaud had helped prepare it and knew it comprised the less spiritual ingredients of henbane, belladonna, thorn apple and mandragore, such as witches used in their flying ointments.

Kalid offered to Renaud a pewter goblet, in which the bitter brew shivered sluggishly. The Lord Aquinas raised the philtre to his lips; the cup seemed full of disembodied voices, of disturbing thoughts. Closing his eyes, he drank, and drank again. Presences waited in the corners of the room, and the candles bent their flames to their breath.

A sparkling mist stole across Renaud's vision. He collapsed backwards into a chair, blinking at the ceiling where an astral doorway seemed to churn and writhe. They were waiting for him; he knew it. Already he could hear their gleeful howls and the thunder of their infernal horses' hooves.

Thomas told Melusine she must not run away again. It wasn't safe for a girl, out there in the darkness. Who knows but some strange beast might come out of the forest and take her life? Melusine knew she was safe from any such attack, but bowed her head, with her hair over her eyes.

She could not explain about the angel, nor how its presence had filled her with a terror so cold, she shivered still in the light of day. As soon as Thomas would let her out of the house, she went down to the church with Old Mag. Here the yews, beaded with blood, dripped dew onto the lichened mulch around their roots. Crows shook their branches, flew rasping into the cold white sky. 'Snow might come,' said Old Mag, lifting a finger to the wind.

Melusine pulled her cloak around her, which did not keep out the chill. The world seemed a drab place that day; too damp, and everything was colourless, but for the poisonous yew berries and the blood of a slaughtered rabbit, whose carcass lay half-devoured upon one of the graves.

Inside the church, Melusine slipped into one of the pews, where the wood was misted with moisture. Her breath was a heavy cloud before her eyes. She clasped her hands and tried to pray, unsure of what thoughts she should form within her mind. It was not an angel of Christus who had come to her; was she welcome now in this House? 'Holy Father, cleanse me of all evil. Protect me...'

The prayer seemed hollow, powerless. Melusine kept her eyes screwed tightly shut, her forehead wrinkled in a frown. She could hear old Mag moving about the church, arranging the holly branches and the late-blooming roses in a vase. But there was someone else here, too. She could sense it. Someone sitting right behind her. She could almost feel their breath, a plume of warmth, reaching out to her through the frigid air. She had not heard the great oak door open, nor foot-steps upon the flagged floor. Whoever sat there...

'Mistress Gifford, young Mistress Gifford, isn't it?'

Melusine's eyes flicked open and there was the stooped dark shape of the priest before her, his small yet piercing eyes fixed upon her like some bird of prey.

'Father...' she managed to whisper.

The priest smiled, although she sensed a predator's edge to the gleam in his eyes. 'I heard you had a bad scare the other night. Ended up here in the churchyard.'

He paused, as if waiting for an answer. Melusine could not speak. Helplessly, she twisted her mouth and rolled her eyes, quite aware of how she must appear to him.

The priest loomed closer. 'What frightened you, my child? What chased you through the night?'

She drew away from him, clouds of breath puffing in between them. She was terrified that he knew what she was, saw her black core. Now, he was trying to urge confession, which would be followed by accusation, pain, even the flame. In her panic, Melusine still had a sense of someone behind her, pressing closer, eager and alert. It was almost as if they wished to speak for her. The priest leaned forward, frowning, perhaps concerned. He must not touch her; if he did she would scream profanities at him, or spew flies. Then was a sound like silver knives clashing, perhaps of laughter, certainly not holy. She was aware of a radiant flash at the corner of her vision, and the metallic clatter of monstrous wings. She carried *it* with her, around her. The priest could not see it, but a certain knowing distaste was creeping into his eyes.

Melusine scrambled from the pew and pushed past the priest. Out, out, into the winter light, where a murderous coven of crows lifted from the yews, rasping hysterically. The sky was full of wings, moving too slow, too fast. And it was there before her on the path - a tall, shadowy figure, its light closed in against the day, yet still inhuman. Behind her and before her. Was there no escape?

She found herself then out in the meadows, stumbling past the cows in their shaggy winter coats, skidding in their frost-rimed dung. Bare trees clawed the colourless sky and the birds wheeled across it in a shape like a crown. Once the creature touched her, she would be lost. She would belong to it and whatever tenuous hold she had on being a normal girl would disappear for ever. Her grandmother had been right. She was a changeling child, born of evil.

The forest was ahead of her now, its forbidding branches a puzzle of darkness that would either hide her, or simply hold her as a prisoner until the dark angel came for her. She had no choice but to run. The air was becoming opaque around her, and so cold. Stumbling, arms flapping, she hurled herself into the shadows of the naked trees.

Renaud saw the girl from his high window. She ran across the fields along the edge of the forest as if the demons of the abyss rode behind her. Her awkward movement attracted his eye and he was drawn to watch. Did some brutish male pursue her, or was she fleeing from a misdemeanour? High overhead, a tangle of crows lifted and fell in a tattered curtain and the sky was so dense. Then it was full of falling stars and the birds were flickering in and out of reality. The snow had come.

Behind him, Kalid stirred in his chair. 'You are close now, very close.'

There is some fault in me, Renaud thought, ignoring his mentor's remark. *Perhaps I am not destined to follow my parents' work. Perhaps I am both awake and asleep, one foot in each world, never fully in one nor the other.* He blinked at the littering snow, his hand upon the heavy drapes, and saw the diminutive female figure spin and whirl into invisibility as the weather closed around her. She looked like a rag on the wind. For a brief moment, Renaud saw a spiralling column of silver light flicker in the place where he had last seen her, but he could not be sure. The *vinum nostrum* sometimes coloured in the world with strange shapes of the mind. He let the drapes fall.

Father Rathford was present for dinner. 'I have had a day to try the saints!' he informed Renaud as they sat down to partake of a sizzling haunch of beef. A servant heaped steaming scallions onto his platter, while another filled a tankard with foaming ale. 'Agues and complaints, and two deaths in the parish. On top of that, young Gifford's bride taking another strange turn - in the church itself! I'll fancy he'll have trouble with her. She's touched - or worse.' These last two words were delivered with a meaningful scowl. 'She's always had a strange way with her.'

Renaud experienced a tremor, but not on behalf of the unknown woman. Rathford's words seemed strangely portentous. 'And now the snow has come.'

'More deaths in store, no doubt - sickly children, doddering ancients and the like.' Rathford tucked into his meal with relish. 'You look tired, milord.'

Renaud could do no more than barely pick at the meat. In truth, he felt weary to his soul. He shrugged.

'Too much peering,' Rathford announced. 'Bad for the eyes and the brain. Put your books away. You should get out more. I do believe you rarely see another body but myself. Perhaps a comely young wife would bring joy to these halls. Think on it. You'll not be short of offers, I'll wager. A spring wedding, yes...' The priest's eyes took on a dreamy cast.

Fortunately, an interruption curtailed the priest's advice: a heavy knocking at the outer door. It boomed throughout the castle.

'Someone in need!' Rathford declared, wiping grease from his chin.

Fate is at the door, Renaud thought, and his flesh went momentarily hot, then cold. He stood up.

Presently, a servant came into the hall and addressed the priest. 'There's some folk at the gate for you, Father.'

'What, they come here? Disturb our dinner?' Rathford's face had gone pink.

'Another death, perhaps,' Renaud said. He knew it would not be that. 'Show them in,' he told the servant.

Thomas Gifford headed the crew, a landowner faintly

known by Renaud. He remembered the priest's earlier words concerning Gifford's wife, and knew this must be no coincidence. After a grovelling apology to the lord and his guest for interrupting their meal, Gifford gave anguished voice to his dilemma. 'She's gone, Father. Not come back this eve. Old Mag took her to the church, but she had a turn and fled into the fields. We have searched, but found only five of Morton's kine stiff and dead in the snow, with no mark of injury. Of her, there's no sign. Father, I am afeared. What must be done?'

They believe she killed the cows, Renaud thought. *It often begins that way, with the death of animals.* Though he had heard little of this story, in his mind he saw the mountain of damning evidence that had been mounting against this unfortunate female. They would all be small things, but together they made a dark picture. He wondered, for a moment, whether she was truly a witch or just some stripling moon-calf, cursed for her inherent difference.

'Thomas, I am aware of your problem,' Rathford said, sighing heavily. 'It occurred to me this very day that all was not well with the child. We must find her, of course, before more ill befalls man or beast.'

'But what is wrong with her?' Gifford asked, his words constricted in his throat. 'Can it be remedied?'

The priest got to his feet. 'I will do all I can. Sometimes evil can be cast out, sometimes not.' He turned to Renaud. 'You must excuse me, milord. This is urgent business.'

'I understand. Of course, this poor maid must be found. I will naturally lend my aid to the venture.'

I should not be going out, he thought, as his steward laced up his stoutest boots, and brought out his heavy winter cloak. *The effects of the nostrum seep back into the brain in the hours of darkness. I should speak to Kalid.* But he had to see this girl. He had thought back to what he'd witnessed from his high window that afternoon, and knew that he'd seen her vanish into the forest. And more besides: the light which had seemed to follow her, an incandescent spirit light, like the anima of a magus.

Outside, the world was hushed and shrouded. Already the snow lay thick upon the meadows, and although the moon was eclipsed by the snow-bearing clouds, the landscape was lit by the ghost-light of the winter blanket. Renaud's hounds leapt before him, yelping like puppies, as gaunt as were-beasts in the unnatural radiance. The priest tramped beside him, muttering. They had broken away from the main band, to skirt the forest that bordered the Aquinas estate. Renaud knew the woods well, having spent most of his days there as a boy. If she was what they believed her to be, perhaps this maiden witch would be drawn to the place where his youthful imaginings had conjured spirits from the trees. His mind had enlivened the life force there, and it would perhaps give succour to the girl.

Renaud glanced back at the castle, before they entered the darkness of the trees. A dim light burned in the turret room; Kalid would be waiting for him. No matter. Privilege of birth had protected him from the zeal of the Church, and it was perhaps his duty to offer aid to this wench, whether she had the way of wyrd or not. If he had been born into peasant stock, perhaps he too would have been hunted across the land, brought to earth, bound and condemned.

Amid the trees, snowflakes hissed down through the canopy. A stag broke cover and thudded away down the brackened path. An omen. Renaud would follow it.

'No night for this,' the priest declared. 'I fancy she'll be frozen to a stone by daybreak. Perhaps we should return...'

His righteous sanctimony was tempered by physical discomfort. He had a hand pressed to his beef-fattened flank. Renaud paused a moment, then said, 'Father, fear not. Return to Aquinas. I will scour this area. If I happen upon the maid, I will bring her to you. If not, perhaps the others will find her.'

The priest looked uncertain. 'I should not leave you to search alone, milord. It is my duty to hunt this blighted soul for the love of Christus and his Eternal Father.'

Renaud laughed sweetly. 'I know this land better than any. And I shall not mention I tramped it alone. Go back, Father, seek the warmth of my hearth. The cold does not discommode me. Please, I insist... If we go any further, you will not be able to find your way back alone in the snow.'

The priest needed no further encouragement. He offered a few perfunctory phrases of apology, then turned his steps back towards the castle.

Renaud watched his figure diminish amid the soft deluge of the weather. Then, he dismissed the priest from his mind and began to jog down the forest path, following the spoor of the stag. As the forest claimed him, its spirit connected with his soul. He became one with all the hunters of the past, who understood the ways of the land. His sense of smell sharpened, as did his hearing. On his tongue, he tasted a thousand subtle scents of beast and plant, even the distant taint of human sweat, which told him in which direction the other men were heading. This way not his usual way of working, and perhaps leaned more towards the traditions of other orders, those more attuned to natural magic, but his father had taught him to use whatever skill lay to hand, and in this moment, all the paraphernalia of his Hermetic art would be of no avail. His abilities might lack puissance, because he lacked connection with his anima, but he had a far greater chance than the other men of finding the girl.

Melusine thought she must soon die. She could no longer feel her toes and fingers, and it was becoming more difficult to keep her eyes open. The angel had cornered her in a bower of briars. She had crawled through the thorns seeking a sanctuary and now a shivering radiance hovered at the entrance to the barbed tunnel, perhaps waiting for her to come out, or die. What had she done to invite its presence? She could hear it speaking to her but its language was a mesh of elemental sounds that she could not fathom. It sounded like water running through the forest, the fall of rain, the bustle of leaves in the wind and the call of a stag. Part of her wanted to go to it, for she sensed in some way it would make her warm again. But another part was afraid. Emerging from this bower of thorns would be like throwing herself over the edge of a waterfall. And yet, they were coming for her, weren't they - Thomas' men, the priest? She could hear their heavy movements through the forest, their hard voices. She could hear everything, even the progress of the king stag that made its way towards her, followed by a hunter. Her perception shifted to this image - it seemed somehow out of place, unconnected with her own situation. They might be ghosts, she thought, or shades of the forest spirit, enacting timeless rituals of life.

Beyond the naked briars, the angel said her name, 'Melusine.' It was distinct and perfect like a word from a song.

Melusine held her breath. Her head swam with the cacophony around her, men's clumsy feet, the breathing of the forest, the crash of snowflakes against the high branches. She put her burning forehead against her raised knees. How could she be so cold, yet so hot?

'Melusine!'

More urgent now, as loud as the sky, yet quieter than the scamper of voles. This was the end of her life and she had a choice. What would take her? The cold, the hands of men, or the voice of an angel? Slowly, she lifted her head. Her vision boiled with light. The angel was so radiant that all the briars looked like fragile burned sticks before it. She could see it clearly now, a tall figure crouching low, silver hair spilling forward, its eyes like white coals. Its face reminded her of a serpent; long, with slanting eyes. In her mind, she answered its summons. 'Leave me! I don't want to go to hell.'

'There is no hell, but in men's hearts,' it replied. 'Come forth, Melusine. Come unto me. Do not shut your mind to me, for we are one, you and I.'

She knew then, in an instant of blinding clarity, that this brilliance was indeed hers. If she reclaimed it - and she had no doubt it would be reclamation - the strangeness of the world would make sense to her. The feelings she had, the differences she possessed, would plait together into a single, shining whole. She could escape her fate, and if it was the Devil's work, then so be it. She did not want to die here in the chilled dark, nor upon a witch's pyre. She would fall backwards into the arms of Fate and see where she landed.

It was difficult to move because she was so numb, but gradually, she uncurled herself and crawled towards the angel. Its hands reached out to her through the taloned branches. When she took that shining hand in hers, she would rise up with renewed strength. She would be reborn. So close now. She could see the clearing beyond the briars, and her head was full of a rushing sound. She lifted one hand, reached out.

A stag crashed through the frozen bracken into the clearing. Even the angel looked round at it: a magnificent beast, the primal archetype of all stags. Its flanks ran with steaming sweat, its eyes rolled and it bowed its regal head with exhaustion, its antlered crown kissing the earth. Behind it came the hunter; a man in a long, flapping coat, his hair wild around his shoulders. He could be no mortal man. Melusine was not afraid exactly, but overwhelmed. Without thinking, she scrabbled her way through the final barrier of thorns and threw herself against the angel. The breath left her body. She was engulfed in a feeling that was beyond heat and cold. It was similar to the way she'd felt sometimes when Thomas had come to her bed, and dreams of a far-off presence had eclipsed her husband's physical being. It was all this and more. The angel was inside her and she inside it. When she stood up, she would be eight feet tall and shining. The man who pursued the stag was *her* hunter, as much as the angel was her angel. As Mistress Mathen had once said, three herbs apart possess little strength, but grind them together and they become something beyond themselves, much greater.

Renaud stood at the edge of the clearing. He was as the Red Slave approaching the White Woman, the body of the alchemist approaching all that is celestial and pure within his soul. She was queen of the snow, and above the trees, the sun glared alongside the moon, his light devoured by ravens. *I have come home*, Renaud thought, and dropped to one knee. All this time, he had searched for his anima in a goblet of alchemical potions, yet here she was, out in the forest, where first he had sensed her existence. He had been blind, lost. And so had she, attaching herself to some strip of a girl, some pathetic witchling, pursued by all that was gross and impure. The time had come now for them to conjoin. She would take him by the hand and lead him into the realms beyond human thought, where all the arcana of his art would be revealed to him. At last.

She was coming towards him, drifting above the white-starred mulch. He dared to look upon her and was surprised to see she did not seem wholly female, but certainly not male either. His heart yearned for the connection. He stood up to face her, opening his arms to take that light into his body.

Kalid sat alone in the high tower, listening to the sounds, far below, of the fat priest picking at the remains of his meal. The mage pressed the fingers of one hand against his eyes, muttering words from an ancient hermetic work. 'I Hermes, cause to come out to thee, O Sun, the spirits of thy brethren, the planets, and I make them for thee a crown, the like of which was never seen; and I cause thee and them to be within me, And I will make thy kingdom vigorous.' He had caught glimpses of what would happen in the magic of the *vinum nostrum*. Sometimes, he had wished to speak, to tell Renaud his suspicions, but the journey of a magus to his or her Guardian was personal, and no man or woman should intrude upon its course. He had sensed young Aquinas was somehow fragmented - an hereditary blight perhaps that had sent his parents, despite their knowledge, to early extinction. His mother and father had sought wholeness with each other, but they had been mistaken. Sometimes, the universe caused strange things to happen, and it was not the first time Kalid had been witness to an event such as this.

It was nearly dawn when the door at the bottom of the tower stairs creaked open. Kalid heard the footsteps rising higher towards him. What he saw soon after in the doorway was a drenched creature, the warmth of the castle having melted all the snow upon its hair and cloak. Its face was the embodiment of beseeching, full of bewildered questions. Kalid stood up, his vision dimmed by tears. He gestured to summon it, 'As a shadow continually follows the body of one who walks in the sun, so the rebis, though he appears masculine in form, nevertheless always carries within him his feminine part, hidden in his body.'

The being collapsed into a chair before the fire, blinking at the flames. It was Renaud, yet it was a female, both afraid and confused. Kalid gave it wine and it took the goblet with quivering fingers.

'You have a crown of planets about your head,' said Kalid, 'it is the symbol of the metals and the astrological temperaments. You are the star of perfection. Drink, my friend.'

'What am I?' it whispered hoarsely.

'The rebis is hermaphrodite, the divine marriage of male and female, of the sun and the moon. Your separate physical parts shared, and were conjoined by, a Holy Guardian, and fate smiled kindly upon you, for you were able to find one another so quickly in this life, which can be long.'

The rebis put its head into its hands, letting the goblet fall and smash upon the floor. Indigo wine soaked into the rugs, between the boards of the floor.

'Fear not,' Kalid murmured. 'I shall take you from this place, into the east, to the great house of Art where your parents trained in their youth. There, you will learn what you have become and of its potential. You will advance beyond the conflict of opposites. Your advent will be welcomed by your brothers and sisters.' He reached down and pressed a hand upon the red hair of the rebis. Bone white, flawless skin showed at its neck where the hair parted. Its frame was at once delicate and robust. It was the dark hunter and the white hart in one body. Slowly, it raised its head and stared at Kalid with wide eyes.

'I did not realise... did not know. The forest... I should have stayed here... stayed in the church... gone home, stayed home...' It shook his head, as if warring personalities fought to express themselves.

'Be calm, my friend,' murmured Kalid. 'Assimilate your separate parts. You are at one now, and have made contact with the divine spark. It is only forward now.'

Forward yes, but the path was littered with dark stones and twists. Monsters lay concealed there, but also light and knowledge. Kalid sighed. He had been right to come here. He had not realised how much he would be needed.

There were no heirs to Aquinas, and the king gave the lands as a gift to another duke, who in due course took up residence with his family. Thomas Gifford presently took another wife, an older woman who chattered all the time. No sign was ever found of Melusine and Renaud, other than a strange, scorched area in the heart of the forest, circled by the neat spoor of a stag. The locals presumed that Melusine had indeed been a witch and had killed the young lord before spiriting herself away from the district. Father Rathford declared she must be thought of as dead, because she'd been no child of God. Thomas was pitied, though few liked to talk to him about his vanished bride. At night, he would lie beside his warm, ordinary wife and think about the small room at the top of the house. He thought about the way she had slept there all alone. Was there evil in her? There had only ever been a stair betwixt them. Sometimes, he would weep and intense feelings would twist in his heart. In his mind, he spoke the words he would never speak aloud. 'Oh, my God, the down, the soft young down of her, the brown, the brown of her - her eyes, her hair, her hair...'